The Panhandle Predicament

Kendra Hoey

Kendra Hoey Novels, LLC

Publisher: Kendra Hoey Novels, LLC

Editor: Elizabeth A. White

Cover Design: Brailey Hoey

For more information about this book or to obtain permissions to use this book, contact Kendra Hoey at kendrahoeynovels@outlook.com

Praise for
The Panhandle
Predicament

"A tantalizing mystery that always hovers just out of reach yet concludes with a brilliantly unexpected twist!"

"This book is a page turner. The characters are depicted so vividly that I could conjure them in my mind almost immediately. A mystery that invokes all the emotions, makes me think critically, and keeps me guessing!"

"This book had me hooked from start to finish, and the twist blew me away! It felt so personal, like a reflection of my own journey to adulthood, including the universal challenges faced by all females."

"Oh my gosh, plot twist! Did not see the ending coming."

For my Dad

For all those Saturdays spent at the bookstore

My Partners in "Crime"

Thank you for supporting me on my journey.

My husband, Jim — An unwavering belief in my abilities

My son, Levi —Invaluable insights and unexpected accolades

My daughter, Brailey — A perfectly crafted design cover and dynamic marketing content

My son, Mason — My personal IT department dedicated to answering endless Mom questions

My editor, Elizabeth — Her magical touch

My friend, Lynn — Imaginative ideas and continuous support

My inspirational author friends, KG Fletcher and Suzy Accola — A successful path to follow in your footsteps

Thank you for believing in me.

Until next time.....

Prologue
Compulsions

Present Day

Trina Scotsdale was, from all outward appearances, a very normal, well-appointed, trustworthy, and reliable woman. A married mother of three with a doting husband, David, and a successful career, she presented a respectable image within her community. But under her well-manicured public persona was a secret fixation with the world of crime, a fixation that fed an unseen, crippling obsession.

As a teenager, Trina had lived through the life-changing experience of participating in the search for a kidnapped girl. Her intimate involvement in those events, and the crushing devastation of having to live with so many unanswered questions when the teenage girl was not found, had implanted a desire in Trina to search for answers. But her curiosity in seeking the why, how and who of things had spawned an unintended consequence—a bizarre habit of monitoring her own evidence trail. This habit ramped up slowly over her fifty years of life, eventually blossoming into a full-blown obsession. After putting more than twenty-five years into the corporate world and desperate to escape both the stress of her job and her crippling obsession, Trina retired.

Trina had treasured her high school summers at her parents' Florida Panhandle beach bungalow on Scenic Highway 30A. She remembered the joy of feeling the sun's heat on her face, walking along breathtaking white sandy beaches, and strolling through miles and miles of paths. When the opportunity to buy her parents' home was offered to her, Trina jumped. She was ready to take on retirement, and reconnecting with her youth felt like the perfect way to get started.

Although the move was intended to break the irrational chains that weighed on her every thought, it ended up having the opposite effect. The absence of corporate deadlines and the need to manage her now grown children's daily lives reopened the floodgates for her passion for reading. Over time, she found herself entrenched in the minds of the various characters who populated mystery novels. Before she knew it, she was exclusively consuming warped tales of murder that depicted salacious stories of horrific atrocities. Trina convinced herself that her fascination was not with the murderers but rather with the detectives. Crafting investigative skills, learning how to interpret crime data and eliciting case-breaking details were all things she secretly wanted to explore but never had the confidence to chase. It explained why reading about dead bodies, people with traumatic pasts and twisted characters who did the unthinkable provided her so much enjoyment. Even though her addiction to reading mysteries cluttered her mind, she told herself she was crafting a skill set that someday may come in handy.

Unfortunately, the more she read, the harder it was to ignore her own trail through the world and her irrational compulsion to eliminate it. Just the idea of being falsely accused of a crime made her rethink her daily actions and filled her mind with dread. Ironically, Trina knew she would never break a law or bend a rule—even the thought of stealing a grape from the grocery store or taking a pen home from the doctor's office sent convulsions of fear through her body—so her desire to eliminate "evidence" made her question her sanity. Despite her initial intention to wean herself off after retiring to Florida, she knew her addiction was far stronger than her willpower. She was destined to continue eradicating her own daily footprint and getting sucked into reading an endless abyss of wicked lullabies.

To add to her burden, Trina couldn't escape an ever-present feeling of guilt. Her entire life, she'd been riddled with the feeling she didn't do, give, or offer enough. Regrettably, moving into her family's beach bungalow generated more guilt. The worst kind: parental. The fact Trina had spent half her youth growing up with sand in her toes and yet had refused to visit her old stomping grounds with her children in tow had been a source of family contention. She could never quite articulate why she felt an overwhelming feeling of uneasiness at the thought of returning to the Panhandle while her kids were young, even though she had explored the pristine area freely in her own adolescence. Now, however, she hoped her grown children would discover all the area's hidden gems and forgive her for failing to share it until they were adults themselves.

Her new home was nestled in a natural sanctuary surrounded by showcase-worthy homes, toothpick tall palm trees and streets lined with bike riding families, dog walkers, and golf carts spilling over with coolers and beach towels. Enjoying their annual week away from reality, adventurous visitors rode e-bikes like REI tour guides through the backroad trails and beachgoers enjoyed the flawless UV index. Each little neighborhood along 30A was proud of their flavor, from the hipster vibe in Grayton beach to the elite vibe in Alys Beach's white stucco neighborhood. Families flocked to Florida to enjoy the fabulous twenty-six-mile pedestrian path that guided you along 30A and all its unique communities and its endless dining and entertainment options.

Trina and David were no different. They loved the peaceful and glorious state protected parks and the adventure of getting immersed in the dense and dynamic trails. As she assimilated into her new carefree life living on the coveted beaches of 30A, she was determined to make a conscience effort to curtail her involuntary habit of hiding "evidence." She would try not to focus on the saliva that splattered on the shopping cart after a sneeze. She would no longer wipe her fingerprints off wine goblets at restaurants, and she would not obsess about finding the piece of hair that fluttered to the floor after pulling her sunglasses off. Trina could already feel the huge weight being lifted as she slowly began to kick this habit.

She had owned up to her addiction to salacious crime stories, and now had freed up her mind to enjoy the beauty of 30A in her retirement. She felt stronger and more in control, and she planned to keep it that way.

The Beach Bungalow

1988

R iding a three-speed bike on streets barely wide enough for one vehicle to pass was a daily after-school adventure for Judy, Jane, and Trina Scotsdale. They peddled through their Massachusetts small town on their way to their friends' houses, whiplashed by cars that whizzed past. Eleven-year-old Trina, the youngest of four siblings, loved her afternoons riding bikes through windy backroads, stopping to examine flower blossoms, and fallen bird nests while letting the cool air immerse her in nature. There were two main paved streets going down to the center of town, but most of the side streets were gravel and dirt, making bike riding a true athletic experience. Houses spread out every quarter of a mile left the natural forests up close and personal to bike riders. If you weren't getting bullied off the street by passing cars, you would be bludgeoned in the face by tree branches. Trying to listen for the sound of an engine before deciding to continue around a sharp turn was the only way to guarantee survival because Trina's sisters surely were not waiting around to see if she made it to her destination.

Judy was headed to the abandoned barn to meet up with her boyfriend, Jimmy, for an afternoon of smooching. Jane was going to her friend Sarah's to work on her history project, leaving Trina to bike to the penny candy store on her own after her sisters peeled off for their destinations. The store sold basic groceries like milk, bread, and peanut butter, in addition to liquor and canned goods. The owner of the store, Mr. Jones, was always pleasant but watched the neighborhood kids like a hawk. Trina jumped off her bike and gently propped it up against the side of the small building. She saw three other bikes scattered on the dirt parking lot but didn't recognize any. She walked inside, waved at Mr. Jones, and saw three boys standing near the penny candy bins.

Jason Brown, Christopher Bishop, and Steve O'Neill were negotiating who got to take the last piece of root beer barrel candy. Butterflies danced in Trina's stomach. One year older than her, Trina loved Christopher's wavy long hair and admired his casual attire of flannel shirts and jeans. For a twelve-year-old, he already had style. Trina was too young to have a boyfriend, but having older siblings, she had witnessed enough backyard make-out sessions to know what was in her future. Trina walked around the back of the bread and canned goods aisle, hoping the boys didn't see her. She stood in the back near the Hamburger Helper boxes and picked up a can of baked beans to appear busy in case they glanced her way. She could hear the boys still arguing about the candy. Mr. Jones, losing his patience, told the boys to make their decisions.

Preoccupied with trying to look busy, Trina failed to notice Christopher approaching the end of the aisle. He turned the corner and bumped into her, knocking the can of baked beans out of her hands.

"Oops. Sorry. I didn't know anyone was there. My mom asked me to grab a can of green beans for dinner tonight." He handed her back the can she had dropped, then reached behind her. As he grabbed a can of green beans, his arm brushed along Trina's.

Trina smiled and said, "You should get this kind, they taste like actual green beans. That brand tastes like plastic."

"Really? Do you eat plastic often? How do you know what it tastes like?" he joked.

"Actually, yes. Plastic pizza night on Wednesdays is my absolute favorite. I cover my pizza with lots of plastic pepperoni." She giggled, amazed at herself for speaking so casually.

"Eww, gross. OK I'll grab this one. Hey, where is your sister, Jane? She was supposed to meet my brother after school to help him on a project," Christopher said. They could hear the bell ring on the front door as his two friends walked out with their brown paper bags filled with penny candy.

"She went to Sarah's house to work on a school project. Maybe your brother was supposed to meet over there."

"Oh, Paul probably forgot. He's always getting things mixed up. Hey, our parents told us they bought a beach house, and I guess your parents bought one too. It sounds like we'll be spending more time together over the summer. Catch ya later," he said and walked to the register to complete his purchase.

"Bye. See ya later." *A beach house*? She had no idea what he was talking about. She walked over to the candy section and filled her bag with Swedish Fish, Jolly Ranchers, Dum-Dums lollipops and one candy necklace. She paid Mr. Jones and waited outside for ten minutes for her friends. They didn't show up, so she decided to bike home and ask her mom about the beach house. Her family had been driving to Florida for summer vacations for the last three years, but her parents hadn't said anything about buying a house. Trina crunched up her paper bag and held it the best she could while still holding the handlebars. She made it home around quarter of five. Judy and Jane were already home and Jane was helping her mother set the table.

"Hey, Mom, what's for dinner?" Trina said as she plopped her bag on the kitchen counter.

"Meatloaf and mashed potatoes. Go clean up and then help your sister. I want you all at the table by five fifteen because your dad has an American Legion meeting tonight at six thirty."

Trina cleaned up, finished setting the table, grabbed her Judy Blume book *Blubber* and sat at the table reading and waiting. Her brother, Tanner, came in the front door, dropped his smelly gym bag, and sat down immediately at the table saying, "I'm hungry."

About ten minutes later, her dad, Richard, came home and dinner began, with multiple conversations going on at once. Her dad was sharing a success story about signing a contract with a new customer. Judy was asking permission to go bowling with Jimmy Thursday night, while Jane pointed out she and Sarah needed a ride to go to the football game on Friday night. Tanner was complaining that tomorrow's practice was going to be extended an hour since his team was playing their biggest rival. Trina sat quietly and picked at her meatloaf. She had seconds of mashed potatoes, but even ketchup couldn't disguise the onions that were overpowering the meatloaf. When there was finally a lull in conversation, Trina jumped at the chance to investigate Christopher's story.

"Hey, Dad, did we buy a beach house?" Trina asked, not realizing this might have been a big family surprise.

Her mom looked up from her plate, holding a forkful of green beans resting mid-air. Her dad shot her mom a confused look, then said, "Where did you hear that?"

"I ran into Christopher Bishop today. He said both our families bought a beach house. Is that true? Did you buy the bungalow that we rent every year?"

Her dad dropped his fork and pushed his plate forward on the table. Her mom shrugged, let out a sigh, and began clearing the table. Trina's siblings immediately burst into parental interrogations.

"What?" Tanner exclaimed. "We bought a vacation house? Was it the yellow one by the dune lake? I could go fishing every morning."

"The Bishop family? Paul and Christopher? Ew," Jane complained, her arms crossed over her chest and big pout on her face. "Did you ask Sarah's and Patricia's families? I would rather spend summer with them."

Judy had a grin on her face. "Can I bring Jimmy? I would love to take him to the bonfires. Pennie would be so jealous!"

"OK, enough. Everyone, calm down." Her dad raised both arms in the air with his palms spread out and slowly lowered them. Nancy, their mother, came back into the dining room and stood behind Richard.

"Your mother and I decided that since we like to spend our summers in Florida, it was more economical to buy a place than pay rent for three months each year. We found a great bungalow near Grayton Beach in a quiet neighborhood along County Road 30A. The Bishops really enjoyed visiting with us over the last two years and decided to buy one too. They also found a house in the same community. So, yes, we will be spending our summers down on the Panhandle. Now, our summer house rules have not changed. I still expect you to get summer jobs. You will not be lollygagging at the beach every day. I may have to fly back home periodically for work, so all of you need to support your mom and help her maintain the beach house. We were going to surprise everyone at Christmas next month, but I guess that blew up in our face," Richard said, standing up and putting his arm around Nancy's shoulder.

Trina's mom smiled and rested her head on her dad's shoulder. "We are so excited. We hope to make great family memories together."

The rest of the evening was quickly derailed as the siblings sat around making summer plans. Judy was plotting ways to decorate her new bedroom while Judy was flipping through a Sears magazine looking for bathing suits. Tanner had taken out his fishing rod and showed their dad the tackle box supplies. Conversations crisscrossed between lavish tans, cute boys, and seafood dinners. Tanner called his friend Jonas to talk about getting a job working beach bonfires. Jane and Judy wrote down a list of restaurants where they could apply for waitressing jobs. Richard and Nancy sat on the couch holding hands basking in the excitement that tonight's news had generated. Trina didn't need to find a job yet, so she sat on the couch reading a book thinking about spending summers with Christopher.

***

Before they knew it, winter was over, and spring had sprung. Nancy took them shopping at Swansea Mall to buy new bathing suits, beach towels and flip-flops. The girls found their one-piece bathing suits at Caldor department store, and their mom bought one for herself at Sears. Finding warm weather supplies this early in the year in Massachusetts was difficult since summer really didn't hit there until June. However, their mom had a way of finding things. After several shopping trips, their kitchen counters were disappearing under containers of suntan lotion, beach umbrellas and other beach paraphernalia. Trina was worried that she wasn't going to be able to go to a bookstore every week and asked her dad if she could stock up on summer reading. Since he was an avid book lover too, he let her buy two books a week for the months leading up to summer and told her to hide the books in the garage. He didn't want the others to know he was splurging on his baby girl.

Memorial Day weekend arrived, and Trina's family fought over what they could squeeze in the Chevrolet Celebrity and on the luggage rack. The kids knew they would miss spending summer with their hometown friends, but they had enough experience spending time down in Grayton Beach that they knew they would meet many other kids their age. The road trip was long and not very fun, but thoughts of their destination kept the family's irritation with each other at bay. The Scotdales arrived at their new home during the evening. The late hour didn't stop them from finding the closest boardwalk and running to see the beach. They ran through the soft, silky sand and laughed as Tanner ran directly into the Gulf with his clothes on. It was truly the start of years of making memories as a family.

Trina always thought the beaches were so much prettier in the Panhandle than they were up in New England, which were often filled with seaweed, rocks, and thousands of tiny shells, making taking a stroll uncomfortable. The sand in Florida was as white as snow and felt like walking on a cushy quilt. New England beaches were also normally overcrowded since temperatures only remained hot enough for two to three months every year. You could reach out and rub elbows with strangers on checkerboards of blankets and portable radios. The Panhandle beaches got busy, too, but there was so much more available beachfront property it never felt crowded.

It was almost midnight by the time they came back from the beach, wet and sandy but exhilarated. Their parents had moved most of their belongings into the appropriate bedrooms. Thankfully, their parents had bought the place furnished, so they had everything they needed. It was a three-bedroom bungalow, but with four kids, someone had to sleep on the pull-out couch. As the oldest, Tanner should have gotten one of the bedrooms, but he could not have cared less. He threw his bag of clothes on the floor and crashed on the couch with his shirt off and wet shorts on. Judy and Jane fought over the bedroom with the single bed, knowing whoever didn't get it would have to share the bunk bedroom with Trina. They decided to take turns—one month on, one month off. Trina didn't care because she knew she could crawl up to the top bunk and read in peace.

Even though it was late, Trina used a flashlight to read her new book, *Flowers in the Attic*. She was completely engrossed in reading about the Dollanganger family and stayed up till 2:00 a.m. to finish the book. She was in heaven. She already knew that buying this house was the best decision her parents had made.

The first week at the house was chaotic. Her parents had several maintenance projects to tackle, and they had no qualms asking the kids to pitch in. The bushes had to be pruned, the garage needed organizing and each room required a thorough cleaning. By the end of the first week, the major projects had been tackled and the kids were released from family obligations. The house quickly began to feel like home. Richard and Nancy became preoccupied with integrating into their Gulf Trace neighborhood leaving the kids free to entertain themselves.

Tanner began training for his new job, not returning home until late in the evenings. Judy and Jane spent a couple of days applying for summer jobs, while Trina helped their mom with some of the smaller projects that remained. Trina did not like clutter or disorganization, so she would spend hours organizing kitchen shelves, repacking beach blankets in the wagon and color coordinating bathroom towels in the hall closet. Their mother tended to be messy and never really had a rhyme or reason as to why she stored things the way she did so if someone needed to find something, they would ask Trina where to look. Trina would spend the morning cleaning up the kitchen, only to come downstairs a couple of hours later and find piles of laundry, newspapers, and random supplies from the store spread out all over the house. Trina would struggle to find common kitchen items like a can opener or Tupperware because Nancy moved things around constantly. It was like she didn't understand the simple concept of matching similar items together. When the kids found garden tools tucked under beach blankets, grill tongs under the bathroom sinks and packages of toilet paper in their bedroom closet, they learned it was useless to try to understand the pandemonium of their mother's disorganization. The chaos was baffling, but Nancy's fun-loving personality made up for her junk drawer living mentality.

Feeling like they had found their summer community, Nancy and Richard hosted the first official community potluck. Neighbors gradually turned the backyard into a standing room only gathering. The picnic tables filled with casserole dishes, trays of premade sandwiches, coleslaw, corn on cob and coolers full of beer. Richard and Nancy mingled effortlessly with guests making everyone feel welcome.

Trina hid away in her room at the onset of the party, not wanting to hang out with a bunch of adults. But when she peeked out of the window from the top bunk and saw Christopher standing by the bean-bag bull's eye boards, she decided to join the party. She grabbed a can of soda and a plate of food and snagged a spot under the umbrella at a picnic table. Three girls about her age were hanging out with Christopher, his brother, Paul, and two other boys she had never seen before. Too shy to approach, she ate her hot dog and kept reading her book.

Tanner grabbed his mini surfboard and took off with Jonas and a couple of other boys to the beach. Judy seemed to have gotten over missing Jimmy, as she was sitting with a curly-haired boy in the far back of the yard near the shed. Jane was surrounded by a gaggle of pretty blondes and brunettes in bathing suits, hair in ponytails. After about thirty minutes of frisbee tossing, most of the kids grabbed towels and joined the rest of the kids at the beach.

The three girls Trina noticed earlier came over and asked if she wanted to come. "Hey, my name is Monica," a naturally pretty girl with brown, wavy, shoulder-length hair said. "This is Wendy and Angela. We all live in the neighborhood, but I am the cool one. The rest of these girls just follow me around," Monica said, laughing and poking the other two girls on their shoulders.

"Oh, you are so cool, Monica. We couldn't live without you. If you didn't have a cute older brother who drove us around, we wouldn't even be hanging out with you." The girl who spoke, Wendy, had short black hair and wore a ripped T-shirt hanging off one shoulder, and a bright blue bathing suit underneath.

The third girl, Angela, waved her arms up and down in front of Monica. "Monica, you are a beach goddess. Tell us your command and we shall follow." She poked Monica's arm playfully.

Trina joined them, and without even consciously thinking about it, the four of them linked arms together as they left the party and walked toward the boardwalk. Questions peppered back and forth. Where are you from? How many months will you be in Florida? Did Trina like her siblings? How strict were her parents? Who did she have a crush on? What did she do for fun? Trina was fascinated by the girls' energy, honesty, and their flair for sharing stories. Two additional local girls, Dawn and Tanya, joined them and all six spent the rest of the afternoon together. The night came sooner than expected, as Trina was caught up in enjoying herself. She belonged and it felt great, like she was floating on a cloud.

By the end of the bonfire, the conversations came around to Christopher's quirky smile and messy hair. Trina was proud to say he was from her hometown, but she didn't reveal her crush. She knew her chances were slim with so many pretty girls around. As the light from the bonfires faded, the kids dispersed from the beach and Trina headed home after saying goodbye to her new friends. The backyard was a wreck. Her parents were still dealing with the remnants of the bonfire on the beach, so Trina began cleaning up. Surprisingly, Tanner was already home, sitting inside eating leftovers. Her sisters were nowhere in sight.

As Trina began picking up empty bottles and paper plates, she heard someone say, "Do you have any plastic hotdogs left? I'm starving." Trina turned and saw Christopher standing behind her. His hair was wet and dripping and he had no shirt on, only his bathing suit trunks. Trina's lips slipped into a wide grin. "The hotdogs got devoured, but I think there's plenty of plastic corn on the cob left. I hear you can take a bite and stretch the plastic out like a mozzarella stick." She picked up a couple of half empty soda cans and threw them in the trash.

"Man, I was craving a gooey hotdog. Do you mind if I check out what's left in the kitchen before I head home? I'm starving," Christopher said as he bent over and picked up some dirty napkins. "Looks like you have a bunch of friends already. I think we're going to like spending summers here. What do you think?"

"I think so too. Tanner is in there devouring most of the leftovers. Good luck pulling food out of his hands."

Christopher waved thanks and walked into the kitchen.

Trina smiled. A beach bungalow and books. Friends, sun, and sand. A boy crush. Summer couldn't get much better than this.

A Dead Person's Trash is Another Person's Treasure

Present Day

Not a cloud in the sky and a cool breeze coming off the Gulf, Trina took the last sip of her morning coffee and began planning her daily walk. She was eager to get some Vitamin D and release the tension in her neck from spending all day yesterday cleaning the house. Since she was planning to walk to work tomorrow on Scenic Highway 30A, today she would venture to the nature trails in Blue Mountain Beach. Since moving back to Florida, Trina had picked up a part-time retail job. On her days off, she looked forward to her routine of exploring nature with her energetic dog, Freckles, in tow. The daily escape provided her with the freedom to enjoy the balmy weather, to listen to a good book and to partake in a little neighborhood cleanup.

Surprisingly, cleaning up her neighborhood was as rewarding to Trina as solving her fictional murder mysteries. It frustrated Trina to see the remnants of human laziness spread over what was intended to be nature's artwork. She had become as compulsive about picking up trash as she was about reading about blood spatter, knife wounds and rape kits. Remembering how quaint and uninhabited her beach community used to be, she treasured the coastal beauty that surrounded the beaches and state parks and was committed to ensuring it remained clean for all to enjoy.

She pressed play on her current crime novel, grabbed a trash bag, Freckles's leash, and a pair of gloves. She was about to walk out the door when she remembered she should take the bear horn since she was headed to the trails. She'd heard a local woman's dog was killed by a bear, so she wasn't taking any chances on having an unexpected companion. Anxious to get going before the temperature rose, she searched for her bear horn but couldn't locate it. A little hesitant to leave without some form of protection, she opened the junk drawer and pulled out the can of mace her daughter had left the last time she visited. Freckles was impatiently jumping on her legs, so Trina headed out.

"Be back in an hour," she hollered at her husband as she walked out the door.

Before leaving the driveway, she cycled through her mental checklist simultaneously shaking her head in disappointment. Although she knew she was being ridiculous, she couldn't help but worry about leaving a digital and physical trail of today's adventure. Since moving to Florida, she had made an exerted effort to loosen up and live more freely but today the feeling was too powerful. Ignoring her own admonishments, she silently eliminated random preposterous thoughts as they popped into her head. She turned off the Life360 tracking app her family used to share their locations but kept her phone on in case David called her. She double-checked her pristinely white sneakers ensuring she wouldn't leave a muddy trail behind and reminded herself of which houses to avoid eliminating any risks of being captured on neighborhood security cameras as she walked past. Feeling calmer, she took a deep breath of fresh air and lost herself in her current crime story.

She passed a couple of vacationers who were out early riding their bikes, and she chatted with a couple of neighbors as they walked past with their dogs. Petting a dog released all her anxiety and helped set her mood for the rest of the day. After mingling with her neighbors, she turned right down Route 83, and Freckles instinctively pulled her faster toward the Point Washington State Park public entrance.

Donning a pair of gloves, Trina picked up stray water bottles and random pieces of paper as she strode through the trail opening. She concentrated on her audiobook, with Freckles effortlessly navigating the path forward through the woods on the narrow dirt path. The deeper they walked into the state park, the hotter the temperature rose. Trina's hands were getting uncomfortably sweaty, so she removed her latex gloves and stuffed them in her skirt pocket. Remembering the warning that black bears were known to roam the woods, Trina stopped walking for a moment, intent on listening for any sounds of movement. It was rather hard to believe there were bears in Florida within one mile of the beaches, but Florida bears found safety in the thousands of acres of state parks and were not shy about intermingling with people, trash cans and front porches on the hunt for food. Hearing only the sound of silence, she allowed herself to believe there were no predators around.

Even though most of the trails were easy to follow, sections of the path were as curvy as a rollercoaster and populated with huge tree roots that could trip even the most nimble gymnast. She took a moment to untangle Freckles's leash and reacquaint herself with where she was on the path. The dog loved to run free on the trails, and her eagerness to explore the smells and sights made Trina feel guilty when she looked down into her pleading eyes. Knowing she had the mace in her skirt pocket and that this portion of the sandy path was relatively straight, she decided to give Freckles a few minutes of freedom. Freckles normally protected Trina like a security guard, so Trina was relatively confident the dog would behave. She released Freckles from her leash, and they reengaged in their casual stroll through the woods.

About a minute later, Trina saw a flutter of movement up ahead. Before she could process the resulting repercussion, Freckles took off chasing a squirrel that had serendipitously crossed the path in search of safety. Watching with horror as Freckles scurried off into the thicket, Trina regretted her decision to unleash the dog. As she watched Freckles jump high over a two-foot-tall palm bush and disappear away from the clearing, she admonished herself for her foolishness.

She called for Freckles and clapped her hands, offering promises of bones and treats. When Freckles did not return, Trina frantically began fighting her way through the branches and Florida palms. The deeper she ventured, the harsher the environment became. Attempting to gain stability and maintain her speed, she cringed as she left handprints on tree bark and footprints in muddy puddles. Trina's anxiety spiked as she began to catalog the DNA trail left behind with each thorny vine that ripped into her calves. She tried not to look at the blood seeping down her legs and onto her sneakers. Trina wiped cobwebs off her face and pushed her damp hair off her forehead, unconsciously fretting over loose strands that escaped. Concentrating on establishing a visual, she pushed forward, trying to catch her breath and control her nerves.

As she pulled branches down and stepped over weeds reaching higher than her waist, Trina was frustrated with her own mental distraction. With each step she took, she tallied the Hansel and Gretel path she was leaving, her blood and DNA sprinkled on leaves and sticks marking her path forever. Truth be told, people who commit wrongful acts were less likely to fret about being caught than innocent people were. She knew she couldn't be found guilty of walking in the woods but couldn't stop worrying about the trickles and droplets. The combination of salty sweat dripping from her forehead and the sting of each new bloody scratch was sending her mind into a tailspin. Why did she let herself obsess? When she moved to Florida, she'd promised herself she would stop being so foolish. She needed to focus on catching her dog. She stopped, closed her eyes, and exhaled a deep breath. Focus, Trina. Focus.

After fifteen minutes of painstakingly navigating the deep forest, Trina finally caught sight of Freckles' shiny black coat propped up while she stared up a tree, presumably at the squirrel. Unfortunately for Trina, the dog was still fifty feet deeper into the woods. Trina continued to climb over dense weeds and thorny bushes, wondering if she would be able to find her way back to the path. Her thoughts progressed into the future. In her head, she predicted her husband's response if she had to call him and tell him she was lost in the trails. She could hear him now: "Really, Trina? Why did you let Freckles off the leash? You know she chases anything that moves." Trina really didn't want to have to make that phone call.

"Freckles," she admonished as she approached the tree where her dog was resting with her mouth hanging open.

As she manipulated her body up and over natural barriers, Trina saw a glint of something shiny lying on the ground near the squirrel's tree. She sighed and changed direction slightly away from Freckles to reach the spot where she saw the shiny object. Why would someone litter way out here so far from the path? There were service roads webbed throughout the trails for the county park employees who maintain the nonpublic portions of the park. Maybe one of the workers dropped something when hanging trail signs or setting boundaries for the periodic preventative forest fires.

Freckles, taking note of Trina's arrival, lost interest in the squirrel and joined her. Freckles stuck her nose down to sniff what Trina was reaching for, and Trina quickly reconnected the leash with a large sigh of exhausted relief. The chase was over. She would never do that again.

Bending over the apparent piece of trash, Trina extended her hand to pick up the scuffed oblong metal object, which was not as small as she initially thought it was. She tugged and discovered a rusted and decrepit belt buckle attached to a decayed leather belt. There was some denim material still wrapped around the remnants of the buckle. As she pulled at the dirty and moss-ridden denim, it appeared to be from a pair of jeans or jean shorts. After a little tug-of-war, Trina yanked it out of the ground. It was not an entire piece of clothing, but a scrap of a pocket. Trina was about to plop the whole thing in her trash bag when she noticed a little piece of faded red paper sticking out of the seam of the pocket.

Her curiosity heightened, she tugged gently, separating the denim material from the paper, revealing a red book of matches. The faint image of the words *Red Bar Grand Opening* was printed on the cover. The Red Bar was one of the most beloved and recognizable restaurants in Grayton Beach, Florida. Trina recollected celebrating the opening of the now-famous restaurant back when she was in high school working as a waitress at a local dive bar. Gosh, what year did the Red Bar open? Ninety-four? Ninety-five? Her memory was fuzzy, but she recollected that the Red Bar's opening had created some competition within the local restaurant industry. She remembered the excitement the new dining establishment had created, and of course her family had enjoyed eating there over the years.

She was somewhat surprised the matches were still intact considering they were out in the elements, though, they had remained hidden in the jean pocket. Instinctively, she flipped the matchbook cover open. On the inside was a handwritten note, faded but still legible. It said, *# 4 – Last Shift*. The message was meaningless, but the matchbook was a cool historic find. Trina dropped the denim material, the buckle and belt in her trash bag while looking at the old book of matches. She wished she'd put her gloves back on, which would have protected the old matchbook from additional deterioration, but it was too late to worry about that now. She opted to put the matches in her skirt pocket for safekeeping. The grand opening matchbook could be a collector's item since the restaurant was now one of the top ten dining destinations when visiting 30A. It would make a great decoration on the shelf with her antique art.

Tired, hot, and sticky, she was ready to begin the hike back to the path and head home. She looked down one last time to make sure she hadn't missed any pieces of trash. The sun's rays hit the ground slightly differently than they had a minute ago, and Trina recognized another object embedded in the mud and dirt at the foot of the tree. Her heart exploded with adrenaline as she released a guttural sound. She almost choked on her chewing gum as she sucked in a deep, mortified breath. She fell backward, landing on the dirt, then scooted back on the ground as fast as her arms could push her. Trina sat hunched over her bent legs, breathing in and out faster than a woman in labor.

Poking out of the ground were bits and pieces of a human skeleton. Bones covered by broken branches, an accumulation of pine straw, leaves, mud, moss, and all things nature. The portion that was exposed was a human forehead, one eye socket visible. She was staring at a dead person! A body was buried in the earth about five feet from her toes, right here in the sanctity of the peaceful Panhandle.

Freckles reacted to Trina's body language and hovered up into her face. Trina sat for what seemed like an eternity feeling like she was on a freight train headed straight for a cliff, in complete shock. What was she supposed to do? She questioned the reality of what she was seeing. Was that really a skeleton or just a Halloween decoration?

She inched forward about a foot away from the skull and stared down. It was, without a doubt, an actual human skeleton. It was not laid out perfectly like in the movies. The portion of skull buried in the mud was sideways like the person was taking a nap. She could make out three, maybe four rib bones poking out from the earth. She looked around a little more and saw a knee bone and the tip of some toes. The bones were crooked, like the person had fallen from the tree and broken in half on impact. How long did it take skin and organs to decompose? Was this a female or a male? Was there more than one?

She stood up slowly and examined the ground to make sure she didn't desecrate the body by accidentally standing on it. Even though it was well camouflaged, the eye socket was hauntingly staring back at her. Her addiction to fictional crime had just become uncomfortably real. She felt nauseous. She was about to spit her gum out when she stopped, thinking about her own genetics embedded in the piece of spearmint. She spit her gum into her trash bag, took a couple of deep breaths and tried to concentrate.

Now that the initial shock had subsided, Trina's brain kicked in high gear as it regurgitated crime novels. What would Sherlock Holmes do? How would James Patterson's Detective Alex Cross protect the scene? Would Detective Megan Carpenter from *Snow Creek* take pictures to document the skeleton's position? If Harry Hole from *Nemesis* had picked up a piece from a crime scene, would he put it back? Would Detective Mitchell Lonnie from *Spider's Web* call the FBI or the police? Trina had a decision to make. Her discovery was now a critical piece of a mysterious puzzle.

The realization hit her in waves, like when pretty snowflakes turn into a blizzard. Finding evidence of a dead body in a small, safe, crime-free beach town was insane. This was really happening! She couldn't think. She was overcome with fear, dread, and the desire to run. She needed to call her husband. Would the police think she was guilty of something if she called her husband before she called the police? The smart thing to do was to dial 911.

She closed her eyes. The detective skills she had been refining were finally going to get put to work. She began to feel empowered, and a little sick to her stomach. Shamefully emboldened with morbid glee, she decided she was going to solve this mystery before the real detectives did.

She picked up her phone and made the call that would change her life forever.

Becoming a 30A Local

Summer couldn't have come soon enough. Trina was looking forward to enjoying her three-month-long friend reunion. The Florida sun painted her body with cozy, relaxing warmth. The clear, light-blue skies, ninety-degree temperatures and pristine glistening water of the Gulf of Mexico openly invited her as a welcome sign that she was back. She felt like she was living a fairy tale whenever she was back in Florida, and she was eager to bask in the freedom summer promised. Although living at the beach felt like she was living in her own special cocoon of safety and happiness, her outlook on the approaching summer months had been tempered with normal teenage anticipation. As a rising high school freshman, she was feeling more mature and socially accepted but she always worried about fitting in. But as soon as she spoke with her Florida squad of girlfriends, she felt at ease. Dubbing themselves the Beach Bomb Babes (BBB), the girls plotted and planned their Memorial Day Weekend.

The 30A area was getting more crowded with each passing year but the Scotsdale bungalow would feel much roomier. Tanner, who recently finished his freshman year of college, had landed a summer job working on a private yacht and would not be joining the family. For his three sisters, Tanner's absence translated into finally having a full food pantry and a couch free of his smelly laundry. Although they would miss Tanner and his rambunctious friends, the remaining Scotsdales still planned on taking advantage of many of the area's hidden gems. The word about this oasis dream vacation area had spread to neighboring states. Families from as far away as Arkansas and Texas and as close as Alabama and Georgia were filling up rental properties and dropping thousands of dollars on their family vacations. Although residents liked to see local business owners thrive, between the overactive land developers and creative entrepreneurs opening new retail establishments, the simplicity of the area was gradually disappearing. But the local youth, including the BBB, knew how to escape the crowds. They already made plans to hike in Point Washington State Park, fish on the coastal dune lakes and paddleboard on nearby clear-water springs.

Despite being thrilled to be back in Florida, the one negative of turning fourteen was Trina was encouraged by her parents to find a part-time job. Although she wasn't a fan of having to work all day with her sisters, Trina figured she had an easy in at the Salty Bar, where her sisters worked last summer. Knowing that her freedom was approaching an end, Trina was eager to enjoy her Memorial Day weekend with her friends. Her mother packed a cooler with sandwiches, fruit and lots of water, and her beach bag was filled with books, *Teen Magazine*, and Coppertone sun lotion. Spending hours sitting on the beach, floating in the Gulf, and playing beach volleyball was the perfect way to reintroduce herself to the Florida way of life. The BBB mingled freely with familiar faces while acquiring names and phone numbers of several newfound friends. Monica, Dawn, and Tanya had remained preoccupied with the three

Alabama high school football players while Wendy and Angela concentrated on their tans.

Trina was polite and conversational with the new kids but as soon as she caught sight of Christopher with his long, lean body and friendly smile, she was distracted. His head was a mess of blond and brown wavy hair that bounced off his shoulders when he jumped to spike a ball. He wore blue swim trunks with a little picture of a dog on the lining, and his olive complexion fit right in with the full-time Florida boys. Although his friends kept him busy tossing a football and playing frisbee, he seemed to purposefully find time to sit near Trina. She adored his contagious personality. He naturally struck up conversations, laughed at his own jokes and mingled effortlessly. When his friends decided to head back into the water, he opted to stay and talk with Trina. After chatting about generic topics, their conversation migrated to Trina's eagerness to enter high school in the fall. Christopher recommended she join the school newspaper club and the yearbook committee. She was surprised that he remembered the article she had written about animal shelters that had been published in the local community newspaper back home. His attentiveness was exciting and a little overwhelming.

Their conversations flowed easily, and Trina's crush was getting deeper, less superficial. She wasn't only attracted to him; their passions and interests were surprisingly aligned, more than she realized. She was completely focused on his storytelling. His adorable expressions enhanced his unique commentary, and he had Trina laughing so much her belly ached. He loved to volunteer at animal shelters and had rescued more wild animals than his mother could handle. When he recounted the events relating to a tiny cardinal, Trina forgot they were sitting on the beach surrounded by friends. His description of his tender and delicate rescue, his month-long recuperation efforts, the family's frustration with a free-flying house guest, and the culmination of the bird's residency after leaving an unwelcome gift at the dinner table had Trina enraptured. His animal stories were inspirational, and she nervously shared some of her own. Her stories were not as comical as his, but he listened intently, which warmed her heart.

By the end of the weekend, Trina couldn't think of anything else but Christopher. She sat on her beach towel pretending to be reading a book while peering over the top of the pages watching his every move. When it was lunchtime, she volunteered to hand out sandwiches, saving him his favorite, a cold PB&J. She even allowed herself to be buried in the sand when he asked for a volunteer.

She wasn't sure if he was attracted to her or not. She had grown a couple of inches during eighth grade, and her hair now swung just below her shoulders. Her face had transitioned away from its youthful round shape, and her cheek bones were more pronounced. She had perfectly almond-shaped eyes, with eyebrows that highlighted her hazel eye color. This was the first summer that she filled out her bikini. Her long legs silhouetted her new shape. She had the innocent look of a young Sally Field with the body of Jamie Lee Curtis, but she had yet to gain self-confidence. She felt less attractive in comparison to the popular girls at school, but she couldn't deny Christopher was making genuine efforts to spend time with her, which gave her a taste of self-esteem.

After the long weekend, the reality of getting a job hit Monday afternoon. Tuesday morning Trina left with her sisters for her first job interview. She was nervous but having her sisters' support gave her the necessary confidence. The cook at the Salty Bar, Danny Flanigan, was friendly. He told her if she was willing to accept cash, she could fill his open dishwasher position.

Judy laughed. "Danny, Trina is a neat freak. The dishes will be so clean you'll think you've bought new ones. Give her two days and the shed out back will be organized alphabetically, and the food in the freezer will be color coordinated by the end of the week."

"Impressive. I'm more of the creative type, but Trina if you like to do that sort of thing, feel free."

"Hey, Danny, can we get Trina to clear our tables?" Jane asked while she clocked in.

"Your sister's priority will be keeping up with the dirty dishes, but if she's not backed up, she can help you bus tables. Trina, do you need to be home earlier than your sisters when you work nights?" Danny asked, wiping his greasy hands on his apron.

"No, Mr. Flanigan. I can work the same shifts. I also have a couple of friends who would love a job if you had extra hours available."

"I could use some more help. It seems like each summer we're getting more visitors, which is great for business. We expanded the patio over the winter to add six more tables. You girls should stay busy all summer. Tell your friends to stop by this week, and I'll see what we can do. And you can call me Danny. I don't like to be called Mr. Flanigan. It makes me feel too old. Now, wear this apron to keep your clothes dry, and I'll show you the mechanics of dishwashing. Judy and Jane, can you fill the salt and pepper shakers and wrap forks and knives? We open in twenty minutes, so let's get the place ready for the lunch crowd."

By the end of the first week, Trina was exhausted but thrilled at the same time. Her hands were raw and withered by the end of each shift, and she always needed a hot shower to eradicate the stinky smells from her pores before crashing into bed. It was backbreaking work, but she loved feeling like part of a team. The kitchen staff, who were all middle-aged men except for an awkward seventeen-year-old kid, Billy, treated Trina with respect. They saw how hard she worked and always felt guilty for handing her nasty pans to scrub at the end of the shift. Her sisters gave her a hard time now and then, but overall, it was a great first job.

Monica and Angela, two of Trina's original BBB crew, were both hired as well. The three of them loved working together and soon bonded with not just employees, but also with locals and vacationers who stopped in for meals several times a week. However, Monica's natural knack for putting people at ease had earned her admiration. She possessed zero inhibitions and could distract a disgruntled customer with humor and charm. Her social antics were not just geared towards the patrons. Monica placed friendly bets with her coworkers too. A dollar to make the grumpy old man smile or two dollars to convince one stranger to high-five another. Trina didn't know how she thought of the unique challenges each night, but the hours flew by so much faster. Although Trina could have gotten a job with Dawn, who worked at the ice cream shop, or Wendy, who worked at Goatfeathers Seafood Market, she enjoyed the camaraderie of the restaurant staff. Working at the Salty Bar was more physically draining, but Trina found it rewarding to see cash piling up in her shoebox at home.

The more she worked, the more comfortable Trina became at the restaurant. Initially, unaccustomed to being the center of attention, Trina attempted to escape the prying eyes of customers or shied away from casual conversations with the kitchen staff. But within a couple of weeks of engaging in small talk, Trina was able to relax and enjoy her new relationships. Trina felt the most comfortable with Danny. Although she was one of the youngest workers, he treated her like an equal. Danny was an arduous, hands-on chef and manager. He opened the restaurant early each morning and would be there until close, which sometimes was close to midnight. Occasionally, Trina would witness Danny taking a cigarette break or a shot of whisky to lower his stress levels, but overall, the staff would agree he was an expert at managing the kitchen.

An average-looking guy, Danny's light brown, slightly feathered hair was offset by brilliant blue eyes with a hint of hazel. About six-feet tall and slightly stocky, he normally wore jeans and a white T-shirt under his chef apron. He made an honest effort to get to know each employee, understand their moods, recognize when they were overwhelmed and insisted the staff take periodic breaks on busy nights. His relaxed personality and straight forward communication style made the restaurant an enjoyable workplace. Even though Danny's jokes were horrible, the staff couldn't help but enjoy the comic relief on stressful nights.

Danny became like another big brother to Trina especially since Tanner was not around. She admired Danny's excitement and fearlessness for creating new dishes. He was always trying new toppings on oysters, sampling different methods of frying fish and devising fresh takes on pasta salads. Trina went home full every night because he was constantly giving her samples and letting her munch on the kitchen mistakes. When he staffed the shift higher than was needed, he'd ask Trina to organize the shed supplies, and no matter how busy he was, he would make sure Trina took her breaks to rest her back. Even when the restaurant was packed and he was preoccupied with orders, he found a way to make sure Judy and Jane didn't overextend their 'sister' power.

Danny's brother, Jerry, who demanded to be called Mr. Flanigan, managed the business side of the Salty Bar in addition to operating four vacation rental properties. He was not nearly as nice as Danny, and he treated the waitresses more like secretaries than servers. Jerk Jerry, as the staff nicknamed him, was like an irritating splinter—minimal in stature but painful in its intrusion. Jerry was extremely handsome. About 6'2, he had bleach-blond hair with a tailored haircut. He normally wore one of his Flanigan Brothers, LLC aqua-blue, short-sleeved shirts, which wrapped tightly on his well-toned arm muscles, and a pair Levi's and loafers. Although he rarely smiled at the employees, he had straight white teeth and a dimple in his left cheek. His good looks were offset by his holier-than-thou temperament, which made most staff disperse into hiding spots whenever they saw him drive up. Even though he spent limited time at the Salty Bar, he demanded that his designated parking spot remain guarded by a No Parking sign. Danny, who basically lived at the restaurant, had to park his Jeep Wrangler down the street to ensure customers had available parking spots. The only good thing about Jerry's precious reserved parking spot was that the staff had a heads-up when he arrived.

Trina, Angela, and Monica absorbed the brunt of Jerk Jerry's foul temperament. As the most inexperienced staff, the girls were forced to cater to Jerry's demands and ridiculous requests. "Trina, come grab these boxes from the backseat of the Jeep. Angela, wash the sand off my tires. Monica, empty my cigarette tray. Don't touch my door handles with greasy fingers. Fetch the dirty sheets and bathroom towels the cleaners dropped off. Rewash the restaurant windows. Wipe the shelves in the stockroom. Make twenty-five extra toiletry bags for next week's rentals. Stop chatting with customers." Jerry was nonstop with demands as he smoked cigarettes at the bar.

The only time he turned off his overbearing demeanor was when he was in front of customers. Luckily for the staff, he only stopped in on Mondays to pick up cash for the bank deposits, check on restaurant inventory and grab supplies from the shed for the rental properties. Once or twice a week, he grabbed a late dinner and a couple of cocktails, but he wasn't in the habit of staying through the entire dinner shift. Poor Danny worked sixteen-hour days in the hot and sweaty kitchen while his brother sat at the bar flirting with the newest ladies in town.

Both Danny and Jerry were married, but the casual observer wouldn't know it. Danny's wife, Janice, hung out at the bar every night. She was not startlingly pretty but not unattractive either. She had a subtle way of flirting with the men, the way she crossed her legs with a miniskirt on or leaned over to grab something revealing cleavage. Trina felt bad for Danny because he seemed like such a nice, hard-working husband.

Maybe having cheating spouses was a Florida thing, because Jerry's wife, Sherry Lee, wasn't much better. She snuggled up to men with her notorious tight, candy-red dresses and left the bar with other men more often than she did with her own husband. The staff was convinced Jerry and Sherry Lee were in cahoots to increase revenue because they each had their own personal antics that resulted in wallets being emptied. Sherry Lee enticed men with her undivided attention, and Jerry used his good looks to tease women into believing he would shower them in free cocktails, which he never did. Between Sherry Lee's overtly physical contact with men and Jerry's gregarious smile and good looks, they milked their customers out of an unwarranted amount of their vacation spending money.

Danny's and Jerry's marriages were odd, to say the least, but she was just as shocked at the cunningness of the kitchen and waitstaff. The general mentality was if they didn't get caught, it never happened. Food, liquor and even salt and pepper shakers disappeared on a nightly basis. Danny looked the other way. He knew how hard the team worked and let things slide but Jerry would walk you to the door if he caught you in the act.

A few weeks into summer, the older kids planned their first park party at the trail entrance near Grayton Beach. Judy and Jane sat out back smoking cigarettes waiting for Trina to finish. Danny had released the kitchen staff, and he approached Trina and Angela. The girls had everything completed except emptying the trash and refilling the ice machines.

"Girls why don't you two go ahead. I can wrap up. I still need to check the inventory and restock the bar. I know there's something going on tonight I'm not supposed to know about. You've both worked hard, so go and enjoy a fun night out. Please be careful. Make sure you stay with the group." Danny ushered them out the back door, handed them a six-pack of coca cola and winked.

Trina felt gross and really wanted to go home and shower, but her sisters didn't give her that option. Judy and Jane pounced on them. "Let's go," Judy said. "We're going to be the last ones to show up. I have some clean clothes in the back seat of the car. And spray some perfume on; you both stink."

They drove to the service road trail entrance, which was a dirt path wide enough for a small vehicle to pass through. The path was populated with several beat-up cars, a couple of ATVs, and a spaghetti-like pile of bikes. The local police usually did not prowl the parks at night, so it was a great way to throw a secret party. Judy and Jane were chatting away in anticipation.

"Pennie said she was bringing two friends from her hometown," Judy said while applying lipstick in the dashboard mirror. "Johnny told me he invited that tall, knock-out brunette who came into the restaurant the other day. Let's hope she doesn't bring a bunch of other pretty girls to the party, because I heard that hot, college basketball player and his buddies from Georgia were coming."

"I bet some of the guys are already passed out from too many tequila shots," Jane said as she took off her work shirt and changed into a cute pink tank top and jean shorts. "We have some catching up to do. I can't wait to see Tommy."

"Trina, you, and your friends need to hang separately from us," Judy said as they got out of the car. "We don't want to look like we're babysitting."

They began walking toward the low rumble of conversation in the dark night. Once the girls saw an orange bear sign on a tree, they stopped.

"This is the spot where we go off the trail," Judy said. "Normally, Derik sets up in the No Trespassing section of the woods to keep us hidden. Walk carefully. Your legs and arms will get some scratches and cuts. The guys are pretty good at finding a decent sized clearing in the woods but getting there can be treacherous."

After about a minute of walking, they could see a low beam of light up ahead. Trina and Angela were nervous, but once they entered the clearing, they recognized about a half dozen kids their age and a pretty good chunk of their siblings' friend group. Tanner, who had come down for a long weekend, was already at the party and gave Trina a brotherly warning to stay clear of the alcohol and boys. Trina was tired after a long night of work but tried to put on a brave face. This was her first real party. She was going to be starting high school soon and wanted to fit in. She and Angela walked over to Monica, who of course had a group of guys near her. She said something to make them laugh. Trina didn't know how she talked so effortlessly with the older kids, but she was glad she could benefit from Monica's social skills.

Beer continued to flow, and though they didn't feel quite ready to drink yet, the BBB crew were thrilled to be there with the older kids. It was rather entertaining watching the transition as the alcohol took hold. Girls were laughing more. Guys were challenging each other to perform stupid party tricks. Soon, couples had formed and make out sessions were in full swing. Dawn was watching two boys who were competing against each other funneling beer. Wendy and Tanya were sitting with two rising high school sophomores, and Monica was sitting next to Christopher.

Trina was doing her best not to keep watching Monica while she was trying to listen to Angela. Jealousy was a new feeling for her. She completely understood why Christopher would like Monica. Everyone loved Monica. She was honest, humorous and an absolute blast to hang out with. Trina would have to get used to the idea of Christopher and Monica together if the two of them ended up together.

To distract herself, Trina concentrated on the murmur of various conversations and absorbed the information. Some of the guys were anticipating the return of some hot chick who vacationed down here every 4th of July and there were plotting on ways to break through her brother's protective barrier. A couple of girls were talking about how they went skinny dipping at Blue Mountain Beach last night. Pennie was hanging all over a surfer dude. He was smoking a joint and didn't seem to be paying any attention to Pennie, but she wasn't letting any other girl get close to him.

Angela decided to go hang out with Wendy and Tanya, leaving Trina sitting by herself. It was getting late, and Trina was hoping these parties didn't last until the wee hours of the morning.

"What do you call a piece of pizza made with chewy plastic mozzarella cheese, topped with pliable pepperoni and homemade Italian tomato sauce?"

She turned and saw Christopher standing with his hand held out, the palm facing up but closed tight. Trina's smile broke out wide and her chest heaved in pure joy. "Well, is it hand tossed and gooey?"

"Not sure about hand tossed, but definitely stretchy," Christopher said, sitting down next to Trina.

"Then I would call it my little slice of heaven," Trina said, shyly looking down at her legs stretched out in front of her instead of directly into Christopher's eyes.

"Perfect. Hopefully, you like it enough to wear it." Christopher opened his hand and moved it toward Trina. Resting on his palm was a thin, silver-link necklace with a small charm in the shape of a slice of pizza. Trina's eyes opened wide in pure astonishment. She didn't take the necklace for fear she was misreading the gesture.

"Can I?" he asked as he reached out to hang the necklace around her neck and clasped it behind her head. "It is a little dorky to give you a pizza necklace, but I wanted to always remember the first time I really noticed you. Your story about plastic green beans and pizza stuck with me. Thankfully, you get my quirky humor." He smiled and Trina smiled back. "I really think we should hang out more this summer," he said as he reached out to hold her hand.

"Yes, definitely. That would be great. I would love to! And thank you. I love it," Trina said in a whisper, still in complete shock. She took a moment to let it all sink in. She scanned the party for Tanner who must have left early. Relieved she didn't have to worry about being observed by her protective brother, she turned back to Christopher. "I can't believe you remembered my plastic pizza story," Trina said more confidently.

"It definitely stuck with me," he said as he squeezed her hand.

Trina was as ecstatic as she was confused. Earlier, it looked like Monica and Christopher were deep in conversation. She was thinking they were going to hook up, and here he was giving her a gift. Not letting go of his hand, she reached up to touch the necklace with her free hand and smiled. They sat together and chatted about work and the upcoming July 4th fireworks show. Eventually, Trina asked what he and Monica had been talking about. He revealed he was asking her for advice on whether to approach Trina tonight. Trina blushed intensely, then leaned in and rested her head on his shoulder and squeezed his hand. She couldn't help but feel nervous. She had not anticipated Christopher's mutual attraction and was doing her best to hide her excitement.

Midnight approached and the group was getting rowdy. Although Trina didn't want to leave Christopher's side, she was getting tired. Her legs were exhausted from standing all day at the restaurant, and she had to work the lunch shift tomorrow. She stood up, stretched, then walked over to the blanket that held the remnants of bags of chips and open pizza boxes. Christopher stood beside her while scanning the crowd trying to locate his brother.

Trina felt a heavy swipe across her lower back and left arm, then she was pushed over like she'd been hit by the linebacker of a football team. She fell to the ground and rolled to her back. Then it seemed like everyone was screaming.

"It's a bear!"

"It's a big black bear!"

"Oh my god, run!"

"Run! Run!"

Standing in front of Trina was a huge black bear. When it reared up on its hind legs with a pizza box in its paws, the screams got louder. Trina was transfixed, gazing starstruck at this huge, majestic animal. A hand reached out and pulled Trina up, and she heard Christopher say, "Run now! Follow me!"

Chaos ensued, with everyone scrambling and running as fast as they could in the dark in the thick of the woods. Everyone was focused on escaping and distancing themselves from the bear. Trina ran, one foot in front of the other, holding Christopher's hand. Although it was very dark, moonlight illuminated enough of the woods so that they could step out of the way of big pine trees and follow the trail of cups that were scattered all over the forest in the wake of departing partygoers. Her sisters and friends were holding on to each other's clothes as they tried to navigate the thorns and bushes in the woods and find the service road. Their legs and arms were torn to shreds by the vines and sharp palm leaves, but no one cared. They were not sticking around to see what else the bear wanted.

Christopher led Trina to her sister's car, squeezed her hand, smiled, then jumped into Paul's car. The kids on bikes bolted out of the woods the quickest, with it taking a few more minutes for the cars to back safely out to the main road. When they got home after midnight, they were filthy dirty, and their legs were scratched up and crusted with blood. Trina and her sisters piled into the bathroom and couldn't stop talking about the craziness of having a bear crash the party.

Judy was the first to jump in the shower as the adrenaline slowly dissipated. Jane wiped her makeup off while talking about some guy she met tonight. Trina sat on the closed toilet, waiting for her turn in the shower. She was still in shock. Not at the bear, although that was shocking. Christopher's gesture had her mind swirling. She replayed the night over and over in her head.

Judy finished and Jane jumped in. Judy dried off and left the bathroom, telling Trina to set her alarm for the lunch shift tomorrow since they were both scheduled to work. Trina brushed her teeth while she waited for Jane to finish her shower. Jane told Trina she was done but would leave the water running as she stepped out of the shower. When Trina took off her shirt, Jane let out a high-pitched squeal. "Trina, your back! It's bloody! Did the bear do that?"

Judy returned into the bathroom when she heard Jane. "Trina, holy moly! Oh my God! You have a six-inch scratch across your back. That looks like it really hurts. Why didn't you say something? Let me get some Neosporin and some Band-Aids."

Trina had no idea she was hurt. The unexpected turn of events had her focused on her escape and safety. She didn't even process that the bear had knocked her over. Now that it was brought to her attention, she started to feel the stinging on her back. She twisted her head and tried to look at herself in the mirror. She couldn't see it clearly, but she could sort of make out a red streak across her skin. Trina washed up in the shower, dried off and let her sisters take care of her back while she stood there silently. Her sisters thought she was thinking about the bear, but she was holding her *my slice of heaven* pizza charm in her hand and thinking about everything Christopher said. She was truly in heaven.

Trina climbed into her bunk bed, exhausted, and bandaged, but enchanted. Anticipation and happiness floated in and out of Trina's thoughts. As she drifted off to sleep, she dreamt of eating a big piece of chewy pepperoni pizza while holding Christopher's hand.

What Did She Have for Breakfast Today?

"9 11, what is your emergency?" That is what Trina should have heard, but she chickened out and called her husband, David.

"There is no way you found a human skeleton, Trina. I bet it's a pile of deer bones," David said, a loud nail gun zapping in the background. He was building something in the garage, and her story of finding bones hadn't distracted him from his mission. He always found a project to work on between business conference calls, which gave him the opportunity to tinker with his workshop tools. He was truly talented. He could fix pretty much everything and had saved them lots of repair costs over the years. David's hardware store and Home Depot receipts stacked up as quickly as her Publix and Amazon ones.

"I am not joking! I'll send you a picture. No, wait. I can't take a picture. The police will confiscate my phone, put me in a room and grill me as to why I found the need to take a picture." Trina rambled as she sat near the body on the damp forest floor. Sweat was now pouring down her cheeks, as it was getting close to 9:00 a.m. and the Florida sun had fully risen. It gets so hot in Florida, walking outside in the heat and humidity felt like trudging through a room full of human-sized marshmallows—thick and sticky. She wiped the sweat with the back of her hand.

"I'm telling you; I found a belt buckle and a pair of jeans. Or maybe shorts, I don't know. But there are bones. Lots of them. Enough to build a classroom skeleton," she said emphatically as she cradled the phone between her ears and shoulder, still holding the dog leash and trash bag in her hand.

David exhaled a long, drawn-out sigh. "Trina, how did you discover bones in the middle of the woods? And are you sure it is not an animal? The bears eat things all the time. How do you know its human?" he asked patronizingly, like asking a teenage daughter if she put the right gas in her car.

"First of all, a human rib looks different than a deer's rib," Trina stated with confidence, though she really didn't have a clue what a deer rib looked like. "The skull is human. It's sort of buried under mud, leaves, and pine needles, but I swear I can see a human eye socket. I have to call 911," she said, more to herself than David. "OK, I am going to dial 911. I'm going to be here for a while. Oh my God, I can't believe I am calling 911. I've never called 911. Will the police wonder why my mouth is so dry when I try to answer their questions? Can you come pick Freckles up and bring me some water? I'm sweating like crazy, and my lips are so chapped. Oh gosh, what if the police think I'm sweating because I'm guilty? Can you bring me a dry shirt? Bring me my blue and white V-neck T-shirt that's in the dryer." Her random commands escalated. "I'll be here for hours. Can you take the marinated pork tenderloin out of the fridge and put it in the crock pot on low? Don't forget to spray the inside of the crock pot with Pam. Also, can you change the laundry? I put a load in before I left."

She continued to ramble, acting like she hadn't just discovered a murder scene. Thinking about normal things like household chores calmed her nerves. Finding a dead body should have been more important than prepping dinner and shifting the laundry but talking about basic tasks was a good distraction.

"Trina, stop!" David interrupted. "Hang up the phone and call 911. I'll be there as soon as I can. I need to wrap up what I'm working on but then I'll head that way. Where are you again?"

"I don't know where I am exactly. Freckles ran off into the thick brush. I don't hear the traffic on 30A, and I can't see the back of any houses that bump up to the state park. Umm, let me look and see if I see anything familiar." She scanned the woods around her. Thank goodness she was wearing her prescription sunglasses, otherwise she would not see details in the distance.

She scanned the trees, looking for anything. Freckles began to show signs of impatience. The dog was eager to take off back into the woods, but Trina held on to the leash. "Wait," Trina said. "I think I see something behind me."

Trina's hand holding the garbage bag wiped the sweat from her forehead. Some sweat dripped down her hand into the bag. She sucked in a huge gulp of air, making a squeamish sound—her sweat had dripped onto the denim. Were the police going to think she had something to do with the crime if her sweat DNA was on the worn and fragile piece of clothing? She irrationally dropped the bag on the forest floor, wanting to separate herself from the evidence. Trina tried to clear her head. How can she secure the evidence? She heard David banging something in the background on the still open call. She decided to tie the trash bag to a tree branch near the dead body. The bag would help her find her way back, because that would be embarrassing if she couldn't find the skeleton when the police arrived.

After the bag was secured to the branch, she walked toward the orange color she saw up ahead. How she was doing this so calmly she had no idea. She was literally in the thick of the woods, vines and palms and pointy things scraping at her as she pushed her way forward within a stone's throw from a pile of bones. When she finally got close enough to see what the orange color was, she realized she had reached one of the dirt-and-sand-packed paths state park workers had cleared so the public could ride their RVs through the woods for a trail adventure. An orange sign dangled on its last leg about five feet up a tree.

It was a very old sign. Barely hanging on the tree, the sign could have been a victim of a hit-and-run by someone's 4x4 as they drove rampantly through the woods. Trina flipped the sign over since the visible side was blank. *Whoa, flashback.* She remembered this sign. Well, not this exact sign but the message. Freckles jumped up and licked Trina's arm. As Trina pet her with one hand, she read the imprinted message on the front of the sign. "No Trespassing: Bears Live Here." The sign had a silhouetted image of a black bear climbing a tree.

She tried hard to remember when and where she'd seen the sign. Had she seen it previously walking in the trails and therefore she should remember where she was currently standing? Or had she remembered this sign subconsciously from another time? Knitting a memory together like a winter scarf, Trina thought back to when she was attended parties as a teenager. The local high school kids liked to pick the No Trespassing areas of the state park so the cops wouldn't find everyone drinking. Although the sign brought back some fun memories, they had no relevance to pinpointing her current location.

David brought her back to reality. "Trina, did you figure out where you are in the park? How are you going to tell the police how to find you?"

"Well, no," she said slowly, still reminiscing about the sign from her youth. "I thought I saw a trail marker, but this is just an old sign. It isn't going to help you find me." She did, however, have one important piece of information. "I did find a service road. There can't be that many service roads in the park. If I tell them where I went in and how long I walked, they should be able to find me." As she relayed this information to David, she realized it might not help him find her. Freckles whined at her feet. The dog was not going to last much longer out here in this heat. "Can you remind me how to pin my location using Google maps? I'm somewhere in the middle of the Longleaf Greenway in Point Washington Park, but I haven't reached the Grayton side yet. Freckles ran off about ten minutes after I entered the trail from Route 83 side."

"I'm not sure a Google pin will work out in the woods. Let's hang up, then I'll call you once I get over there. By then, the police may have found you. I'll follow the blue lights. But, Trina, are you sure you want to do this? You could let someone else find it. Are you sure you want to take this on?" he said with concern. "It's not like people find dead bodies around here every day."

"David, seriously. I literally found a once upon a time living and breathing person out in the woods! I don't have a choice."

"OK. OK. You're right," he said with husbandly exasperation. "Call me when you're off the phone with 911." He hung up.

Trina took a deep breath and recollected the strong fictional female characters she had read about and virtually bonded with over the years. Female FBI profilers, police chiefs and coroners. These women had the confidence and stamina to dig in until justice was served. *I've got this!* She took one more deep breath, gave Freckles a reassuring pat and dialed 911.

She surprisingly communicated her gruesome discovery clearly and relatively calmly to the 911 operator. Knowing that her call was being recorded, she tried to breathe after every other word to keep her voice from shaking. The operator told her to wait there until the police crew arrived. Trina cautiously walked back through the brush to the bag hanging on the branch to take one more look at the body. She was second-guessing herself. One more look would guarantee she hadn't imagined this whole thing. It would be devasting if she needed to call 911 back and tell them she had really found the bones of a squirrel. Gosh, she wished it was that darn squirrel's body. That animal had caused the entire chain of events to begin with.

Trina realized her hands were shaking. No, not just her hands, her whole body. She felt like she was going to throw up, could feel the bile creeping up her throat. *No! No! No!* If she got sick out here, it would contaminate the crime scene. What she ate for breakfast would end up in a police report. She held her hand to her stomach as the cramps ramped up. Don't do it, Trina, do not let yourself throw up! Taking a deep breath, she closed her eyes and pushed the air out of her open mouth. The sun was rising fast, and beads of water ran down Trina's back. Freckles tugged on the leash as they both heard vehicles on the dirt road.

This was happening. Oh my God, where was David? She could not do this alone. What was she going to say to the police when they arrived? What if they asked her why she was walking in the woods and not on the trail? What if they yelled at her for touching the belt? Her mind was spinning, thoughts racing through her head like an intense ping-pong match. She tried to calm herself down. Why was she worried? She couldn't be found guilty of picking up trash, could she?

Trina cycled through memories of books she had read. What steps would FBI profiler Violet Darger from *The Girl in the Sand* take if she found a skull? Should she put the denim and the buckle back on the ground? Would animal control confiscate Freckles and take doggie paw prints? Oh geez, she was so bloody nervous. She felt guilty. Really guilty. But why? Why did she feel like she needed to get used to wearing silver handcuff bracelets? Thank God handcuffs were not made from gold. She'd never been a fan of gold.

As her thoughts jumped from good to bad to silly, the sound of dirt churning under tires got louder. Soon, she glimpsed the top of a vehicle. One car, then another one. Wow, there was a whole line of them. As the realization hit her, she felt the nervous energy bouncing around in her stomach like a ball stuck in a Chucky Cheese vacuum chamber. She tried to control it, but she couldn't stop it. Trina's insides joined the world of the outside. She took a quick look down at her desecration. The bones that were previously only covered with mud were now covered with her horribly unhealthy breakfast choice. A damp nose touched the side of her cheek. Freckles sniffed her, then turned to stick her nose directly into the wet bones. Trina yanked on the leash. Things were bad enough already. She couldn't let Freckles further disturb the scene.

The soulless eye socket staring directly up at Trina and the reality of what was about to happen snapped Trina out of her fog. Someone's life had ended under this tree, under the glorious blue skies of Florida. Fate had sandwiched her love of fictional crimes in between a layer of 30A history, skeletal remains, and a spicy smear of mystery. She stood up and wiped her mouth, her fascination with evidence retargeted. It's time to forget about her DNA. The police will be focusing on finding someone else's. She now had a newly defined focus. She was going to help them solve this case.

My Slice of Heaven

Everyone was talking about the bear attack. As the grapevine embellished facts surrounding Trina's bear encounter, the beer and bear parties became notorious among the local youth. After Trina was examined by a local physician, her parents relaxed. However, Richard and Nancy still grilled details of the encounter out of Tanner, Judy, and Jane. Trina's siblings downplayed the incident focusing on the rarity of an animal encounter and promised they would carry a bear horn for protection. Trina didn't care about the potential of restricted nighttime activities, but she wasn't happy her mom was making her wear a one-piece bathing suit until the scratch healed. For the first week, the scratch stung every time she dressed and washing dishes for hours didn't feel great either, but she eventually got used to the discomfort.

Every day, familiar faces stopped in for lunch and dinner to catch a glimpse of Trina's scratch. Trina felt like a Ripley's Believe it or Not Freak Show main attraction. The size of the bear and the ferocity of the bear's contact seemed to grow with each rendition. Bragging that it was her idea to bring Trina to the party, Judy proudly boasted it was her little sister who survived the bear attack. While Judy exaggerated the amount of blood that gushed out of Trina's wounds, Jane at least focused on Trina's bravery after the attack.

Trina didn't think about the bear; she was focused on Christopher's valiant efforts to pull her to safety. The day after the attack, before the news had spread, Christopher stopped in the restaurant for lunch to check on Trina. They walked out to the back of the restaurant and sat on a pile of boxes filled with kitchen supplies that hadn't been unpacked yet.

"I wanted to call you this morning but figured you slept in. How are you? Did you get hurt?" Christopher asked, his hand softly touching her lower back.

"I have a scratch on my back and my arm. It all happened so fast. If it wasn't for you, who knows what would have happened to me! Jane and Judy cleaned it up last night, and my mom is taking me to a doctor after work today."

"Is it OK if I peek at it?"

Trina nodded.

He lifted the back of her T-shirt and carefully untaped the gauze. "Trina, wow, that bear raked its paws across your entire back. You were so calm. Are you sure you're not in pain? That is going to take a while to heal, but man, you are going to have a great story to tell your children someday."

"I don't think I'll tell my children I used to party in the woods. No need to give them crazy ideas."

He gently lowered her shirt and slowly turned her around, wrapping his hands around her upper arms. "I am so glad I was there. Maybe you should take it easy for a little while until that heals. Do you want to watch sunset on the beach tonight?"

"Sunset would be great. I get off at three, and I should be home by five from the doctor's office. Thanks so much for checking on me. And thank you again for the necklace. It was totally unexpected and so thoughtful," Trina said, touching the tiny pizza charm that hung on her chest. She knew she was never ever going to take it off.

Christopher and Trina were two peas in a pod after that, spending every spare moment with each other. They took long walks on the beach, explored nearby state parks, chased lizards, and admired eagles and ospreys flying high above the huge pine trees. Between their part-time jobs, they had to finagle their schedules to find a few hours each day to be with each other. Since Christopher worked till noon each day on a fisherman's boat; he was able to visit her at the restaurant most days she worked. He was there often enough, he now entered through the back kitchen door instead of the customer entrance and quickly became as recognizable and welcome as the staff at the Salty Bar. Sometimes he sat at the bar waiting for Trina and other times he helped Billy in the kitchen while they talked about their fascination with snakes and love of rock-n-roll.

Danny also engaged in conversations with Christopher and treated him like one of the kids under his tutelage. He accepted Christopher's offers of assistance by having him move supply boxes, fill the ice machine, and clear a table or two. He wasn't on the payroll, but Danny gave him free meals as a thank you. Danny told Christopher to keep their arrangement between the two of them since Jerry was stringent with staff policies and would not have accepted a trade of meals for service. Jerry would have flipped if he knew Danny let Christopher help in the kitchen, and he would have blown a gasket if he knew Christopher was allowed in the supply shed.

Trina didn't really understand why Jerry was weird about access to his shed. When she first started working there, she was repulsed by the extreme disorganization. Within a couple of days, she sorted and separated the supplies, so the kitchen supplies were on the left side of the shed and the rental property supplies were on the right. She organized hotel-sized soaps, shampoos, and conditioners so they were lined up like rows of tin soldiers. The bathroom towels were folded with military precision, with the folds facing the same way making towels easy to grab. The individually wrapped toilet paper rolls were now stacked so neatly on three vertical shelves it looked like an igloo built with perfection. Danny was in awe of her tidiness and requested she take on organizational duties weekly.

Jerry, on the other hand, was initially not a fan. He treated access to the shed like a coveted treat reserved only for select few. But after one look at Trina's handiwork, it was difficult for Jerry to argue against it. Trina enjoyed the freedom of organizing, but she did not enjoy working in the shed when Jerry was around. Even if he didn't say anything, his body language and the intensity of his silent observation made working in his vicinity uncomfortable. Trina learned Jerry's weekly routine and did her best to work around his schedule. After grumbling about the restaurant's cleanliness or bitching at staff loitering at the bar area, he would retreat to the shed to sit at his office desk and make the daily cash deposits, reconcile the credit card receipts, and order supplies. His desk was sparse, and he locked up paperwork in a tall filing cabinet behind his desk. When he left for the night, he locked up the shed and dropped the keys off with Danny. Although Trina had never approached his work area, Jerry made an extra effort to remind Danny that Trina was not allowed near his office and no one else besides Billy should have access to the shed.

Knowing that Jerry was militant about staff following rules, Christopher found ways to visit the Salty Bar unobtrusively when Jerry was there. Hiding in one of the smallest booths in the back, he read stories about primitive time periods reveling in the details of how humans lived hundreds of years ago, fascinated by the cutthroat way human beings forged progress, fought for their religious freedoms, or blindly followed the monarchs and clan chiefs. Trina didn't enjoy his reading choices, but his diversity of book genres did expand her own personal reading.

Their passion for books and animals had a way of merging their inner thoughts more deeply than frivolous typical teenage conversations. When their friends were talking about crashing parties, Madonna's latest outfit or a funny *Simpsons* episode, Christopher and Trina looked at each other, sending thoughts of boredom or disdain through eye contact. It was like they had their own nonverbal language that conveyed to each other they would rather be hiking in the woods or hanging out on the beach with a good book.

The month of June melted away as Trina divided her time between work, Christopher, and her friends. After watching her kitchen and living room disappear under piles of paper plates, napkins, hamburger buns, holiday decorations, new yard games and boxes of sparklers, Trina eagerly awaited the annual neighborhood cookout. On the morning of July 4th, the weather was picture perfect. The Florida sky was painted a deep blue and there were small, thin wisps of featherlike clouds highlighting the amazing view. By eleven in the morning, it was hot and humid outside, but the Gulf was still cool enough to feel refreshing. All three sisters had the day off because the Salty Bar was closed for the holiday. Their mother had tasked them with making potato salad and plates of pigs-in-a-blanket while she hand rolled meatballs. Their dad, who was spending two weeks in Florida between work trips, was preoccupied with preparing the fireworks show and cleaning the grill.

Jane had invited Tommy to the fireworks show, and he was bringing his beautiful sister, Jasmine. Although Tommy and Jasmine's family had been vacationing for years in Blue Mountain Beach during the month of July, Trina had not met Jasmine. Trina was curiously eager to see Jasmine because the rumor mill had painted a vision of an untouchable goddess. Wary of the attention Jasmine would garner at the party since most boys were infatuated with her, Judy tried to convince Jane there were already too many people coming. Jane distracted Judy with tales of all the good-looking friends Tommy was bringing with him. Trina did her best to stay out of the drama and focused on taking advantage of the day since it would be the first day all six of her BBB girlfriends would be able to spend an entire day together since Memorial Day. Trina and Christopher agreed to enjoy the day with their friends and catch up with each other at the fireworks show that evening.

Noon arrived and the backyard was popping. The community's love for July 4th celebrations was apparent in the red, white, and blue outfits, sparkly face paintings and glittered sun hats. By the afternoon, fifty or more people were teetering between their backyard and the beach. The older kids were stealing beer and wine coolers from their parents' stash, partaking in beach volleyball games, and laying on all sorts of colorful beach blankets that were scattered along the water's edge. The BBB and four of their new friends formed a circle with their towels, allowing them to carry on multiple conversations at once. They shared stories of stingy customers, boy crushes and pesty siblings.

Dawn and Tanya told the girls about the new cute guy who worked at the Grayton General Store. Old Grandpa Joe, the name the local kids gave the store's owner, told Dawn Bobby was his grandson from North Carolina. Tanya described him as a Rob Lowe lookalike with blond hair and blue eyes, but with the mystique of Judd Nelson's character from *The Breakfast Club*. Dawn said he didn't talk to them, but in her words, "Oh man, I felt like he was undressing me with his eyes!" The girls laughed in unison and soon bet on which girl would become his lucky girlfriend. Initially, they threw out Monica's name, but she reminded them she had eyes on Ricky. Several bets were put on Pennie because she could be so tenacious when she wanted something. By the end of the conversation, they decided tomorrow was a great day to ride bikes to the General Store to grab some soda, snacks and maybe his phone number.

The sun was blazing by midafternoon, and the girls lathered up with their third application of suntan lotion. Jane was walking down the beach with Tommy and a beauty queen who must have been Tommy's sister, Jasmine. As they got closer, all the girls were sitting up on their beach blankets, staring at Jasmine. Tommy was a good-looking guy but there was something startling about Jasmine's presence.

Jane walked over to the circle to make an introduction. "Jasmine, this is my younger sister, Trina, and her friends. I'll let you all introduce yourselves. Tommy and I are going to join the volleyball game."

Jasmine said hello and took out a beach blanket from her bag.

Monica jumped right in with her open and honest admiration for Jasmine's beauty. "I had heard that you were a knockout, but you are the true definition of bodacious!"

Jasmine sat down next to Wendy's blanket "Well, thank you for your fabulous description, but I really am nothing special. I just lucked out that I look like my mom and am also tall like my dad. I hope to grow into my lanky legs or stop looking like I'm going to fall over from being chest heavy." Her humble response put everyone at ease. It was a nice surprise that she gracefully accepted the compliment but, at the same time, poked fun at her early womanly figure.

By the end of the day, Jasmine had fit right in. She was shy but friendly and was not conceited even though she was the best-looking girl on the beach by far. The center of conversation had quickly shifted to watching the various childish actions the boys took to garner Jasmine's attention. The entourage of high school boys that repeatedly walked by their spot on the beach to make eye contact with Jasmine was so ridiculous that it became funny. Since Jasmine was not interested in their attention, the girls felt bound to protect her, and the group turned Jasmine's fan following into their beach entertainment. Tommy never strayed far from his sister's vicinity, and therefore not a single boy made successful contact.

The weather had been absolutely stunning all weekend, and the memorable 4th of July festivities brought their close-knit community even closer. The long days relaxing on the sand, floating in the clear aqua water and the progressive bronzing of their skin elicited peaceful contentment, and no matter where you were sitting on the beach, the evening fireworks show lit up the night sky for miles in both directions. The camaraderie of their neighborhood, million-dollar beach views and days filled with stories, laughter and suntans made Trina and her family believe their bungalow was the best investment they ever made.

As the busiest week of the summer, the days after Independence Day were exhausting. The Salty Bar staff members were required to work doubles that week to keep up with the steady stream of customers. Although their savings accounts were growing, their feet were aching and their patience with unruly customers was waning.

Jerry Flanigan showed up at the restaurant on Thursday, which was a rare occurrence. Billy and Trina were tasked with emptying his Jeep and restocking the restaurant supplies that Danny had requested. Billy washed his hands, took off his work apron and grabbed Trina on his way out.

"Hey, Trina, what are you reading nowadays? Your choices are more interesting than your boyfriend's and all that historical mumbo jumbo. I like reading about killers on the loose like you," Billy said as he walked around the back of the Jerry's Jeep.

"I'm in the middle of an Agatha Christie book right now. What authors do you like? Do you have any recommendations?" Trina inquired.

"Have you ever read *Lifeguard* by Richie Tankersley Cusik? After reading that book I learned to never trust people in a position of perceived power." Billy grabbed a heavy box of fresh vegetables.

Grabbing a small box of napkins and a light box of plastic cups, Trina said "Never heard of that one. If you still have the book, bring it in and I'll add it to my summer reading list." Trina walked in behind Billy. They both dropped the boxes off and walked back outside. Now that her hands were free, she instinctively reached up and grabbed her *my slice of heaven* charm.

"Christopher is a nice guy and all," Billy said as he grabbed a small box for Trina and piled two big boxes in his arms, "but you deserve someone a little older. More mature. Do you know I saved over $2,000 this summer? I could treat you to a nice dinner and take you to the movies. I would buy you a real necklace charm, not a pizza one. You are a pretty girl. You deserve someone who will treat you right."

"That's super nice of you to offer, Billy. I am honestly flattered. You're a nice guy, and I bet you'll find the perfect girl. Maybe someone who likes Aerosmith and snakes," Trina said, feeling a little awkward. She thought of Billy as a friend, so she pushed the uncomfortable thoughts out of her head.

He seemed to accept her dismissal, but he kept tooting his own horn as they continued their task. After they emptied the first few boxes, they struggled to have the proper leverage to get the remaining items out of the back. Trina climbed up into the open Jeep so she could push boxes toward the rear. She was immediately struck by an overpowering smell of perfume. It reminded her of the Love's Baby Soft perfume her sisters both liked to use. Trina didn't like to wear perfume, so the smell sort of suffocated her. She wondered if Sherry Lee, Jerry's wife, wore Love's Baby Soft. Seemed like an odd choice for an adult woman but what did Trina know about perfume. Maybe adults liked that fragrance too.

After moving three crates of fresh produce and two boxes filled with napkins, plastic cups and condiments, Trina was struggling to push a box that held four large bottles of fryer grease. She had to lean up against the seat and push her feet on the box to get it all the way to the edge. Billy was making a trip inside with the last box of condiments. When the box slid, it pushed the thin felt fabric that lay over the back of Jeep. Trina climbed out and tried to straighten the fabric because she knew Jerry would get angry if his Jeep was not left meticulously clean. When she reached to adjust the fabric, she noticed a small delicate necklace clinging to the back. The necklace was made with petite chain links and had one small seahorse figurine. Trina assumed the necklace belonged to Sherry Lee, so she hung it around the stick shift so Jerry could return it to his wife. Thirty minutes later, they had placed all the boxes either in the restaurant cooler or supply closet with the overflow being dropped off in the shed. Trina was too tired to organize the shed, so she asked Danny if she could take a late lunch break before the dinner shift.

While Danny was making her a quick grilled cheese sandwich, Trina sat in one of the booths. Her sisters had already had their lunch break, so they were preparing the salad plates for dinner service. While she waited for her lunch, Trina opened her book, *Murder on the Orient Express* by Agatha Christie. The plot was intriguing and had Trina struggling to figure out who the murderer could be. Billy brought out Trina's grilled cheese, and he was nice enough to drop off a soda as well. As Trina sat reading and nibbling on lunch, she fiddled with the slice of pizza charm, oblivious to her surroundings.

"What's the deal with the necklace?"

Trina looked up to see Jerry standing by the booth holding the daily deposit bag in one hand and a plate with a burger on it in the other. He slid into the booth opposite Trina. Reflexively, she gave the pizza charm a little squeeze.

"I noticed you've been wearing that necklace a lot lately. You know we only serve pizza on Friday nights." He placed his deposit bag on the far-left side of the booth, set his plate down and immediately took a bite of his hamburger.

"Yes, sir. I know that," Trina said, feeling uncomfortable with her boss sitting across the table from her. She unconsciously raised her index finger to her mouth, because whenever she was nervous, she nibbled on her fingernails.

"Tell me why you wear it so much." He took another big bite out of his burger and followed with a couple of French fries.

"It was a gift. It reminds me of someone," Trina said, removing her index finger and taking the last bite of her grilled cheese.

"Well, if it's from that boyfriend of yours who's always hanging around, you should tell him to bump up his game a little and buy you a gold necklace. Gold would complement your eyes." Jerry smiled at Trina, knowing he was making her uncomfortable. Trina rarely saw the man smile. It creeped her out.

"I better get back to work, Mr. Flanigan. My sisters will get mad with me if I sit for too long." Trina grabbed her book and empty plate and scooted out of the booth.

"Don't get too smart reading those crime novels, Trina. You're too young to put dirty thoughts in that sweet head of yours."

"I'll try not to. Oh, Mr. Flanigan, when I was grabbing the last box of supplies, I found a small seahorse necklace stuck to the felt pad in your trunk. I put it around your stick shift so you can return it to Sherry Lee. Enjoy your lunch, Mr. Flanigan."

Jerry's eyes widened and his mouth opened to speak but no words came out. She hoped she hadn't overstepped by moving the necklace. Trina bowed her head, spun around, and walked to the back of the kitchen. She placed her plate in the dirty dish bin and leaned up against the wall by the time clock. Now that was weird. Jerry never sits with employees. She reached up and felt her necklace. How the heck did he even notice it? Normally, she was bent over the dishwasher or had her head hidden in the storage closet stocking shelves. She did not like knowing he was so aware of her presence.

"Trina, are you OK? You look like you might faint." Danny was standing over by the kitchen grill running a cleaning brush back and forth over the top of it. "Did you eat your lunch? You might need to take a little bit more of a break. The steam from the dishwasher could be overheating you."

"Oh, no I'm fine, Danny. I just need a glass of water. I'll take a quick drink and start helping Angela stack the bar glasses. Thanks for asking, though." Trina ran both hands over her cheeks, then filled a glass with water. She took two big gulps and then grabbed a tray of hot steaming glasses out of the bar dishwasher and rested it on the counter to begin unloading.

Angela, who was kneeling next to the bar stacking beer mugs, looked up. "What did Mr. Bossy want with you? I don't think I've ever seen that man eat lunch in the restaurant. Normally, he hides away in that shed of his."

"He was asking me about my book. But yeah, I scooted out of there as quickly as I could. He's a good-looking guy but creepy as a Peeping Tom the way he looks right through you."

Trina slid wine glasses into the slots that were hanging above the bar, then the girls finished emptying the glassware and did a final walk through the restaurant to make sure they had every dish cleared. Billy was sweeping the restaurant and Judy and Jane had finished salad preparations and had begun slicing pieces of pie to prepare plates of dessert for dinner service.

The night was insanely busy. The staff hustled with little chance to rest. Around 9:00 p.m., the bartender asked Trina to restock the glasses. She did her best to stay out of the bartender's way because she knew he had to shuffle quickly to attend to the long stretch of customers. Working at the bar, she was able to listen in on several conversations. Two local fishermen were rehashing stories of the day's catch. A couple in their thirties, still wearing their bathing suits from a day in the sun, were on their fourth round of Captain Jack Swirls, which was a rum, coke, and ice cream concoction. Three single ladies sitting on the far right were batting their eyes and flirting with Jerry, who'd decided to stay at the bar.

Sitting in the center were three middle-aged men who were property owners in the area. The scrawny guy with a balding head was complaining this week's tenants had broken the hot tub twice and he had to spend $125 on repairs. Another man, Brooks, was sharing his plan to install a camera at his rental properties pools so he could watch videos of his female tenants. The third guy, Walt, was relatively quiet, but Trina noticed how he watched every female in the mirror's reflection. Trina was so glad she normally worked in the kitchen. Adult men could be so creepy.

Eventually the crowd died down and it was time to focus on finishing up dishes. Angela had pushed the last tray of dirty plates into the dishwasher and was scrubbing the last kitchen pan. Trina walked around the restaurant and pulled the trash bags out of the bins. Trina pulled the big trash bag out the back door and was about to heave it into the dumpster when she heard a faint sound. She stopped and listened. It sounded like a whimper, then a female voice said, "No. I don't want to kiss you! Please let me go!"

Trina heard a grunt, a slight sound of impact and then a rustling sound, as if someone was trying to back up or move. "Hello? Are you alright?" Trina said with trepidation. She heard scuffling, then the sound of someone running.

"Damn it!" a male voice said, followed by what sounded like a fist hitting the side of the shed.

Trina didn't wait to see who it was. She turned and jogged back to the restaurant. Her chest was pulsing from the instant jolt of fear. Danny and the girls were standing in the back of the kitchen by the time clock.

"Hey, Trina, you're all set for the night. I'm going to clock you out. Have you seen Billy?" Danny asked. "He didn't clock out, but he left about ten minutes ago."

"No, I never saw him."

Judy and Jane pulled Trina toward the door. "Let's go. We're supposed to meet Ricky and Tommy for a late-night beach stroll. Bye, Danny, see ya tomorrow." Judy and Jane started gossiping as they briskly walked down the side street toward their car. When Trina turned the corner to catch up, she caught sight of Billy leaning up against the shed smoking a cigarette.

"Goodnight, Billy," Trina said.

"Yeah, really great night, Trina." He banged his left foot against the shed and took another puff of his cigarette, then dropped the cigarette butt and squashed it into the ground. Billy walked up to Trina and said, "Just because you have a boyfriend doesn't mean you can scare away my chances at finding a date."

Billy had never been rude to her. He was usually super nice. She realized that must have been him she had interrupted. Trina was learning so much this summer, including not to assume everyone was as nice as they appeared to be.

How Not to Act at a Crime Scene

"No, Freckles, no!" She yanked on the leash to pull her dog away from the now involuntarily garnished bones. She straightened her back as streams of salty sweat raced down her face. Unconsciously wiping her cheeks, she squinted at the rays of sun in between the numerous tall pines and mentally braced herself.

She gave herself a mental pep talk as she stomped over vines heading toward the sounds of vehicles moving closer. As her right foot landed on the hard packed dirt road and her left hand supported her on a pine tree, she turned her head to peer down the road and immediately regretted calling 911. Red and blue lights brightened the green and brown hues of the forest like a colorful fireworks show. She unconsciously raised her index finger to her mouth to nervously nibble on a fingernail. The sight of so many police cars made Trina feel sick all over again. Struggling to control her stomach revulsions, she bent over and coughed out a tiny burst of leftover anxiety. She wiped her face and kicked dirt over the mess with her sneakers. Trina prayed the sun's rays had blinded the cops' view, otherwise their reports would include descriptions of Trina's hug of the virtual toilet.

A police officer and his partner exited the closest vehicle and walked toward Trina as the sound of other doors opening echoed around her. Trying to appear rational and professional, she reached out to shake hands and then quickly retracted it, remembering she had not sanitized them.

"Um, hi. Hello. I assume you are here to check out the dead body I found this morning?" Trina sputtered to the first officer who approached. "I didn't touch anything. Well, that's not exactly true. Let me clarify—I didn't touch the skeleton." She felt like a child who swore to their parents that they hadn't eaten the last bit of cookies and cream in an empty half gallon ice cream container.

Trina pulled Freckles away from the cop and kept babbling. "I totally found this by accident, Officer, but it is most definitely a human skeleton. Animals don't have skulls that look like that. The skull is at an odd angle too, like maybe he fell from the tree. I didn't see much clothing but maybe over the years it all decomposed. Well, I assume years. I really don't know how long that poor person has been lying there."

"Talk to Officer Cody and Sheriff Smith, ma'am. My job is only to secure the perimeter of the crime scene," he gently stated, a sly grin hiding underneath his polite smile. This kid looked like he just graduated college. Trina couldn't help but notice his precision haircut, thin but well-groomed mustache and exquisitely sculpted forearms. She thought of her daughter, who was single, and wondered if he was single too.

"Excuse me, ma'am, did you hear me?"

Trina became conscious of the presence of another man to her left who was speaking to her. He was crouched down petting Freckles, whom Trina hadn't realized had escaped from the clutches of her grip and was panting heavily and licking the man's face.

"Oh, I am so sorry, Officer. I was lost in my thoughts. What did you say?" She grabbed the end of her dog's leash, which was now covered in prickly sandspurs. "Freckles, come here, girl." Trina bent down to eliminate any unnecessary discomfort that might have lodged in her dog's paws.

"I was asking if you are alright. My name is Officer Cody Jenkins. When we drove up, you looked like you were not feeling very well. Take a seat. We can wait a minute until you get yourself together." He was a decent-looking man. He had a crew cut, brown eyes and a youthful, muscular build underneath his clean, freshly ironed uniform. Trina assumed he was from the south based on his polite manners and gentle approach.

She withered inside. She felt like a piece of clothing that was turned inside out and wrinkled from the washing machine. All hot, tumbled and needing time to straighten out. She wanted to hang her head in shame. Her first interaction with law enforcement, and she was not making a great first impression. She needed to prove to them she was a valuable resource, but her nervous energy was manipulating her words and actions like a puppeteer.

"I am. Fine, that is. Totally fine. Thank you all for coming so quickly. I didn't realize the entire department was going to be here. I've never met a real cop in person before. I've watched lots of Netflix crime shows but to meet a cop at an active crime scene is making me a little skittish. Not because I did anything, don't misunderstand me. I only found the skull; I didn't kill it." The guilt-ridden comments tumbled out of her mouth. Normally, she was polished and competent. Now, she sounded like a bumbling idiot.

Within minutes, there were eight people standing in a semicircle around Trina on the service road. Most were wearing police uniforms. Two were dressed like paramedics. Trina counted two females: one in regular clothes and one in a police uniform. She silently appreciated their presence.

Officer Cody took command. "We received a call about human remains you believe you found. Are you OK if we ask you some questions or do you need to rest for another minute?"

Before she answered, Trina processed that he had said *believes* she found. Why was it so difficult to believe a woman knows what a dead body looks like? She was going to prove them wrong. She turned around and walked briskly through the brush tugging Freckles behind her, totally forgetting about any evidence she may be trampling on.

"This way! I'll show you the skull and rib cage. This is definitely a person not a deer or a bear." She marched toward the skeleton like an expert hiker, stomping over the briers and bushes to navigate back to the litter bag hanging on the tree. "I don't know how fast skin decomposes, but this person must have died years ago. Not only did I uncover a skeleton, but I also discovered a piece of denim and a leather belt with rusted buckle. I bet if we dig in the mud, leaves, and twigs, I could help you find the rest of this poor person's clothes." She was almost back to the original spot when she realized several voices were shouting out commands.

"Ma'am, stop!"

"You can't go back there!"

"Lady, we need to mark off the crime scene!

"Miss, please you have to stop!"

She was about to turn back when she felt a tug on the leash. Before she could regrasp the loop, Freckles took off chasing another squirrel. Trina yelled, but the dog successfully escaped her grasp with the leash trailing behind her. Trina heard the officers, but she was sure she could grab the end of the leash before Freckles got too far. After a couple of long strides, Trina bent down to reach for the tip of the leash and tripped over a huge tree limb. Falling with her hands out in front of her, Trina heard the devasting sound of a crack underneath her as she hit the ground. She leaned her chin down to see a skull staring back at her. Hoping she hadn't broken any bones, hers or the skeleton's, Trina pushed herself up to a standing position with the unwelcome clarity that she was causing more harm than good.

Cody, one female and another gentleman were standing several feet away from the crime scene, breathing heavily from trying to keep up with Trina. She heard someone say, "Well, I'll be damned, there is a skeleton," followed by cussing and frustrated whispers.

Staring at the bones in a complete fog at what she had just done, Trina caught a glimpse of her bottle of mace, which had fallen out of her skirt pocket when she fell. Not wanting to ruin the crime scene any more than she already had, she extended her arm to grab the mace off the ground. Someone else's gloved hand reached down at the same time and grabbed the can. They both picked it up, and the pressure of the dual grip caused one of them to press down on the button. *Pfsssssst!* A quick spray shot out opposite her, straight into the face of some tall, gray haired, older gentleman. He was wearing a brown-colored shirt with a bright metal star clipped to the front. Trina winced at the same time he hollered in pain as he bent over with both hands over his face.

She heard a loud grunt, followed by a long, slow breath. The man raised his right hand with his index finger pointed up in the air, and the woods became completely silent. No one spoke a word. He reached into his pocket and grabbed out a cloth with his left hand. Someone handed him a bottle of water, which he opened then slowly and consistently poured over his eyes. Minutes ticked by in silence with all eyes on him.

The man, who Trina later learned was Sheriff Sam Smith, finally spoke to the first officer. "I'll be fine," he said, eyes red, puffy, and barely open. "Cody, please escort the lady to the service road and ask Joe to mark off the crime scene. Everyone else, let's suit up and commence protocols. Detective Jenifer let's do our best to try to keep this off the airways and get the medical examiner here ASAP. We need Miriam back here to take photos. We also need the lady's shoe prints, fingerprints and to document all evidence she touched. Detective Trenton, please initiate your inquiry with the misses. Please send medical back here to help me with my eyes. Let's go team. We need to dot every I and cross every T. This is not going to bode well as we enter spring break season."

"I am so, so sorry," Trina said. "I normally carry my bear horn but happened to grab my daughter's mace this morning. I am so sorry, sir. I didn't realize you were reaching for it. Did it spray you directly in the eyes? Can you see?" she asked him, hovering like a mother who had just watched her child fall on the playground.

"I'm sure it was an accident. Excuse me, ma'am, please stay back," the sheriff said as he walked around her, still squinting.

"I'm sure the medical examiner can put his body back to its original state even if his bones are broken. Well, it could be a female. The denim I found could have been a denim skirt. Ummm, now that I think about it, that belt didn't look feminine, but you never know. Do you want me to show you exactly where I found the belt?" Realizing that no one was really listening to her, she stopped talking.

One of the females approached Trina but remained standing about three feet away. "Ma'am, my name is Detective Jenifer Townsend. Please turn the nozzle down to the ground and hand the mace to me so we can catalog it," she commanded firmly. Jenifer reminded Trina of Rachel Zane from the show *Suits*. Very professional, very attractive and targeted with a mission. "Officer Cody will escort you away from this area."

Trina lowered the mace and handed it to the detective. "Can I go look for my dog? My husband is on the way to take her home for me. Will he be able to come back and see the body? He will never believe me unless he sees it with his own eyes."

"No, ma'am. This is now a secure crime scene. Wait right here for Officer Cody."

Trina stood there feeling like a disciplined schoolgirl. A multitude of activity swarmed around her like bees in a hive, and Trina swiveled her head taking it all in. The sheriff had re-opened his eyes, which made Trina feel slightly better, and he was bent down examining the body. Crime scene tape was being wrapped around trees, and a tent was being propped open over the skeleton and surrounding area. Several people had contamination suits on and blue booties, and a uniformed female officer was snapping photos with a professional camera.

Officer Cody approached Trina, grasping her arm with a gentle but firm grip on her wrist and guided her back toward the service road.

Trina heard Freckles barking somewhere in the woods. "Sir, I really need to find my dog. Chasing her is what started today's events to begin with," she explained.

"Ma'am, I will retrieve your dog. You need to stay here. Can you please sit tight? Don't go anywhere. Detective Trent will be over in a minute to ask you some questions."

"Would it be possible for me to take a quick picture of the crime scene. My kids will not believe me unless I show them proof. Can I call my husband and find out if he is on his way?" Trina's nervous energy had her adrenaline bubbling to the surface. Why couldn't she shut up? She must be in shock. Maybe she was going to have PTSD after this. She'd literally found a dead person, threw up on the person, then broke that person. She felt like she needed a hot shower and a glass of wine.

Cody grunted with frustration. "No, miss. You cannot take pictures and no phone calls right now. Let me grab your dog. I will be right back. Here comes Detective Trent."

A broad-shouldered man casually walked over to Trina. He was talking on his cell phone and had a small pad of paper in his hand. She heard him say, "Yes, that's the one. Enter from 83. You might have to park near the trail entrance, but you can't miss us. Tell Betty she may need some assistance with this one. We can't assume there is only one. Thanks. I'll check in with you in the hour." His face resembled a puzzle made from a handsome, older Tom Selleck with the jaw and muscles of the Rock. He was about six one, had hair peppered with gray, and wore a kind expression.

"Good morning, miss. It's a hot one today," he said as he wiped his forehead. "I really appreciate you calling the station this morning. I'm sure you're still in shock. Don't worry about your little mishap. Pretty much all rookies and even some old-timers have let their lunches go on their first encounter with human remains. Don't let anyone know I told you this, but I had an incident once too."

His kind demeanor put her at ease.

"Let's find a comfortable spot for you to sit and we can begin. My name is Detective Trenton Oliver. Most folks call me Trent. It is a pleasure to meet you," he said as he ushered her over to a downed tree that lay horizontally to the side of the service road. He sat down on the log, and she followed.

"Quite a good-looking pup you have. I caught a glimpse when we first arrived. I'm sure Officer Cody will get your dog back to you soon."

Detective Trent's tone was gentle and soothing, like jazz music. His mannerisms reminded Trina of stepping into the old Grayton General store when Grandpa Joe used to welcome them as kids when they bought their weekly ice cream cones. Grandpa Joe could make you smile even if you didn't buy anything. He magically could convince kids to confess their sins. Little had they known that good Old Grandpa Joe had been sharing their summer mischief with their parents during their weekly shopping trips.

"I apologize, but with so much going on, I didn't catch your basic information yet. Would you mind giving me your full name, phone number and address? Then we can get down to the details of how you ended up here today."

Trina would have told this man her dirty little secrets if she had any. He was so good at making her feel comfortable. "What was your name again?" she asked without answering his questions. "I have the worst memory. I'm lucky if I remember to call my kids on their birthdays," she said, gushing unnecessary details once again.

He chuckled. "Call me Detective Trent. Yes, ma'am, I get that about forgetting things. I have this pad here to help me remember all the details. So why don't we kick things off with your name."

"Oh, right. My name." she paused with a sigh of relief to be able to give him information she was comfortable with. Trina gave him her name, phone number and address.

"That's in the Gulf Trace community about a half a mile down the road from the Red Fish Taco restaurant, correct?"

"Yes, that's correct. I go for a walk pretty much every day, usually on the 30A path, but occasionally I take Freckles, my dog, out on one of the trails. Assuming this poor person died years ago, I gladly offer you my knowledge of the area. I know you don't need my help, but I recently moved back into my parents' vacation home. I didn't live here full-time growing up, but my summers and most holidays were spent living and working around here. My parents are well connected with the local community even to this day. Everyone knew everyone back then before 30A blew up into this huge vacation destination." Trina proudly shared her family heritage with Detective Trent, who seemed to listen with actual interest.

"Miss Trina, I appreciate your kind offer. Sometimes it's the little details that get overlooked. I will keep your number handy in case we need your help. For now, let's get back to today. Can you tell me how you came upon the body? No detail is too little," he gently guided her.

She began to rehash the dog chase story while explaining her litter pick up routine. Eventually, she described how the metal was shining in the sun and how the denim piece came up once she pulled out the belt.

"Where did you say you put the denim and the belt?" Detective Trent asked.

Trina turned to face the crime scene and was amazed at how quickly the forest had become a scene from *NCIS*. Technicians, police officers, medical examiners and other seemingly important people were milling about. She looked the other direction down the service road and was astonished to see twenty plus random people lined up behind yellow tape that was strung across the service road behind the cop cars. Several people were snapping photos, and some were taking videos. That's when Trina noticed David waving his hand behind the yellow ribbon.

"Oh, there's my husband. I'll go let him in," she said as if this was her crime scene.

"Sorry, your husband is going to have to remain over there with the other onlookers. Where did you end up putting the denim and belt? Also, did you pick up or touch anything else?" Detective Trent coaxed.

"See that bag hanging on the tree over there? I dropped the denim, the belt, and the buckle in that trash bag. There are also two empty water bottles in there and some scraps of paper I found as I was walking onto the trails. Sorry I mixed up the crime scene stuff with normal trash, but I had no idea it belonged to a dead man."

"Not a problem. We appreciate your community service. How about the deceased? Did you touch the bones, even briefly, out of curiosity? I would totally understand if you did. We just need to know in advance," he stated calmly. "Also, are you OK if we take an imprint of your shoe and eventually get your fingerprints to rule those out of the crime scene? Nothing to worry about, I assure you. Normal procedure."

He was so kind and understanding. She would have agreed to give birth to his child if he had asked. OK not literally; she had given birth to three already, that was enough. "Um, I didn't do anything wrong, so sure, you can take my shoeprints. However, to clarify, I did not touch the bones. Emphatically did not. It scared the living daylights out of me when I saw it," she confessed.

"Understandable. Ah, here comes Cody now with your dog." Trent

"Miss, here's your pup." Cody handed Trina the leash. "She was a little nervous to come with me, but she seems fine."

"Cody will process the imprints of your shoes now, and we'll arrange a time for you to stop by the office for fingerprints," Detective Trent said as he gave Cody a simple nod.

Cody took imprints of her shoes with quiet efficiency.

"Why don't you go home with your husband," Trent said once Cody was finished. "We have what we need for now. I'll reach out for some follow-up questions if needed. Thank you again for notifying us of your grim discovery. I'll walk you over to your husband."

Trent's hand gently rested on her lower back as he shepherded her with the kindness of a priest guiding someone to a coffin as they say their last goodbyes.

As they approached the taped off area, everyone in the crowd raised their phones. Alarmingly, the phones were not pointed at the crime scene but at her. Once they were in earshot, questions filled the normally peaceful forest.

"Miss, did you find the body?"

"How come you were in the woods?"

"How many bodies were there?"

"Did you see any bullet holes in the body?"

"Was it a man or a woman?"

"How long do you think the body has been out here?"

"What is your name? Are you a vacationer or do you live here?"

"Why was the Detective questioning you? Why did they take your shoe prints?"

TV shows depicted this familiar scene with flashbulbs popping and microphones pushed in faces, but to have them pointed directly at her was an out-of-body experience. She could feel the interrogation in both their questions and their eyes.

Trina cataloged every single mistake she had made. Her footprints. Her blood dripping all over the forest from the thorny cuts. Her fingerprints and DNA on the denim, the belt buckle and even the trees. Her saliva mixed in the throw up. Freckles had licked the bones. Oh geez, how could she forget the broken bones? Or that she had spit her gum in the trash bag. Never mind all that, the simple fact that Trina had discovered the body. A body that was nowhere near the pedestrian trail. Oh, the metal bear sign. She'd forgotten to tell Trent she touched the sign. She was about to tell him when they reached the yellow tape in front of the observers.

"Good morning, everyone," Trent stated calmly to the crowd. "So nice to see some familiar faces today. Please lower your phones for this nice lady and let her depart without further interruption. Sheriff Sam will be communicating with the press as soon as we have some basic information. It's going to be a long day. We all know how warm it gets, and we have a lot to accomplish today. Please make a path through for this lovely lady, and I will speak to you all later. Appreciate your kindness and respect."

The crowd, obviously familiar with Detective Trent, peacefully cleared a path as wide and welcoming as when one of the local dune lakes opens to the Gulf.

Detective Trent grabbed ahold of the yellow tape and lifted, then gently pushed her through. David quickly grabbed her hand and pulled her away from the crowd. She followed like a lost puppy with her actual dog behind her. They walked past several South Walton cruisers, the sheriff's car, an ambulance, a yellow and red South Walton Emergency Response vehicle, and a couple of vans. A few questions were tossed in the air as they passed, but their obvious intention to ignore them quickly silenced the attempts. After walking for a couple of minutes, David pointed at his truck up ahead. They rushed over to it and jumped in.

"So, do you believe me now?" She sighed, exhausted. She adjusted Freckles on her legs so that the dog could face the window, panting saliva all over it.

"That place was crazy. I can't believe how fast people showed up. It took me ten minutes to find a place to park. Are you OK? You look like you've been in a bear fight—scratches all over you, blood on your legs and your clothes are filthy. You also smell funny. Did you climb through the woods on your stomach or something?"

Popping down the mirror in the passenger side sun visor, Trina stared at herself in horror. She looked like she had competed in a *Survivor* competition. As someone who normally looks naturally polished, it was a shocking visual. She glanced down at her legs and hands and cringed at the red scratches encrusted in dark red blood and mud. Oh gosh, evidence, evidence, evidence, evidence, evidence.

Licking her extremely dry lips, she reached into her pocket for Chap-Stick as David drove toward the intersection of Route 83 and 30A. When her hand found the bottom of her skirt pocket, she sucked in a deep breath of air. Trina slowly pulled out the book of matches with the words *Red Bar Grand Opening* on the cover.

She forgot to give the police the matches!

What Happened to Her?

With one week left, Trina crammed for exams and wrote her final essay before wrapping up freshman year. High school had been more challenging than she had anticipated. Between juggling the newspaper club, the writing group and spending weekends with Christopher, she'd been fully engulfed in high school life.

Now that classes were over, it was time to pack up and drive to Florida. Trina's parents had left earlier in the week with a carload of groceries and suitcases. Trina rode with Christopher and his brother, Paul. Jane's friend Sarah, who was going to stay with them for the month of June, rode with Judy and Jane. Tanner stayed in Massachusetts to work at a local construction company and planned to visit for two weeks mid-summer. The annual road trip began with cars so packed you couldn't see out the back window.

The eagerness and anticipation for reaching the beach overtook any angst they had after spending two days in the car. There was something about the blue skies and the warmth of Florida that made everyone feel giggly, relaxed, and pumped up about being back. By the time they pulled into the driveway, their legs felt like spaghetti and their backs were sore, but one look at the beach bungalow and the pain was forgotten. They scrambled to unpack, took turns in the bathroom changing into bathing suits, then with a quick parent hug and a mad dash into the pantry, they were off. Running to the end of the boardwalk, the girls chucked their flip-flops off and jumped in the sand. Judy and Jane continued down into the water, while Christopher and Trina stood at the bottom of the stairs holding hands. They breathed in the fresh air and absorbed the beauty of the picture-perfect horizon. Christopher wrapped his arms around her, gave her a deep kiss and then said, "First one in the water gets a free ice cream tonight!" Trina took off running before he finished his sentence.

A constant trickle of Florida friends joined them at the beach with portable radios, packed coolers, and a year's worth of stories. A few unfortunate souls were scheduled to work and missed the unofficial Panhandle reunion. Beers were flowing, skin was glistening, and the year's Top Ten Songs were keeping the energy high. Being back at the beach made them all more sensory aware. The sounds. The smells. The views. The waves. The laughter. It was like a magic eraser that cleared the brain of all thoughts except complete satisfaction. Everyone's focus was on soaking in the sun and being back in their happy place.

After several hours of sunshine and heat, the gang walked to Tanya's house to enjoy the pool for an afternoon cooldown. Marco polo games, belly flop contests and pool volleyball made for a busy afternoon. Sarah had already latched on to a new guy named Denkin, a rising college freshman from Louisiana. He had a strong southern accent and teased Jane about her northern one. His southern drawl made everything he said seem more gentlemanlike. Of course, once everyone started paying attention to accents, the other Florida native kids asked the Scotsdale sisters to say the infamous New England phrases "park the car" and "wicked."

Eventually finding a quiet spot in the backyard to dry off. Christopher whispered in Trina's ear that she was the best-looking girl at the party. He squeezed her hand and gave her a peck on the cheek, then opened his backpack and pulled out a small green pouch.

"Trina, the past year has been filled with so many cool memories. I love that we know how to have a good time just as much as we love to push each other to try new things. My grades are so much better because of you, and I think you'd agree that my daily nagging to get you to join the writing club paid off. You'll be running the show as next year's newspaper's editor."

Trina smiled proudly and held his gaze.

"Spending summer with you without school hanging over our heads is going to be amazing. I'm ready to dive in starting with our first of many trips to Sundog Books. But you know what I'm really looking forward to is doing absolutely nothing but being with you."

"You, Trina Scotsdale, make me a better person. You make me see things I wouldn't normally see, and you make me do things I wouldn't normally do. From our first night together holding hands running through the woods away from a bear to our all-night study session last week, I want you to remember that I will always be there for you." Christopher handed her a green felt pouch.

Trina tugged on the strings and shook the pouch upside down. A small black bear charm tumbled out into her hand. "Oh my gosh, Christopher! You are the cutest!"

Christopher unhooked her necklace, added the new charm, then hung the necklace back on her neck. Trina reached up and touched his cheek and stared thoughtfully into his eyes.

"How did I get so darn lucky? I don't deserve all those sweet words, but you can't take them back now. No going backward, only forward. I can't wait to make new memories with you." Trina stood on her tiptoes and kissed him. The kiss started slowly as a thank you, but as he held the back of her head and hugged her hip, she melted under his touch. They lay down on the beach towel and forgot that the backyard was filled with their friends.

"Yo, you two," Christopher's friend hollered from a raft in the pool. "Nobody bought backstage passes. Are we getting a free VIP show?"

Christopher reluctantly separated and chuckled. "OK, OK. I got to go to work anyway." He stood up and extended his hands to pull Trina up. He gave her a tight embrace, kissed the top of her head, then headed off to his car.

Trina was in a daze of contentment. She hated to see him go, but she appreciated his energy for working hard. Instead of having to wake up early like he had last year, this summer he would be working the night shift setting up beach bonfires. Trina released a deep, thankful sigh. He had grown a couple of inches this past year and was beginning to portray himself with more confidence. His face had lost its youthful innocence. His messy, wavy locks accentuated his face and gave him the surfer boy look. He was a hottie for sure, and she was smitten as much today as she was when she first met him. She grabbed hold of her new bear charm and smiled. He was a keeper.

Friday night ended late, and the girls slept in till almost noon the next day. They enjoyed a few hours at the beach and then returned home to shower for work. After spending fifteen minutes searching for work aprons, they arrived at the Salty Bar just in time for the dinner shift. Rushing to the back door of the restaurant, they blasted through the opening and ran up to Danny, who was standing over several pans of hand-formed crabcakes. The sisters gave him a big group hug.

"Danny! Did you miss us as much as we missed you?" Jane asked.

Danny dropped the crabcake he was forming and let out a big, "Eeeewwwww! Girl hugs! Yuck!" He jokingly pushed them off without touching them with his work gloves. Billy was standing over by the sink peeling shells off a big bag of Gulf shrimp. He gave a head jerk hello and returned to his duties without much fanfare. A deluge of words hit Danny as all three girls excitedly summarized a year's worth of personal life updates. Filtering through the shower of stories, he did his best to acknowledge their accomplishments. After they clocked in, they walked around the restaurant *oohing* and *aahing* at the decorative enhancements. New oyster and heron artworks hung on the wall, a garland of boat rope embellished with seashells hung around the bar, and the old salt and pepper shakers had been replaced with new surfboard-shaped ones.

The three sisters effortlessly transitioned into working on their restaurant tasks. Getting accustomed to the onslaught of direct customer interactions, Trina realized she could no longer hide in the back now that she was a food runner. Smiling and courteous, she was a natural. She put enough effort in to keep customers happy but didn't linger out front unnecessarily. Within a couple hours, she'd been recruited by a local property management company and hit on by a table of fisherman. Judy had eyes for the one with curly black hair, so Trina did her best to divert his attention from her to her sister. Trina knew if Judy had a boyfriend, she would be much more pleasant to live with during the summer.

On the ride home, Judy was super chatty about the cute fisherman named Jack who lived on the bay about ten minutes away with his older brother. Judy had convinced him to take her phone number, and they arranged a tentative day to hang out. Jane, oblivious to Judy's new infatuation, was focused on counting her piles of crumpled cash. Trina, who had meticulously stored her tips in her apron, was thrilled that she came home with so much cash and hadn't bent over a steamy dishwasher all night long.

Trina showered and climbed into the top bunk with her newest book, *Black Echo* by Michael Connelly about an LAPD detective named Harry Bosch. Fascinated by Bosch's tenacity to dig into the murder and find justice for the victim, she couldn't put the book down. There was something soothing about reading before drifting off to sleep, even if she was reading about drugs, death, and puncture wounds.

Several days later, Dawn, Tanya and Trina went on a walk on their morning off. Although they wore sunglasses, shorts and tank tops, the girls were sweating in the humidity within minutes of leaving their neighborhood. Open-air vehicles filled with bikini-clad girls and shirtless cute boys whizzed by generating excitement for the upcoming Fourth of July weekend. The Grayton Beach community had a flare for creating patriotic fanfare for the nation's celebration and the girls were eager to generate new holiday memories together. The sweat continued to pour down their faces and their thirst pushed them forward. With the corner store in sight, their pace quickened.

Dawn and Tanya sprinted across Defuniak Street during a gap in traffic to reach the corner near the general store, but Trina heard a strange sound and stayed put. She stood still listening, searching for the source. Catching a glimpse of movement, Trina walked away from the street and into the woods where she found a deer whose rear hoof was wedged in a piece of broken fencing caught in between two trees. The deer was frantically trying to escape and was making the agitated and frightened noises Trina heard. Trina's protective instincts kicked in. Approaching cautiously, she pushed on the four-foot wooden fence fragment but was unable to dislodge it. The deer moaned. Listening to the animal's fear and adrenaline motivated Trina to keep pushing at the board.

"Trina, are you insane?" Dawn said as she and Tanya approached. "You disappeared into the woods without even telling us what was going on."

"Oh my gosh, the poor deer is caught. Do you need help?" Tanya said as the girls walked up behind Trina.

"I almost have it. The board is breaking. I think one more good whack should do it." Trina leaned on her friends as she gave the board a strong kick. The board broke and the deer sprinted away. Trina stood there panting, hands resting on her knees.

"Trina, you are crazy. I'm glad the deer is free but you're lucky you didn't get hurt."

"Dawn, you might need to take that back," Tanya said. "Look at the back of her calf. She has a couple of splinters." Trina winced as Tanya pulled out three splinters lodged in her lower calf leaving a light trail of blood. "Let's go to the store. I bet they'll have some Band-Aids."

The girls made their way out of the woods and across the street to the Grayton General Store. As soon as they walked in, they noticed the cute guy standing behind the register.

"Hi there. Would you happen to have a Band-Aid and a couple of paper towels?" Dawn said as she sauntered up to the counter to get closer to the good-looking teenager. "Our animal loving friend just saved a deer's life in the woods. She's bleeding, and it would take us a while to walk back home."

"Oh. Yeah. Hold on a sec." He popped his head down and stood up with napkins and a first aid box in his hands. "Are you okay? What happened?" He came out from behind the counter and walked up to Trina.

"It was no big deal. I heard a strange sound in the woods and when I saw a deer's hoof stuck in a broken piece of fence, I had to do what I could to help free it."

"One swift karate kick, and thanks to Trina, the deer gets to live another day" Tanya said.

The kid knelt and wiped the back of Trina's leg. Dawn and Tanya smiled at each other and winked at Trina.

"You didn't have to do that for me but thank you, appreciate it."

The guy nodded. "Anytime."

Tanya, who hadn't stopped gawking at him, said, "Hey, you're Old Grandpa Joe's grandson from North Carolina, right? It's nice to meet you. My name is Tanya, this is Dawn, and the crazy animal lover is Trina. We get together on the beach sometimes for volleyball, and the first party is going to be this weekend. You should come." Tanya smiled, hoping he would ask for more details.

He nodded but otherwise had no response as he walked back behind the counter.

"Sorry, I didn't catch your name," Dawn said while she grabbed a bag of chips and a bottle of iced tea and placed them on the counter. She already knew his name but wanted an excuse to talk with the boy every girl had a crush on.

"My name is Bobby. Nice to meet you," he said as he rang up Dawn's items. He didn't make direct eye contact. Tanya bought a bag of Doritos and a lemonade and tried to engage Bobby in conversation, but he did not open up. Dawn and Tanya shrugged and exchanged a defeated look. They walked out as Trina put her package of Fruit Gushers and an apple flavored Snapple on the counter.

Bobby looked at the door, confirming they were alone. "Pretty impressive saving a deer. You must like bears too. Are you an animal lover?" he asked, pointing to her charm necklace.

"Yes, I guess I am." Trina touched her charm, handed him some cash, and grabbed her items.

"You have gorgeous eyes. Hope you don't mind me saying so. Where are you from?" Bobby stared intensely into Trina's eyes. It was like he was trying to analyze and understand. She felt like she was under a microscope the way he concentrated so completely, but his gaze was methodical and purposeful, not creepy.

"Thanks. We live in Massachusetts, but we have a beach house right down the road. We have been coming here every summer for several years. How about you?"

"From North Carolina but stay with Gramps during the summer. He's getting a little old and needs help. I can't complain about the views." He smiled and nodded at Trina.

"Very nice to meet you. We have a pretty big group of friends our age who get together all the time. Maybe we will see you around. Have a great day. Thanks again for bandaging me up." She opened her Snapple, walked out, and strolled over to where her friends were sitting on the top of a picnic table under the trees.

"Well, well, well, Miss Trina. Why did it take you so long to check out? Were you checking out Bobby or was Bobby checking you out?" Dawn and Tanya laughed, leaning in toward each other bumping shoulders.

"Oh, stop it! I only have eyes for Christopher." Trina plopped next to them, touched her charms, and smiled. "You two are free to flirt away."

They sat for another ten minutes chatting about ways to get Bobby to come to the next party, finally deciding to ask one of their older brothers to invite him. The girls threw their trash in the bin and began walking back down the path toward home. They weren't going to have time to go the beach today since the deer incident delayed their plans. They only had forty minutes to walk home and get ready for their evening shifts.

Vacationers were in rare form during the dinner shift that night. The Salty Bar overflowed with people young and old, and customers were tan, sweaty, and thirsty. Pop music blared from the patio and special summer cocktails dominated the tables. Danny's recent happy-hour promotions generated numerous orders of oysters, barbecue nachos, beer on tap, and steaming hot pretzels. The kitchen ran out of oysters by the end of happy hour and there was a wait list for dinner service, though tables were turning over quickly. Trina felt like she had taken 10,000 steps walking back and forth between the kitchen and the dining rooms, staying busy bussing tables and handling most of the food running.

The effects of alcohol became more obvious as drunk men began to show signs of belligerence. Trina recognized the four property managers who were pounding rounds of beer at the end of the bar. Brooks, the one she remembered who stalked his rental tenants, kept grabbing Trina's arm and asking her if she had a boyfriend. Politely declining his various advances, she relocated her position to the other side of the bar but still overhead him tell his friends that if the food tasted as good as Trina looked, the place would be sold out every night. The bartender, recognizing that she needed a rescue, interrupted the conversation. It was on nights like this Trina felt like she wanted to go back to being a dishwasher.

About an hour later, Trina was dropping off a load of dirty dishes when Jerry Flanigan came storming into the back of the restaurant. "Danny, someone parked in my spot! Why do you let staff park in my spot? No one is allowed in my parking spot! Billy, there are bikes clogging the front of the restaurant! You can barely even walk through the front door. You need to go move them, so we don't have a customer suing us for falling at a blocked entrance."

Assuring Jerry that the car did not belong to a member of the staff, Danny suggested that a customer had most likely ignored the no parking sign. Jerry continued to ramble, accusing workers of being disrespectful to him. "I work all day running rental properties, maintaining the cash flow, and dealing with irrational vacationers who make unreasonable requests. And do you know how hard it is to find consistent house cleaners who are worth a damn? All you have to do is cook some burgers and fries and hire teenagers to wait on tables. The one thing I ask is that

I always have my parking spot. Is that too much to ask?" He paced back in forth in the tiny walking space in the kitchen.

Danny was trying to continue cooking, as the tickets were piling up, while periodically making eye contact with his brother.

"I don't get any respect around here," Jerry continued. "Do you know how difficult it is to keep us in the black? We barely break even in the restaurant with the price of seafood and rising hourly pay. Speaking of rising costs, you need to do a better job of monitoring the bar. Liquor seems to be disappearing more rapidly than the nightly register reports reflect." Jerry continued to pace. "Have Billy bring me my normal dinner. I'll be in my office. Next time I come here, there better not be anyone parked in my spot. I had to park a mile away. Absolutely ridiculous!" Jerry stormed out the back door and headed to the shed.

"Show's over, everyone, let's get back to work," Danny said, shaking his head and sighing. The staff moved on, but Jerry's interruptions had a ripple effect, and several kitchen mistakes were made. A couple of appetizer orders were overlooked, and some fish dishes were overcooked. They managed to rectify the customers' concerns with a round of free drinks and 10% off the bill. Overall, the night was a success, but the staff were ready to go home after a very long night.

By the end of the week, the local youth were eager to head to the state forest for a party. Portable boom boxes blasted Billy Ray Cyrus, Red Hot Chili Peppers, and Guns N' Roses. Boys played beer pong on makeshift tables, while girls gossiped in small groups. By the end of the night, almost everyone was hooked-up with someone. Sarah and Denkin were snuggled up near a big pine tree, Judy was nestled up with Jack and Pennie had latched on to a local football player from South Walton

High School. Wendy and Tanya hung out with Bobby, who'd surprised everyone by coming to the party. He had not moved his mouth once in response to her friends' conversations, but rather, he stood leaning against a tree observing everyone. Wendy and Tanya didn't seem discouraged.

After midnight, the crowd began to fizzle out. After getting dropped off back at home by Paul, Christopher and Trina went to her backyard to find a quiet spot. They hadn't had many days off together, so it was nice to find some time to spend alone. They sat on the top of the picnic table rehashing observations from the night, laughing at the antics of several of the boys and acknowledging Pennie's determination to win her prize. Christopher leaned in closer to Trina and whispered amazing compliments into her ears, staring intently into her attentive eyes. When he kissed her, he kissed her slowly and softly.

Each tentative kiss was followed by an intentional separation, but he kept his mouth so close to hers she could smell his spearmint breath. Another soft, slightly longer kiss and then Christopher broke free but maintained eye contact. His left hand was wrapped warmly around her neck, his right hand on her lower back. He slowly pulled her lean body toward him. He kissed her more intently. His warm, muscular body pressed up against her, and the teasing touch of his tentative kissing caused her pulse to quicken. She molded herself into Christopher's embrace, lost in his rapt attention. The kissing intensified, their breathing and heartbeats becoming their love language.

Slowly, his hands rose up her back underneath her cotton T-shirt. His mouth wandered down her neck. His kisses were warm and welcoming. She couldn't help but lean in closer. Skin to skin. The desire to become one was innate. His hands slowly, gently moved lower. She felt nervous and excited. She'd never felt this way before. She liked it and didn't want him to stop. Sounds of desire were escaping from Trina's mouth, embarrassing her. She'd never experienced this level of intimacy before.

He was kissing, pressing, holding, and expertly handling. Trina was holding the back of his wavy hair with her hand. Their bodies were pressed against each other. She raked her hands over his chest, feeling each muscle. Each flex. Feeling his heartbeat.

Slowly, Christopher pulled away. "Are you OK? Was that too much, too fast? You know I will never ask you to do anything you don't want to do," he said, still breathing heavily.

Trina had her hand on his chest, and her fingers were warmed by the vibration. "No. You have never rushed me. You have a way of making me feel... I don't know the right words. Maybe comfortably excited? Does that sound weird? You just make me feel like I am wrapped in an invisible embrace that sends goosebumps up and down my body." She stood on her tiptoes and kissed the top of his nose. "You are truly my slice of heaven." Trina tilted her head down and leaned into the nook of his neck.

They enjoyed a couple of minutes of holding each other and listening to each other's heartbeats. Eventually, they regretfully said their goodbyes. Trina opened the side door to the house and tiptoed up to their bathroom to take a quick shower. She stopped at the top of the stairs and held her necklace. She could have easily let things escalate with Christopher, but she knew it was better, safer, to have stopped. But, wow, those feelings. The adrenaline spike. It was overpowering!

Trina heard the side door close, followed by Judy and Jane tiptoeing up the stairs. They were giggling and laughing, and a little tipsy. "Oh my god! Jack is so cute! He's almost nineteen and works as a fisherman with his brother. What a sexy name—Jack. I like the smell of a hot and sweaty fisherman," Judy said as they approached the second-floor landing. "He asked me to go out Sunday night after my lunch shift. I can't wait."

Trina walked into the bathroom and turned on the shower to hide her flushed face from her sisters. She hadn't quite jumped in the shower yet when her sisters walked into the bathroom.

"What's up with you, Trina? You have quite a big smile on your face. What have you and Christopher been up to?" Jane said, laughing.

"I'm smiling because you two sound like you've had just a little too much to drink," Trina said, jumping into the shower and hoping she'd distracted them from the truth.

"You know safety comes first. If you need supplies, let me know," Judy said in a motherly, joking but concerned way. "It's way better to be prepared than to be caught in the heat of the moment."

"Thanks, sis. Make sure you follow your own advice since you sound like you have the hots for the fisherman," Trina said as she shampooed her hair, trying to change the direction of the conversation.

"It is so nice to be with a more mature, older man. I don't have to watch him do crazy stunts or crush beer cans against his head. We can have a normal conversation. I can't wait for Sunday," Judy said.

The girls kept chatting away while they got ready for bed. Exhausted and exhilarated, Trina fell asleep with her hand wrapped around her necklace. She couldn't stop her mind from rewinding the scenes from earlier that night. She knew she was going to have the best dreams of her life.

The next day, the girls had to work the night shift, so they slept in. The smell of bacon woke the girls up at noon, as their mom was nice enough to make them a hearty breakfast. She whipped up fresh omelets made with ham, cherry tomatoes, grilled onions, pepper and grated white cheese. Handmade biscuits toasted perfectly were served with local blackberry jam. They came bounding down the stairs and rushed over to hug their mom. Nancy placed three breakfast plates on the table.

Placing a folded newspaper on the kitchen table, Richard said, "I can't imagine what would have happened if he wasn't caught," taking a sip of coffee and waving the girls over to the table. "You girls need to always stay together, especially when you're working late at night. It only takes a minute for something horrible to happen."

"What happened? What are you talking about, Dad?" Jane asked as she took a big bite of omelet, cheese dripping down the side of the fork.

"A man was caught attacking a girl. He had her pinned down behind a dumpster about two miles west of here. She was walking home alone on the side road when he grabbed her. Thankfully, a worker from a nearby market heard her screaming when he was leaving his shift and successfully rescued her. The girl escaped physical harm, but I'm sure she'll have nightmares for weeks. You girls need to be careful. Evil lurks in the shadows, and our beach town is not as safe as we think. Honestly, girls, this makes me realize we have been too lenient. We've gotten too comfortable in our surroundings. We shouldn't have let our guard down. We need to set a nightly curfew," he said, clearly deeply concerned.

"The girl was only sixteen years old," their mom said. "It could have been any one of you. Or one of your friends. Poor thing. I'm so glad he was stopped before something horrible happened."

"That is so scary," Trina said. "I can't believe he was so bold to attack someone on a busy street. Didn't he think he would get caught? I'm going to call Wendy. She was working last night. Since she works in that same area, I want to see if she heard any other details. I'll be right back." Trina stood up and walked out of the kitchen to find the phone.

"Dad, I totally understand your concern," Judy said, sounding every bit the mature and responsible older sister. "Unfortunately, working the night shift at the restaurant, we don't even get off work until nine thirty or ten most nights. But remember, we are never alone when we leave. Usually, the guys from the kitchen and the bartender leave at the same time. There's usually four or five of us all walking to our cars together. Believe me, I'll make sure we're all more aware of our surroundings, and I promise to keep an eye on both Jane and Trina."

"I agree, Dad. We promise to watch out for each other," Jane said. "We'll always make sure we're in a group before we walk to the car. I wish we had a way to stay in touch with you while we were out. What if we call you when we leave the restaurant at night?" Jane offered as a compromise, hoping to scratch any thoughts of curfews out of her dad's mind.

"That's a good start. If we have any more incidents, we may need to re-address. Your safety is our number one priority." He stood up and gave each a hug as Trina returned to the table.

"Wendy didn't have any additional details but she's going to see what she can kind find out today." They continued to chat about the incident as they finished breakfast. They were in shock something like this could happen on 30A. Everyone was always so nice. So trustworthy. So genuine. Their little cocoon of safety had burst open like a pandora's box.

That night at work, everyone was talking about it. More facts had come out, and it was determined the girl had left a bigger group of friends about a quarter of a mile from the intersection of South Highway 393 and 30A. She was only a five-minute walk away from her family's vacation home when he attacked her. The man had gotten reprimanded at work that night and must have seen her walking and decided to take his rage out on her.

Utter disbelief was the prevalent emotional response from patrons. However, as the night progressed, the girls heard the undertones from various drunk male customers. Claims that it's difficult to behave surrounded by tanned, bikini-clad youth. Accusations that girls flaunt their figures in their faces. How else were they expected to react? A couple of times, the waitresses had to go tell Danny what was being said because it was making them uncomfortable. Danny had the bartender cut off any of the customers who were being disrespectful. The rude men would apologize and say it was the alcohol talking, but the girls knew, unfortunately, that liquor loosened the tongue and truths spilled out.

As much as the girls normally liked garnering attention from the various attractive guys who stopped in the bar, the lessons of real life were hitting hard. It was natural to want to trust people, but this attack shined a bright light on the risks of going out alone. No one wanted to believe someone would hurt another person, especially an innocent one. But the reality was that many men had base instincts that were only contained by human laws. They needed to be more aware of potential dangers that hid behind the faces of strangers, and even the faces they had come to know.

Trina listened to both the customers and the staff and tried to absorb the facts and the gossip in hopes it would keep her safe in the future.

Unfortunately, her discomfort with the male gender continued to swell as the night went on. She felt every brush of a stranger's hand when she delivered their food. She zoned in on every smile that lasted more than a fraction of a second. She broke eye contact with every male customer, blinking away admiring stares.

The last straw was when Jack stopped in to say hi to Judy. He paid too much attention to Trina any time Judy was preoccupied with customers. Initially, she didn't know if it was the edge on the night itself that was making her feel more alert to his attentive eyes or if he was truly being inappropriately too complimentary. But when Trina stood on the stepladder to grab some liquor bottles off the top shelf for the bartender, Jack stood up from his chair and eyed Trina up and down. He whispered loud enough for only Trina to hear, "Your legs are as long as the Destin pier. I'd go fishing if I wasn't already hooked." Trina was so embarrassed, she quickly finished restocking and politely excused herself to help deliver food to the tables.

Trina knew her physical appearance had changed dramatically this year. Her long legs, natural brown tan and big, almond-shaped eyes caused double takes from several men at the restaurant. Even though she didn't wear makeup and normally had her hair up in a ponytail, her olive complexion peppered with freckles invited more than the average glances. She also had a curvier figure than her sisters, and her smile could light up the room. Even her sisters agreed she was the ugly duckling that had turned into a swan. Trina didn't like the attention and would rather blend into the background.

Christopher frequently reminded her that though her stunning looks turned many heads, it was her heart and mind that drove him crazy. That's what she remembered whenever random guys hit on her. Tonight, however, she was a little more uncomfortable than usual. With each glance, each annoying comment tossed her way and outright disrespectful physical contact made, she felt victimized more than she had ever felt before. She was so happy to go home after work and crawl into bed. She was lucky she had Christopher to protect her. She should talk to Judy about Jack's rude comments, but she didn't want to burst her sister's bubble. This was the first guy in a long time that made Judy happy. Maybe she could keep her distance from Jack. That would be better than hurting Judy's feelings.

The next day, Trina worked the lunch shift with Jane and Angela. When they showed up, Danny was outside at the shed talking to a girl and an older woman. Danny was helping them load their minivan with supplies.

"Hey, Trina," Danny said. "I helped stock the rental property house cleaners with supplies. Can you take a quick count and make sure we're not running low on anything? I had a late-night last night and am running behind on prepping for lunch, so I'd really appreciate your help." He dropped the last box of supplies in the minivan trunk and walked off toward the restaurant.

Trina went into the shed to scan the shelves, write down a list of low inventories and make sure everything was still organized. She flipped the light off in the rental supply room and walked toward Jerry's desk. She noticed a light-pink piece of fabric sticking out from the side of the metal filing cabinet drawer. She tried to open the drawer to fit the material back in since she knew how anal Jerry was, but the drawer was locked. When she spun back around, she glanced down at the floor. A pair of loafers were tucked under his desk surrounded by a glittering of sand. Trina grabbed the broom and dustpan and swept the mess up. She wondered when Jerry had been in the shed. He normally never left things out of place. All she could do was clean it up so he wouldn't blame her for leaving a mess. She finished, put everything away, and locked the door.

As she walked into the kitchen, she handed Danny the keys. "I cleaned up a little and left Jerry a list. He must have taken a walk on the beach last night because he left his loafers back there full of sand. I did my best to clean up, so he won't blame you or me for the mess," Trina said.

Danny looked at Trina with a strange, almost confused look on his face, as if she'd caught him with his hand in a cookie jar. But as quickly as the look appeared, it disappeared and was replaced by the typical Danny smile. "Thanks, Trina. You're awesome. I'm sure Jerry must have been in a rush the other day after his parking spot meltdown. I appreciate you taking the initiative to clean up. And thanks for helping with inventory."

Trina acknowledged his appreciation and asked him to adjust her timecard since she hadn't clocked in yet. The lunch crowd kept her busy enough that she didn't have time to think about the week's bad vibes. She was happy to go home at the end of her shift and spend the afternoon on the beach with Wendy and Monica. The girls talked about the attacker, the disgusting habits of men and future ways they could all watch out for each other. The topic of men eventually led to discussion about how lucky Trina was to have Christopher. Wendy said she would accept second best if she could get Bobby to pay her any attention, but he was proving to be a hard nut to crack.

As the week ended, community plans for the upcoming 4th of July weekend slowly took over residents' conversations. Trina was anxiously anticipating a day off relaxing in the sun followed by Christopher's first bonfire for the holiday weekend. He was excited to be working at one of the prominent locations at Grayton Beach and thrilled to be able to work at the same beach Trina would be hanging out at. Trina's dad helped organize the fireworks show, while her mother arranged the community potluck.

The Florida sun was sending warm, fuzzy, vacation vibes throughout the Panhandle, shining brightly against a sky painted stunning shades of indigo, royal and powder blue. A gentle breeze provided relief to sunbathers, and the waves breaking from the Gulf of Mexico delivered entertainment to raft floaters. The college students, who'd secured their spots on the beach as early as four a.m., were cracking open coolers and jamming to music. The beach was overflowing with RVs, Jeeps and 4x4s. Paddleboards and surfboards were sprawled all over the landscape, along with beach blankets, sunshades, and flip-flops. Everyone was in their happy place.

The BBB arranged their beach towels in a circle near the volleyball nets. Jane was thrilled to see Tommy, and it wasn't long before the two of them were nestled on a blanket. Jasmine stopped by to say hi to the BBB girls but departed to reconnect with some friends further down the beach. Judy hung under an umbrella trying to stay sweat free as she waited for Jack to arrive after his morning work shift. The girls launched into crisscross conversations, all playing catch-up after working so many shifts. Trina eventually moved her towel over to the bonfire area so she could watch Christopher. He had taken his shirt off as he carried firewood and other supplies to the designated areas. He had a nice, deep tan and Trina thought he was looking fine. She had no problem sitting there watching him work up a sweat.

The crowds settled in to get ready for the show. Various boom boxes played holiday melodies including Neil Diamond's "America," Lee Greenwood's "God Bless the U.S.A.," and "Living in America" by James Brown. Chills ran up and down Trina's arms as she listened to the patriotic songs and watched a stunning display of red, white, and blue glimmering in the sky and off the reflection of the water. It was like watching two shows at once. Christopher and Trina held hands while they lay on their backs, fascinated by the displays of colors and coordination of various pyrotechnics. Lots of oohs and aahs were heard from the crowd. The celebration of freedom, friendship, artistic and natural beauty was pervasive, and the feeling of community was strong.

As the show ended, people began packing their tables, blankets, coolers, and chairs. Everyone was still feeling high from the exhilaration of a packed day of community events. Trina helped Christopher pack up chairs and clean up around the bonfire. Once he had filled the truck, he told Trina he had to drop the first load off. He promised he would be back in fifteen minutes to grab the remaining items. Trina walked over to her friends, who were still sitting around drinking and listening to music.

After a while, Jane came running over with Tommy. "Trina, have you seen Jasmine? Has anyone seen Jasmine?" she asked frantically without really waiting for an answer. Tommy continued up the beach, asking everyone he encountered if they had seen Jasmine. Within minutes, it seemed like the entire beach was alive with activity again. Beams of flashlights were scanning the area, and an escalating hum of Jasmine's name was in the air.

Jasmine had been seen earlier sitting by the water, watching the show. Prior to the fireworks finale, she left her friends to find a place to go to the bathroom. One of her friends said she'd suggested Jasmine go to the dunes, but she didn't watch to see which way she went because she was focused on the show. After the show was over, Jasmine's father noticed she wasn't sitting by the water's edge. Now, nobody could find her.

Adrenaline coursed through Trina's veins. What happened to Jasmine? Where was she? A large group of adults were methodically walking up and down the dunes calling Jasmine's name. A description of Jasmine was rapidly spreading from person to person. As the minutes crept by, more beams of light lit up the beach like another light show. Parents gathered their kids under a protective hug. Fear was etched on everyone's face, even in the dark. When the search on the beach was proving to be unproductive, the crowd migrated to the boardwalk.

Tommy was frantic. He continued to run up and down continuously yelling her name, pleading to anyone within earshot for help. Demanding that someone must have seen where she went. Each time she heard the desperation in his voice, a little piece of Trina's heart ripped apart. This couldn't be happening. Jasmine's going to walk out from behind a dune and they'd laugh about this for years to come. She had to. This couldn't be real. This was something that happened on TV, not in real life.

Rumors spread like wildfire. Did she leave the beach with a guy? Did she go out into the Gulf and get swept away in a wave? Was that man who assaulted the girl out on bail? Did someone else take Jasmine? How could she have disappeared so quickly? It didn't make sense that she could vanish when there were so many people on the beach. But deep in her heart, Trina knew the fireworks would have distracted everyone, and no one would have paid attention to a girl walking away from the water. To make matters worse, so many people had been drinking all day and wouldn't have thought twice if there were any strange noises coming from the dunes. But how could she just disappear? Jasmine knew this area just as well as the rest of them. She had been coming down to the Panhandle for years. It didn't make sense.

The local police had joined in the search, but progress was difficult as the night progressed. Even when the search moved to nearby streets, it was too dark to truly search since local turtle protection laws prevented excessive lights near the beachfront. The only shimmer of light came from the moon and sporadic reflections from interior rooms of nearby homes. The night seemed to stretch out like a stressful, slow-moving freight train that was coming to a crashing end. The search continued past two a.m. People didn't want to stop looking, but there were no glimmers of hope. Finally, around two thirty, the crowd dispersed. The majority agreed to re-engage at sunrise.

The car ride home was silent. No one wanted to admit something had happened to sweet, kind, beautiful Jasmine. The Scotsdale family sulked into their house and sat together around the kitchen table. Their parents asked the girls various questions. When was the last time anyone saw her? Had she been hanging around with anybody they didn't recognize? Did she seem abnormally nervous? Had she ever talked about anybody that sounded suspicious? Of course, these questions were merely asked to make the parents feel like they hadn't given up. Finally, around three thirty in the morning, they decided to call it a night but agreed to get up early to rejoin the search.

Trina lay in her top bunk squeezing her charms. What had happened to Jasmine?

She's Not Dreaming

Present Day

"Trina, what's wrong?" David asked, concerned but trying to keep his eyes on the road.

"Um, I sort of... forgot to hand over a piece of evidence from the crime scene." Trina showed him the book of matches.

"What? Where was that? How are matches evidence? Do we need to go back?" he asked, though his subconscious desire to go home to escape the cameras had him not slowing down.

"No, no I don't want to go back. The skeleton is the key. They asked me to go to the station to have my fingerprints taken later. I'll hand the matches in at the same time. How important could it be when they have a dead body to dig up?" she said confidently, backing up her decision to not return to the crime scene.

"Fingerprints? Why do you have to have your fingerprints taken?" David blurted out.

"I found a piece of what I thought was litter but ended up being the dead guy's clothes. Since I grabbed it, they need to rule me out. It's normal procedure," she said as if she was used to this.

David drove the rest of the way home in silence. As soon as they got home, she let her elderly, aging dog, Phoenix, a short-legged dachshund, out to do her business. When she entered the kitchen, she grabbed a Ziploc bag to safely store the Red Bar matchbook. She did not want to contaminate the evidence any more than she already had. Trina dropped the bag on her desk in the next room. Looking at the grime on her arms and legs and remembering the horror of her discovery, she wanted a hot shower to wash away her memories of the morning. She told David she was going to go clean up.

"Wait a minute. I totally understand your need for a shower, but just walk me through what happened out there first. Cops and journalists surrounded you. Your picture is going to end up on the evening news. Plus, now you're telling me you'll be fingerprinted like a criminal." David stood with both hands on the kitchen counter and a stunned expression on his face, still in shock she had in fact discovered a body.

Trina sighed and kept walking toward the bedroom but hollered behind her, "I need a rinse off. As you so kindly pointed out, I'm covered in muck from head to toe. Give me fifteen minutes and I'll tell you everything."

While she was in the shower scrubbing dried blood off her legs, she couldn't help but feel nervous, sick to her stomach and a tiny bit excited at the same time. She's not dreaming. She had found a body. She was going to go down in history books as the dog walker who found a dead person on 30A. Why was it always the jogger or walker who discovered the dead? Why not a park employee or birdwatcher?

She guessed it didn't matter who found the gravesite. What mattered was who the person was and unraveling the facts surrounding their death. Trina's desire to answer those two questions was already burning a personal motivation deep within her mind. She was meant to find this skeleton. It was not a coincidence or even fate. It was her calling. She had always been fascinated by crime. The diabolical differences between the 1% of humans who stab, shoot, or strangle another human being and the 99% of the rest of humanity who feel guilty after squashing a mosquito. With no guilty conscience, murderers grab a cup of coffee and a bite to eat right after they steal someone's heartbeat. That juxtaposition of imbalance was so strange it was almost alluring.

Who had she found? David was right in that there were not a lot of murders in their small beach town. Who could this be and why was no one looking for this person? What if she'd found a famous person? What if a hunter shot and killed someone? Oh gosh! A pang of motherly sadness hit her. What if she'd discovered the remains of someone's child? The skull was mostly covered up, so she didn't know how big or small it was. It could have been a child.

Her mind jumped uncontrollably from one conclusion to the next attempting to magically solve the case with random guesses, while simultaneously retracing each mistake she'd made. Never should have let the dog off the leash. Never should have removed her gloves. Why did she eat pizza for breakfast? So stupid to spit her chewing gum in the bag. On and on her mind rambled.

Randomly, a memory from her past popped up in her head. "Oh my god," she exclaimed to the fog and steam in her shower. Both the dogs' heads lifted from their dog beds at the sound of her voice. "David!" she yelled from the shower, knowing full well he could not hear her down the hall and in the kitchen.

Trina quickly finished scrubbing the dirt and blood off her body and turned the water off. She combed her wet hair and grabbed some clean clothes. Resting both hands on the vanity countertop, she took a good look at herself in the mirror. She looked cleaner but didn't feel much better. Her highlighted hair was shoulder length and styled very simplistically. She didn't invest much time in making herself look good. At this stage in life, looking good was more about feeling good on the inside than primping to impress others. She stared at her image and pondered the events of the day and considered the memory that had just popped into her thoughts. She brushed her teeth and walked out of the bathroom.

"Come on, girls," she said to Freckles and Phoenix. "I think I might be able to actually point the detectives in the right direction."

Trina rushed toward the kitchen and began speaking before she even turned the corner. "David, I think I might know who I found." But David was not in the kitchen. Trina walked toward the garage, as David was most likely back to building his mystery project. "David, are you out here?"

"Back over here. I'm trying to build a new fence post for the neighborhood sign," David said from a squatting position over a piece of wood.

"David, I know who the body could be. I don't remember if I ever told you this story. When I spent my summers here as a kid, I remember a teenage girl who went missing. We referred to her as the July 4th Girl. Her disappearance was the talk of the town when I was getting ready to enter my sophomore year of high school. She went missing after the beach fireworks show which had everyone frazzled. The whole town, including my family, helped search for her, but as far as I know, she was never found."

David gave no reply, only continued to measure his piece of wood.

"Jasmine was her name. She was a beautiful, petite blonde and always super friendly. She had an older brother, Tommy, who was extremely protective. Jasmine once told me her brother would kill her if she ever was caught with a boy. I only talked to her a couple of times, but she always seemed like a sweet girl. I was shocked when she disappeared! Gosh, I haven't thought about Jasmine in years."

Trina gushed these memories to David as she paced back and forth in the garage.

"I bet I found the July 4th Girl. I could actually become famous! Well, maybe not famous. That's a horrible thing to say since it would mean Jasmine was killed. Ugh, what a horrible, horrible thought," Trina said with sincere regret. She closed her eyes and rolled her fingertips in small circles on the side of her head to press the stress out. After a minute, she said, "David, I've decided that I want to work with the detectives and help solve this case. I think I could really help solve this 30A mystery. Can you imagine if I found that missing girl?"

David was now sitting back staring at her in utter disbelief. "Trina, hold on a sec. You do not need to get more involved than you already are. You need to slow down and think this through."

Trina kept pacing, not really listening. "I remember that our friends were mad that our parents put curfews in place. They wouldn't let us out of their sight. I mean, I totally get it now as a mom, but back then it was like our world came to a crashing halt. Her disappearance motivated us to be more vigilant, that's for sure."

She looked over at David to see if he had been paying attention. She was hoping he would share the same excitement for solving this murder. The dogs had come into the garage and jumped on her leg for their midday treat, and she bent down to pet them. David was about to say something, but Trina kept rambling.

"I'm going to need to go look through mom's boxes in the storage shed and see if I can find old newspaper articles from the year Jasmine disappeared. Maybe I can go through old photos too. As you know, my mom kept everything. There should be plenty of pictures of the local kids, neighbors, and vacationers. Even some of the customers since my boss liked to hang pictures on the bulletin board."

She headed for the door as she finished her train of thought. Walking toward the shed, the realization hit her that she hadn't opened the shed since they bought the house from her parents. Trina hadn't been ready to tackle what she assumed would be her mother's disorganized chaos hidden behind those doors. Today was a perfect reason to dig in. Her parents had owned the house for over thirty years, so there were likely a lot of memories in there.

When her mom first told Trina they were getting ready to sell the place, Trina was reluctant to consider moving to Florida. Although her siblings had continued to benefit from vacationing with their own children at the house when her parents still owned it, Trina had not been back since she was eighteen. She always loved the beach house, but for some reason, she never wanted to go back once she'd left that last summer before college. She couldn't recall any specific reason she never thought about returning. Now looking back, she assumed that once she left for college, her own life moved her in direct directions. Her college summers were focused on internships, and she had accepted employment in Atlanta upon graduation. Returning to Florida was never a priority.

After she had kids of her own, Trina kept them busy in various summer camps to help them remain occupied while David and Trina worked. Being a dual income household, Trina arranged annual family vacations, but those trips never included a week on 30A. The kids had enjoyed many beach vacations, just never at her parents' place. Her mom always begged her to send her grandchildren down for the summer, but Trina always seemed to find an excuse as to why they couldn't come. She admitted she always had an inner fear that something bad could happen to her kids down on 30A, and since she wasn't going to be able to be there to protect them, she wasn't going to send them. Maybe Jasmine going missing had more of an impact on her than she'd realized.

As she reached for the door handle, Trina heard David talking.

"Can you sit still for one minute? You still haven't told me how you found the body." He stood behind her with an oily rag in one and a long tool in the other.

"Oh, well there really isn't much to tell. I chased Freckles into the woods. I saw a piece of trash on the ground near where I caught up with her. When I scanned the area for more litter, I saw a head and half of a body lying under some mud. I called you and then the police came. And you know the rest of the story. I did find some of the guy's clothes in the dirt. Well, I guess based on my new discovery, it could be girl's clothes," she said, convincing herself since she really wanted to be the one to solve the crime.

"You make it sound like discovering a body is an everyday activity," David said as he plopped down in a patio chair.

"Sorry. I don't mean to diminish the importance of my discovery. Someone lost their life out in those woods. I just want to help bring closure for some poor family. If I can find any clue that might help, I want—I need—to help."

She yanked open the shed door and stared at all the bins and boxes and miscellaneous items scattered on several racks. The excitement at participating in the investigation of a murder had Trina forgetting all about her own obsession with covering her tracks. She had a new focus, and she was ready to search for anything that could be an important piece of the puzzle.

As she was moving a couple boxes around, Trina's cell phone rang in her pocket. She glanced at the phone screen, as she was not expecting any phone calls. The number was from an 850 area code, but it was not a number she had programmed. She ignored the call and placed her phone in her back pocket. She continued to move boxes, slowly creating a walking path deeper into the shed.

"Do you really think it was that girl?" David asked from the shed doorway. "Did you take any pictures of the clothing you found? You normally take pictures of everything. Was there something specific you found that makes you think it's the 4th of July girl? Did you find something that reminded you of her?"

"No. Just my gut instinct. I know that sounds ridiculous."

"Well, I hope you're wrong. Let's hope Jasmine was located years ago and this is just a random accident in the woods. Also, Trina, don't you think you should reconsider giving your fingerprints?" He asked as he scratched the dogs' ears. "Don't all those shows you like to watch tell you to talk to a lawyer before giving police officers anything? I don't think you should get involved more than you're required by law."

Trina's phone rang again. She checked the screen, but it was another unknown number, so she declined. Not even ten seconds later, another call came in. Trina was getting irritated by the interruptions and answered the phone.

"Hello, can I speak to Trina Scotsdale please?" a woman asked.

"This is Trina. Can I help you?" she said as she held the phone to her ear with her raised shoulder and kept moving boxes.

"Trina, my name is Samantha Hunter. I work for WJHG News Channel 7. I was wondering if I could ask you a couple of questions? It will only take a minute," she asked politely.

Before Trina could reply, another phone call rang in the background. Trina declined the second call. So, the news vultures had already figured out who she was and how to reach her.

"Who is it?" David asked.

Before Trina could answer him or the lady on the phone, both dogs turned sharply to the fence that lined the backyard near the driveway and began a symphony of barking. While still squeezing the phone to her ear, Trina walked around her husband and the boxes in her path and peaked through the fence. She could see a car parked in the driveway.

"Sorry, ma'am, I have to go. No comment at this time." She couldn't believe she'd said *no comment*. Never in a million years would she have thought she'd be saying that well-known statement. She clicked off the ringer on her phone to stop future intrusions.

Both David and Trina walked through the house to get to the front door. As they approached the foyer and peered through the window, Trina recognized Detectives Trent and Jenifer on their front doorstep.

"Oh no, it's the detectives," she whispered, trying not to move her lips in case they could read them through the windowpane. She turned to face David. "What do I do? Should we call a lawyer? Why would they come to the house already unless I'm in trouble for vomiting all over the body? Is there a law against breaking a dead person's bones before they have examined the body?" She was shaking as she reached out and held her husband's wrists with both her hands. "Oh my gosh, they linked me to the crime scene because of my blood, fingerprints, and chewing gum."

"Trina, calm down. You didn't do anything. They are here to ask you a couple of follow-up questions, I'm sure that all." He looked out the window and smiled at the detectives, putting his index finger up to signal to them to wait.

"Wait a second, what do you mean you broke the skeleton's bones? And you threw up? You obviously had more details to share about your morning than you let on. Let's find out what they want," he said with all the kindness of a husband of twenty-five years. He grasped her hands and turned her around slowly and smiled. "Go lock the dogs up so they'll stop barking, and I'll let the detectives in," David stated, taking control of the situation.

Trina ushered the dogs to their bedroom as she heard the front door open. After securing the dogs, Trina took a quick glance at herself in the mirror. She was clean but not prepared for company. She tried to fix her hair and rub color in her cheeks. She closed her eyes and took a couple of breaths before returning to the foyer.

"Detectives, so nice to see you again. I didn't think I would be seeing you so soon. Did you need me to verify what I ate for breakfast?" She nervously laughed, trying to hide her anxiety. "If you're stopping by to grab old photos from back in the day, I really haven't had time to go through them yet."

Detective Trent smiled, and Trina heard a very faint chuckle under his breath. The smile was genuine, and his laugh was not judgmental. Now that she had a better look at Detective Jenifer, she couldn't help but notice that Jenifer was a natural beauty.

Trent cleared his throat. "Well, I appreciate your confidence in our team to already be in the investigative stage of this case, ma'am, but we are not quite to that step yet. Would you mind if we came in? We would enjoy a little A/C after this morning's activities. You must be Trina's husband. I apologize, sir, for not taking the time to formally introduce myself back there in the woods, but I wanted to provide you both with a clean escape from the hounds. I figured it would be easier to ask Trina some questions away from the lens of the media and curiosity seekers."

Trent extended his hand to David. "My name is Trenton Oliver. You can call me Detective Trent. This is my partner, Detective Jenifer Townsend." They both shook David's hand as he opened the door completely permitting them entrance into the house.

Trina walked them over to the kitchen table, which was covered in her mom's recipe books. When Trina noticed the recipe books, she said, "Oh gosh, David, I don't smell the tenderloin. Did you forget to put that in the crockpot this morning? I bet you forgot to switch the laundry too." Trina made the realization aloud and turned abruptly to walk to the refrigerator to grab the marinated pork.

"Trina, why don't you worry about that later. I'm sure the detectives have busy schedules. Let's find out what they need so they can be on their way," David said.

"Okay, sure. I can take care of that later." Stacking the recipe books up in a pile, Trina sat down at the table next to David looking across at both detectives.

"Thank you both for letting us further interrupt your day. You have a lovely home. Great location for enjoying the beach. Trina, you deserve a community award today. Discovering a body and staying emotionally calm enough to call 911 takes a lot of courage. We really appreciate your help. We just have a couple of follow-up questions, then we will be out of your way," Detective Trent said.

"Thank you. It was really nothing. Anyone would have done the same."

"Let's get right to it. You mentioned you ended up in that section of the woods because your dog ran off while off leash. Is that correct?" he asked.

"Yes," she admitted. "I let her off leash but only to walk with me for a little bit. She normally is very good, but she is determined to catch every squirrel she sees. And unfortunately, she saw one and took off."

"That's what we thought. I totally understand her hunter instinct. I have an English Springer Spaniel, and I have a hard time controlling her when we take her for walks on the beach. Those sandpipers and herons that love our Gulf are great enticements for dogs to chase. When you finally caught up with your pup, did you see the human remains immediately?" Detective Trent asked.

Detective Jenifer jotted some notes while keeping a polite smile on her face.

"No. As a matter of fact, I saw the glint of metal. I assumed it was a lighter or a pair of sunglasses. I find that kind of stuff all the time when

I pick up litter. I find those lighters and e-cigarette containers all over the path. Um, anyways, when I pulled up the belt buckle and small piece of denim, I honestly still hadn't noticed the body." Trina picked at her fingernails. She could hear her heart beating. It felt like a drum concert was going on inside her chest. "Um, can I get you something to drink? I forgot to ask you that when you came in." Trina stood up, not waiting for them to answer.

Trent "No, thank you, we're both good," Detective Trent said.

Trina spun back around and began fidgeting with her hands. "OK. Umm, so when did I see the body? I was checking the ground for anything I might have missed. When there's one piece of litter, there's usually two. I was standing right where I found the belt buckle and was just scanning the ground. That's when I saw the skull sticking out of the ground."

Detective Jenifer finally spoke up. "Trina, did you notice any other items around the body? Did you find any other objects besides the belt and denim that we found in your trash bag? Any other metal objects?"

Trina turned slightly to face Jenifer. Her curiosity was piqued by the sound of Detective Jenifer's voice. It had no hint of southern in it. It almost sounded Northern, like maybe she was also from New England. Trina would have to keep that information in her back pocket for future bonding. She noted again that Detective Jenifer was truly a beautiful woman. So professional. Kind of made Trina feel underdressed in her own home.

Trina responded to the question and countered it with one of her own, trying to dig for information. "No, I don't recall seeing any other metal objects besides the belt buckle. Were there other pieces of metal buried in the ground that I missed?"

Trent picked up again. "We can't share anything we might have discovered this morning, Trina, but we appreciate your inquisitiveness. Did you see anything else that you might have touched but didn't have a chance to pick up? We want to make sure we can rule out your fingerprints properly."

"I usually do a great job of picking up all the trash left behind by vacationers. I can fill a bag or two every day even though I generally walk the same path," she said, feeling the need to defend her litter picking skills. "It's sort of amazing and sad at the same time. Of course, not as sad as finding a dead person." She felt bad for complaining about litter when the focus should be on the body. "But, no, I didn't find anything else I can think of. I only picked up the belt and denim." Thinking back to her chaotic morning, her mind focused on trying to visualize the scene. Maybe she missed a gun or a knife. How did she miss that?

"One more question. I know we were able to take a print of your sneakers earlier this morning. Those woods are very thick and hard to navigate. I want to make sure we properly document your path in the woods. Have you ever been to this particular section of the woods?"

His gentle coaxing to gather information was pure cloudlike. His deep voice, tempered with a slight southern twang, made him easy to listen to. She wanted to please him with her answers, to prove to him that she was an asset to have on his investigative team.

"Oh gosh. I don't think so. Does that matter? Even if I have chased Freckles to that area before, I really couldn't tell you for sure. Normally she's on a leash. I only let her off the leash occasionally. I guess there's a chance I could have chased her over there before, but I don't really recall. The trees all look the same to me. If I hadn't found that service road, you would have received a different kind of 911 call because I would have needed help finding my way back home." She smiled at the thought of having to call 911 to get back home. "But my footprints shouldn't really matter, right? This girl has most likely been there for ages."

Detective Trent leaned slightly forward. "Trina, we don't believe you had anything to do with the loss of this person's life. But we are required to follow certain protocols. Sort of like the ones you watch on crime TV shows. We want to make sure we have a complete picture of what happened this morning." As he said this, his phone rang. He excused himself and stepped out onto the back porch.

Detective Jenifer stood as she asked, "Trina, what makes you think that you found a girl?"

Realizing that she divulged her secret a little early, Trina responded, "Oh, I'm taking a wild guess. It could be an old man for that matter. I don't really know how to identify a skeleton just by looking at an eye socket." Trina told herself that she should keep her July 4th Girl idea to herself until she could gather a little more information on the case.

Detective Jenifer nodded her head in agreement and asked if she could use the bathroom. David stood up to walk her down the hall. Trina sauntered over to stand near the back screened-in porch and heard a small portion of Detective Trent's conversation through the windows.

"...confirmed that we have a partial taillight and maybe enough of a bumper to identify it. Do we have a turnaround time on trying to isolate the VIN?" he asked the person on the phone as he walked toward the shed in the back of the yard.

Since Trina couldn't hear the rest of his conversation, she walked back toward the kitchen and approached Jenifer, who had returned from the restroom. "Detective Jenifer, it is so nice to meet a female investigator. I admire you for working in a field that has historically been filled by men. I look forward to working with you on this case," Trina said as if she had joined the team. "How long have you been working with Detective Trent?"

"I appreciate your recognition, but you might be surprised to hear there are several women working at our local South Walton Police headquarters. Not all of them are detectives but are still as valuable to our team. This is my third year with Detective Trent. He's a mentor as well as a partner. I'm lucky to be on his team. It's a tough job, but I wouldn't change a thing."

Detective Trent closed the porch door as he walked in. "We better hit the road. We have a meeting with the sheriff at three o'clock and need to meet with the team beforehand," he said as they walked toward the front door.

"That's it," Trina said bluntly, slightly disappointed that was all they needed from her. She was also a little bummed because she hadn't had enough time to adequately bond with Detective Jenifer.

"Yes, in terms of questions. However, if you would be so kind, we would greatly appreciate it if you could stop by the office to give us your fingerprints. I understand that you didn't touch the bones, but you picked up the denim, the belt buckle and belt itself, so we need to get your fingerprints documented. I totally understand if you want to run this request by a family lawyer. We need your fingerprints for the purpose of elimination. Obviously, it's your call." Detective Trent finished his statements as he turned around on the front porch to shake hands.

Jumping at the chance to show up at the police station, Trina said, "How about Friday morning? I'm scheduled to work on Wednesday and Thursday. Is that OK if I wait until Friday? Do I simply walk into the police station, or do I need an appointment?" Trina could feel her stomach getting a little jittery at the thought of being fingerprinted. She instinctively wanted to bite a fingernail, but she consciously held her hand down by her side so she wouldn't appear nervous.

"I'll let the front desk know to expect you on Friday. Thank you both for your time."

As he turned to walk away, Trina breathed in sharply and said, "Oh, Detective Trent, how is the sheriff? Did his eyes recover from this morning's accidental mace spray?"

Trina felt David nudge her and heard him whisper, "Mace? Trina, what else did you do?"

"He's doing fine," Detective Trent said. "Though I think he decided to keep his sunglasses on for the rest of the day." He put his arm out to let Detective Jenifer walk in front of him toward the car. "Again, thanks for your help today. We'll be in touch if we need anything else," he said as he reached the car door.

Detective Jenifer nodded and said, "Yes, thank you, ma'am." She opened the door and climbed into the passenger side, and before she closed the door, Trina heard her say to Trent, "Let's grab a quick bite at Blue Mountain Bakery and bring back a box of goodies. I think we're going to need to bribe the team to work late tonight."

Trina stared at the car as it pulled out of the driveway. She could see her neighbor across the street, Trudy, staring out the window with a phone to her ear. Although she loved Miss Trudy, the feeling of being watched sent chills down Trina's spine. She'd have to tell Trudy all about it another day. She wasn't ready to tackle that conversation yet.

"Well, that wasn't so bad. He seems like a nice enough guy," David said, totally under the same relaxed spell that Detective Trent had put over her every time he spoke. "They both seemed very professional. Maybe this won't be such a big deal after all." David walked to the garage, already forgetting to ask her about the broken bones and the sheriff's eyes.

It is not a big deal yet, she thought. But when she tells them who the dead girl is, then this will become a very big deal for this little beach town.

Trina walked through her office on the way back to the kitchen with the intention of finding the tenderloin in the refrigerator. As she passed her desk, the matchbook caught her eye. "Oh crap! I forgot to give them the matches." Not only had she forgotten to give them the matches, but she also totally forgot to tell them about the matches. She had been too preoccupied by Detective Jenifer's questions about finding metal objects and simply forgot to mention the evidence she had in her possession. Detective Trent was never going to let her get close to this case if she messed up on simple things like finding evidence and reporting it. She turned around to peer out the front window to see if she could still see the detectives' car, but they were already gone.

Although the thought of having the police take her fingerprints went against everything she did daily to protect herself, she knew that gaining Detective Trent's trust would give her a perfect opportunity to learn more facts about the case. Voluntarily providing her fingerprints would prove she was eager to help the team process the crime scene. But was she making the wrong decision for selfish reasons? Her library of crime fiction novels demonstrated that innocent choices often escalated down an irreversible path. She had worked diligently her whole life to eliminate her evidentiary footprint. Once her finger pressed on the black ink, there was no going back. Should she go against everything she believes in?

Giving herself a pep talk, Trina sat down at her desk, staring at the red book of matches. She focused on the skeleton. Someone had lost a loved one. There was a family out there waiting for answers. She remembered Tommy's face when Jasmine disappeared, the desperation in his voice. She needed to do whatever she could to help bring this person back home to their family, no matter who it was.

Friday might be the only chance she had to get a closer look at the evidence. Although, she wasn't sure she could get any closer to the evidence than landing on the dead body.

Watching Wishing Wanting

1992

A t five a.m., the entire family was down in the kitchen dressed and ready to help search for Jasmine. They were exhausted, basically walking zombies, but no one complained. DeFuniak street in Grayton Beach was filled with cars parked on both sides of the road. Trina's dad drove around the backstreets a couple of times to find a place to park. When they walked to the central meeting spot, the local police were addressing the crowd.

"Jasmine was last seen approximately five minutes before the firework show ended last night. We have confirmed that at least three people saw her approach the boardwalk heading away from the beach. Early this morning, her brother found her hairband near the very end of the main boardwalk. As of now, that is all the information we have. We are forming five teams. Two teams are going to focus on the beach and surrounding dunes. The remaining teams are going to scan residential property along the beach. Please look for any clues. We will be passing out pictures of Jasmine, including a description of the clothes she was wearing last night. The local community should be fully aware of the search, so we shouldn't have issues walking on private property. A member of the police force will escort each group. Please keep in mind that today will be a very hot day. Several members of the community have agreed to leave coolers on the roadside filled with bottles of water to keep everyone hydrated, and we appreciate the community's support. Let's keep positive thoughts. Any questions?" The South Walton Sheriff scanned the crowd.

A couple of people asked questions, and the groups dispersed.

The Scotsdale family joined one of the teams canvassing the neighborhoods. Everyone was on high alert, and no one was chatting. It felt surreal to be searching for her friend that she had seen only yesterday. All Trina could think about was finding Jasmine alive. She must be somewhere.

After three long, exhausting hours of walking the streets, the teams met back at the central location. There was no news. Nothing. Tommy was sitting on the sidewalk with his head hung low. His parents were hugging nearby. The feeling of utter helplessness was pervasive. What could she say to make Tommy feel better? What else should she do to help? She had no good answers. It was the worst feeling ever.

Trina's parents left to go home, shower and grab some coffee. Trina, Jane, and the rest of the BBB were showing signs of shock, desperation, and fear. They didn't say it, but Trina could tell everyone wanted to stay together. As a group, they decided to walk to the store to grab something cold to drink. They walked holding hands in silence, dazed and numb.

Bobby was sitting behind the counter. He nodded his head at them as they walked in. The girls milled around the refrigerated sections for several minutes making their selections. One by one, each girl paid for their drink. Bobby didn't say a word to anyone. Trina and Dawn were the last two to check out. Dawn paid first, grabbed her drink, and walked to the exit. Trina gently placed her drink on the counter and nodded at Bobby.

"Hey. How are you holding up?" Bobby asked, making direct eye contact with Trina. "I assume you were part of the search party. Based on the looks on everyone's faces, I assume she wasn't found. Did anyone find anything to figure out which way she went?"

"Sadly, no. Absolutely nothing. It's so weird. We were with her and then she was gone. I saw you sitting behind the bonfire. Did you see her last night?"

"I'm not sure if I ever met her. I haven't really gotten to know that many kids around here. I'm taking a couple of summer classes, so between work and school, I don't have much free time. It would be a real bummer, though, if something bad happened to her. Are you going to be OK, Trina?"

Trina was shocked he remembered her name. She had only spoken to him once and seen him maybe twice at parties. "As OK as you can be in this situation. Thanks for asking," Trina said as she turned and headed toward the exit.

"I heard she was a real knockout. I would recommend that you pay extra attention to your surroundings. I don't think you realize how beautiful you are, Trina. If Jasmine was half as beautiful as you, it makes sense something bad could have happened to her. There are some nasty guys who hang around this area during the summer. I've seen my fair share of them while working the night shift. I wouldn't be shocked if some of them would take advantage of a girl walking alone. Promise me you'll be careful?" Bobby said with true sincerity.

Trina had turned around to look at Bobby when he threw out the unexpected compliment. She was flabbergasted. She smiled and said thanks, then walked out the door because she didn't know how else to respond. It was nice and awkwardly uncomfortable at the same time. Bobby had sounded protective, but was he protective because he knew something? Should she trust him? Did Bobby hurt Jasmine? Her mind was in overdrive. She was overanalyzing the situation. Not everyone had bad intentions. She walked over to her friends, who were standing in a small group by the street.

"Is everything OK, Trina? You look a little shaken up," Jane said, putting her arms around Trina's shoulders.

"Yeah. I'm fine. Just frazzled by this whole situation. Let's go home. I need to rest before work tonight."

The group methodically walked back to their respective homes. Trina went up to her room and climbed back to bed. She wrapped herself in her comforter and closed her eyes. Could someone have taken Jasmine? Who would have taken her and why? Have they hurt her? Is she locked up somewhere? Will they let her go? Was she attacked? Could Bobby really hurt someone? What about that property manager who stalks his tenants? Or the drunk fishermen who come to the Salty Bar? Or that weirdo who sits at the bar and watches girls in the bar mirror?

Trina's thoughts flittered from one person to another. She eventually drifted off, but it was not a sound sleep. Her dreams were filled with images of someone attacking someone, but she couldn't see the attacker's or the victim's faces. She could hear cries for help but couldn't see who was being attacked. Her heart was beating out of her chest. Then she felt someone shaking her. Someone was touching her shoulders. Squeezing them.

"Trina. Trina, wake up!"

Trina bolted straight up from her slumber. Jane was standing on the edge of the bottom bunk shaking Trina's arms. "Trina, you need to get ready for work. You have been sleeping for hours. Hurry up, we're going to be late."

Trina wiped her face with her hands and felt that her cheeks were moist from tears. She shook her head to get the sleep out of her head and shuffled over to the bunk bed ladder to climb down. She spent ten minutes in the bathroom freshening up. She couldn't find any clean aprons in her room, so she had to go searching in Judy's room. She threw on a semi-clean T-Shirt and a pair of jean shorts, combed her hair and walked downstairs.

"Hey, Mom, would you mind throwing a load of laundry in. I think we have been working so much we don't have any clean aprons," Trina said as she grabbed a granola bar from the pantry.

"Of course, honey. Please come home right after work tonight. Your dad and I are too nervous to let you girls go out after work. With the recent attack and now Jasmine's disappearance, we're extremely worried," she said as she hugged both sisters. "I already mentioned this to Judy when she left for her lunch shift. Maybe tomorrow morning we can all sit down and talk about it."

Jane and Trina nodded. They were too dazed to really hear what their mom had said. They drove in silence and had to park the car farther away than usual. There were still many cars down by the beach, people still searching for Jasmine. As they walked closer to the restaurant, they could see different crowds of people standing around talking in small groups. They walked by two police cruisers and a couple of television vans. Trina hoped somebody had found something, hoped they'd get some updates tonight at work.

When they walked into the restaurant, Danny asked Trina to grab supplies from the back of Jerry's Jeep since they were running low on several basics and fresh vegetables. The lunch shift had been twice as busy with so many people participating in search parties. When Trina and Jane clocked in at the time clock, they saw Judy wiping down tables out front. They walked over and asked if she'd heard any news.

"No. People have been searching for her all day. This place has been a revolving door for customers. Danny had to call in an extra cook to keep up with the orders. I've been listening to local gossip all day, but there has been no sign of her. Jane, you should check in with Tommy tomorrow. He never came into the restaurant, but I could see him across the street. He's been a wreck all day. He looks like he hasn't slept a wink since last night. Maybe Danny will let us bring dinner over to their family's house."

"I tried calling Tommy's house for the last hour. No one answered the phone," Jane said. "But I'll ask Danny about making a couple of meals. Great idea. You should go home, Judy. You look beat."

Trina walked back into the kitchen and asked Danny for the keys to the shed so she could grab the hand truck. She stepped outside the back of the restaurant. The sun was glaringly bright and immediately Trina could feel the heat and humidity of summer. She didn't know if she had the energy to work today. She was hot, tired, sad, and completely on edge. She took the hairband that she kept on her wrist and pulled her hair up into a ponytail. She wiped sweat from her brow and inhaled a deep breath to stabilize herself. Maybe a busy night would take her mind off of things. She needed a little bit of sanity.

Trina walked over to the shed and slid the key into the door. When she pushed the creaky door open, Jerry bolted upright at the sound of the door. To Trina's astonishment, when he stood up, she saw that he was not fully clothed.

"Get out! Get out of my office! You're not allowed in my office when I am working! Get out!" He adjusted his shorts and started to walk around the desk toward Trina, but she bolted out of the shed and ran back into the restaurant. She grabbed Jane, who was sitting at an open booth wrapping forks and knives in napkins and pulled her into the restroom.

"Oh my god! Jane, I think I just walked in on Jerry, um..." Trina said with severe embarrassment.

"What? You walked in on Jerry and what?" Jane said, looking at herself in the mirror and washing her hands.

"I think he was, um. I think I caught him in the middle of... you know!" Trina exclaimed.

Jane stopped and turned, mouth agape. "What? Are you sure? Where was he? Was he alone? Did he see you?"

"Yes, he saw me. I went into the shed to get the handcart," Trina said. "What do I do now? Danny wants me to grab boxes out of Jerry's Jeep. I don't want to go back into the shed. How can I ever look him in the eyes again?" Trina said shamefully.

"I cannot believe it! Although it's not surprising. His wife's too busy sleeping her way through the Panhandle. Oh, Trina, you poor thing. It will be hard to erase that image from your mind. Are you OK? Do you want me to tell Danny you want to go home for the day?"

"No, I don't need to go home. I mean, I walked in on him in his private office. It's not like he was doing it in front of me on purpose. But ewwwww! God, I am never going to get that image out of my brain," Trina said, holding her hands over her face and standing back against the bathroom wall.

"I'll go ask Billy to help us carry the boxes. Let's tell Danny we decided to do it together to get it done faster since there is so much prep work to be done before the dinner shift. OK? Stay away from Jerry. God, I knew he was a weirdo. How could he be doing such a thing, especially today of all days. Like really! A poor girl has gone missing."

As they walked out of the bathroom, they heard the sound of a car peeling out of the front parking lot. That must have been Jerry. He left before they could even grab the supplies.

Danny came over to the girls. "Hey, Jerry said he had a call at one of the rental properties. Some sort of emergency. He said he left the boxes out front. Can you go grab them? I asked Billy to help so they're not sitting out in the hot sun. Jerry said he left the door to the shed open. Lock it up when you are done. Drop the vegetables in the kitchen because I need to start dinner prep. Hey, are you girls OK? Sorry, I should have asked with everything going on. You both look as white as a ghost."

"Sorry, Danny. It's been a long day, as you can imagine. We'll take care of everything. Although if tonight is as busy as the lunch shift, we may need an extra set of hands. Is Tammy coming in tonight too? If you need more help, Trina's friend Wendy might be looking for extra hours," Jane said, squeezing Trina's hand to let her know she had not forgotten what just happened.

"Yes, Tammy is coming, and I also asked Roxy to come in for the first couple of hours. Trina, have your friend stop in tomorrow to fill out paperwork. Thanks, ladies. I appreciate you coming tonight. I'm sure you really don't want to be working, but we really need help. I'm trying to focus on the task at hand and not think about the situation. See if you can do the same. If you need to take extra breaks, let me know. We all may need to take breathers tonight," he said as he walked back into the kitchen.

"Thank goodness Jerry left," Trina said as they walked out to the front to grab the boxes. "That would have been so bloody awful! I don't think the last twenty-four hours could get any worse."

They completed the task and dove into the chaos of the endless stream of customers who walked through the door. Trina didn't know how she was getting through the shift. All she could do was watch every single man who walked into the restaurant and analyze every move they made. Is the tall, slim, gruff-looking customer hiding his eyes because he has a guilty conscience? Does the contractor with his sleeves rolled down have scratch marks on his arms? Are those bloodstains on the fisherman's shirt? Is that weird guy with the long hair looking for a girl to kidnap?

Do all men think horrible thoughts? How could she ever trust a man again? The property managers give her the creeps. Judy's new boyfriend continues to hit on her. Bobby locks eyes with her every time he sees her. Billy has hit on her. Jerry pays attention to what jewelry she's wearing, and now she knows what he does in the shed. Ugh. She needed a shower to cleanse herself of that memory.

While those horrible thoughts were bouncing around in her mind, she kept wishing Christopher was there to make her feel better. She didn't get to see him last night once the search began, and she hadn't seen him today at all. She wanted to hold his hand, needed a bear hug. But she knew he would be working late again tonight. They won't get a chance to talk until tomorrow.

Trina tried to focus on staying busy, which wasn't difficult as the restaurant was a constant stream of people. Tonight, however, very little drinking was going on. The tables were filled with groups of adults who were all eating like they hadn't eaten in days. Most had spent the day walking and searching. Although every table was filled and the bar had no open seats, the conversations throughout the restaurant were at a low murmur. It was like everyone was trying to be respectful of the situation and simply eat for the pure human need to replenish the body. Trina stayed busy delivering food, stacking clean dishes, and seating customers. The night flew by, and the restaurant emptied out before ten.

She was eager to go home, take a hot shower and scrub her entire body clean. She felt guilty because she couldn't help but feel preyed upon merely being in the presence of men even though it was poor Jasmine who was the real victim. She didn't know if she would ever feel 100% safe again. As emotionally traumatized as she'd felt over the last twenty-four hours, however, she was also energized to help. She wanted to write down the names of all the people she saw last night. She wanted to make a list of all the little things she had observed throughout the day that didn't feel right. Who had left the bonfire? Who else disappeared about the same time? Who had a motive? Who had the means? Did she have enough information to make a list of who could be guilty? She felt like she was living inside one of her books, and she wanted to rewrite the ending chapters. If only she could see Jasmine again, she would give her a protective hug. As Trina sat in the passenger seat as her sister drove home, all she could think about was hoping this nightmare would end.

Their parents were still awake, sipping wine with two other couples from the neighborhood, when Jane and Trina walked in the kitchen. The girls said hello but noticed how the conversation stopped when they entered the room. The girls grabbed glasses of water, excused themselves and went upstairs to the bedroom. They were too exhausted to deal with their parents tonight. Trina had a hard time falling asleep. Her mind was in overdrive. She ended up taking a pad of paper and jotting down random thoughts to make her feel like she was emptying her brain. Eventually, she finally fell asleep after midnight.

The girls slept in the next day but awoke to Nancy calling their names to wake up. Thankfully, none of them had to work. They really needed a day off. Smells from the kitchen wafted up to the second floor, and the sisters dragged themselves out of bed and went downstairs. Their mom was cooking bacon on the stovetop, and they could see their dad cooking hamburgers at the grill. From the looks of it, he was cooking a lot of hamburgers. The kitchen table was covered with potato salad, corn on the cob, a big bowl of watermelon and a stack of paper plates and napkins.

"What's going on? How come it looks like we are having a party?" Judy said as she slinked into a dining room chair and grabbed a juicy piece of watermelon.

"We invited several of your friends' parents over today, along with your friends of course. We would like to talk to you girls as a group, so we decided to make lunch out of it. Everyone should be here in ten minutes.

Can you girls get dressed and come back down to help me make pitchers of lemonade and iced tea?"

"Who's coming over?" Jane asked.

"You'll see. They'll be here shortly. I think I hear someone pulling in the driveway now. Go skedaddle, girls. Please. For me. Thanks."

The three girls ran up the stairs.

"A group meeting with our friends' families? This is not good. This must be about Jasmine," Jane said as she pulled her hair into a ponytail.

Judy pulled her pajama top off, picked up a shirt off the floor and sniffed it before putting it on. Trina grabbed a cotton short-sleeved shirt and a pair of jogging shorts. She didn't even want to try to guess what this lunch was going to be about.

A couple minutes later, they walked back downstairs to find about eight of their closest friends and their respective parents. Their friends quickly tackled the sisters and started chatting. Did they know what's going on? Did their parents tell them anything? What kind of meeting was this going to be?

The mothers asked everyone to grab a plate of food and meet out in the backyard. Twenty minutes later, their dad and three other dads stood up and excused themselves as they interrupted lunch.

"Hey, everyone. We really appreciate everyone coming together today," Trina's dad said to the crowd. "As you know, the last two days have been extremely difficult for this community. The most precious thing in the world is our children. Jasmine might not have lived here full-time, but she's an extremely important member of our town. We're all hoping for good news, and we'll continue to keep everyone up to date with any new discoveries."

Monica's dad began speaking. "We're lucky to be surrounded by a group of responsible, hardworking, and trustworthy kids. We feel like we need to set new boundaries, but this is not about you. This is about the unknown. We didn't want to set rules for one family and not another since we know you all spend so much time together, so we worked on a set of new standards as a group. We're only doing this to keep you away from harm. We want you to be able to continue enjoying your summer, but at the same time, we need to believe you will be safe."

Dawn's dad took over. "We would like for each of you to come home after work instead of going to the beach or going into the woods for late-night parties. When your shifts end at work, we want you to call home to let us know when you are leaving."

Trina's dad jumped back in. "We have all agreed that all our homes are open for gatherings. If you want to get together for a pool party or backyard barbeque, we freely and willingly offer up our homes for the rest of the summer. Until we know what happened to Jasmine, we need to keep you protected. If we have beach bonfires, we need everyone to check in with an adult before, during and at the end of the bonfire. No more walking home on the beach or walking on the dark streets at night. If anyone sees anything out of the ordinary, we ask that you immediately tell an adult. We don't understand what's going on in our community, but these small changes will provide us a little bit of comfort until we get some answers."

The conversation kept going. Reasons why they were setting new rules. What they were allowed to do and what they couldn't do. The information droned on and on for what seemed like forever. Finally, their parents thanked them for listening and left the kids alone outside to process the information.

They were all in shock but understood. If Jasmine had disappeared, any one of them could have been taken. The reality was none of them felt safe anymore. However, they were still devastated their Florida freedoms were being taken away. No more beer and bear parties. No more skinny-dipping late at night. No more drinking wine coolers by the water's edge. No more spontaneous fun. No more.

Since she spent most of her free time with Christopher, Trina wasn't as devastated with the new restrictions. However, hearing the parents set down ground rules made the events of the last twenty-four hours sink in. Jasmine was gone.

Her First 'Steak' Out

O nly two days had passed since her morbid discovery in the park and already the rumor mill had spun out of control. Trina had gained a little bit of small-town notoriety. A revolving door of faithful customers stopped in the store, Grayton Loft & Gifts, where she worked, but it wasn't long before Trina realized shopping wasn't their real intent. Trina began to feel like the town therapist as everyone wanted to share their opinion, with most expressing fear that a killer was prowling the Panhandle. The ladies at the nail salon were convinced a lone, lost vacationer had died in the woods while the coffee shop employees assumed a hunter became the hunted. Oddly enough, a post on Nextdoor linked the discovery of the body to corrupt commissioners and overdevelopment of the area. As an investigator in training, Trina soaked in the theories like a sponge, just in case there was a tiny fraction of truth in any of them.

Although the onslaught of business was generated out of curiosity, Trina enjoyed the quality time she had with the familiar faces who visited the store. Chatting with the local women was one of the best parts of her retirement job. She spent her time processing inventory items, ringing up purchases and striking up conversations. No stress, no deadlines, no corporate managers. Even though this strip of Florida heaven was relatively small, she had met people from all over the United States who came down for a 30A beach vacation. Trina frequently swapped stories about recent wine festivals, the daily live music offerings, new restaurant happy hour specials, and the long list of art events hosted by the Cultural Arts Alliance. Although there were several negatives to living in a tourist destination, her new hometown offered plenty of alternatives, which went a long way to easing the locals' frustrations. Trina had made several friendships by finding common interests, and though the extra attention on her now was because of the discovery in the woods, she couldn't deny she enjoyed realizing how many connections she had made in the short time since moving back to Florida.

The news cycle moves fast, and even just a couple of days later, the story had already started losing traction on social media and in the local newspapers. Her name had, shockingly, never made it in print as far as she could see, though most locals had found out through the grapevine. She didn't mind the unexpected rise in traffic at work, but she had to stop looking at her incoming calls and texts because she was receiving a high percentage of messages from unrecognizable numbers and decided it was in her best interest to keep the details to herself and not respond to random inquiries. Nevertheless, Trina heard the various theories as they bounced around the rumor mill, and the unknown threw her thoughts into a constellation of varying directions. The more theories she heard, the more motivated she was to solve the case.

The past two nights, she had scoured the shed and successfully identified seven cardboard boxes filled with newspapers, scrapbooks, and photo albums. She spent hours reading and getting lost in the nostalgia of her youth. Although eager to establish a link to her past and uncover a clue, once she began examining images from her teenage years, she began to feel overwhelmed. She had many positive memories of her summers on 30A, but a nagging feeling overcame her. She wondered if the trauma of living through Jasmine's disappearance had left an invisible wound of deeply buried memories. The negative emotions seeping into her thoughts forced her to step away.

Organizing always made her feel better, so she sat at her desk and began to clean out her drawers and the filing cabinet of old paperwork. She created a pile and sat at the shredder mindlessly eliminating her personal paper trail. Once that task was completed, she decided to rewash her summer wardrobe ensuring no hair fibers, fragments of skin or DNA were present. The cleaning made her feel refreshed and gave her comfort. She convinced herself that she shouldn't delve deeper until she'd visited the police station.

When Friday rolled around, Trina woke up to a vibration of nerves coursing through her body. The realization she would voluntarily walk into the police station and create a permanent ID tag was extremely intimidating. She had spent her life protecting her movements, eliminating breadcrumbs and magic erasing her existence. Now, she was handing over the sacred keys to her personal identity. Voluntarily, at that.

David and Trina had discussed the risks a little bit more. They'd decided there was no legitimate reason to not help eliminate herself from the crime scene through fingerprints. To keep her mind occupied, she focused on menial household chores and ran various errands to delay the inevitable. All day long, she coached herself, mentally preparing for the task ahead. While out, she stopped at the bakery and grabbed herself lunch in hopes of calming her nerves. She ate a steak salad on the patio under a red umbrella, enjoying the cool breeze and beautiful blue skies.

Her thoughts wandered back to the case. She wasn't ignorant of the fact the police had most likely created a list of potential victims but maybe she could be the first one to find the needle in the haystack. Once that mystery was solved, she could start scanning internet sites to review missing person cases from this area over the last twenty years. She wished she knew how long the body had been buried out in the woods. That would narrow down her search parameters.

Taking a sip of her favorite local brew, Noli South Kombucha, she couldn't stop thinking about Detective Jenifer's question. Why would she think Trina had found another metal object? Maybe the metal object wasn't a knife or a gun. Or it could be the car part Detective Trent referred to during his call at her house. She shouldn't assume this case was the only case he was working on, but the combination of Detective Jenifer's question and his conversation made her think otherwise. If they found a car part near the body, it's possible the body was a joyrider who took a 4x4 into the woods and bashed into a tree. As a mom, Trina felt anguished at the thought someone's child dying in the woods alone.

As she sat alone on the patio, she let her mind explore several possible alternatives. There had to be a way to elicit more information from the detectives. If she could confirm the body was, in fact, a female, she would feel more confident sharing her presumption. If she could cajole them into casually talking about the case, maybe they would slip up and unknowingly pass along important distinguishing details to help her help them.

Trina couldn't explain this desire, this invisible force pushing her to try to uncover the truth. She was not one to believe in fate. Why did the squirrel run so far into the woods up that specific tree? What were the odds? On top of that, even after making it to that tree, she had a one in a million chance of seeing a belt buckle hidden under nature's camouflage. No, there was an invisible force pushing her to that spot. She was destined to solve this case. However, the longer she sat, one realization became clear. She had absolutely no experience solving crimes, and she was either stupid or crazy to consider there was even the tiniest possibility that she could.

Trina pondered that thought as she chewed on another bite of her lunch. Solving the case might be a tad bit ambitious. Instead of trying to be the lead character in this story, maybe she should strive to be a good supporting character. Sort of like the gadget man in Bond movies. Maybe she could discover a small lead but vital clue that changed the whole investigation. Now that she thought about it, she still had the matches. Detective Trent would most definitely appreciate her value once she turned over a time capsule of evidence. That would surely build trust. The matches could be the grain of sand that toppled the sandcastle. Forgetting about her lack of experience, Trina felt confident she could help the detectives. She'd already messed up the crime scene, so what's the harm in doing a little investigation on the side?

Maybe she could bribe her way to Detective Trent's office. Trina jumped up from the patio seat and stood back in line at the counter. She asked for a to-go box and ordered a box of donuts, muffins, and scones. That might do the trick. She packed the rest of her lunch, waved to Lynn and Josh, who worked in the kitchen, and headed out the door.

She turned on the radio in her car and connected it to her playlist. Rolling her windows down, Trina felt empowered as she sang the lyrics to the song "Stronger" by Kelly Clarkson. She arrived at the small police station on U.S. Route 331 and parked under one of the only remaining trees that provided a little shade. The building's sign read *Walton County Sheriff's Office*. There were five police cars parked in the lot, six non-descript vehicles and one South Walton Emergency Response van. She had never been to a police station and felt a little awkward being there. Guilt, that's what she felt. It was like seeing blue lights in her rearview mirror and instinctively slowing down even though she wasn't breaking the law.

She opened her windows, not wanting to keep the AC running. She wasn't quite ready to enter, so she opted to keep eating her lunch to mentally prepare for what was to come. She sat there munching on lettuce and steak thinking about the endless possibilities while she stared at the front door. If they were going to take her fingerprints at the front desk, how would she gain access to the detective's office? She tried to visualize scenes from TV crime shows. While she was devising a plan on how to get past whatever blockade she found inside, she chuckled to herself as she took another bite of steak salad. "I'm on my first *steak* out." She wondered if this was what it felt like on actual police stakeouts. She bet no one had ever staked out the sheriff's office before. She considered the irony as she sat there eating her salad and watching the periodic activity at the front door from the safety of her car.

Well, if she was ever going to assist the detectives, she needed to get hands-on investigatory experience. Her first obstacle would be getting past the front desk. Baby steps, Trina. Baby steps. She remembered one of her favorite fictional detectives. *Patterson's Detective Alex Cross was a rookie at one point too. Go bribe your way in and gather information.*

She finished her last bite of salad, grabbed the box of goodies and her purse. Confidently striding toward the front door, Trina hummed the lyrics to Kelly's song, giving herself an extra boost of self-esteem. *What doesn't kill you will make you stronger, indeed.*

Trina took her sunglasses off and hooked them to the front of her shirt. As she opened the right door with the sleeve of her shirt, the left door swung outward, and Officer Cody and another policeman walked out. The officer with Cody said, "We're supposed to have a taskforce update in the war room around three today." Cody recognized Trina and gave her a polite nod but kept walking to the parking lot.

The war room at three o'clock. Need to find the war room. As she entered the building, she saw a waiting room with about thirty chairs spread throughout the room. The television mounted on the wall was on, but the sound was muted. Three people were sitting in chairs, and two officers were standing off to the side by a coffee machine. There was a reception window with a sliding glass panel, and a woman was sitting behind it with her back to Trina. A small logbook was open on the counter, and a digital clock hung on the wall.

Deep breath in. Deep breath out. Deep breath in. Deep breath out. Trina walked slowly but with purpose to the reception window and rested the box of goodies on the small counter. She knocked lightly on the glass pane and said, "Excuse me, ma'am."

The woman spun around in her chair and slid the window open. "Trina, oh my dear! I heard all about it. How are you holding up, young lady?"

Betty Bringston was staring back at her. Betty was about ten years older than Trina and had lived in the Panhandle her whole life. Trina met Betty within the first couple weeks of moving back to town. Betty had been walking her dog at the same time Trina was walking hers, and they became friends. Betty stopped by the shop at least once a month to check out home decorations and chat with Trina.

"Oh my gosh, Betty. I totally forgot you work at the police station. I'm so used to seeing you out with Bojangles for a walk or stopping in the store after you get your nails done. It's sort of odd to see you in uniform. It's like my brain can't process the uniform and your friendly face. Oh no." Trina gulped. "I didn't mean to insinuate that police are not friendly," she said, embarrassed and trying to backpedal on her unfortunate wording.

"Don't you worry, dear. I am not easily offended," Betty said sweetly. "I completely understand where you're coming from. My neighbor Phil never wears a shirt when he works in his yard. When I see him all dressed up at a wine tasting, it always takes me a minute to place his face as my next-door neighbor." Betty laughed, making Trina feel slightly better for in advertently insulting Betty's profession.

Betty swung around and looked behind her to scan who was milling around, then turned back to face Trina. "Why don't I buzz you on back and I'll take care of you as quickly as I can. It's lunchtime so the place is empty. I know why you're here, and you don't want to stay any longer than you need to." She hit a button and the door to the right popped open.

149

Trina grabbed her box and sauntered through the door, thinking this was too easy. She had an "in" at the police station she had forgotten about; she'd hit the jackpot.

It was about ten minutes after twelve, and the station was relatively quiet. The center of the large room behind Betty's desk was filled with twenty low-walled gray cubicles. Lining the walls were small offices with glass doors. She assumed those belonged to detectives. Across the back wall was one large office, but the shades were completely drawn. She assumed the large office belonged to the sheriff, and Trina intended to steer clear of him; he might not be ready to forgive her for the mace accident. She could see down the hall on the right there were six floor-to-ceiling panes of glass, which seemed to be lining a conference room—the war room.

After quickly taking in the surroundings, Trina reached over the counter to give Betty a hug. "Girl, you look good in blue! And exuding professionalism and importance to boot. It's so nice to see where you work after all this time."

"Oh, Thank you Trina, you are too complimentary. I was deeply sorry to hear about your discovery. Only you would uncover a skeleton on your walk. You seem to always find the strangest things, though this one surely hits the top of your list. Well, I know you're here to get fingerprinted. Detective Trent told me to expect you. I would have called you to find out if you were managing okay, but I didn't want to cross the line between business and friendship. I figured I'd wait until I saw you today. How are you faring?" Betty's empathy for Trina's situation was obvious and genuine.

"The shock has lessened, but what I saw in the woods is still filling up my dreams at night," Trina shared with a sigh. "So, I obviously have never been fingerprinted before. What does this process entail?" She held up her right hand with her fingers spread out, her eyes wide open.

"Super easy. Come around to this side of the desk, and I'll take care of you right here. I already had paperwork waiting for you." She approached Trina and commenced the fingerprinting process. "What's in the box?" Betty asked as she pressed and rolled one of Trina's fingers in a box on the fingerprint card. "It smells delicious."

"I know this is a little strange, but I wanted to thank the detectives and officers for being so kind to me at the crime scene," Trina explained. "They were extremely patient and respectful. Everyone really helped me get through the initial shock. I was hoping to hand deliver this to Detective Trent to give him my thanks. No one can turn down a Black Bear Bakery treat. Would you like to be the first?"

Betty efficiently finished taking her fingerprints and handed her a hand sanitizing wipe to clean her fingers. "I'll pass. The delicious smell is enough for me, but I'm sure the team can use a little sugar to get through the next couple of days. They're putting every effort into identifying the remains. This team is sharp, so I have no doubt they will solve this case soon enough. Do you want to wait for Detective Trent? He isn't in right now, but he's expected back by 12:30 for a meeting. I can show you to a chair right outside his office."

She posed it as a question but clearly assumed Trina's answer was yes, as she began to lead Trina down the narrow hallway without waiting for a response. Betty pointed to a chair next to one of the bigger offices on the left wall, almost exactly opposite what Trina assumed was the war room. As Trina sat, they both heard knocking on the glass panel at the reception desk.

"You wait right there. Detective Trent is always on time. He should be here any minute," Betty said, glancing at the clock on the back wall before heading off toward her position at the front desk.

Once she confirmed that Betty was situated back out front, Trina slowly looked around to assess her location. She could hear an officer talking on the telephone but couldn't see him. There was a muffled conversation occurring behind one of the closed office doors. Overall, the place was quiet. Feeling like she was relatively alone in the room, she focused her sights on the big conference room. It was enclosed in glass walls with long-slated blinds lining about 60% of the way across the length of the room. Trina squinted to focus on what was inside the two uncovered glass panels. A big whiteboard with writing on it hung on the back left wall, and on the adjacent exterior wall was a pegboard of sorts filled with plastic bags containing various items.

Her excitement spiked. This was the real deal. She was staring across at an active investigation room. Knowing that the discovery of a body was not a common occurrence in Santa Rosa Beach, she felt confident she was seeing evidence related to the skeleton. This must be where the meeting will be held later this afternoon. Trina exhaled loudly. *How badly do you want to know what else they dug up near that skeleton?* Did she have the nerve to walk over there? No. She was not bold enough to strut over there and stare in the windows. However, she was close enough to take pictures using the zoom feature on her iPhone. Could she convince herself to snap photos?

A guilty conscience zapped Trina. She wasn't comfortable breaking rules, never mind laws. She hadn't read enough legal fiction to provide her with a sense of legality versus ethics of sneaking photos of confidential evidence. Struggling with this mental tug-of-war, she glanced around the room one more time aiming her iPhone toward the gap in the blinds. She hit 3x magnification and snapped eight pictures in quick succession. She closed her eyes and pushed out a gust of hot, nervous energy.

She couldn't believe she had broken an unwritten rule—maybe even a law—within the confines of the police station. Her pride was quickly replaced with guilt as she scanned the room to see if she was caught on an internal security camera. She didn't see any lenses pointed her way. If there was a surveillance system, she hoped no one would watch the camera feed unless an issue occurred. As she sat there waiting for Detective Trent, she wondered why this case was making her act so compulsively. So out of character. She normally would never even consider taking any risky actions, never mind following through with it.

A door opened behind her and several people walked into the room chatting away. Trina slightly popped her bottom up off the chair and peeked at who walked in. She didn't recognize any of the faces. Soon after, the sheriff's door opened. Trina saw only a very small sliver of the sheriff sitting at his desk before two officers walked out of the office and closed the door behind them.

The back door opened again, and both Detective Trent and Detective Jenifer walked in. She was wearing a white V-neck shirt with a pair of lightly faded jeans and had her hair up in a ponytail. He had a gray golf shirt on with a pair of khaki pants. He was a handsome fellow, but unfortunately appeared a little more frazzled than the last time Trina saw him. He was carrying a cup from Seaside's busiest coffee shop, Amavida, in his right hand and had a Grayton Beach Fitness workout bag in his left.

Although Trina was sitting about thirty feet away, she overheard Detective Jenifer say, "At least we're getting pushed up to priority one by the coroner. We should get his initial finding before the three o'clock meeting. I'll check emails and see if we've heard anything more about the vehicle. See you at two." She walked away toward a cubicle down the hall.

Detective Trent walked toward his office. He rounded the last cubicle and saw Trina sitting there. "Mrs. Scotsdale, what a nice surprise. Wow, it's Friday already, isn't it? Thank you for coming today. Did Betty take care of you?" he asked.

"Yes, she sure did. She processed me faster than a deer crossing 30A during midday traffic," Trina joked, trying to keep it light and friendly.

"Wonderful. Well, you're sitting in the hot seat here outside my office. Did you steal too many mints from the reception desk?" he joked back, smiling.

"Well, I'm not accustomed to sitting in a police station, that's for sure. I wanted to thank you personally and the team for being so patient and kind with me the other day. Truly a commendation to everyone for their professionalism considering the disastrous path I seemed to have left in my wake on Tuesday." Smiling widely, she held open the white cardboard box showing the baked treats she had brought with her. "And I do need to confess. Do you have a moment to spare?" she said with a slight grin and a cocked head.

"Oh my, you discovered our weakness for sweets already. You are quite a good investigator, Trina. I'll have to keep you in mind if we ever have an opening. Of course, I can give you a couple of minutes. Come on in." He unlocked his office door and held it open for Trina like a proper southern gentleman.

Walking in his office, Trina noticed three chairs—two sitting opposite his desk and one off to the side. She did a quick glance and decided she would get a better view of his desk if she sat in the chair to the side, which faced out toward the war room. Trina sat down and placed the box on his desk. "Detective Trent, what is your weakness? Fresh hot blueberry muffins or a glazed donut? Maybe one of each?" she asked as she held the cover of the box open.

"You got me at hot blueberry," he said with a friendly smile.

She stood up and placed her sunglasses on his desk while she leaned over to place a muffin in a napkin in the palm of his hand.

"Not too many people tell a police detective they want to confess without their lawyer present. What do you want to share with me today?"

"I feel so bad about this. I honestly totally forgot about it until I was ready to put a load of laundry in the washer this morning." Knowing full well holding onto the matchbook provided her with a solid excuse for coming to his office, she emphasized the right words to make it believable. Lying and sneaking photos! She was more devious than she realized. She was slowly developing similar skills to the fictional female detectives she so admired.

"When you and Detective Jenifer asked me if I had found anything else, I guess I was not completely honest. However, let me sugarcoat that by saying I honestly forgot that I had found something else. Let me get right to the point. Inside the pocket of that small piece of denim was an old, worn-out book of matches from the Red Bar's grand opening. From what I can remember, the Red Bar opened in the late nineties, which might help you narrow down the period of his or her death," she said, hoping she was successfully planting a seed that she could be a valuable local resource.

"Obviously, in order for me to physically have possession of this, I did, in fact, touch the matchbook with my fingers," she shamefully confessed. "When I came home from the trails on Tuesday, I threw my dirty clothes in the laundry, totally forgetting that I had put the book of matches in my skirt pocket. But please believe me, I put it in my pocket before I saw the skeleton. I thought I'd found an old and rare book of matches from the Red Bar. Then when I found the body, I totally spaced out on the matches. I didn't remember I had them until I was checking my pockets this morning before starting a load. Luckily, I found it before I washed it, although I guess it has gotten pretty damp being stuck in someone's pocket out in the woods for years." She pulled out the sealed Ziploc bag and placed it on his desk, watching him intensely for a reaction.

Calm as a cucumber, you could almost see his mind churning, Detective Trenton made her think of Gil Grissom from *CSI*. As a top-notch professional, he would not jump to conclusions about the evidence until he had ascertained all the appropriate facts. He picked up a pen and turned the Ziploc bag over to see the other side, looking at the matchbook as if he had forgotten Trina was standing there.

Feeling guilty for keeping this from him for three days, she quickly added, "Words were written on the inside. Something about number four or five and getting off work. I am sorry for not remembering this. I'm bribing you with sweets so you can forgive me. Am I in big trouble?" she asked him seriously because she really didn't know if she'd broken a law by not turning it over sooner. Trina nervously rubbed the scar on her upper right shoulder. If she wasn't nibbling on her fingernails, she ran fingers over the scar as a calming mechanism.

While he seemed keenly focused on the book of matches, she took advantage of the opportunity to scan his desk. Granted, everything appeared upside down from where she was standing, but she could still see handwritten notes on a legal pad. Trina was typically forgetful when she listened to information, but she had a knack for remembering things if she saw it. One quick glance and she cataloged that his notes said: Missing Person 1990-2000; Camel Cigarettes; VIN – Pending.

He seemed to finally come to the realization that Trina was still in his office. "Mrs. Scotsdale, this is a very helpful piece of the puzzle. Where did you say you found it again?" he asked as he picked up his phone and hit a couple of digits. "Jenifer, when you have a moment, please." He spoke gently and calmly into his office phone while maintaining eye contact with Trina, then put the receiver of the phone back and glanced at the matchbook again.

"It was inside the denim pocket. I really am very sorry. I'm sure this could break the case wide open," she offered, emphasizing the words *break* and *wide open*. "Trent," she said, as if they were old buds sitting over a beer at Chiringo's happy hour. "I pulled out my parents' storage boxes of photos and newspapers covering over thirty years. Once you identify the year in which he or she died, I would happily sift through photos and newspaper articles if you think it could help," she offered to make up for the three-day evidence sharing delay. She desperately wanted him to find value in her assistance. "Many of the small, local newspapers printed limited quantities and most likely have not yet been digitized."

"No worries about forgetting the matches. You were exposed to a gruesome discovery. No one can expect you to remember everything, which is why we follow up with all witnesses several times after incidents. Memories come back in pieces like a slow-motion puzzle. Thank you so much for bringing this in today, and for providing us with your fingerprints. Unfortunately, I need to cut our little meeting short, as I need to meet with the team to prepare for our afternoon meeting." He swooped his hand around her lower back and gently nudged her out the door. He strode beside her most of the way toward Betty, then turned back around and returned to his office, greeting Detective Jenifer, who was waiting for him.

Trina waved goodbye and turned toward the exit. As she pushed the door open to enter the foyer, Betty said, "I hope Detective Trent was appreciative of your sweets. He has his hand full this week trying to figure out who the dead man is. Let's hope the team can solve this mystery sooner rather than later."

Trina told Betty that she would see her and her dog, Bojangles, soon. As she walked outside, she processed and felt the crushing blow that Betty said—dead *man*. She wondered if Betty said that generically, like any dead body could be referred to as a man, or if they specifically knew it was a man. If it was a man, her gut instinct was wrong. She'd been so confident that it was Jasmine, the July 4th Girl. Thankfully, she had not shared her idea with the detectives. They wouldn't have a reason to think any less of her for trying to solve this murder too quickly. Now that she thought about it, she didn't even know if this was a murder.

She rushed back to her car, squinting in the afternoon sun. Trina sat in her car with the window down and took a huge breath of fresh air. "OK so not too bad. I think he believed me about finding the matches this morning," she said to her empty passenger car seat. She needed to gather her thoughts now that she had collected information. She pulled out her phone and studied the pictures.

She zoomed in on the pictures since the fine details were hard to see. She could make out the word Jeep written on the white wall. Beneath that were the following phrases: Missing persons, Make Model, Denim – Stores sold, Belt- Mfgd, and Medical examiner report. Alright, this gave her an idea about their initial investigation approach.

The pegboard picture was blurry in comparison. It looked like a white, scalloped piece of material in one plastic bag and a small pad of paper in another. There was also a bag with several other small items, but the image was too blurry.

Not too shabby for her first day on the job as a rookie detective. Although no one was expecting her to dig into relevant facts of the case, she felt a sense of satisfaction with her efforts. She needed to get back home and write down the details to confirm what she knew and what she needed to know. She started her car and was ready to pull out when she realized she'd left her sunglasses in Detective Trent's office.

She was about to get out of the car and go back inside the police station when she smiled slyly to herself. Her sunglasses would provide her with the perfect excuse to come back and see the detective in a couple of days. She bet lunchtime would be the perfect time. Maybe she should bring

Bojangles a bag of dog treats. She'd already bribed the detectives, why not bribe her friend who happened to be the gatekeeper at the police station?

Send-Offs, Shifts and Sex on the Beach

1993

J udy stood squished in the middle of her family as they squeezed
love into their embrace near the International gate at Logan
Airport. She released herself from the confines of arms and heads,
grabbed her backpack and waved goodbye, taking one last glance
before entering the hallway to catch her flight to Paris for her French
summer exchange program. Mr. and Mrs. Scotsdale stood wiping
tears from their eyes as they proudly watched their daughter begin
a new journey. With no time to wallow, they walked Tanner to the
parking lot and snuck in an extra hug. Tanner pulled his baseball cap
down and nodded goodbye as he drove off to his new apartment in
the north end of Boston, where he would begin an internship with
a prominent architectural firm. Jane and Trina sat in the back of the
car on the way home, holding hands and listening to "I Will Always
Love You" by Whitney Houston. A family of six had been quickly
reduced to four, and the impact of sibling absences would undoubt-
edly alter the vibe of their summer vacation at the bungalow.

Jane and Trina were eager to reunite with the beach crew for a summer in Florida. After Jasmine's mysterious disappearance last summer and the resulting social gridlock, their remaining beach days were filled with parental chaperones, backyard cookouts, and game nights. Rummy, War, Crazy Eight and even the Scotsdale favorite, Spit, occupied many nightly competitions. The kids had initially longed for the ability to sneak out for moonlight beach strolls or late-night parties in the woods, but by the end of the summer of '92, their Florida friendships had unexpectedly solidified.

Their "confinement" to each other's houses had prompted long nights of honest and thoughtful conversations, as well as fits of laughter, spawning new nicknames and private jokes they would remember for a lifetime. While the intimate dialogues cemented friendships, it also generated a welcomed comfort for sharing fears, anxieties, and dreams. Their initial resentment of parental restrictions soon morphed into appreciation for the opportunity to truly bond with their summertime friends. They'd all departed Florida last year with stronger friendships, fresh perspectives, and a desperate hope that Jasmine's 30A mystery would be solved.

Although the Scotsdales opted to stay in Massachusetts over the past winter holidays, Christopher and Paul had enjoyed Christmas with their family back in the Panhandle. Christopher picked up a couple of work shifts, while still having plenty of time to enjoy his hobby of exploring state parks and hiking trails. During his nightly phone calls with Trina, his excitement for sharing unique wildlife sightings—evidence of a bear's den or an armadillo skeleton—was contagious. She savored every detail and longed to be by his side. Sitting in her bedroom back at home, she lived vicariously through Christopher's stories of 30A.

Three weeks of separation were tortuous for Trina, and she counted the hours until Christopher returned right before the start of the second semester. When he walked into school on the first day, his winter tan highlighted the contented aura that exuded from him after being in Florida for three weeks during the dreary winter months. She soaked in his stories of encounters with wildlife, enjoying ice cream on the boardwalk and early morning paddleboard adventures. She spent the rest of the semester dreaming about returning to the white, silky sand and plotting moonlight walks on the beach.

The time for vacation arrived, and Jane and Trina stuffed their suitcases full of cute new bikinis and bright summer T-shirts. Trina also filled a backpack full of books. Although she'd devoured several crime novels over the course of the school year, she had an insatiable desire to consume more. Ever since Jasmine disappeared, Trina had become fascinated with how detectives solved crimes. She couldn't get enough of mysteries, kidnapping stories, and FBI re-enactments describing attacks and horrific tragedies. Unfortunately, the events of the evening of July 4th had taught Trina that sometimes unfathomable fiction could become someone's unbelievable reality.

Frustration at the lack of a resolution and the slowly fading hope that Jasmine would be found had flipped a switch in Trina. She had become more cognizant of her surroundings and interactions with men. Any awkward male body language set off her internal alarm bells. Lingering eye contact generated an invisible protective shield around her physical proximity to men. She trained herself to be aware of unwelcome company as she walked aisles in the grocery store, became hesitant to accept kind gestures and reluctant to engage in small talk. She forced her friends to travel in groups, reduced her exposure to strangers and limited her outdoor exercise routines. Her parents never had to ask her to check in because she was diligent about communicating her whereabouts. Trina was not only cautious, but she was also compulsively alert and proactive about taking actions to ensure her safety. As she finished packing for the road trip, she was confident she was mentally prepared for any situations that may arise.

Their parents left for Florida around four thirty in the morning, and Jane and Trina finished stuffing the trunk of their car an hour or so later. Christopher's car needed repair work, so the annual tradition of dipping their toes in the sand together upon arrival would be delayed. The hours of highway driving passed by slowly. Cranked music, funny stories and silly license plate games passed the time. They consumed prepacked ham and cheese sandwiches, devoured bags of Doritos and treated themselves to watermelon slushies at convenience stores. Jane divulged that she dreamed of opening her own pastry shop back in their hometown and was nervous to tell their parents. Knowing their dad was a successful businessman, Trina convinced Jane their parents would support her desire to be an entrepreneur. As the hours in the car became a seemingly endless loop, Trina revealed that her feelings for Christopher were growing stronger, more concrete. Because Jane was an avid listener and did not indulge by providing unsolicited advice, Trina eventually revealed she was feeling anxious about taking the next step in their relationship. Jane listened nonjudgmentally and eventually provided Trina with some sisterly advice.

Arriving in Florida after midnight, they unloaded the luggage, touched their toes in the sand and crashed into bed in separate bedrooms eager with anticipation for their first day back in Florida. Danny had requested the girls show up at two in the afternoon to go through paperwork and review menu changes. Although she had not officially taken customer orders, Trina felt like she knew the Salty Bar menu better than most since she had frequently tasted Danny's dishes and had worked around the kitchen staff for years.

She was proud to wear her first waitress apron, and as she walked into the restaurant by Jane's side, she felt a little taller, a little more important. Danny was showing Dawn and Tanya how to use the time clock and Monica and Wendy were standing at the supply closet reviewing menus. Loud welcome screams erupted as Monica, Angela, Dawn, and Tanya ran over to Trina and Jane to give them hugs. Comments flew back and forth—Trina's new hair length; Monica's cool pixie haircut; Angela's flashy earrings; Tanya's skinny waist; Dawn's athletic muscles; Jane's maturity. After several minutes of reunion excitement, Danny reminded them the clock was ticking.

Jane was tasked with training the girls on the menu and walking them through the intricacies of taking orders. The girls were tested on their knowledge of commonly ordered cocktails and were briefed on ways to add appetizers, suggest to-go orders of desserts and recommend higher priced alcohols. As Jane walked around the restaurant, Trina was barely listening to her sister. She was extremely confident in her ability to be a waitress. Her thoughts were focused on all the money she could earn over the summer. She wanted to buy her own car and was planning to accept as many shifts as Danny would give her.

On the wall across from the hostess stand, Trina noticed that Danny had hung a bulletin board filled with customer photographs Trina had taken over the last two summers. Trina's hobby of snapping pictures had developed into a fun way to promote the relaxed atmosphere and great food at the Salty Bar. The pictures were previously taped on the mirror behind the bar, but she liked how they were now displayed as a mixed-matched collage of images. She recognized many of the customers she had befriended over the years, and the images made her super excited for the next couple of months.

Jane was the only returning experienced waitress, so Trina wasn't surprised that she was assigned the patio. Patrons absolutely loved sitting under umbrellas with a perfect view of the beach accompanied by the sounds of waves crashing along the shore. The other coveted section included four tabletops and two booths near the bar, and Trina was shocked Danny had enough confidence in her to assign her that section. His support on her first night made her excited to begin her first shift as a waitress.

It wasn't long before she was in her own groove and was comfortable meeting the endless loop of customer faces. After a big rush of beachgoers filled up all the tabletops outside, Jane asked Trina for help.

"Trina, I'm slammed. Can you take the customer around the back corner? I don't think I'm going to get to him anytime soon," Jane said as she slipped next to Trina at the food pickup window. "I got three parties of six each, and they all ordered appetizers, cocktails and dinners," Jane said as she grabbed a tray full of oysters Rockefeller, fried shrimp and three Caesar salads.

"Not a problem. I'll deliver table thirteen's dinner and head outside." Trina delivered the plates to one of her tables, grabbed a glass of water and a menu, and headed out the side door to the back end of the patio. As she approached the table, Trina's adrenaline spiked.

"Excuse me, miss. I heard the hottest waitresses in town worked here. I'm in desperate need of an order of Florida's famous plastic pizza, or a plate of chewy elastic spaghetti and meatballs," Christopher said. He was sitting at the small round table in the back corner. Trina couldn't help but notice there was a small box with a bow on it. She slid into the empty seat across from Christopher after reaching over and planting a peck on his lips.

"Sneaky! You told me you weren't coming until Monday. You must have left right after we did. When did you get here?" Trina said, holding his hands across the table.

"The repairs on the car were done much quicker than I expected, so Paul and I decided to come on down. I thought I could surprise you on your first official shift as a waitress." He held up the box. Trina stood and gave him the tightest hug, holding him for twenty long, intimate seconds. She let him go, sat back down and gently took the box out of his hands.

Trina untied the bow and popped the box open to find a delicate, intricate charm in the shape of a tiny book. Trina read a little notecard aloud: "For my favorite, veracious reader. I cannot wait to write our own chapters this summer." Christopher stood up and bent over the small table to give Trina a kiss.

"Christopher, you truly spoil me! You are seriously the most thoughtful boyfriend. How did I get so lucky to have a boyfriend as sweet as you?" She held the tiny book in her hand and studied it with fascination.

Before he could respond, Trina said, "Where on earth did you find a necklace charm in the shape of a book?"

"While I was here over winter break, I had stopped in at The Zoo Gallery to look for Christmas presents for my family. When I saw that, I just had to buy it for you." The Zoo Gallery was a unique retail establishment in Grayton Beach that had been in business since 1979 selling art, jewelry, pottery, and custom-designed T-Shirts. It was the Scotsdales' favorite store to shop at to buy special mementos reminding them of their special vacation home.

"It's perfect! I have no doubt you and I will fill pages and pages of our own crazy chapters this summer. You mean the world to me, Christopher. Thank you." Trina slipped the new charm onto her necklace and stood up and grabbed his hand.

"Although I would love to sit with you all night, I need to get back inside. Can I place your usual order?" Trina said as she straightened her apron and fixed her hair.

"Yes, please, I'm starving. One greasy burger with seasoned fries. How is it going on your first waitressing shift? Are you killing it?"

"So far, so good. Danny gave me the bar section. I can't believe he trusted me on my first night with the best section. I think I already made a couple hundred, and we still have a few hours to go! I'll place your order and be right back," Trina said as she squeezed his hand.

"Give everyone that big, adorable Trina smile and you'll be a rich woman by the end of the summer. I'll stick around for a little bit after I eat before I head out."

Trina walked back into the kitchen and placed his order. Christopher had a special way of making her feel soft and squooshy on the inside.

She was the luckiest girl on the beach. She spent the rest of the evening smiling and laughing with customers, floating on a high, dreaming of fun times ahead.

The night ended later than they expected, as the late-night crowd ordered dinner and cocktails. By the time Jane and Trina pulled into the driveway, it was almost midnight. Monica, Angela, and Dawn pulled in right behind them. The girls were all crashing at Trina's house since the group had early morning plans to drive up to the Vortex Springs, a nearby natural water park. Their friends had brought their bags of clothes with them in preparation for the next day's adventure.

Even though they were exhausted from their first night back at work, the girls were filled with excited energy as they sat on the floor counting aprons full of cash. Monica credited her new sexy white apron as her unique moneymaker. Angela admitted that she sucked up to families with kids, and Dawn confessed to smothering her customers with excessive kindness. Trina listened to all her friends' suggestions, but she had observed the bartenders and wait staff over the years and had been silently taking mental notes on how to be financially successful. On her first night of waitressing, Trina brought home way more than the rest of the girls, but she let Monica believe she was the night's big breadwinner. Trina didn't care about the recognition; she just wanted to be able to buy her first car before school started in the fall. Plus, she loved watching Monica parade around the room in her tight apron re-enacting her evening. After an hour of gossiping, the four girls squeezed themselves into the bunk bed, falling asleep one by one.

"Girls, breakfast is ready," Trina's mom called up the stairs around nine.

The girls let out a collective groan. The energy from the previous night had dissipated, and they didn't want to crawl out from their comfortable, snug spots. Eventually, they roused themselves and took turns in the bathroom. As they walked downstairs, the smell of cinnamon buns stirred their bellies. In addition to the warm buns covered in homemade vanilla icing, Trina's mom had made sausage, egg and pepper muffins and had cut up a bowl full of fresh cantaloupe and honey melon. The girls barely spoke as they piled their plates with food and ate like they hadn't eaten in weeks.

"Thank you so much, Mrs. Scotsdale. I didn't realize how hungry I was until I sat down," Monica said as she finished the last bite of her second cinnamon bun.

"You must give my mom this recipe," Angela said. "These sausage muffins are amazing. I could eat ten of them."

"Mom, is Jane up? We were supposed to leave by ten to get a couple of hours at the springs before work tonight," Trina asked as she sipped her orange juice.

"She ate already and ran to the corner store. We didn't have much coffee left in the pantry, and I wasn't sure if any of you ladies would need a pick-me-up."

About five minutes later, Jane walked in with a small grocery bag and plopped it on the counter. She walked over to the table and sat down, grabbing a piece of cantaloupe. "Girls, eat up and pack your things. The boys are headed over to load our coolers and paddleboards. Make sure you pack suntan lotion and a change of clothes for the ride home. Hey Mom, can you help me pack a couple of sandwiches while they get changed? I already grabbed grapes, chips, and water," Jane said as she pulled bread, ham, and cheese out of the refrigerator.

The girls headed upstairs after clearing their plates. The excitement for the day had reawakened their tired bodies. They changed into bathing suits, T-shirts, and shorts, grabbed beach towels, and walked downstairs as the boys pulled up. Christopher and Paul had one car, and Ricky and Sean were going to drive the second and third car. Everyone piled in and they headed up to Vortex Springs. The weather was spectacular, and the girls teamed up with the guys to paddleboard. After paddleboarding for half an hour, they found a spot to tether together in the majestic aqua-blue water. Conversations teetered back and forth between stories about crushes that never came to fruition, and movies they'd recently watched.

Ricky said, "I love that scene in *Sandlot* where the kid with glasses makes out with the hot lifeguard chic. I was never that gutsy as a kid."

"Yeah," Paul chimed in, "I'm more like Wayne in *Wayne's World* when he met Kim Basinger at the laundry mat. Zero confidence to sneak a kiss with a beautiful girl. Do you know how hard it is to approach an attractive girl? I hate that we have all the risks of getting rejected. Girls expect us all to be as romantic as Tom Cruise, when we're all as awkward as George McFly."

"Whoa, hold on, Paul! At least we would appreciate a guy who treats us as good as Tom Cruise even if he looked like George. You boys can keep dreaming about dating Cindy Crawford but it's never going to happen. Especially with Ricky's cheap pick-up lines," Monica said jokingly.

"At this point, I'll take any girl who pays attention to me for longer than five minutes. We need fresh blood around here. No offense, ladies, but you're like sisters now. I can't wait to meet a bunch of new, sun-tanned goddesses this summer," Paul said.

Angela and Monica splashed water all over Paul. Christopher shook his head and pushed Trina's paddleboard away. "I am not chiming in on this conversation. I don't want to accidentally say the wrong thing. We're going to float down the springs one more time before we need to leave. Catch up with you all in twenty minutes," Christopher called out as he and Trina floated away.

"I hope our parents don't go back to last year's curfew rules," Paul said to the remaining group. "I need to spread my wings. Spending another summer hanging out in our parent's backyards isn't going to cut it."

"No shit, right?" Ricky agreed. "I don't think I can deal with curfews all summer. Although I heard some interesting gossip last night at work that might steal our freedom again. A girl from Alabama went missing down here after New Year's. Weren't you and Christopher here over winter break? Did you guys hear about that?" Ricky asked Paul.

"What? Another girl was taken? I didn't hear that. Who was she?" Monica asked.

Ricky shared his gossip with the group. "Not sure if it's true story or not. One of my coworkers said the girl spent the night with her boyfriend on the beach. Supposedly, he dropped her off near her car, but she never made it back home. At least that's the story I heard."

"I'd think our parents would be all over that if it was true," Angela said.

"I don't recall hearing about another disappearance," Paul said. "Christopher and I were working double duty over the winter break, but I would think we would have heard about that if it truly happened. Just in case, don't tell your parents."

As they floated along the springs commiserating over the potential of another summer under parental observation, they decided to pack it up around two o'clock. They regrouped near the cars, changed in the restrooms, then hopped back in the cars to make the drive back to Santa Rosa Beach. The girls slept the entire way home. After their first exhaustive shift at the restaurant followed by an entire day in the hot sun, they were beat. The boys dropped the girls off at Trina's house at quarter of three, leaving them no time to go to their respective houses to grab clean aprons. They borrowed aprons from Trina and Jane and headed to work.

When they clocked in, the restaurant was already full of patrons taking advantage of the new happy hour specials. Billy, who had been promoted to Danny's assistant chef, had his head down over the grill with Danny and barely said hello to the girls. Based on the rack of pending orders and the absence of empty booths, Trina knew it was going to be another hectic night. The lunch staff gradually transitioned each table to their replacements and shamefully rattled off a list of the uncompleted dinner prep work. Gearing up for the approaching stress of a long night, the girls all chugged a cup of coffee and quickly teamed up to tackle the current tables.

Before diving in, Monica gathered all the waitstaff together. "Girls, tonight customers are going to complain, the kitchen's going to fall behind, and we are all going to mess up. Just remember, at the end of the night, everyone will eventually go home full and happy. Don't let the small mistakes erase everything we do right. Let's have a friendly competition to make tonight fun for us behind the scenes."

With spontaneous creativity, Monica threw out three silly but achievable challenges for the night. The stranger the challenge, the more motivated Monica was to check it off by the end of the night. Trina was not as daring as Monica in her plots to have a financially successful night, but she always enjoyed the behind-the-scenes entertainment. While the challenges were created to inspire friendly competition, in reality, everyone knew Monica would most likely win, and they all looked forward to watching her bewitch the customers with her unique charm.

Around nine o'clock, Trina had a lull, so she walked throughout the restaurant snapping pictures. Initially, Trina took photos as a pastime. But once Danny witnessed her knack for capturing genuine smiles of customers enjoying their annual beach vacation, he asked her to hang the pictures behind the bar. After initially voicing skepticism toward the photo documentary, Jerry Flanigan eventually relented when he overheard a competing restaurant owner say they were going to steal the idea.

Trina tried not to think about Jerry's negativity as she walked around to each table. She was glad he hadn't shown up while she was working to dampen her mood. She wasn't ready to communicate with him after the embarrassing interaction last summer. Connecting with people, listening to their tales of nasty sunburns, lost sunglasses, and buckets of sand dollars made Trina remember how lucky she was to be able to spend her summer on 30A. As she asked families to smile and randomly snuck candid snapshots, she chuckled to herself remembering how Jerry refused to let her take a photo of him. He said posting a picture of him on the wall would be unprofessional. Considering how often he flaunted his importance as the most successful restaurant owner, she thought it was ironic he would not want to hang an eight by ten of himself for all to see.

Any casual observer would assume Danny didn't exist the way Jerry talked about running the restaurant and their rental properties. He made it seem like he was the glue holding the businesses together. The staff knew the real story. Danny was the only reason the Salty Bar filled up every night. Danny's talent in the kitchen and his accommodating, compassionate management style were the only reasons the bar was a success. Trina tried to push Jerry out of her mind and focus on the images she was capturing. Paying attention to natural smiles and periodic laughter had a contagious effect.

The night soon ended, and the staff shut the doors before eleven. As the girls cleaned the front of the restaurant and performed their nightly restocking duties, they began chatting about the night.

"I overhead the tabletop of fisherman talking about a new restaurant called the Red Bar that's scheduled to open up on the beach next summer," Dawn shared. "They're advertising that they'll be hosting nightly live music and offering a limited, elevated menu. Supposedly, Jerry bet the locals that the place wouldn't last a year."

"Jerry is such an ass!" Jane said. "He is so self-absorbed. He touts that the Salty Bar offers the best food, but he won't even let Danny buy quality ingredients. I bet Danny could concoct amazing, award-winning dishes, but under Jerry's scrutiny and penny-pinching, he will always struggle to compete with a new place."

"All Jerry cares about is his ego. I would never work here if it wasn't for Danny," Trina added. "I don't even know how they are related. Danny is so kind, so helpful. He treats all of us like his equal. The only finger Jerry lifts is to tilt a mirror in his direction.

"I have a great idea," Monica said. "Let's make Jerry work! Anyone who can manipulate Jerk Jerry into completing manual labor will get paid ten dollars. Are you all willing to contribute tip money to see Jerk Jerry clean up throw up or wipe down a toilet? Who is with me?"

The girls erupted in laughter as they accepted the Jerk Jerry Challenge (JJC). They left the restaurant that night giggling at the crazy list of tasks they were imagining. Trina, a little apprehensive at the thought of having to deal with Jerry, volunteered to try to capture a picture of Jerry in the act. She would enjoy watching him sweat a little, but only if he was helping the staff not alone in the shed.

As soon as Trina got home, she grabbed the phone and called Christopher. She recounted the mayhem of the busy night and told him about the new restaurant opening soon. "I really hope Danny can convince Jerry to expand their menu. He needs to spice things up. Oh, by the way, I finished my roll of film in the camera tonight, so I need to drop that off for processing. And listen to this crazy idea. Monica wants us all to find ways to trick Jerry into doing manual labor. I can't wait to see Jerry sweat, just a little."

Christopher threw out a couple of ideas Trina could take back to the girls and told her to make sure to buy a couple extra rolls of film for her camera to be better prepared to catch Jerry working.

"Does Danny know about this secret challenge?" he asked. "I bet he could think of dirty kitchen tasks like scrubbing the fryer. Speaking of

Danny, I guess I should tell you about what I saw tonight at the bonfire. At first, I wasn't sure if I was seeing what I thought I was seeing since it was hard to clearly see through the bonfire's smoke and haze. But once I walked around the beach chairs, I clearly saw Danny's wife cozying up next to several different guys. She seemed to jump from man to man until she found one who paid her attention. Right before I put the flames out, Janice walked across the beach with one of the local property managers toward the dunes. She had her head resting on his shoulder and was holding his hand. When I was loading up the truck about forty-five minutes later, I saw her walking toward the parking lot alone. I wonder if Danny has any idea his wife might be cheating on him."

"That breaks my heart for Danny," Trina replied with disappointment. "I wonder if that's why he spends such long hours at the restaurant every day. He gets there early in the morning and stays late every night. I would hope that Janice would appreciate his dedication to his job. Maybe they just don't have a healthy relationship. Thanks for telling me, although I almost wish I didn't know. I'll have a hard time keeping that secret from Danny."

"Unfortunately, that wasn't the first time I've seen her with another guy. I can't prove she's cheating, but she sure doesn't hide her willingness to explore. I'm so glad I don't have to worry about that. I have the most beautiful, trustworthy, smartest girl on 30A. Danny deserves a woman like you, but he can't have you."

"Very funny, Christopher. Danny's old enough to be my father. I'm sure if he gets the wandering eye, he will stay in his age bracket. But I'm flattered that you think so highly of me. I guess that means I don't have to worry about you having a wandering eye either. Honestly though,

I would never worry about you cheating. You wear your emotions on your sleeve, and you are a horrible liar," Trina said, stifling a laugh. "Remember when you tried to lie to me when you said you studied for the AP Calculus exam? As soon as the lie left your lips, you backpedaled and confessed you got distracted the night before and watched TV shows instead of studying. You couldn't even make eye contact with me until I forgave you for fibbing." A tiny laugh escaped her as she remembered his one bad attempt at keeping the truth from her.

"I wasn't that obvious, was I?"

"Yes! It was so obvious. I can read you like a book. I can guess what you're thinking before you even utter a sound. And besides, you've told me a million times that you only have eyes for me. Even when you're surrounded by beach babes in bikinis, you only look at me," Trina gloated.

"Trina, if I wasn't so tired from a long night, I'd come over there and show you how right you are. But right now, my back is aching, and I smell like smoke. I need a shower and then I am going to crawl into bed. But let's plan an official date this week. You're not scheduled every night shift, right?"

"I know it will be rough working so much, but I really want to buy a car before junior year. If we can't have date nights, we can always spend time together during the day. This week, I only have Thursday night off. What about you?" she said.

"I can switch my Thursday shift with Paul and take his Friday night shift. I'll pick you up around two on Thursday." They agreed and said their goodbyes.

Trina grabbed a glass of water from the kitchen and strolled leisurely upstairs. She threw a pile of dirty laundry in the washing machine, grabbed a book, and climbed into bed. She realized quickly she couldn't concentrate on reading. She was thinking about Danny's wife. How could Janice do that to poor Danny? He was such a nice man and so determined to make the Salty Bar a success. She didn't understand why Janice would choose to be dishonest and deceitful. Her actions made Trina realize how lucky she was to be with Christopher.

He showered her with attention and made her feel like she was the only important person in the room. In the middle of conversations, he would throw out random compliments; she had the softest skin, and her eyes sparkled when she shared a good story. Trina loved telling him stories. He was like a kindergartener sitting with the librarian for story time. He listened to every word and seemed to always ask the most intriguing questions. She loved how he made eye contact even if they were across the room. She appreciated it when he held doors open or waited until she took her first bite to eat his meal, and how we spent his free time at the restaurant patiently waiting for her to get off work.

Since he was a couple of inches taller than her, he frequently kissed her on the top of her head, just letting her know he was there. He liked to surprise her by dropping off "thinking of you" gifts at her house. He remembered that her favorite candy was chewy caramel and that she had a weakness for vanilla milkshakes. She loved how interested he was in everything Trina. Whether she was telling him about an argument with her sister, a nasty customer, or a new book she was reading, he never judged and added commentary that made her think about each situation with a different perspective.

The more she thought about Christopher, the more eager she was to see him again. The last time they were alone together, their physical attraction had been put to the test. It was the night before she was leaving for the airport to drop Judy off. Christopher had picked her up and taken her to an early dinner, then drove her to a nearby park so they could sit by a lake. They lay on the blanket chatting about school and Christopher's upcoming senior year. After a little while of quiet time, he laid her back on the blanket and stared at her. He gently touched each part of her body and whispered words of adoration.

"Your eyes have so many different tones of hazel and emerald, green. When you're excited, your eyes glisten like a shining star," he said as he gently touched the skin around her eyes. His index finger slowly traced her cheekbones to her lips. "Your nose is perfectly shaped like an artist carved it especially for your face. Man, you know how much I love when you smile. Your face lights up the entire room. No one can keep their eyes off you. You have no idea how stunning you are, Trina. My absolute favorite part about you are those soft and delicate lips. Perfectly shaped. Naturally pink and delicious. They taste like flowers."

He continued to slowly roll his fingertip over the top and bottom lip. "When you kiss me, Trina, my insides melt. Your lips have a power over me that is so hard to control. You are so very sexy. Your face is like a piece of exquisite artwork, and I am the luckiest guy around to have you hanging up in my heart!"

He leaned his face down to press his lips up close to hers, then straddled Trina with his legs and planted a slow and soft kiss, hands on either side of her head. He leaned over to her right ear and whispered, "Can you close your eyes for me? I could talk all day about how beautiful you are, but I want to show you."

Trina wrapped her hands around his back and closed her eyes. Christopher oh so slowly moved away from her ear and gently moved her hair off her forehead. He kissed the top of her head and moved gracefully to her closed eyes, left then right. He whispered, "You are so beautiful. Absolutely perfect. You're the first thing I think of in the morning, and you are what I dream about at night. You make me want to be a better person, Trina."

He kissed her nose. The pace was painstakingly slow. Trina's grip was getting tighter around his waist. She could feel her heart beating. He finally reached her mouth. Once, twice, three times he gently kissed her lips. His tongue gradually parted her lips as his hand held the back of her neck. Trina lowered her hands and gave a gentle squeeze of his ass. His kiss suddenly became more passionate.

The switch was unexpected and instantaneous, his kiss becoming intense. His lower half was pressing against her, and she could feel him through his shorts. He left her lips only to explore her chest with the same tenacity. Sounds escaped from her mouth that she had no control over, and she pressed against him. He made eye contact with her and took his hand and explored her.

She kissed him with a passion that matched the energy that stirred inside her. She was enjoying his pace, his eagerness wrapped in gentleness. He leaned into her and whispered again. "Trina, you are my special girl. I could keep you here all night long if you let me." He moved adeptly, and she was reaching her limit. The sounds that escaped from her lips caused him to want to please her more. She said his name. She wanted him. Her body needed him. The energy was electric.

She needed to push him away but, at the same time, wanted to pull him closer. Should she go all the way? The next step had too much meaning for Trina, so she pulled them apart and lay to the left of him on the blanket, breathing hard, her heart racing. They had ended that night at the lake holding each other and staring at the stars.

Now, lying in her bed in Florida thinking about that night, she could feel her adrenaline spiking just thinking about it. She didn't know how much longer she could wait. She was only a rising junior, while Christopher was a year older. She didn't really think it was smart to go all the way, but he was making it so hard. She knew he cared for her, and she cared for him. She also knew that her body responded to him in ways she hadn't imagined. This summer was going to be a challenge for sure.

She fell asleep with her hand holding her *my slice of heaven* charm.

A Murder or A Mystery

"Honey, really," Trina said to her daughter Hazel on their weekly facetime call. "I have no secrets. I have no valid reason for not bringing you and your brothers to the beach bungalow when you were younger. I guess I grew tired of the sand and the sun after spending so many years here. Plus, it's not like Dad and I didn't plan some of the most amazing beach vacations over the years—San Diego, the Caribbean, Jamaica. Not sure why you keep bringing this up. Dad and I don't plan on moving again, you can enjoy 30A for the rest of your life. The real mystery that you should be curious about is who killed the person I found last week buried in the state park." Trina tried to kid with her daughter to divert the conversation away from her uncomfortable interrogation.

"Yeah, okay. I guess I'll let it go for now. And yes, I agree finding a dead body is way more mysterious. I'm glad I was not with you when you found it. That would have totally creeped me out! Do they know who it is yet? Come on, Mom, with all those crime books you read, you should have this all figured out by now," she suggested playfully.

"Just because I read lots of mysteries doesn't mean I have the skillset to untangle a real one. Plus, they haven't released any pertinent details.

I guess I have to leave it to the professionals." She knew her casual reply was masking her true desire to do just that.

"Speaking of untangling a mystery, can you help me figure out my monthly budget? I always seem to be a few dollars short each month."

This was Hazel's second year living on her own and Trina and David did their best to help teach her appropriate life lessons. They continued chatting while Trina folded clothes in the laundry room. Once Hazel's friends showed up to pick her up for their Sunday night yoga class, they said their goodbyes for the week.

Hazel's conversation had Trina contemplating what further details the detectives might have uncovered. She remembered hearing that they were supposed to get the medical examiner's initial report on Friday. She wondered if they had determined if this was, in fact, a murder?

She never really thought about it until now. Death investigations lead down three distinct paths—accidental, natural, intentional. Was this the death of an innocent person? Or maybe the death of a not so innocent person.

Trina dropped the folded clothes onto her bed. She called the dogs and took them out for their morning jaunt. After spending a couple minutes in the backyard, she grabbed a cold drink from the refrigerator and headed to her desk to review the list she had written on Friday.

- Body abandoned — Point Washington State Park

- Decomposition — Death maybe 10-20 years ago

- Denim/Leather Belt — Male or female

- Grand Opening Matches — The Red Bar time relevance

- Number 4 — Significance?

- Bear Sign — Location near body

- Metal object — Vehicle? Gun? Knife? Other weapon?

- VIN # — Vehicle Make & Model

- Male or Female — Confirm or deny

- Scalloped white material — Clothing or tablecloth

- Missing Person 1990-2000 —Jasmine (July 4th Girl) or another girl?

- Camel Cigarettes — Victim's or murderer's?

- Items in plastic bag — Get a second visual

- Medical examiner Report — Murder, accidental or natural?

She stared at the list trying to figure out what she could do to help the investigation. Until she knew more about the sex of the person and how long ago they'd died, she could be going down too many wrong paths. She needed to find a way to pull information from those close to the case.

She walked into the garage looking for David. He was painting a piece of wood that was resting on a pair of sawhorses.

"David, I think I am going to run out to grab a cup of coffee. Do you want anything?"

"Where are you going, Amavida or Black Bear?" he asked as he stroked brown paint on the plank of wood.

"Black Bear."

"Grab me an Americano and one of their crème puff pastries. Oh, and grab an extra couple of pastries. I met this car guy, Sean Hampton, last week at Frank's Hardware store. We ended up talking for an hour or so. He's refurbed several vintage vehicles and has developed quite a car collection. He wants to come over and see the new engine I bought last month. He said he was going to swing by this morning." He finished painting and wiped the side of the brush against the inside of the paint can.

"Should I grab him a coffee too?"

"Nah, just an extra pastry should be fine."

"See you in little bit. Dogs should be good until I get back," Trina said as she headed for the car.

Luckily, everything was relatively close to where they lived, so these little splurges didn't take a lot of time. She pulled into the parking lot a few minutes later and found a decent parking spot. Glad there was no line out the door, she walked into the bakery, waved at Josh, who was wiping down a table, and placed her order at the register.

Lynn walked out from the kitchen wiping her hands on her apron and came over to greet Trina. "Hey, Trina, how are you holding up? I heard about what happened last week." She reached out and gave her a quick hug.

Trina moved out of the way for the next customer and stood with her back to the patio door that was propped open to let the breeze in. "A shocker for sure. I lived near Boston and in Atlanta for most of my life, and I never found anything this crazy before. I really hope they find out that this was an accidental death instead of a grisly one," Trina said as she grabbed a couple of napkins, sugar packets, and a stirrer.

"No surprise that the local gossip has generated all sorts of random theories. I didn't realize you weren't a native Floridian. I thought you grew up here. I've only lived here for five years so I don't know much of the history. Have you ever heard of a murder taking place here or any other strange happenings?"

"I grew up *parking the car in Harvard Yard*," Trina said jokingly, restating the common New England accent expression with extra emphasis on the A sounds. "However, I did spend all my summers in Grayton until I left for college. I honestly don't remember hearing about any murders. Let's hope the black bears aren't getting so hungry they're eating people now!"

Trina heard her order number being called out from the kitchen, and she and Lynn headed back toward the counter. Lynn walked over to get Trina's order and said, "Now that would definitely generate gossip if bears started eating vacationers. I'm not sure how I would have reacted if I discovered a body in the woods. I think I'll stick to the pedestrian path until they figure this out. Glad you're doing well. See you soon."

Trina took her bakery bag from Lynn and waved bye as she headed to the exit. As she reached the door, she bumped into Detective Jenifer, who was also leaving, a coffee in her hand. The detective's papers fluttered to the floor. They both apologized and laughed as they both gained control of their belongings.

"Oops! I can't seem to do anything right when I'm near the police," Trina apologized, bending down at the same time as the detective to help gather the loose papers. As she handed the sheets to Detective Jenifer, Trina glanced at them and saw the words *apron styles* and a list of local restaurant names listed on one of the pieces of paper.

"Totally my bad," Detective Jenifer said. "I was reading and not paying attention to where I was going. Hey, was that you who just spoke with a Boston accent? I thought you were from Florida." Detective Jenifer placed her coffee cup on one of the small tables as she straightened her papers.

"I grew up in a small town in Massachusetts but spent all my summers down here as a kid. For most of my adult life, I lived in Atlanta but occasionally my northern accent sneaks out. I will always hold New England close to my heart."

"It's always nice to hear it. I spent about fifteen years growing up in Salem. My family relocated to North Carolina, and job opportunities brought me to Florida. We'll have to enjoy a cup of chowder together and discuss all things Massachusetts," Detective Jenifer said, offering a genuine neighborly gesture to Trina.

"I would love that! Although, I doubt we can find the real thing down here. The Gulf makes killer crabcakes but haven't tasted a chowder that can beat New England."

"So true. Nothing like a bowl of chowder and a good football game."

"Maybe after you and Detective Trent solve this case, we can grab a coffee. I think news of a buried body has sent chills through the community. Once you solve the case everyone will feel a little safer." Trina smiled.

"Agree."

"I would be happy to help in any way that I can. I don't know if the person who was found was a 30A local, but if you want to bend my ear for any local knowledge, please don't hesitate. I grew up having backyard cookouts with many 30A families over the years. After working at a local dive bar in Grayton, I can tell you town gossip flowed freely. I know I have no police background, but you never know what little tidbit of information might point you in a different direction."

"I always like to say we don't discriminate but rather evaluate so I am always willing to collect information from all relevant sources. However, since you're offering, I would love to accept your help. Do you have a quick minute? I would like to show you a picture to see if it jars any memories."

"Of course." she said casually, hiding her true excitement.

"Let's grab a table on the porch." The detective grabbed a cover for her coffee and walked out the patio door. Trina followed her with David's pastry bag and her two-cup coffee holder.

Detective Jenifer sorted through her papers and pulled out two pages with pictures on them. She laid the papers on the table and spun them around, so they were facing Trina, then slid the papers closer to Trina's side of the table. "You mentioned that you worked at a restaurant when you were younger. Do any of these aprons look familiar?"

The pictures were of two styles of aprons. One was a short white apron that would tie around the waist. It had a scalloped bottom and a small pocket on the left side. The other was a basic apron with three pockets that covered the entire width of the fabric. Trina took a moment to look at the pictures. They were not from an actual crime scene but rather looked like images pulled from the internet. Both aprons brought a sense of familiarity to Trina.

"The white scalloped one is rather unique. It sort of reminds me of something that character Alice who worked at Mel's Diner would have worn on that TV series when I was growing up. Sorry, I guess that doesn't help you." Trina grimaced. "I can't say that I remember any restaurants down in this area requiring girls to wear that style of apron. At least not when I was working here," Trina said, disappointed she wasn't being helpful.

"Do you remember what waitresses wore back then? I'm curious if they even wore aprons down at the beach establishments back then," Detective Jenifer asked while pulling the papers back to look at them herself.

"From what I can remember, most servers wore black basic aprons. However,..." Trina said, letting that word sit there for a delayed moment, hoping to build anticipation.

The detective remained composed, patient, and professional.

"One of my friends used to wear an apron similar to the scalloped one. I remember that she liked the way it hugged her hips, claimed it resulted in more tips. Boy, I haven't thought about Monica's sexy apron in years!" Trina smiled at the memory. "Granted, this was a very long time ago, but she's the only waitress I know of who wore a white apron similar to that."

"Interesting. Did her apron have scalloped shapes all the way around the bottom like this one? What is Monica's full name?" Detective Jenifer asked.

"I realize this is above my pay grade, but if you think the body could be Monica based on finding a white apron, thankfully, you would be wrong. Monica is alive and well and living a fabulous life in Raleigh, NC."

"Respectfully, I cannot divulge what we have or have not found. However, it would be helpful if I could get Monica's full name. She might be able to point us in the right direction about where an apron like that came from. Do you have any recollections of anyone else wearing a white scalloped apron?" she pressed.

"Nope, Monica was the only one. Although the more I think about it, Monica's apron also had small black polka dots scattered on it. Bear in mind, I also didn't visit all the restaurants back then. We were still teenagers and had limited mobility. We tended to hang on the west end of 30A, and we worked 40-50 hours a week. Sorry it's not what you wanted to hear," Trina apologized sincerely. "If you think she can help you, Monica's full name is Monica Mill. She's married now, so her last name is Foster. I can text you her contact information if you would like," she offered obligingly.

"Thank you. Yes, please. Here's my business card. Please pass along her contact information. One more question. This is a shot in the dark, but do you remember taking customer orders on specific pads of paper? I know that's a strange and rather vague question, but I'm just curious."

"Oh wow, now you *are* testing my memory." Trina spent a minute truly digging into her memory before she responded. "Funny enough, I do remember the pads we used at my summer job. The top of the pads said GUEST CHECK, and they were light green with a red line across the top. I remember taking a box of them out the owner's Jeep once when we had to unload supplies. The box was falling apart, and the pads fell all over the parking lot. The owner was so angry at me. I had to go through each pad to make sure it wasn't wet or ripped. Isn't it funny how small, meaningless events in life can stick in our memories?"

"It is. What was the name of the bar you worked at again? I don't think I have that in my notes," she said as she flipped through her own note pad.

"The Salty Bar. It was the local dive. Lots of my friends worked there, including Monica."

"Great. Thank you, Trina. Every little detail helps."

"I know you can't tell me much about the case, and I respect that. But I'm curious if you believe this is a missing person's case?" Trina did her best to squeeze out a tiny bit of additional information. At least now she could focus her attention on thirty years ago since Detective Jenifer seemed to be interested in finding details from that specific time.

"I wish I could share, but at this juncture, I can't divulge information. I'm sure when we're ready, you'll hear it locally before you see it on the news. I know how fast word gets around." Detective Jenifer stood up.

"Very true. When you identify the missing person, it will be posted on Nextdoor before it makes it on the nightly news." Trina smirked, and Detective Jenifer nodded in agreement, though Trina wasn't sure if that was confirmation the body was in fact a missing person or that information was spread quicker on social media than in the official news.

She decided to take this opportunity to try to throw Detective Jenifer a small bone. "The reason I asked is when I was about fifteen, there was a girl a little older than me who went missing down on Grayton Beach. We referred to her as the July 4th Girl. I don't think they ever found her. I'm sure your team is already digging into missing persons cases, but I mention it just in case that one hasn't landed on your radar yet." Trina watched the detective's face intently for any response.

Detective Jenifer's face was blank. Detective Jenifer was a tight seal to crack.

"I'll make sure our team is made aware of that. What year did she go missing?" Detective Jenifer asked.

"Let me think. I am guessing it was around nineteen ninety-two or maybe ninety-three. Her first name was Jasmine."

Detective Jenifer received a text. She glanced at her phone and stood up. "Thank you so much for your time. I really appreciate it. I've got to run to a staff meeting. I'm sure I will see you around. We'll have to grab that chowda." She winked at Trina, tucked her papers under her arm and walked across the patio toward the parking lot.

Trina grabbed her purchases and headed to the restroom thinking about her conversation with the detective. As she scrubbed her hands with soap, Trina recounted her actions since she left the house. Did she open the front door of the bakery or follow someone through it? Did she touch the side of the credit card machine when she swiped? Did she leave fingerprints on the papers when she picked them up off the floor?

She needed to stop obsessing about leaving a trail. *You promised yourself. Nobody cares if you touched those things. Stop obsessing!* But then her new reality hit her like a slap in the face. Her fingerprints were now official police records, so everything she touched could be traced back to her. Maybe she should start wearing gloves all the time. No, that would be ridiculous. Somedays she thought she was breaking her bad habit, then on other days it was all she could think about. *Focus, Trina.* She dried her hands and forced her mind to think about the more important mystery. How could Monica possibly be tied to the crime scene? Tossing the paper towel in the trash can, she headed back out into the restaurant, pushing the door open with her shoulder.

If they found a white, scalloped apron near the body, it must be a coincidence. Maybe Monica had a romp in the woods, and it just so happened they were fooling around near where the body was later recovered. Monica was way too squeamish to have done anyone any harm. She would jump on a chair if a bug walked across her path and wouldn't even hurl an insult never mind throw a punch. She truly was one of the nicest and kindest people Trina knew. There was no way Monica had anything to do with this case.

Trina headed to the car and felt how cold their coffee cups were now. So much for a splurge of a fresh cup of coffee. After driving home and microwaving David's coffee, she made two additional notations. She scribbled Monica's name next to the apron discovery and estimated the time of death to the late '90s. She found David and another man in the garage. He looked to be a couple of years older than David. He was wearing a blue T-shirt with a picture of a vintage car on the front, and his shorts had a couple of greasy stains on them.

"Hi there. Nice to meet you. I'm Trina. I brought sweets from the bakery. I didn't know how you take your coffee, but I would be happy to make you a fresh cup, or I can offer you something else to drink." She extended her hand to shake his, passed over the bag of goodies to the man and handed David his warmed-up coffee. She noticed the grease in the man's fingernails and how calloused and rough his hand was when she shook it.

"Nice to meet you. My name is Sean. I hope you don't mind me barging in on you and David. He was showing me this beautiful engine. I appreciate the offer of coffee, but I had my caffeine already today. I will, however, accept your offer of a sweet." Sean opened the bag and pulled out a strawberry scone.

"Sean was telling me about all the cars and trucks he's rebuilt over the years. I can't wait to see his collection, but I'm honestly more fascinated with how he found them to begin with. He's found several abandoned gems along the back roads, purchased cars from police impounds, and found financially constrained sellers desperate for cash. He gets the steal of a lifetime, then turns these vintage cars into instant auction best sellers." As an avid car lover, David was obviously fascinated by Sean's talents.

She nodded, but this didn't really fascinate her.

"I would love to show you both my collection," Sean responded. "If you're free next week, we're hosting friends for shrimp and grits. My wife, Mary Anne, would love to meet you. I can show David my auto restorations and you can join Mary Anne and her friends in a mahjong game.

"David's two favorites: cars and home cooking. That would be awesome. We would love to come," Trina said. They spent the next fifteen minutes talking about cars, food, and community, then Trina politely excused herself.

With the July 4th Girl the focus of her thoughts, she decided to dig into the old boxes of newspapers. Mentally, she thanked her mother for her packrat mentality when she found two boxes packed with old publications. She separated the magazines and made a neat pile of newspapers. She focused on the newspapers that were more likely to have news content and less advertisements.

She perused the articles about local businesses, rezoning meetings, and various charitable efforts. The crime section was scattered with petty thefts, car accidents and drunken escapades. After about two hours of flipping through papers, Trina found several pages that had been separated and bundled together with a paper clip. The first headline in the bundle caught her attention.

The 1992 article chronicled the disappearance of Jasmine and surprisingly the details were close to her own personal recollection of events. It provided basic personal facts and historical context of how many years her family had vacationed in the area. Her older brother was quoted as saying he searched all night long after the fireworks show and was desperate to find his sister but had only located her hair bow near the end of the Grayton Beach boardwalk. The second clipping reported that over one hundred volunteers participated in a search over several days, but no additional clues were revealed to help locate the missing girl. The third article was a follow-up story confirming that the police were stumped.

A 1990 newspaper clipping summarized a story of another missing female Panhandle vacationer. She'd disappeared after her family attended a beach bonfire over the summer. A search was conducted but only her sweater was found at the end of the boardwalk near the Blue Mountain Beach. Trina was truly shocked to learn that another girl had gone missing in the same general area. In 1990 she would have only been in middle school. Her curiosity was piqued.

Trina flipped to the last set of newspapers. Another woman had gone missing about six months after Jasmine's disappearance. The Alabama family had frequently spent their weekends at their small cottage on the bay about ten minutes from 30A. The twenty-year-old frequently spent weekends visiting her boyfriend, who lived in Grayton Beach. After grabbing dinner at a local restaurant, the missing girl and her boyfriend had attended a small bonfire one night over Christmas break. The boyfriend had requested extra holiday shifts, so she had cut her visit short. Unfortunately, she had not let her parents know, and neither of them realized she'd disappeared until they called him several days later asking about her whereabouts. Her boyfriend assumed she'd made it home safely, but once they put their stories together, they realized she disappeared the night of the bonfire. He told police he walked her to the end of the street where she had parked her car and assumed she had gotten into the car and drove back to Alabama. The only evidence they subsequently located was her car key ring and flip-flops, found near a mailbox two houses further up the road from where her car was found. Her suitcase and personal belongings were still in the back seat of her car.

The rest of the remaining articles were follow-up stories to the original articles. Apparently, none of the girls were found and no person of interest was ever identified. There was a very good chance Trina had uncovered the body of one of these missing girls.

This new information kick-started another burst of energy within Trina. She needed to help them solve this case. She had been on 30A at the same time these poor girls went missing. There had to be a clue somewhere in her past. How could she lean on her friendship with Betty to get more details? Should she lean on her friendship? She felt a twinge of guilt, then thought about Jasmine.

Time to go pick up dog bones. A little thoughtful gift for Bojangles could go a long way.

Growing Up Not Out

"Trina, I need you to come sit at the table with your sister," Trina's mom called to her from downstairs. Trina was standing over a pile of dirty laundry in her bedroom, of which about 50% belonged to her friends. Now that Trina had her own room, it seemed like her friends slept over at her house more nights than they slept at their own. They swapped bathing suits as much as they swapped clothes. Trina didn't mind. She enjoyed having friends to share her evenings with, and when they didn't have the lunch shift, they could hit the beach first thing in the morning.

Jane had told their parents last night that she'd decided she didn't want to go to college so she wouldn't be working on college applications this summer. Supporting Jane's decision, they had talked about potential locations for a café in their hometown. Trina assumed this morning's conversation would be a continuation of last nights. Maybe they were curious if Trina would start college applications next year.

"Coming, Mom!" Trina grabbed a clean apron from the closet and a pair of jean shorts. She braided her hair into one long, thick braid. Summers were so hot in Florida. Working the lunch shift today, she knew she was going to be sweltering within the first hour. Trina walked down the stairs and met her mom and sister at the kitchen table.

"Girls, I wanted to grab you both before you head off to work today. Dad and I have been talking, and although we trust you both 100%, we're still concerned about your safety working the night shifts. We decided we want you both to carry a can of mace for your own protection. Your dad will teach you how to properly use it so you both feel comfortable and don't accidentally hurt yourself. We hope, of course, that you never have to use it. Better safe than sorry, as the saying goes."

She handed them small cans of mace attached to a small flashlight and a clip that provided easy attachment and detachment capability.

"Normally, I would never promote hurting anyone or ask you to carry a weapon, but the events of the last year have changed my perspective. Go ahead and see your dad now. I know you're getting close to your lunch shift." She leaned over and kissed both girls.

Jane and Trina grabbed the cans and walked solemnly into the garage. Their dad was leaning over a car engine.

"Hey, girls. Good morning. I see your mom gave you your new safety gadgets. I know this is a strange request, but we still struggle to sleep at night whenever you two are working late. This is more to make your mom and me feel better than it is that I think you'll ever have to use it." Their dad then proceeded to show them a safe and secure way to use the protective spray. After fifteen minutes, he gave them both a hug.

On the short drive to work, Trina said, "Well that was unexpected."

"If carrying mace makes them feel better and allows us more freedom, I guess it's an even trade."

"Agree. It might actually be nice to have because it is really dark at night when we leave work," Trina said.

Jane pulled up on the side of the dirt road to park their car. They chatted a little more as they approached the back of the Salty Bar. Billy and Danny were both sitting outside. Danny was smoking a cigarette, and Billy was drinking a soda. They both looked tired.

"What's up?" Trina said. "We haven't even opened for lunch yet and you both look exhausted."

"The fridge went on the fritz," Danny said. "We had to empty the entire walk-in and put everything in coolers while the repairman fixed it. Luckily, I slept on the cot in the shed last night after a late night and came in early this morning. We would have lost thousands of dollars' worth of food if I hadn't been here to find the problem. We spent the last hour restocking the fridge and emptying coolers. We're both wiped out, but the problem was resolved."

"We're expecting a big crowd for lunch today. Janice arranged a meeting of local property managers to discuss pooling their properties to get better rates on pool maintenance, landscaping, and bathroom supplies. I think a bunch of local vendors are coming too, so get ready to work hard today, girls."

"No problem, Danny. Let us know if you need anything special done to help the lunch go smoothly," Jane replied.

"Trina, Jerry is on his way here. I'm sure he will want to check on supplies. Can you make sure the pantry shelves are fully stocked so he can assess what needs to be ordered?"

"Sure, I'll do that first thing. Are you sure you're OK, Danny? I know you had a rough morning, but you look wiped out. Is there anything else we can do for you?" Trina said as she grabbed the key from Danny's hand.

"No. All good. Long hours are taking a beating on me. Thanks for asking though. Come on, Billy, we have marinades to mix and veggies to chop. We're behind as it is."

After clocking in, Trina checked the restaurant stock levels then headed outside to the shed. She unlocked the shed door, was glad to see it was empty, and began piling up the needed supplies. She took two trips back and forth and had returned for a final trip to grab a bottle of fryer oil when she heard footsteps behind her. She was kneeling with her hands on one of the containers, and she froze in place with her back to whomever walked in. She heard a man clear his throat. Trina grabbed the bottle, took a deep breath before standing up, then turned around. Jerry Flanigan was standing behind his desk with his hands resting on a box he must have just placed there. Trina waited a beat to see if he was going to say anything. He didn't, and he wasn't making eye contact either.

Trina decided to bite the bullet. "Hello, Mr. Flanigan. I'm done restocking. I'll get out of your way," she said and walked briskly toward the door.

"Trina," he said with a slight nod. "Today is a very important day. We need to make a good impression. Several of these men are my chief competitors, and these vendors can make a huge impact on my bottom line. Please work with your sister and the rest of the staff to make sure no mistakes are made."

"Yes, sir." She nodded, walked out, and quietly shut the door behind her. She breathed out a big sigh and scrambled back inside, glad that interaction was over. She had better warn the girls that Jerk Jerry was here, and he was not in a pleasant mood.

Monica, Jane, Angela, and Dawn were prepping side dishes in the kitchen when Trina came in. "Guess what, girls. Today we have the pleasure of hosting Jerk Jerry for lunch. Get ready to have every move we make watched like a hawk," Trina said as she joined them at the counter.

"Awesome, let the JJC commence," Monica said.

"Seriously, Monica? Are you crazy? Jerry doesn't lift a finger around here and you really think you can manipulate him into completing a task in front of his competitors?" Dawn asked.

"Peer pressure works on adults, too. He will want to impress the other restaurant owners so maybe we can embarrass him into working. He walks around this place pointing out all the flaws and imperfections. He needs a reality check. If he spent one shift in our shoes, he wouldn't complain half as much. Come on, ladies, let's get creative!" The girls plotted and planned as they wrapped up the prep work.

Before they opened the front door for the day, Trina walked over to the hostess stand to check out the reservation list. After assessing the reservation counts for her station, she walked over to the picture board, where she noticed a picture she hadn't seen before. In the very center of the collage was a picture of Tommy and Jasmine sitting with their family in the restaurant. The picture was more focused on Jasmine than the rest of the family. Trina didn't recognize the picture as one she had taken. Trina got up closer to the image and realized there was a number two written in small print on the lower left of the picture. Odd. Her thoughts were interrupted when Danny called out from the kitchen food window.

"Hey, Trina, go ahead and open the floodgates."

Trina snapped out of her thoughts and called out to the team. "Are you ready for crazy, girls?"

"No!" they screamed and then they busted out laughing.

"Let the crazy commence," Trina said as she opened the front door.

Eighteen property managers and six vendors quickly filled the main tables, and over the next twenty minutes, the normal lunch traffic filled in the remaining open booths. The girls did their best to split the guests up among several different sections so no one waitress was overwhelmed. Janice, Brooks—the creep who'd had the plan to install cameras at his rental properties to spy on guests—and four additional property managers sat in Trina's section. Monica had Jerry, a couple of vendors and two property managers. The remaining meeting participants were seated at various tables throughout the restaurant. Appetizers and drinks were served, and the staff replenished cocktails as they waited for the main dishes.

As Trina did a walk-through of her section, she couldn't help but notice Janice had her hand resting on Brooks's thigh. No one else would have noticed, but Christopher's recent stories had Trina on high alert. She felt protective of Danny and wanted to make Janice stop. She stood behind her and rested her hand on Janice's shoulder.

"I see that you are all fans of Danny's fabulous appetizers. Great job, Janice, for recommending Danny's specialties. We sell out of those spicy teriyaki chicken skewers every day during lunch, and Danny's Louisiana-style shrimp never lasts past the first round of lunch customers. Does anyone want another round of drinks before your main courses are ready?"

Trina put on her best smile and leaned a little bit more on Janice's shoulder until both of Janice's hands were back in her own lap. The nods and agreement were enough to make Trina feel like she'd straightened Janice out. At least for the rest of lunch. Jerry engrossed in a conversation with a bathroom supply vendor was oblivious to his sister-in-law's actions.

Trina met up with Monica in the kitchen as Monica placed a tray of eight ketchup bottles on the counter. "Are you ready to put Jerk Jerry to work?" Monica said as she slid a platter of appetizers off the grill window.

"What do you need me to do?"

"I need you to require my assistance as soon as I place Jerry's table with food. Follow my lead," Monica said as she walked back to her table.

"And here is your fried shrimp lunch special, sir. I believe that is everyone's lunch. I'll be back to check on everyone in a couple of minutes," Monica said as she placed the food.

Standing right behind Jerry, Trina asked Monica for assistance as requested. "Monica, I need an extra set of arms. The food for Janice's tables is ready."

"Sure thing!"

Monica and Trina scurried off to the kitchen, but instead of grabbing the lunch plates for Trina's table, they watched Jerry from the kitchen serving window.

Within a minute, the important vendor Jerry had been trying to negotiate with tried to squeeze ketchup on his plate, but nothing came out. Jerry noticed and looked around the room for a full bottle of ketchup. Not finding any, he stood up and went over to the condiment section in the main dining room. He picked up several bottles and shook each one, each seeming to be empty. He looked around the room for a server or someone to come to his rescue. Monica had held back the three other waitresses to make sure Jerry was left on his own. They could hear Jerry apologize to his table, then he walked over to the waitresses' serving station and refilled a ketchup bottle. He quickly walked back to the table, where the girls saw one of the property managers ask Jerry a question before he could even sit down. Jerry looked around the room again, still not finding a person to point a finger at. He returned to the serving station, grabbed napkins and a jar of mustard from the counter and returned to the table.

Monica and Trina high-fived each other and covered their mouths to stop themselves from laughing aloud. They turned back to the serving window and quickly grabbed Trina's food for her table. The first Jerk Jerry Challenge was a success! He didn't have to sweat or complete any manual labor, but it was a tiny step in the right direction. The staff enjoyed a good chuckle, and that raised spirits for the rest of the shift.

As the meeting was ending, the girls handed out warm cookies to each of Janice's business guests. Danny didn't bake very often, but when he did, he usually created masterpieces. He wanted the property managers and vendors to leave the Salty Bar with a token of appreciation. The sweet smells wafted through the main dining room, motivating all the tables to place an order. Trina made sure to reinforce Danny's hard work as she thanked each guest. She was happy to hear positive feedback and decided to share the positive experiences with Danny. As Trina approached the kitchen, she overhead Jerry talking.

"Adam is such a bastard! He tried to negotiate a side bulk pricing deal with Freeport Clean. I overhead him and was able secure the same pricing. He's going to be so pissed when he finds out but screw him. I also secured a new contract with the pool maintenance company, so that should save us a couple hundred a month. Brooks told me about his new Seagrove rental properties. He's normally a tight ship during his renovations but he is letting Janice walk through them. Not sure why, but I'm not going to argue. I might consider adding one more property if the price is right. Anyways, everyone seemed pleased with lunch. Girls could have been quicker with food service, and they need to keep condiments stocked. We shouldn't have empty bottles on the tables. Make sure to check before the lunch shift clocks out. I'm headed to shed to check supplies." Jerry left, not giving Danny the opportunity to reply.

Trina walked over to Danny. "You and Billy did a fabulous job today. I don't think we've ever had that many people arrive at the exact same time before. I didn't hear any complaints. Also, I heard several customers raving about your new shrimp and scallop bisque. Those bowls were licked clean," Trina said as she piled herself with supplies.

"Thanks, Trina. It means a lot to hear feedback. I'm glad Jerry had no real complaints. You all deserve a treat, on the house! Tell everyone to grab a plate," Danny said as he passed bowls filled with fresh shrimp and pasta to Billy.

Normally, they ate hamburgers or tacos for lunch, so getting seafood was a big splurge. They grabbed their plates and sat out on the back patio. As they ate, Monica collected her reward for a successful challenge. Impressed by her cunningness, the group started crafting ideas for next time. Holding up a wad of cash, Monica had them all laughing as she sauntered back and forth modeling her magical white apron. She showed them how to master charm, sex appeal and a certain hip sway.

Their break was over, and the girls headed back inside to finish the final clean up. While rolling silverware for the dinner shift, Trina told Jane that Danny looked excessively tired. She wondered if he ever went home to sleep. It was like he spent twenty-four hours a day at the restaurant. Maybe he knew about Janice's side adventures. That would explain why he was sleeping in the shed. The girls bounced ideas back and forth and decided they would make more effort to compliment Danny and let him know how valuable he was. Finished with their prep, the girls clocked out and walked toward the exit.

As they approached the door, which was near the supply closet, they could hear someone say, "No! Please let me go!" Jane and Trina looked at each other and silently agreed to open the closet door, which was sitting open about an inch. Jane grabbed the door and pulled it open. Billy was standing with his arms stretched out on either side of one of the new dishwashers, pinning her in. The girl looked at Jane and Trina and immediately ducked down under Billy's arms and ran out the supply closet.

"Billy, what were you doing to that poor girl?" Jane yelled.

"Nothing. I was only telling her that she looked cute in her little shorts. I didn't hurt her. I only wanted to smell her. She wears this baby powder perfume. It's hard not to notice."

"You're like five years older than her. Keep your hands to yourself," Trina said.

"Go out there right now and apologize to her, Billy," Jane said.

"You girls have all the fun. I sweat over a hot grill all day while you get to socialize and go to parties. I just wanted a little fun," Billy said as he sulked past them.

Jane and Trina followed him and made sure he properly apologized. They then took the girl aside and told her if he ever approached her again, she needed to tell Danny right away. She seemed a little shaken up but felt better after the girls talked to her.

Even though it was only three thirty in the afternoon, Trina, and Jane both held one of their new cans of mace as they exited the restaurant and walked toward the car. Witnessing Billy being so aggressive with the new girl had them on edge. Once again, Trina was so thankful she didn't have to deal with anyone but Christopher. She needed one-on-one time to erase her mind of all the bad. Their Thursday date couldn't come soon enough.

***

Christopher had a full day of adventure planned when he picked her up. After grabbing lunch, they hopped on bikes and explored the trails. Trina was enjoying watching his inner child as he climbed trees, dug under rocks, and crawled on his hands and knees to find lizards. By the time they were done and ready to head to the beach, they were both covered in dirt, ant bites and sweat.

They dropped their bags and blankets on the water's edge and ran into the Gulf. They attracted attention as they ran into the Gulf with their clothes on, in desperate need to cool off and clean up. They floated and splashed around for twenty minutes and then headed back to the sand to rest. After talking about the various animal species they saw while walking the trails, Trina decided to bring up a sensitive subject.

"Kind of crazy to think you only have a couple of months left before you apply for college. What's your top choice?"

"Penn State is my number one, but the University of Florida or Washington State University would be awesome too. I need to draft my application essays. Not really looking forward to that process. Senior year is going to be stressful. You are going to help me spruce up my essays, right?" Christopher said as he lay on his side looking at Trina, who was sitting with her knees bent as she looked out into the Gulf.

"Of course. I would love to read your essays. But you're not going to need my help. You've won the school's writing award two years in a row. However, we can pretend you need my help so we can spend more time together." She leaned over and gave him a nice, soft, sandy kiss.

"Why are you mentioning college already? Are you ready to get rid of me?" Christopher said, nudging her shoulder in a way that made it clear he was joking.

"If you want to take a year off after you graduate and homeschool me my senior year, I wouldn't complain," she said with a big smile on her face.

"Don't tempt me. If I was your teacher, I would not hand out any textbooks, hands-on learning only. Grades would be determined based on student participation. Stamina, flexibility, and satisfaction levels would be my grading rubrics. Oh, and I only would accept one student a semester." Christopher leaned Trina back on the beach blanket. He stretched her arms over her head and slowly dragged his finger down her wet T-shirt. "Do you think you can pass my class?"

"With flying colors. Do you offer this class in AP level? I want to go straight to the collegiate level course," Trina said, making direct eye contact.

"You have no earthly idea how I would love to be your exclusive tutor. You would definitely be the teacher's pet." He bent down and kissed her ear while still holding her hands up over her head. "Do you want a sampling of my coursework?" he whispered into her ear. "My first lesson plan requires my student stay in complete control no matter what is thrown at them. Let's see how you would do. Consider this a sneak peek at my class syllabus."

Christopher's kisses navigated down her slender neck as he made his way to her clavicle. Her eyes were closed now, and she could feel and hear his warm breaths. He reached over and grabbed his folded beach towel and threw it over the top of both of them. Christopher let his lips caress her shoulders. She opened her mouth to speak.

He shushed her. "No sounds, class. You must listen to your teacher." His body leaned into her hips as he left a trail of kisses down her neck.

"Christopher, I am going to fail this class." Trina said so softly it was almost a whisper.

"I will throw away my college applications right now if you say it," he said as he planted a long, sensuous kiss. He released her and sat up, gently straddling her belly. The beach towel fell down his shoulders and landed on her thighs. "Trina, whenever you're ready, I will skip all the classwork and go straight to the final exam. But I'm enjoying helping you prepare for the test. Come on, help me cool off so I can walk this beach without people staring at me." He pulled her up and they ran back into the Gulf.

Trina was glad their relationship had moved slowly, but lately she could feel the sexual tension every time they were together. She was growing up. Not simply by getting older, but also in her desires, and she was nervous at the thought. The reality that Christopher was a year older than her was hitting her hard. Should she give in to temptation, knowing that he was going to leave her within a year?

The internal battle rocked her heart. He made her so happy. He made her feel sexy and smart. He was the puzzle piece that filled all her empty spaces. What was she going to do when he left her for college? She didn't want to think about it. She needed to concentrate on the here and now. She dove into the water and came up right next to Christopher. She jumped up on his back, and he spun around and playfully dumped her back in the Gulf.

She'd save growing up for later.

Building Trust

T rina pulled in the driveway after running to Publix. A red convertible with a news logo on the driver's side door was parked on one side of her driveway, and a woman was talking on the phone pacing back and forth. Trina didn't like the idea that a reporter was at her house, or the fact she was walking back and forth near their trashcans. She searched her memory for all the things she had thrown away over the last couple of days. What if she'd rifled through her trash to look for personal information? This lady looked too professional to be digging in trash cans, but Trina couldn't help but let the thought drift through her mind.

The lady smiled and put her index finger in the air to signal she was almost finished with her call. Trina opened the kitchen door letting her dogs run outside. While the dogs did their business, Trina grabbed her grocery bags and plopped them inside the kitchen door. As she watched this stranger walking in her driveway, she noticed her neighbor Trudy peeking out of her window across the street, which reminded Trina that she needed to pay her a visit.

The woman said her goodbyes and walked briskly over to Trina. As she walked, she grabbed a small pad out of her shoulder bag. The woman was a petite blonde with a sharp, angled, short haircut. She wore a white buttoned-down cotton shirt with khaki fitted shorts, simple pearl earrings and a silver necklace with a small sand dollar pendant. Her nails were French manicured but short and businesslike. She had a stunning smile that emphasized her gleaming white teeth and mauve-colored lip gloss. She reached her hand out to Trina upon approach.

"Mrs. Scotsdale, my name is Samantha Hunter. I'm a reporter from Channel 7 News. I was hoping to ask you a couple of questions if you have a moment." She shook Trina's hand, then politely stepped back and crouched down so she could pet Freckles and Phoenix.

"I don't have any information to share that hasn't already been published," Trina said as she gathered the dogs and scooted them back inside.

"I respect that, Mrs. Scotsdale. Could you at least confirm that you discovered the body by happenstance?"

"Well, I would say it was pure luck but finding a body is the opposite of luck. But yes, I was chasing my dog and unfortunately discovered the bones," Trina replied.

"I understand that in addition to retiring and moving to Florida recently, you used to live here back in the day. Is that true?"

"Well, yes and no. I spent my summers vacationing here at my parents' house," Trina said, pointing back to the house. "I actually grew up in Massachusetts."

"You were one of the lucky ones to have enjoyed this part of Florida before everyone else discovered it. I've only lived here for eight years, but it's been a dream to live in such a serene place while still being able to follow my passion for journalism. I'm sure you're happy to be back." Samantha stood up and readied her pad and pen. "I had a couple of questions to help me put the finishing touches on my story. From the research I've conducted, there were two girls who went missing from this area in the early 'nineties. Do you remember hearing about their disappearances when you were here during the summer?"

"Have you heard confirmation the body is one of the girls you mentioned?" Trina asked, turning the question back to her.

"No, the police have not released the sex of the body or the identity. However, from my personal sources, I understand the initial reports indicate the body has been buried in the state park for twenty-five to thirty years. It took a little digging, but my research thus far has led me to old news articles that discussed two girls who disappeared from 30A around the same time. It's also possible that there were more disappearances I have yet to uncover. I wondered if you were familiar with the stories because there wasn't an abundance of information written about them." She openly shared her research challenges.

"Ms. Hunter, I wish I could tell you more. I do remember that the summer before I entered high school, a local teenager disappeared the night of the 4th of July fireworks show. She spent time with my friends a couple times over the years, but I didn't know her well."

"Do you know if she had a boyfriend?" She flipped through her notepad.

"No, I can't say that I remember."

"One more thing, Mrs. Scotsdale. Can you confirm that you used to work at the Salty Bar?" Samantha put her pen up to her mouth and squinted slightly, like she was trying to assess Trina.

"Wow, you *have* been doing your research. Yes, I worked at that dive bar. I was hired as a dishwasher and eventually moved up to a waitress.

I returned each summer and worked all through high school," she answered with slight nostalgia. "Not sure why where I worked matters, Ms. Hunter."

"Every story sells better when you can paint a more descriptive picture of the characters. If we confirm that you have in fact found one of the missing girls, the fact you basically lived down here during their disappearances will add more weight to the story. Do you remember who owned the Salty Bar? I heard a couple different owners ran the place before it was sold and converted to an Vrbo vacation home."

"From what I can recollect, we used to work for two brothers. One ran the kitchen and managed the staff, while the other one took care of the business side of things. I assume they were the owners, but they could have been working for an owner. Again, why does this matter?" she asked, now with a little hint of irritation and the onset of concern. *Why is she so curious about me? She should be focused on identifying the victim not the dog walker.*

Before Samantha could answer, Trina heard David open the mudroom door. "Trina, what's going on? The dogs are barking like crazy."

Both dogs came running back outside, jumping at their feet.

"David, this is Samantha Hunter from Channel 7. She's reporting on the story and had a couple of questions for me. I think we're all done. Is that all, Ms. Hunter?" she stated, not really asking.

Samantha thanked her and was on her phone before she was even back in her car.

Trina let out a breath she hadn't realized she had been holding. The presence of a reporter in her private sanctuary was unnerving. Why was

Samantha so interested in her personal history? She also wondered why Samantha only found two missing girls instead of three.

As Samantha backed out of the driveway, Trina saw Trudy standing in front of her mailbox. She coaxed the dogs to stay by her side as she walked over to meet up with her neighbor.

"Trudy, how are you doing today? Staying out of the heat and humidity?" she asked as she bent down to greet her neighbor's little pug, Suzy Q.

"Doing my best to stay inside as we approach the spring break rush. You know I like to hibernate during this time of year. What's this gossip I hear about you picking up a body on your walk? Is it true?" Trudy, a retired schoolteacher, was a fabulous neighbor. A little nosy, but overall, very pleasant. She'd lived on this street her entire life and had seen more changes than most see in their lifetime. Her husband had passed away about four years ago, and she occasionally joined them for dinner bringing Trina and David baskets of fresh vegetables from her garden.

"Well, Miss Trudy, there is some truth to the gossip. Freckles and I did find the remains of an unfortunate soul. I did not, however, carry the body home with me. I'm diligent in my community clean-up efforts, but that might take it a little too far."

Trudy grabbed her mail, and Trina and the dogs walked alongside her back to Trudy's front door.

"Crazy is what that is. This town used to be so calm and relaxed until developers got greedy and built too many homes. I truly hope you didn't uncover a secret that's going to make us all shut our doors for good." Trudy opened her front door for her dog.

"Trudy, do you remember that bar my sisters and I used to work at when we were kids? Do you remember who owned it? I was a little young and can't quite remember."

"I didn't frequent that place very much. I never understood why your parents let you work at that dive. I believe the Flanigan family owned it. From what I can remember, one of the owners died from cancer and the one left unexpectedly. Rumors were all over the place that he had affair with too many barmaids and his wife kicked him out. She managed the bar for a couple of years, but she struggled to keep it afloat while also maintaining the various rental properties. I think she cashed out and ran soon after. Why do you ask?"

"I was going through my mom's old boxes and was thinking about the bar. Strange how you can spend so much time at a place and forget so much. Your memory is better than mine, Trudy. I guess I should do a better job of eating my vegetables so I can remember life's little details as well as you." Trina smiled as she patted her thighs to try to gather her dogs to get ready to leave.

Trudy said her goodbyes as Trina closed the door, then walked back across the street. Compulsively, she peeked in her trash cans confirming that the one plastic trash bag was still tied shut. She felt instant relief and went inside.

Once inside, Trina located the bundled newspaper articles and skimmed through them one more time. She found David and asked him what time they were heading over to Sean's place for dinner. It was still before noon, so she had plenty of time to run up to the police station to see Betty and possibly the detectives.

The parking lot at the station was fuller than the last time she was there. She would have to get a little creative this time. As Trina sat in the car gathering her courage up, she received a call.

She didn't recognize the number but answered it anyway. "Mrs. Scotsdale, this is Detective Trent from Walton County Sheriff's Office. How are you doing today?" Trina paused and looked around the building for a security camera.

"Detective, hello. I'm holding up well. Thank you for asking. What can I do for you?" she asked, wondering if he was watching her on video surveillance.

"I wanted to let you know the matchbook you brought in helped confirm the medical examiner's time of death, so that was a helpful piece of information. I did also have one small question for you. If you have a moment?" he asked.

"Well, as a matter of fact, I just pulled into the parking lot. I realized I forgot my sunglasses in your office and wanted to retrieve them."

"Your sunglasses. Hmmmm. Oh my gosh, you are correct. I see them on the corner of my desk. Come on in. I'll let Betty know to bring you back to my office."

He hung up, and she gathered the bag of dog bones and the various missing girl newspaper articles she'd brought with her as an additional peace offering. She entered the building and walked up to the front desk. Betty saw her coming and slid the glass pane open.

"Trina, come on back. Detective Trent is waiting for you."

She walked through the side door and gave Betty a quick hug, then Betty walked her to the detective's office. Betty opened the door for Trina to enter. Trina thanked her and took a seat.

"Hello, detective, I hope this isn't too inconvenient. I'm happy to find that my sunglasses were safely tucked under mounds of your paperwork. They must have slipped off when I was bribing you with muffins." She smiled and placed the glasses in her purse.

"I have been a little preoccupied. I apologize that I didn't even notice them," Detective Trent said as he angled his computer monitor slightly to the left. He was wearing a blue, button-down, short-sleeved shirt and looked freshly shaven and alert.

"Detective Jenifer mentioned that you provided her with some insight about your time here when you were a kid. We appreciate your input. We had a brief conversation with your friend Monica. Thank you for her contact information," he said with a slight nod, conveying his appreciation with simplicity and sincerity. "Also, you might be interested to learn the Red Bar grand opening matches were a very limited version indeed. I bet that set would have been a great collector's item for you, but of course they'll need be stored in evidence, permanently."

"Speaking of evidence, Mrs. Scotsdale, we're continuing to evaluate the surrounding area where you came across the human remains. The reason I called you into the station today was to obtain a little clarification. During the processing of the scene, we came across a couple of items that were buried in the dirt and surrounding debris. We know that morning was a little hectic for you considering you weren't expecting to find what you did, so we thought it might be smart to confirm our understanding of what you came into contact with out there. Would you tell me again all the items you picked up or touched, please?" he asked.

"Sure. No problem," Trina said, though she wondered why he was asking her to repeat what she'd told them twice already. "Let's see... I picked up the buckle first, which was connected to a leather belt. When I pulled the belt out, a small portion of denim clothing came out of the mud. Inside the pocket was the book of matches. I didn't touch any of the bones, but as you know, I did fall on them." Trina gave her answer slowly, pausing after each item to make sure she didn't forget anything.

"Great, can you think of anything else?" he asked as he glanced at his computer screen.

"Ummmm. Let me think. Oh, I know! There was a no trespassing sign out by the service road. I picked that up and turned it over in hopes it would give me a trail location. That's it. I didn't touch anything else that I can think of," Trina said with a sigh of relief. He must have found her fingerprints on the sign. *Phew, that's a relief.*

"Thank you for your clarification," he said, glancing once more at his computer monitor.

"Sure. Not a problem. Detective, there is one more thing I would like to share. One of the things I mentioned to Detective Jenifer was that a girl went missing after a Grayton Beach fireworks show many years ago. Coincidentally, I had a visitor earlier today. A Miss Samantha Hunter from Channel 7 News. She asked me about two girls who disappeared from 30A," Trina said, baiting him to see if he would seem interested in the journalist's inquiries.

"Oh, yes. I am familiar with Ms. Hunter. What was she asking exactly?"

"I know how easy it is to be misquoted, so I kept my answers short, but she was trying to dig a little to help beef up her story. Coincidentally, I have been digging through my mom's storage boxes, including one filled with old local newspapers. I found several news articles surrounding the circumstances of the missing girls. Mrs. Hunter only mentioned two but there apparently were three That could have been a mistake on her part, or maybe she couldn't find any information about the third one," Trina said, trying to expose a potential gap in information.

"After she left my house, I flipped through the newspapers again and discovered one of the disappearances was documented in an Alabama newspaper. Her family owned a second home in Florida on the bay but were from the Gulf Shores. I don't know if her disappearance was published in a Florida newspaper." Trina handed the stack of newspapers clippings over to Detective Trent.

His eyes scrunched up a little as he reached for the articles. Trina decided not to say anything while he read. She sat there for three to four minutes. It was killing her to sit for that long with no conversation. What was he thinking? Did he not know about this other girl? Was this related to the current investigation? While waiting, she peered out of his office at the conference room, but the blinds were completely closed. Detective Trent put the papers down on his desk.

"Mrs. Scotsdale, would it be OK if we kept these clippings? I'll have Betty make copies and then return them to you. I know these were your mother's possessions. We will ensure they are kept intact for you. I can have someone drop them off at your house when we are done with them."

He made his request so graciously, how could she refuse? "Yes, of course. May I ask if the person found was a female? I haven't heard anything officially reported yet."

"Normally, I would never divulge information outside the force, but you have been very helpful Ms. Scotsdale. I trust that you won't share this information prematurely, as we plan to make an official statement later today. The body was male, not female. However, I would still like to make a copy of your articles, if you're still fine with that," he said as he glanced at his iPhone checking the time.

"Really? The body was a man? I wasn't expecting that." The police found a white waitress apron, and Detective Trent appeared to be interested in the missing girl articles. How did this tie together? This was not going in the direction Trina had assumed. It did explain the leather belt, but the rest of the pieces of the puzzle were severely misaligned.

"Thank you for your willingness to share information, Ms. Scotsdale. You have been very helpful. I think that's all I need from you today. Let me walk you back out." Detective Trent stood up and opened the door for Trina. He walked her almost to the front desk, shook her hand, then headed over to the sheriff's office at the end of the room.

Betty was assisting a gentleman at her desk window. Trina whispered, "Bathroom?" to Betty, who pointed down the hall on the same side of the building that held the conference room.

Trina's heart pumped a little bit quicker. Should she risk it? If she got caught sneaking into the police investigation room, she could get in serious trouble. She walked briskly down the hall. There were people milling about, but no one seemed to be paying any attention to her. *What the hell, Trina. Are you crazy? Just do it before you talk yourself out of it.*

Trina opened the conference room door. She walked quickly to the whiteboard wall and noticed two things she hadn't seen before. Inside one plastic bag were various bathroom vacation supplies—small toothpastes, mouthwashes, and soap. She saw a *Freeport Clean* label on the soap. The items were dirty and looked like they had been left outside for a long time.

She continued scanning and saw *1989 Jeep Wrangler Renegade* written on the board. There were pictures of three different Jeeps underneath. Trina knew absolutely nothing about vehicles, but she did know Jeeps were one of the most common vehicles driven down here. That was true today and even more true when she lived here twenty-five years ago. Without a VIN number, whatever they found would be like finding a needle in a haystack.

Trina finished her quick lap around the conference table and then exited the door on the other side of the room. When she closed it behind her, an officer was walking by.

"Can I help you, ma'am? Why were in the conference room?"

"Oh, I am so sorry," Trina said with the sweetness of a grandma. "Betty was on the phone, and she pointed down here. I need to find the restroom. I totally opened the wrong door. I don't want to bother her; can you point me in the right direction?"

"Two more doors down on the right." He pointed down the hallway.

"Thank you so much."

Trina washed her hands in the bathroom, waited a couple of minutes to make it appear she had in fact used the facilities, then returned to the front desk. While she waited for Betty to finish, Trina glanced at Betty's computer screen and saw a website listing soap distribution companies. So that soap in the bag must be unique enough to warrant investigation. Betty finished helping the individual and turned to Trina.

"Miss Trina, did you find the bathroom alright? Sorry I couldn't assist you; Mr. Swanson was complaining about vacationers who trashed his

AIRBNB. Are you all set with the detectives? Can I help you with anything else?" Betty asked.

"I think I'm good." She didn't want to push her luck today trying to acquire more investigation details; however, she could still develop a tiny bit of goodwill. "I did bring Bojangles a surprise." Trina handed Betty a bag of DreamBones, Bojangles's favorite treat.

"Oh, my goodness. She will be so happy!" Betty smiled and placed the bag of treats under her desk. "Let's try to meet up for a walk. Do you have free time in the next week or so?"

"Sounds perfect. I'll text you when I have a free morning. See you soon, Betty." Trina waved goodbye and walked out the door.

Trina walked to her car, rehashing what Detective Trenton had told her. It was so unexpected that the skeleton was a male. She'd been positive it was going to be Jasmine. Who was this man she had uncovered and why was he in the woods? What was the significance of the Jeep? Her thoughts bounced from one to another trying to figure out how she could move forward in her investigation now that she knew it was a man.

Once she felt like she was hitting a brick wall, her mind traversed back through the details. She had been so focused on finding out the identity of the dead person, she forgot to focus on the trail of evidence left by the killer. Why would soap and other bathroom supplies be important? Although she frequently worried about leaving a trail of evidence behind, she had forgotten to consider that if this was a murder, the killer would have left an evidence trail. She hadn't seen anything on the whiteboard to signify a weapon. What about DNA? Maybe the clothes fragment had DNA on it? The more she learned, the more she wanted to know. Piece by piece the puzzle was coming together. She just didn't know what the final image would reveal.

Trina drove home and completed a couple of household chores, then flicked on Channel 7 to wait for the five p.m. news report before they headed over to Sean's house for dinner. Sheriff Sam Smith's news conference lead the broadcast.

> *"Human remains were discovered in a wooded area of Longleaf Greenway Trail in Point Washington State Park approximately two weeks ago. We have identified the remains as a male approximately thirty-five to forty-five years of age. His death most likely occurred between 1988 and 1996. Based on the medical examiner's initial report, the cause of death has been categorized as accidental. South Walton's Criminal investigation team continues to research to confirm the individual's identity. We have requested external assistance to help us develop an accurate facial composite. At this time, no further questions will be answered."*

Trina sat staring at the screen. She'd heard the report, but she was still processing the information. Accidental? Did he fall out of a tree? Did a bear attack him? Did he go on a crazy RV ride? This information gave her more questions than answers. She wondered what was causing the delay in his identification.

"Trina, we need to head over to Sean's." David stepped into the living room holding the pile of today's mail in his hands. "They're expecting us around five thirty so we can eat dinner around six. Do we have a good bottle of wine that we can bring?" he asked as he peeked into the wine cabinet.

"Yes, grab a bottle of Austin Hope. Let me throw a different outfit on. I'll be ready in a couple of minutes," Trina said, walking into the bedroom. She washed her face, combed her hair, and changed her clothes. She selected a slimming black pantsuit and put on eye makeup and perfume.

When she came out of the bedroom, David said, "You are still as lovely today as you were twenty-five years ago. You look spectacular. I'm going to look like the old guy who snagged a young bride." David gave her a peck on the cheek as he ushered her to the garage.

"Thanks, honey. You don't look so bad yourself."

David opened her door and then slipped into the driver's seat. On the ride over to Sean's, she continued to mull over the information from the newscast. It was not a murder. That should send waves of relief through the community. However, his identity and cause of death remained a mystery.

She was disappointed the investigation looked like it would be solved without her help. Maybe she should concentrate on her retirement job at the retail store and forget this detective stuff. Her yearning to become a detective melted like ice in the heat of the summer. She would have to accept the reality that she did not have the same resources the police had at their fingertips.

They arrived at Sean's and spent the first hour enjoying a glass of wine and a fabulous dinner. Then the men took off into the garage and Trina and the other two ladies sat outside on the patio playing a game of mahjong. Sean's wife, Mary Anne, was masterful at the game, but her neighbor, Maetri, was a novice player. The ladies chatted about various subjects, and the conversation eventually evolved to Trina's part in the discovery of the skeleton.

"It's so sad he remained undiscovered for so long," Maetri said. "I moved here from Raleigh in the early 'nineties with my family. My parents craved the peace and serenity of the Panhandle. I guess we all gain a false sense of security living in a small town. We forget that bad things can happen everywhere. Remember when South Walton seized three thousand grams of cocaine and arrested twenty-one people for drug trafficking? We assume that kind of stuff only happens in big cities but how wrong we are. I can't even look at the Sex Offender list. When you open a map and see more dots than you see streets, it becomes too overwhelming to process! The news that this man's death was accidental is at least a little bit of a selfish comfort. It would be terrifying to discover a murder had taken place less than five miles from where we live."

"I agree. An accidental death takes the edge off the unknown," Mary Anne agreed. "No one wants to hear about a murder taking place in their hometown. I think we all get a little complacent when we live somewhere for a while. I try not to listen to the local news. I don't want to hear about all the stupid things people do, stories of drug deals or thefts that occur right in our own neighborhood. I'm just so happy we don't have to worry about a murderer on the loose. We all assume that our neighbors and friends are trustworthy. The reality is we are all human, and everyone has a little bit of bad hiding deep inside. I know I can lose my temper when I'm following a golf cart full of vacationers down 30A. I have to remember to take a deep breath and remember this too will pass."

Trina agreed for the most part with her new friends. She was glad the police didn't have to solve a murder. She just wished she could help them identify the person so his family could get closure.

The ladies continued to talk and play for another hour. Trina decided it was time to go, so she helped clean up the kitchen and said her goodbyes. She wanted to wipe down the mahjong tiles to clean off her fingerprints, but she talked herself out of it. She didn't want them to think she was strange.

Trina walked into Sean's abnormally large garage to look for David. It was filled with car lifts and seven different vehicles. Two of them had their hoods raised and their wheels off, and the remaining vehicles appeared to be completely restored. Trina could tell they were vintage, but besides that, she only knew what color they were and not what make or model. She found David and Sean looking at an engine.

"Hey, guys, I hate to break up the fun, but David and I need to get back to the house to let our dogs out and call it a night," Trina said, truly exhausted from a long day.

"Trina, come check out this beautifully restored engine. Sean found the body of this old 1969 Bronco in a junkyard in Mississippi and rebuilt it with all original parts. Isn't this beautiful? We should get one of these. Wouldn't this be so fun to drive to the Farmer's Market on Saturdays?"

"It is a beauty, and great color. However, I think we'll have to vicariously enjoy his Bronco, David. You have enough unfinished car projects at home," Trina said with the sincerity of a wife who didn't want another car parked on the driveway.

"And look at this Jeep Renegade. Sean found it abandoned years ago in the Point Washington Trails. Can you believe that? He did an amazing job bringing it back to its original condition. Wouldn't you love to drive one of these? We could apply for a beach permit."

Trina stood in front of the Jeep. It was a chestnut brown with orange, red and yellow stripes along the sides and crème-colored leather seats. It had no doors and was completely open. Although it looked like almost every Jeep on 30A, this one felt super familiar. Trina noticed her heartbeat was steadily increasing, and she was feeling a little nauseous. She walked closer to the Jeep and peeked inside. Was this déjà vu? Why did this Jeep feel extremely familiar to her? She had eerie jitters running through her veins, and the hair on her arms was standing on edge. She didn't know what was going on, but the feeling was very uncomfortable.

Sean laughed at David's obvious excitement. "This was one of those random *my lucky day* finds. I went for a bike ride in Point Washington, oh, it must have been about twenty, twenty-five years ago. I was a little more adventurous back then and had gone off the trail and randomly came across this Jeep. The Jeep was in decent shape. The front end was crunched in like it had slammed into a tree. A friend of mine towed it out of the woods, I worked with the DMV to identify the registered owner, then negotiated a great deal with them to purchase it at a discount since it was wrecked. Now, I keep it as an exhibit of my first true rebuild. I don't take it out too much. Trying to keep mileage low on it. But I love to show it off as a reminder of how far I have come in mastering rebuilds."

Trina was not feeling well. She complimented Sean's work and gave David the low-key but unmistakable *Let's go!* wife look. They said their final goodbyes and headed home. After getting home and letting the dogs out, Trina went to bed exhausted. She was rattled and she didn't know why. Rehashing the events of the last couple of weeks, she shouldn't have been shocked that she was feeling a little overwhelmed. Finding human remains had made her realize how fragile life was. The realization that safety was a self-constructed blanket of warmth, and a crime-free life was a falsely painted reality was not a good feeling. No one was truly safe. Life had taught her over and over: expect the unexpected.

The journalist's queries into her past pushed Trina to dance with her own memories. She normally didn't spend much time thinking about her youth. What was it like living here as a teenager? She was sure they did all the normal stupid teenager stuff. Was Trudy right? Should her parents have let them work at a dive bar with strange men who would spend hours getting drunk, day or night? Had Trina and her sisters ever been in danger? Discovering that three girls had gone missing from 30A around that time was unnerving. Why had that not blown up in the news? That seemed like a disproportionately high number for a small area. How did the missing girls relate to the man's death? *Did* it even relate, or was Detective Trent interested because the simple fact remained three girls had never been found?

She needed to call Monica and find out what the police had asked her. The tone and direction of the questions relating to the apron might help her understand how the information fits together. Crime stories always make everything sound so devious and conniving but maybe it was truly a simple but deadly accident. It was very possible he was a random guy, and the story of his demise was not that mysterious.

Her thoughts bounced around in her head like popcorn kernels in a pan on a hot stove. Did she remember to wash the wine goblets at Sean's house? Why didn't she take the time to wipe down the mahjong tiles? Why did that Jeep make her feel like she was Alice in Wonderland going down the rabbit hole? Should she have shared those newspapers with Detective Trent? Had she sent him on a goose chase? Was she overthinking everything? It all began to feel suffocating.

Tears slowly dripped down her cheeks. *How much DNA is in tears?*

She needed to take a day to clean. She always felt better when she spent hours wiping down surfaces, throwing away items and reorganizing. The process of washing away her trail calmed her and made her feel like she had a fresh start. She'd hoped moving to Florida would free her mind from these invisible chains. Why did she still obsess over not leaving a trace?

Enough

Trina sat in the school gymnasium with tears trickling down her cheeks as Christopher walked across the stage to accept his high school diploma. It was no longer "when he graduates." Christopher had flourished during his senior year and accepted a presidential scholarship from Penn State. He will be leaving for college in August. The reality of it was shocking. She was so proud of him, but she was struggling with the concept of not having Christopher by her side.

Christopher promised to spend as much time as he could with her over the summer. Paul was staying in Massachusetts working as an electrician apprentice for a local firm. Tanner was working full-time, Judy was taking summer classes, and Jane was renovating her newly leased retail space so she could open her bakery in the fall. Christopher and Trina would be spending summer without their siblings and her parents were going to stay one extra week in Massachusetts to help Jane with her café renovation.

Trina had saved $4,900 the previous summer and had worked a part-time job during her junior year. Last month, she bought her very first car, a used 1990 Honda CRX five-speed hatchback. It was white with black trim and black and gray fabric bucket seats. It had a couple of scratches and dings, and 71,348 miles, but Trina was proud of her purchase. Her father had performed a full safety check and gave her the approval to drive to Florida.

Trina was excited to spend the entire week with Christopher alone. She'd asked Danny if she could only work three days during her first week so she could have plenty of downtime with Christopher before he started his new position as the head manager over the beach bonfires. He was excited about the opportunity and thrilled that he was receiving a nice pay increase.

By the time they pulled into the driveway at the Scotsdale bungalow after two days of driving, they were spent. However, the annual tradition of running into the Gulf couldn't be broken. Although the sun was setting, the beach was just as beautiful as they remembered. Sand so clean from a distance it looked like freshly fallen snow. Water so clear you could see your toes as you wiggled them. They enjoyed an hour of frolicking in the water and then headed back to the house.

Walking into the bungalow, the silence of the house hit her. Her parents would not be drinking a cup of coffee at the kitchen counter in the morning. Her sisters would not be arguing over the bathroom. Her brother would not be standing vigil. They were alone. Trina had told her parents that she would not break their trust by having Christopher stay at the house. They hadn't even done anything yet, and Trina was already feeling guilty just thinking about what they could do.

Although it was dark outside, Christopher pulled Trina out to the backyard and turned on the outside shower. With their bathing suits on, they stood under the streaming warm water brushing the sand off of each other. Christopher wiped her skin with slow, gentle strokes.

Starting at the shoulders, he ran his hands down her arms as the water steamed down her torso. Adding a little tender attention with his lips, his focused attention relaxed and excited Trina. The normal five-minute shower turned into thirty minutes of exploration. The security of their temporary solitude created an unnerving energy that heightened their intimacy. Trina's thoughts were a swirling mix of pleasure and control. As the tipping point was nearing, she reached behind her back and turned the temperature to freezing cold. The sharp contrast in temperature briskly ended the moment.

"Whoooooaaa! That is cold! Great way to snap me out of it. But one pull of this bikini string and..." Holding Trina under the freezing-cold water, Christopher started laughing.

"No, you don't, Christopher!" Smiling and laughing, Trina pushed him away and escaped the cold water. He pulled her back to him and made sure to leave her wanting more. They held hands as they sauntered back into the house with towels wrapped around them.

They threw on dry clothes and lay down together on top of the quilt in her bedroom. Trina lay in his cocoon of warmth, his arms wrapped around her, leaving her feeling content. She closed her eyes and thought about his touches, his character, his perfectly matched personality. She was still blown away he was her boyfriend.

Christopher whispered sweet nothings to her, complimenting her natural scent, her baby-soft skin, and generous curves. She let her thoughts drift off while she enjoyed his simple embrace and warm breath. After cuddling for a while, she took a slow long breath, turned, and kissed him on the cheek.

"You better go. Thank you for respecting my parents' wishes. My wishes. I know it's not easy." She knew that spending this last summer with Christopher before he went to college was going to escalate their physical encounters sooner than later, but she appreciated his willingness to limit their journey.

"You are still my slice of heaven, Trina Scotsdale." He kissed her cheek, grabbed his bag of clothes, and walked out the door to head home.

The first week back in Florida was filled with shift after shift after shift. The Beach Bomb Babes were basically running the restaurant. With Jane and Judy absent, the BBB were the most experienced girls working at the Salty Bar for the summer. The big gossip was that the new restaurant, the Red Bar, would be opening next summer. The restaurant was pushing a huge marketing campaign along 30A to get vacationers hyped about what was to come. They handed out red matchbooks, coupons, and flyers advertising live music. To Jerry's dismay, they were on the prowl for experienced waitstaff, dishwashers and chefs, which forced Jerry to raise the hourly rate to secure retention. 30A was hopping with a huge influx of vacationers. Restaurants were booming, the beach was overflowing with tanned bodies, and the bike path was filled with happy families.

Several weeks in, Trina was working the lunch shift with Angela and one other new waitress. They were struggling to keep up with the flow of people. It seemed like folks were ordering more cocktails than normal for the lunch shift, and most tables were seated for groups of five or more, which always added a little bit of strain on the kitchen staff as they struggled to keep up. Plus, Jerry's unexpected presence put an extra layer of stress on the atmosphere. He was meeting with Danny to review the menu. Trina overheard them discussing ways they could elevate the selections without raising costs. They had various price lists from several seafood vendors and local farmers markets displayed on the counter, and Danny was pitching menu ideas.

As the lunch crowd dwindled, Jerry asked Trina to unload the supplies in his trunk. Trina was exhausted after carrying trays of food for the last five hours, and her back was starting to ache. She'd been working double shifts three times a week, in addition to picking up three consecutive night shifts Thursday, Friday and Saturday. She didn't want to complain since she appreciated the money, but the long hours were wearing her down. She and Christopher barely found time to be alone, and summer was flying by.

Trina asked Danny for the key to the shed so she could grab the handcart. Danny said he'd given the keys to Jerry, but he was on the phone with a vendor. Trina didn't want to wait. She was ready to go home for the day. She and the new girl ventured out to Jerry's parking spot, only to find there was a customer's car parked behind his Jeep blocking easy access to the back of the vehicle. The driver of the vehicle had most likely parked there to run in and pick up a to-go order.

Instead of waiting, Trina decided to try to pull the boxes out of the back by kneeling down in the passenger seat. She was able to grab two oblong boxes but was struggling to get the big box full of napkins, toilet paper and paper towels. She tried to pull one of the small boxes through, but as she pulled it, it ripped the box, so she pushed it back in the trunk.

The effort was making her even more tired. She didn't know why Jerry couldn't bring these boxes in when he first arrived. He always made the girls empty his Jeep, and he was such a priss about keeping the Jeep clean. If you accidentally tracked any sand or dirt in his car, he had a conniption. The smell of perfume was always overpowering too. Trina didn't know why Sherry Lee would wear so much. It lingered forever even though the Jeep had no actual windows.

Finally, the car that was blocking moved, allowing them access to the back of the Jeep. Trina stacked two boxes on her coworker's arms and sent her on her way. Trina then grabbed the last two boxes, including the slightly damaged one, and headed inside. She was reaching for the door handle when Jerry stormed out, knocking into her. The boxes she was carrying fell to the ground. The bottom of one broke open, scattering dozens of waitress order pads all over the sand and dirt. The other box, which was filled with prewrapped packages of to-go utensils, burst open from the top, causing half the box to spill out on the ground.

"Damn it, Trina! You shouldn't be carrying boxes in your hands. That's why I invested in a handcart. Now look at what you have done. I pay good money for these supplies. Thankfully, that wasn't food. Can you imagine the money you could have dropped on the ground? Pick this up before customers see the mess. And check each one individually to see if they're clean and usable. Give me my keys, I'm late for a meeting."

Jerry stalked off toward his Jeep, mumbling to himself. "One thing after another. Vendors robbing me blind. Waitresses asking for pay raises. Competitors stealing my business. Danny wants to offer steak on the menu—steak! My wife always wants more money but doesn't even come home at night. When am I going to get the respect, I deserve?" He slammed the door, squealed in reverse, and took off.

Trina stood there in complete shock. He was the one who slammed into her, then blamed her for the mess? She'd worked six nonstop hours on her feet, and he couldn't even lift a damn finger? What a complete asshole! Man, she was getting tired of this job. If Danny didn't need them so badly, she'd quit and get a job selling ice cream. She could earn a decent pay without all the hassle.

As she knelt on the ground slowly picking up the supplies, someone reached down and started to help. She looked up and saw it was Bobby from the Grayton General Store. Trina hadn't seen him since the day after Jasmine had gone missing. He looked older, muscular, tanned and, if possible, even more handsome.

"Hey there Trina, looks like you need a hand." Bobby said as leaned down and took both boxes from her. "Let me get that for you."

"Thanks. I appreciate it. Nice to see you, Bobby. It's been a minute since I have bumped into you. Are you still working at the store?" Trina said piling the rest of the supplies in the top box.

"Yeah. Grandpa's not doing so good. I had to quit school halfway through the semester to take over the store. I'm taking night classes to try not to get too far behind. How are you? You're more beautiful than I remember," he said politely, not in a flirtatious way.

"Oh geez, I smell like greasy burgers and have remnants of a hundred lunches all over my clothes. Not sure how pretty I look but thanks for the compliment. So sorry to hear about your granddad. I bet you'll be able to get back on track in no time. You don't need to carry those for me. I can take them in," Trina said as she reached for the boxes.

"No way. I like to think of myself as a gentleman. Point me in the right direction," he said has he held the boxes in his right hand and held the door open with his left.

They walked into the empty restaurant, and Trina pointed him to the kitchen door. They walked by Angela, who was stacking clean glasses at the bar, and she gave Trina a wide-eyed grin as they passed. Danny was in the back talking to Billy about dinner service, and they didn't even notice Trina and Bobby. Trina held open the door to the supply closet, and after Bobby entered, she followed and pointed out the correct shelf for the boxes. The door shut behind them, closing them in the narrow space together.

"You can drop them there. Thank you so much, Bobby. It was great to see you," Trina said.

Bobby turned to leave, and as he did, he reached for Trina's hand. He locked fingers with her, then reached over and grabbed her other hand. He didn't say anything at first, just held her hands and looked into her eyes. Trina was shocked, but at the same time, she was mesmerized. Bobby was handsome. High cheekbones, a sculpted jaw, and mega green eyes. Looking at them, she felt like she was staring at the treetops of a pine forest that had sun glistening off them.

Bobby slowly began to smile. His smile was stunning. Beautifully straight, white teeth. His stare was intense. Trina should let go of his hands. She should stop looking into his eyes. But she was locked in place.

"Ummmm, Bobby," Trina was able to mumble.

"Shhhh." Bobby lifted his finger and gently placed it on her lips. "I have dreamt of being this close to you for a long time, Trina. Never imagined it would be in a supply closet." He chuckled. His finger hadn't left her lips.

He bent down very slowly. Just as his lips were about to touch hers, he stopped. He moved his mouth over to her neck and whispered, "One day." He squeezed her hand, stood up tall, stared straight into eyes, then walked out of the closet.

Trina stood there. *What the bloody hell?*

She could smell him. She hadn't taken in his scent before, but now that he'd left, she could really smell him. It wasn't a cologne smell. It was more like a rugged, natural, masculine smell. Trina lifted her finger to her lips and ran it over them. She shook her head and then a wave of guilt rushed over her. *Christopher! How could I do that to Christopher?* Well, she hadn't actually done anything, but then why did she feel so guilty? She realized that she was aroused. Now she felt ten times more guilty.

Oh my gosh! She couldn't believe that just happened. *Bobby has dreamt about me?* Trina smiled. She felt guilty, and she felt her heart beating at the same time.

The door to the supply closet opened and Danny walked in. "Trina, what you are doing here? I thought you left already."

"Oh, hey, Danny. Sorry. I was taking a breather. Those boxes were heavy," Trina said, stumbling over her words, then feeling more guilty for lying.

"Go home. You had a busy day. I'll get Billy to put those away. I'll see you tomorrow, right? I think you're working a double?"

"Um, yeah. OK. Thanks. See you tomorrow," Trina said as she walked by him, still in a complete daze.

Trina drove home in a fog. That was one of the strangest, most exhilarating two minutes. She hadn't seen Bobby in almost a year, there she was hot, sweaty, and dirty from a six-hour shift, and he made a pass at her? Well, she thought it was a pass. Wasn't it? Why else would he get so close to her lips? She could taste him. *Snap out of it!* Why was she still thinking about it? She had the best boyfriend imaginable. But Bobby's hands were so strong and warm. His face was worthy of a magazine cover. *Oh my god, Trina. You needs take a cold shower.*

She pulled into her driveway, and there was Christopher with his shirt off washing his car in the driveway. She simply sat there and looked at him. Christopher was good looking too. His hair had gotten lighter in the Florida sun, and his muscles had become more sculpted over the last year. He looked up from scrubbing the wheels, smiled big and wide and waved at Trina. Trina waved back. She was lucky. He was adorable, hardworking, smart as heck, he loved animals, and he treated her like a queen. She needed to forget that encounter with Bobby. Forget it completely.

She sat there for another minute or so and suddenly made up her mind. She was going to pass the monumental relationship bridge. She needed to show Christopher how happy she was they were together. She was ready.

She climbed out of the car with her backpack in hand. She pulled off her dirty apron and sauntered over to Christopher. He stood up, gave her another big smile, then squirted a cold stream of water from the hose at her. Trina screamed and ran around the back of the car. Christopher chased her all around the car with the hose as Trina dropped her stuff and zigzagged in the driveway. She was no match for him, and in no time, she was sopping wet.

"I give!" she said, laughing. She squeezed water from her white T-shirt and pushed her wet hair off her face. "You stinker! Payback is a bitch," she said as she ran up to him and tried to give him a big wet hug.

He playfully pushed her away. "Eww, you're all wet. Don't touch me," he said, laughing. Then he reached out and pulled her back to him, picked her up and twirled her around. "I don't mind a soggy wet piece of pizza. It still tastes just as good."

They kissed, hugged, and laughed. "I like this wet look on you, Miss Trina. You might need to add wet T-shirts to your daily wardrobe." Christopher took her hand and spun her around.

"Oh, stop it. I better go in before my dad comes out and sees me! Are you working tonight?"

"Yes, I have to leave soon, actually. My car was getting so dirty with trekking all these bonfire supplies back and forth. I called your dad this morning to see if I could swing over here to wash the car, hoping I could catch you before I leave for work. What are you going to do tonight? You have the night off, right?"

"I do. I'm working a double tomorrow, so I might curl up with a good mystery novel and go to bed early. I'll miss you." They chatted for another couple of minutes, then picked up the car wash supplies. She leaned over and planted a wet kiss on his lips. Trina told him that she wouldn't be able to see him until Sunday. She said goodbye and grabbed the trash bag he had filled up with car trash.

"I'll throw this away inside for you. See you soon." She blew him a kiss and went inside the house.

She threw her backpack and keys on the counter. The keys, with the mace can attached, slid too far, and fell to the floor. Trina dropped the bag of trash on the floor and bent over to pick up her keys, which she hung on the key hook in the hallway. When she returned and picked up the clear plastic trash bag, she noticed something pink and purple in the bag. She ruffled trash out of the way and saw a girl's elastic hairband. *That's weird.* She didn't wear that type of hairband. She took it out of the bag and walked over to the door to go ask Christopher, but she saw his car pulling out of the driveway. *Paul must have taken a girl home in the car.* She tossed it back in the bag and then threw the bag away. Or maybe Christopher gave a friend a ride. She'd have to ask him next time she saw him.

Trina took a long, hot shower and had a scrumptious dinner with her parents. Her dad didn't spend that much time down in Florida, so it was nice to spend quality time with him. Richard and Nancy talked about hiring a painter to give the bungalow a makeover and possibly replacing the backyard fence. They asked her about Christopher's college plans but were respectful enough not to ask whether they were planning on staying together. Trina didn't want to think about it, so she changed the topic. She explained that she wanted to go to school for business and was thinking about Auburn University, Babson College, and the University of Georgia. Luckily, her grandparents had set funds aside to help fund her and her siblings' college education. Tuition and lodging would be covered, but Trina would have to pay for her personal expenses. She was saving all her earnings since she had wiped her account clean after buying her car.

The night ended with Trina cuddled up in her bed reading a good mystery, then falling asleep with dreams about a cute, tall, muscular, green-eyed boy kissing her.

The next couple of weeks flew by with many work hours, and suddenly there was only one week left of summer. Trina couldn't believe summer was almost over. She was scheduled to work a double, and a bad thunderstorm was forecasted to roll in around noon. Trina plopped her backpack in her car to head over to work. She had recently developed two rolls of film, and she was looking forward to hanging up the pictures on the bulletin board. Unfortunately, her car wouldn't start. She turned the key over and over again, but it wouldn't engage. Her dad was back in Massachusetts, and her mom knew as much as Trina did about cars—nothing. Trina would have jumped on a bike since it would only take her ten minutes to get to work, but her mom offered to drop her off. Her mom said she would call her dad and get advice on how to deal with her car issue. Hopefully, they could figure it out soon since they would be headed back home in one week.

Trina walked through the back door of the restaurant and waved hello to everyone, then helped get ready for the lunch shift. By eleven thirty, the thunderstorm had rolled in. It was a bad storm. Lightning and thunder shook the building, and the thick, heavy rain poured from the sky like a painter pouring paint into a pan. Only two soaking wet customers came in for lunch.

At twelve thirty, Danny let the other two waitresses go home, leaving Trina to handle the rest of any lunch crowd. She spent her downtime replacing and rearranging pictures on the bulletin board reminiscing about past summers. Waitressing was a demanding job. Long days on her feet, interactions mixed with pleasure, humor, and occasional irritation. She did love the camaraderie of working alongside her friends and it felt good to have returning customers request her by name.

Danny came out and sat at the bar. Trina rarely, if ever, saw Danny sit down to eat. He was always running around in the kitchen or stockroom. If he wasn't actively managing a long stream of orders hanging from the countertop, he was prepping for the next shift. Trina was behind the bar wiping down glasses. The only other people in the restaurant were the current dishwasher, a fifteen-year-old boy, and Billy. They were sitting in the back talking about a video game.

The rain was forecasted to last all afternoon and into the evening, so Trina didn't expect to make much money during her dinner shift either. Danny had called the other two waitresses who were scheduled and told them to stay home, that he would call them if business picked up. If the dinner shift was anything like the lunch shift, Trina would be able to handle it alone.

"Trina, have you eaten at Bud & Alley's?" Danny said, taking a bite out of his grilled chicken sandwich. "I'm curious what you think about their crabcakes and fish entrees. Jerry agreed to give me a little leeway to try new menu items out. I might whip a few up tonight if it's slow. Maybe you can be my taste tester."

"My parents went for dinner there last week. My dad likes anything pretty much so take this lightly, but he said the salmon was amazing. My mom enjoyed her chicken, but she's also easy to please. I haven't had a chance to eat there. Are you trying to compete with Seaside restaurants menus?" Trina said, stacking beer mugs on the bar counter.

"Trying to mix it up a little. Maybe a grilled fresh seafood platter. I'm thinking grouper, scallops, and oysters over pasta. Also considering NY prime rib or filet served over garlic mashed potatoes with steamed broccoli. Although Jerry's reluctant to let me serve steak. He thinks it's too risky. He's worried our clientele might not want to spend that much money on dinner. It's a delicate balance. I don't want to overbuy, but underbuying disappoints customers."

"If you don't mind me asking, why do you always defer to Jerry? As the casual observer, you run circles around Jerry when it comes to knowing how to manage the restaurant. Why doesn't he concentrate on the rental properties and let you manage the restaurant?"

"Jerry can be a pain in the backside, but he is a smart businessman. I don't know if you know, but our parents used to run this place. When we were little, we would spend all our free time here watching our mom and dad. It was a really small place back then. This area didn't have as many visitors as is common today. Business relied heavily on locals. The menu was minimal, but our parents built enough of a business to put a roof over our heads. When I was fifteen and Jerry was seventeen, our dad died unexpectedly. We were forced to step in and help my mom. She was stressed out most of the time, so she took her frustrations out on us. Mostly Jerry since he was the older one. He had to quit high school to work with mom full time. Our mom ran the business, but she never wanted to change anything. She wanted to keep it exactly as dad had it. Even though Jerry was inexperienced, he quickly discovered that to stay in business, changes were needed. My mom refused to listen to him. They fought a lot, and it put a huge strain on our family." Danny finished his last bite and took a swig from his drink.

"Mom ended up marrying a man from Louisiana. I had just turned nineteen. Jerry and I did not get along well with our stepdad. Jerry convinced me that we should buy the business from my mom since she was spending less and less time at work. Instead of working out a reasonable family arrangement, my mom took our stepdad's advice and charged us a premium. We're still paying off the bank debt to this day. If Jerry hadn't invested in the rental market, we would be broke. We never socialize outside of work, and we only discuss operational decisions. I most definitely don't agree with his communication style, but I wouldn't be running my own restaurant if Jerry didn't take care of the financial side of things. I'm great in the kitchen, but I suck when it comes to pushing paper." Danny drained the last of his drink.

"Jerry has a hard time trusting people since he's been burnt before, but I know it's just Jerry being Jerry. I find ways to let my aggression out. He finds his way too. We try to stay out of each other's space. Even though we have been working alongside each other for essentially our entire lives, Jerry doesn't think of me as an equal. I guess it's the older brother thing. I will always be the lesser of the two of us in Jerry's eyes. Anyways, sorry to give you the family saga. Let's go be creative in the kitchen." Danny stood up from the bar and grabbed his dirty plate as he walked to the back.

Trina followed him. "I had no idea that you've been running this place for so long. Did you always know you had the skills as a chef, or did that happen as a result of the situation?"

"Sort of both. Jerry was the chef after my dad died, but he wasn't great at it. I took over and he slowly migrated into operations, then the finances once we bought it. I don't really like dealing with vendors and prefer to not have to deal with customers," Danny said.

"And Jerry does?" Trina asked sarcastically.

"Touché.' Not really, but he can turn on the charm if he needs to. Plus, he and Sherry Lee seem to have a system for socializing with customers to elicit increased business. I prefer to cook the food and stay away from the public if possible." Danny took out a grouper filet and scallops and flavored them as he prepared the pasta.

"Yeah, we've noticed. Janice does her fair share too," Trina said, hoping she wasn't stepping over the line.

"Not surprising. Janice and I are— Well, let's just say we're still married... legally," Danny said, not making eye contact with Trina. Billy and the dishwasher walked back into the kitchen, and Trina knew the conversation was going to end there.

She watched Danny whip up his new idea for a dish he decided to call Seafood Sunrise. It was absolutely delicious, and fancier than anything the Salty Bar served currently. Trina had never eaten at a fancy restaurant before, but this food melted in her mouth and the flavors popped. The sauce on the pasta was heavenly. She begged Danny to add it to the menu, saying she could push the dish to every table and say it with complete confidence. It was masterful. Billy agreed and asked Danny to make it again so he could watch.

Only two brave couples came in that night for dinner since the thunderstorm raged on. After they left, she reorganized the supply closet, wiped down every canister, restocked every shelf and alphabetized Danny's spices. She was ready to go home and was hoping no more customers would come in since she had been sitting around for hours with nothing left to do.

Around nine p.m., the front door opened. To her surprise, Bobby walked in dripping wet from the rain. "Hey there, Trina."

"Bobby, hi. What are you doing here?" Trina asked as she nervously wiped down a ketchup bottle for the third time tonight.

"This is a restaurant, right? Or did I walk into a bank by accident?" he joked and gave Trina a dazzling smile.

"Oh yeah. Right. Of course. Here's a dinner menu. Do you want to sit at the bar or a table?"

"I placed an order to go. Billy took it for me. It should be ready," Bobby said.

Danny came walking out of the kitchen. "Hey, Bobby, your order's ready. I'll get Billy to bring it out. Trina, why don't you go home? I'm going to close. It's silly to keep you here when this storm has scared everyone away. Thanks for staying all day." Danny walked back through the swinging kitchen door, leaving Trina with Bobby.

"Excuse me, Bobby, I need to go call my mom. My car broke down this morning, so I need a ride." Trina headed toward the kitchen to use the restaurant phone in the back.

"Don't bother your mom. I can drop you off. I drive by your house on the way home. I gotcha," Bobby said.

Billy walked over holding a to-go bag. "Here you go. Trina, can you ring him up? The slip is attached to the bag." Billy headed right back to the kitchen.

"I couldn't ask you to do that. Besides, my mom is at home sitting by the phone waiting for me to call," Trina said as she rang his order up.

"That's silly. Come on. Grab your stuff." He walked around the bar and called into the back. "Hey, Danny, I'm going to drop Trina off. Is she all set?"

"Yes. Thanks. I forgot she didn't have a car today. Appreciate it, Bobby," Danny called out.

Trina felt awkward, but she was ready to go home, and if she had to wait for her mom, it would be at least fifteen minutes before she got there since her mom wouldn't be ready to jump in the car. She checked herself out at the time clock, grabbed her backpack and said goodbye to the boys.

"It's raining pretty hard. Will you be OK running to the car? I parked right out front," Bobby said.

"Not a problem."

They opened the front door, and the rain was already pelting them before they even stepped out. They ran to his car, frantically pulled open the doors, jumped in, and slammed the doors as quickly as they could but they were both drenched. Trina squeezed her long hair to the side, leaving a puddle on his floor mats. She realized she was wearing a light-blue T-shirt, and it was sticking to her skin like glue. She picked up her backpack and held it in her lap, trying to cover herself.

The ride home was brief but pleasant. Bobby talked about his college classes and asked her about her college aspirations. Trina enjoyed the conversation. They pulled into the driveway in seven short minutes.

"Thanks, Bobby, appreciate it. I hope your dinner didn't get too cold."

Trina was about to open the door when she felt Bobby's hand on her leg. "Wait, Trina."

Trina relented and sat back in the seat, slowly turning to look at Bobby.

Bobby pushed her damp hair out of her face, then let his fingers slide down her cheek and rest on her chin. Then his index finger rose up to her lips. "I know you have a boyfriend. I don't mean to push, but I think you should know."

Trina waited. A few seconds went by. It felt like a few minutes.

"Trina, there is something electric about you. When I'm near you, I feel like I am on fire. When I'm not with you, I can't help but paint images of you in my mind. I love that you are 100% naturally you. No fluff. No frills. All you. And let me tell you, you are plenty. One day,

Trina. One day. And I'm willing to wait. I'm in no rush." He gently pulled down her lower lip.

Trina was spellbound. *Damn it! Why does his touch send jolts through my skin!* Her heart felt like it was just hit by a wrecking ball.

"Bobby, I don't know what to say," Trina whispered barely loud enough for herself to hear.

"Your eyes say it all. I'll wait, Trina. Goodnight." He leaned over and kissed her cheek.

Trina pushed the door open and ran toward the house. She stepped inside and dropped her wet belongings. Raising her hand to her heart, she could feel the pounding.

"Trina is that you?"

"Yes, Mom, it's me. I got a ride home. I'm going to take off my wet clothes and use a towel to dry off before I tramp through the house."

"OK, honey. Goodnight. By the way, your dad found a local mechanic who was nice enough to stop by today and fix your car. It just needed a new battery."

Trina stood in the foyer, slowly taking her wet clothes off. She was emotionally shaken. She had no idea that Bobby thought about her. And his touch. It was crazy how two seconds of skin-to-skin contact could send shockwaves through her. She was a mess. Maybe it felt this way because she knew it was a forbidden touch. She wasn't with Bobby, so his touch made her feel like she was doing something wrong. That must be what she was feeling. Not an actual attraction. That must be it.

The more she thought about it, the more she convinced herself that once she slept with Christopher, her sexual frustration would stop. She wouldn't have such a reaction from Bobby's touches and his words.

She and Christopher were scheduled to spend their last Sunday night together before they went their separate ways. It would be Christopher's last night before he took off to college. That could be the night.

Artist Rendering

Present Day

Trina took time off from thinking about the case. She had been frazzled that night at Sean's house. As much as she wanted to figure out why the Jeep sent daggers through her nervous system, the reality was she only had the strength and courage for fiction. The true Trina Scotsdale, who was scared to take a free mint from the doctor's office mint bowl, was too timid to solve a real murder. For her own sanity, she convinced herself to stick to reading Dan Brown and Lee Child and stay away from real-world crime.

Today, she was in the mood to clean. She decided to reorganize her mom's boxes in the shed, which would result in a truckload of donations. She removed all the big boxes and put them out in the backyard on blankets. She went box by box to see what miscellaneous junk her mom had collected over the years. After about three hours, she had repacked four boxes of donations for Caring & Sharing of South Walton and had reorganized the beach supplies, holiday decorations, yard games and cleaning supplies in separate storage bins. When she had finished putting the keeper boxes in the shed, she approached the tall cabinet by the sink, hoping to find it full of garage stuff that David would have to go through. Devasted to find as many odds and ends lining four wide shelves, she mulled over quitting for the day. As she was about to close the cabinet door, she caught sight a rectangular plastic tub labeled Beach Supplies. She moved various cleaning supplies out of the way, pulled the tub out and placed it on the small card table in the back of the shed.

Trina popped the lid and dumped the contents. The box was filled with the Salty Bar cocktail napkins and various condiments like ketchup and mayonnaise with the restaurant's logo. There was also a set of surfboard salt and pepper shakers and two ashtrays. Trina picked up a hotel-sized bar of soap that was wrapped in plastic. It was labeled Freeport Clean, the same name that had been written on the board at the police station. Why would her mother have Freeport Clean soap? She found about forty small soaps in the bin. She separated them out and dumped the rest of the miscellaneous items back into the box. She closed the shed and went back into the house. Since her parents owned a beach house, they rarely stayed at hotels, so the abundance of hotel soaps was odd.

She sat down at her desk and googled the company. No results were generated for Freeport Clean. The company, assumingly small and local, must have gone out of business before the internet. She opened one of the packages and examined the hand-poured soap. It smelled amazing. Her curiosity was piqued. She picked up her phone and called her mom.

The phone rang four times before her dad picked up. "Hello. Oh, come on! That was an Interception!" Richard grunted into the phone.

"Hey, Dad. Watching a game on rerun today? Is mom around?" Trina asked, knowing her dad would not be able to concentrate on a conversation with a game on. He rewatched hours and hours of old football games even though he knew the final results by heart.

"Nancy, Trina needs you!" He dropped the phone down on a hard surface, and Trina could hear her parents' dog barking in the background. After about a minute, her mom picked up the line.

"Trina, honey, is everything OK? Are you sick? What's wrong?" Her mom always assumed Trina needed help.

"Hey, Mom, I'm fine. I finally found time to examine the contents of the shed. I feel like I made a ton of progress in just one day. You collected quite a variety of beach paraphernalia and holiday decorations. I went through every piece and put together a box or two for charity. You will never believe what I found. Do you remember those pink starfish flip-flops? You used to wear them everywhere. I'm going to keep them to show to the kids. Those should be framed as a historical memento of our first ten years as a family in the bungalow. I also found that huge blue beach towel that was as big as a bed. Remember that one? It has a four-foot-tall picture of a polka-dotted umbrella on it. Judy, Jane, and I used to fight over that towel every summer because it was the biggest one that we owned. It's still in fairly good shape considering Judy would drag that thing everywhere. We used to find it in our car trunks, under the boardwalk and even inside coolers. It was like a boomerang and always ended up back at our house by the end of the summer." Trina laughed with her mom at the memories.

"Oh dear, I do remember that thing. Give it a good wash in OxiClean and Downy softener and it should be good to go. I had forgotten about the flip-flops. I spent many summers in those things. I should have gone through that shed before I left. I hope you're not donating too much. You should try to find a way to recycle before you throw anything away," her mom lectured.

Trina didn't even want to think how much stuff was stored in her parents' closets back home in Massachusetts. If it was up to her mother, Trina and David should keep everything no matter how faded and ragged it looked.

"Hey, Mom, I found this bin that was filled with a whole bunch of stuff from the Salty Bar: salt and pepper shakers, napkins and things that like. Do you know why you have all that stuff?" Trina asked, trying to keep the question simple to get her mom to fill in the blanks.

"You and your friends would come home with your backpacks filled with miscellaneous stuff from work. When I periodically emptied your bags out, I would find condiments, forks, knives and even plates from work. I can just imagine how much stuff the restaurant lost from having all you teenagers siphoning off supplies with each lunch break you took. I stored all the supplies in the shed so we could use it when we packed lunches for the beach."

"I also found bars of soap from a company called Freeport Clean. Do you remember how we acquired so many hotel-sized soaps?" Trina asked.

"I would find soap, little toothpastes, and even small hotel-sized shampoos in your bags when you came home from work. I don't remember any of the specific brands, but don't you remember that the bar owners also managed several rental properties? One of those brothers was a penny pincher and always berated you girls for one thing or another. Slipping supplies into your backpacks was, I guess, a little retaliation. Don't throw those supplies away. Pack them up and store them in your car or in your beach bag. They are great for little emergencies. Don't be wasteful, Trina." Trina was amused that her mother worried about a few dollars' worth of twenty-year-old supplies.

257

"OK. Thanks, Mom. I won't throw them away." Trina said what she knew her mom needed to hear. "I didn't remember taking that stuff home from work. But now that you mention the rental properties, that totally rings a bell. I remember we used to make packages of toiletries and fold bathroom towels."

She and her mom talked for another ten minutes, then Trina told her she needed to run to the grocery store so she could end the call.

Freeport Clean was the name she'd seen when she tiptoed through the war room at the police station. Betty had been researching bathroom supply companies, so she'll have to figure out how to bring this up in conversation on their walk on Tuesday.

Trina kept busy for the rest of Sunday running errands, and Monday was filled with various personal appointments followed by a delicious dinner at Grayton Seafood Co. By Tuesday, she was ready for a nice long walk. The morning was stunning, and the temperature was hovering at seventy-five degrees. The cloudless sky looked like a pair of faded blue jeans. She texted Betty, and they agreed to meet at the Grayton Beach intersection. Trina and Freckles sat at the small picnic table at the Grayton General Store waiting. When Freckles jumped up and wagged her tail, Trina knew Bojangles was coming around the corner.

Betty and Trina hugged, let the dogs sniff each other, then began walking toward Western Lake. The walking path was already busy. New moms with baby strollers jogged by and many couples strolled the path holding hands drinking Bad Ass Coffee. Many ladies walked past with gift bags from Aura well known for selling beautiful gifts and coastal artwork cementing Florida vacation memories. As they sauntered past Uptown Grayton, they listened to live music playing at Crackings while visitors devoured the most sought-after breakfast on 30A. Watching three generational families gather at local restaurants was heartwarming. Grandparents fawned over the newest grandchild, and adult moms and dads gushed over their grown children. Although it was a very busy time of year, Trina didn't mind the hustle and bustle of extra people. Everyone was smiling, laughing, and taking in the simple life here.

Wearing cool beach hats, sunglasses, bathing suits and flip-flops everywhere you went had a way of making people feel relaxed and radiant. Getting a healthy dose of Vitamin D and enjoying the freshest seafood dinners, complimented with creative beachy cocktails, had a way of erasing the stress of life outside of 30A. When folks zoomed by as they pedaled to their destination, you could feel the freedom in their smiles and windblown hair. It was difficult to accurately describe the magical aura that floated around the town, but Trina felt it every day.

Bojangles and Freckles knew exactly which direction to lead Betty and Trina. The dogs strutted proudly down 30A greeting other walkers with wagging tails and open, panting mouths. They were great motivators for maintaining a steady pace. Betty and Trina talked and walked for about thirty minutes over to Western Lake into picturesque Watercolor neighborhood. Natural gardens enclosed beautiful homes clustered around checkerboard layered streets. The front porches were populated with rocking chairs, the sidewalks filled with families, and the beautiful live oaks and longleaf pine trees decorated the yards and lined the winding paths. A pure Zen feeling came over Trina when they walked through these neighborhoods no matter how many times she did it.

Trina had filled a large bag full of litter by the time they reached the end of the Watercolor neighborhood. She found a trashcan to dump the contents so they could have an empty bag for the walk back. As she dumped it, she said to Betty, "Isn't it crazy the amount of trash that falls off the back of golf carts and out of toddlers' hands. People say they care about the environment, but how many plastic bottles do we find along the path? I wish people's actions matched their words. It kills me that people can spend $10 on a disposable cup of coffee and toss the cup on the ground. It makes me think about the difference in generations. My mother won't even let me toss out a bin filled with home supplies she used for thirty years that's only worth five dollars now, yet today's generation is accustomed to single use everything. If the TV breaks, buy a new one. Spend $20 on lunch, only eat what you feel like and toss the rest," Trina said with the hint of disappointment.

"We can only worry about things we can control and do our part," Betty said. "I'm glad you and I keep our community clean, otherwise we'd feel like we live at the ballpark after a game. On the bright side, it sounds like you are making progress on cleaning out your parents' belongings. What kind of ancient treasures have you unearthed so far?" Betty asked as she bent over to pick up an empty White Claw can.

"I invested several hours organizing my mom's shed. That woman was an early recycler for sure. She would keep things and find uses for them like nobody's business. Of course, she only reused one percent of the stuff she kept, but it made her feel good to find another use for things. I did uncover a container filled with random supplies from the bar I used to work at when I was a teenager. There were a whole bunch of these hotel-sized soaps made by a company called Freeport Clean. It smells amazing. When I asked my mom why she had them, she reminded me the restaurant owners also owned a couple of rental homes, and my sisters and I used to bring home supplies in our bags all the time." Trina said this with all the simplicity she could muster, knowing full well Betty was aware of the company name due to her assigned investigatory task.

Betty stopped short on the path and turned to Trina. "What was the name of the soap brand?"

"Freeport Clean. The soap smells like vanilla, eucalyptus and lavender all mixed in one. You could tell it was not mass manufactured. I looked it up on the internet but couldn't find anything about it. It must have been a small local company that the property managers used to supply to their vacation homes. Why do you ask, does that name ring a bell to you?" Trina started walking again so she wouldn't have to look Betty in the face and give away how much she wanted to know if this was tied to the case.

"Where did you work when you were younger? You mentioned a bar and rental homes? Did you work at both?" Betty asked, tugging Bojangles's leash so she would catch up with them.

"I worked at this dive called the Salty Bar. It's no longer around. It was sold years ago and now a massive Vrbo home is there in its place. The bar was owned by two brothers, who used to operate vacation rental properties. They stored the guest bathroom supplies in a shed behind the restaurant. Being kids, we must have *borrowed* supplies because they ended up in one of my mom's mysterious bins in the shed," Trina shared, hoping this was going to jump-start a sharing of information conversation.

"Very interesting. Where these rental properties here in Blue Mountain or the Grayton area?"

"In Grayton. I remember the owners of the bar would occasionally have us help by folding bathroom towels and making toiletry bags, but I don't remember ever actually going to the rental homes. We reaped the benefits of doing the messy work by bringing home leftovers, be it food or bathroom supplies." Trina chuckled at the honesty of her dishonesty as a teenager.

"Do you use that brand of soap at your home?" Betty asked.

"Oh no. This was the first time I'd seen the name Freeport Clean. I thought the soap smelled really good, though. I tried to order a box of soap, but the company must have gone out of business."

"Well, Trina, I can't tell you why, but that little bit of random sharing might be a critical detail to help a coworker solve a mystery." Betty smiled and began walking with more purpose.

"Really? Like trying to figure out who didn't read the Employees Must Wash Their Hands Before Returning to Work sign?" Trina joked, hoping to make light of the subject.

"Well, we have that problem too but luckily that's not my department. But seriously, Freeport Clean is the name of a company we've been researching for a case, coincidentally. Thanks for telling me about what you uncovered in your mom's shed. It may be helpful."

"Wow, what a strange coincidence. I would not have thought a soap company would be valuable information, but for your sake, I hope it points you in the right direction. Which sort of reminds me. I know you cannot divulge any details about the skeleton case so please take this as a friend just passing information along. It may or may not help, but I might as well pass it along. My husband and I met a local car fanatic who refurbishes vehicles. One of his projects had quite a unique origin story," Trina said as they continued down the now bustling bike path.

"Not sure where this is going, but you have my attention," Betty said.

"Ok, bear with me. Normally, this guy buys vehicles by attending car auctions and following Facebook marketplace. But he told us a crazy story about how he came across this particular vehicle. About twenty-five years ago, he found an abandoned Jeep in the Point Washington Trails. The man that died in the woods died of an accidental death, right? Maybe it was a Jeep accident? You think I'm losing my mind bringing this up? I mean, what are the chances the two incidents would be related, right? But I couldn't help but wonder. The Jeep's owner is Sean Hampton just in case the detective wants to reach out to him." When she said it aloud, it sounded ludicrous, and Trina almost regretted sharing it. She shouldn't have said anything. Betty was going to think she was crazy.

"A Jeep huh? Well, there are plenty of adventurous trailblazers around here. Twenty-five years ago, the trails were not as established as they are today, so a risky backroad maneuver could have ended badly. One thing I have learned over the years is to never dismiss a clue until you've proven it is not relevant. Appreciate your input. I'll pass it along to the detectives. Crazier things have happened," Betty said.

After another twenty minutes, they wrapped up their walk and hugged their goodbyes. Trina felt slightly rewarded that her little discoveries might help after all. She ended the day exhausted and happy.

Wednesday, she got up early and went for an hour walk while listening to the book *Running Blind* by Lee Child. She showered and opened the shop by ten o'clock. She had ten boxes of new inventory to process, but the spring break foot traffic kept her occupied ringing up customer purchases for most of the morning. Most of the crowd were unfamiliar faces filled with joyful families who were soaking in the Florida weather, filling their bellies with yummy food, and splurging on gift purchases.

Around two o'clock, the store had emptied out except for a couple who were letting their daughter pick out a stuffed animal and a petite woman with a gray bob who kept looking at the candles, but also over at Trina. When Trina finished ringing up a purchase, Trina walked over to the remaining customer.

"Hello, miss, I apologize for not being able to offer you any assistance yet. It has been a busy afternoon. Can I help you find anything? Are you looking for home décor or a gift for someone special?" Trina asked while she straightened the inventory on the shelf.

"Thank you. I'm only browsing," she said, making brief eye contact and then picking up a candle.

"Well, I am here if you need me. You look familiar. Are you a local or are you visiting?" Trina asked.

"Lived here my entire life. Not too many of us original residents left along the Panhandle. I stop here every couple of months to check out the new inventory so we might have crossed paths. You're a true local too, right?" This time, she put the candle down and looked directly at Trina.

"So nice to meet you. My name is Trina. I consider myself a local. My parents owned a house down in Gulf Trace for thirty years. I grew up spending summers here and recently retired and moved back full time. I bet we bumped into each other at a restaurant or a community event. Or I wonder if we met when we were kids. Maybe we used to work together at the restaurant, wouldn't that be a coincidence," Trina asked with curiosity.

"I wish I worked at a restaurant as a kid. I was always jealous of all the tips my waitressing friends used to bring home. Unfortunately, I spent my summers working as a cleaning girl with my mom. She used to clean rental homes as her full-time job, and she would make me clean with her during the summer months. Not a very fun job as a teenager, but my mother didn't give me much choice. She was a single parent and had developed her own cleaning business. She used to manage about forty homes each month, and summer rental turns were brutal. We'd work ten-to-fifteen-hour days to clean the homes before the next round of visitors moved in. My name is JoAnn, by the way. So nice to meet you." JoAnn smiled and shook Trina's hand.

The two of them chatted about what life was like living on 30A, and they relished in the memories of when it wasn't quite a discovered area yet. They rehashed stories of neighborhood BBQs, beach bonfires, and they both remembered hanging out in the state parks at the secret summer beer keg parties when they were younger. The store was relatively quiet, and before they knew it, they had been chatting for several hours. Occasionally they were interrupted when Trina had to check out a customer, but they were so engrossed in sharing stories, they didn't mind the periodic interruptions.

During their conversation, they realized they both were friends with Wendy, who happened to go to the same church as JoAnn and JoAnn had met Angela and Tanya at one of the Fourth of July parades. To Trina's astonishment, JoAnn revealed that when she was in high school, she had a crush on Bobby, the cashier who worked at the Grayton General

Store. Sheepishly, Trina divulged that Bobby had a crush on her when she was in high school. JoAnn was impressed since Bobby was all high school girls' unreachable crush.

Trina looked at the time and realized she had to begin the closing process. Disappointed that their conversation had to come to an end, they agreed to meet up for coffee next week. After JoAnn left, Trina counted the cash in the register and ran sales reports, then headed home happier than she'd been when she left the house that morning. Meeting new friends was such a rewarding experience. She would never tire of connecting over simple things and enjoying each other's company with no strings attached.

When she got home, she sipped a glass of Cabernet Sauvignon as she turned on the stovetop to make an orzo pasta, spinach, and grilled chicken dinner. David was out in the garage and wouldn't come in until she called him for dinner. She remembered that she'd wanted to call Monica and find out how her conversation with the police had gone. She dialed Monica's number and put her on speaker phone so she could continue to stir the pasta while it simmered.

"Trina! Hey, girl, you read my mind. I meant to call you last week, but I ended up having to take a trip to California to solve a work crisis, then when I came back, I was scheduled to speak at two conventions, so I've been slammed. How the heck are you? Wait, what I really want to know is what the heck is going on down there? I received the strangest call while I was traveling. A sweet-talking detective with the most mysterious southern voice. I felt like I was having a hot conversation with Matthew McConaughey. I could envision sweat dripping through his uniform while he held a pen flirtatiously up to his mouth. Who was that man and why was he calling me asking me about my apron from like a hundred years ago? He said you provided him with my contact information. What the hell?"

Monica was truly the funniest friend she'd ever had. She was as innocent and sweet as a cup of southern tea, but she was as hot and racy as a shot of Fireball at the same time. Monica had a master's degree in public health and was an Executive Level Human Capital Trainer. She traveled all over the world providing boutique level catered training to the top-tier leadership of notable companies across the globe. She had a way of telling the truth in a non-offensive way while still getting the point across. When C-suite executives needed motivation, she could give them a swift kick in the butt while winning them over in the process.

"Girl, you have no idea." Trina filled her in. She didn't mind sharing all the nitty-gritty details with Monica. She could trust Monica with her life. By the time she got to the part about the apron, Monica was laughing out loud.

"I remember how hot I thought I looked in that tight little white apron. I used to squeeze it tight around my waist and then cut a deep V in my T-Shirt to drum up the most tips that I could. That apron witnessed more drunken escapades than I care to remember." She was chuckling on her end of the line remembering their crazy stunts as kids. "I have no idea what ever happened to that thing. Do you think they found my apron or just an apron that looked like mine?"

"I don't know. I remember your apron had polka dots on it. I don't know if that's what they found. What exactly did he say?" Trina asked.

"He texted me a picture of a white apron that had those half circles lining the bottom, and it had the polka dots that you remembered. The dots were really faded, but I could still see them. It looked like mine, but of course I had no way to confirm it. Honestly, it was a wasted call. I told him that I owned one white apron that I had worn for a couple of years, but I had no idea where it was now or where I might have left it. They confirmed where I used to work and asked me a couple of basic questions, but nothing was too invasive. It was sort of weird. Who was the person that you found?"

"I don't know. I wish I knew. I might sleep better at night. I assume the apron is unrelated, but the police had to check to make sure," Trina said.

"We used to sleep over at each other's houses all the time and wore each other's clothes. We also left our stuff at the beach and in the woods after our parties. I could have left the apron in the forest after a late night of partying for all I know. So weird to get a call from the police and think about those things after all these years," Monica said.

"Let me know when you can take a week off and come live the retirement life for a while. I might get you to leave your job before you turn sixty, miss corporate bigwig," Trina mocked Monica playfully as she turned off the stovetop and filled two plates with pasta.

"Love to. I keep saying one of these days I'm going to take a sabbatical. But you know how I love the attention, and if they keep hiring me to speak at these conventions, I can't say no. I'll call you after my crazy season. Love ya, girl." Monica hung up and Trina called David to the kitchen.

They ate dinner and watched a couple of episodes of *Suits* on Netflix and then went to bed. The next day, Trina went to work and was able to process the inventory she had failed to finish the prior day. By noon, customer traffic picked up and she felt happy about a couple of high-priced art sales. Around four thirty, she was making her way around the shop to straighten the merchandise when JoAnn stopped in. She was wearing a hazel tank top with a knee-length khaki skirt. Her hair was pinned on one side, and she had on a long silver necklace with a diamond-shaped pendant.

"Hi, Trina, I brought you a surprise." JoAnn held out a vanilla spiced latte from the Bad Ass Coffee.

"What a pleasant surprise. Thank you. I could use a little pick-me-up. How are you? I wasn't expecting to see you again until we made an official coffee date," Trina said, reaching for the coffee and taking a long sip.

"I had a nail appointment at Happy Nails, so I figured I'd pop in and say hello. I wanted to say that I really enjoyed talking to you yesterday. It was so nice to meet another person who lived down here before it became such a popular destination. Most folks who live here call themselves local, but 90% of them have only lived here for a few years. Even though you didn't live here full time, you sure are well connected enough to consider yourself a true Floridian," JoAnn said, walking over to the counter to rest her purse there.

"I was a tiny bit dishonest with you yesterday. Well, technically not dishonest. I withheld a little detail about my life. My husband is Detective Trenton Oliver. I know you've been working with him recently. I felt bad last night for not divulging that to you during our conversation. Those hours flew by, and I realized when I got home that I never told you. When I asked about your horrible discovery, you were extremely tight lipped. I was very impressed by your commitment to confidentiality.

Trent normally deals with people who love to blab and embellish. You did the exact opposite." JoAnn made direct eye contact with Trina and held a small, shy smile when she complimented her.

"One thing I've learned living around Grayton Beach," Trina said, "is that everyone knows everyone. I'm not exaggerating when I tell you that every single week a customer will come into the shop, and within minutes of chatting, we've identified at least one friend we have in common. It's an honor to meet you officially. Your husband has been nothing but professional, kind, and respectful with me during this entire process. I'll even be honest with you. When your husband speaks, he puts a magical southern gentleman-like spell on me. I would give him my winning lottery ticket if he asked me. He has a special way about him," Trina said with genuine amazement.

JoAnn laughed. "That's the same spell that won me over when I was a junior in high school. He has been sprinkling fairy dust over my head ever since."

Trina smiled, flipped the Open sign to Closed and walked back around to the register. "Have you been together that long? Did he save you from an out-of-town stalker, and you owed him for the rest of your life?"

"To be honest," JoAnn's smile disappeared. "He did."

She paused and looked around the store, checking to ensure all the remaining customers had left, then looked back at Trina. "I've never told a single soul this story, but I feel like I can trust you. Remember when I told you I used to clean houses with my mom? When I was sixteen, my mom asked me to do an extra job for one of our client's rental homes on Monday night of Labor Day weekend. The owner had a quick renter turn and needed a special clean for an early morning Tuesday check-in.

My mom had been working six days straight and needed to rest her back, so I told her I'd take care of it. The house was here in Grayton, so it was no big deal since we lived so close. My mom dropped me off at the property and met with the property owner. I had walked by him as he started to berate my mother for getting there late. I remember listening to him be extremely disrespectful and demeaning to my mother and made me feel like I was a peasant. When I walked past him, I had whispered 'jerk' or something to that effect. I did my best to ignore his berating, knowing I would be on my own once he left. I finished the job around nine o'clock.

"When I was walking home from the rental property, I was assaulted. A man covered my mouth with a cloth and pulled me down the street to a dirt road. He pushed me to the ground and held both my hands above my head. It was so dark outside; it was difficult to clearly see his face. To this day, I swear I recognized his voice, but all I could concentrate on was his horrible cigarette breath and the fact he was kneeling over my body. He leaned in and whispered to me that I was like all the other beach girls who thought they were better than him. He said he was going to teach us one by one that girls were not smarter or more important than professional businessmen." JoAnn paused, and Trina could see how she was reliving the nightmare in her mind.

"Trent and I had started dating at the beginning of that summer, so he had walked to the rental property to walk me home. Luckily, I had dropped my basket of cleaning supplies at the spot where the man grabbed me. When Trent saw the supplies lying on the ground, he assumed something had gone wrong and started looking for me. I was able to spit the cloth out of my mouth and scream. I had no idea Trent was nearby; I was simply screaming for my life. The guy got spooked and took off. Before he ran away, he said to me, "You got lucky tonight, but I know where to find you." JoAnn hugged herself and closed her eyes as she remembered that night.

"I was so petrified, Trina. It was the most terrifying incident of my life. I will always be grateful for Trent. He was my savior then and to this day. He watches out for me like a guardian angel. The reason I'm sharing this with you is because Trent told me you brought in three articles about missing girls. Based on the timeline, we feel like I could have been added to the list of missing girls that night. To this day, I believe it was the owner of the rental property who attacked me. He must have waited for me to finish and took advantage of the opportunity when I was walking by myself. I never told my mom about the attack because I was so scared she could lose her job. I didn't feel like I could report it until I was 100% sure it was the property owner. I waited and waited for weeks to see if I could bump into him again so I could see him and listen to him speak, but he never showed up. About four weeks after the incident, my mom received a call that those rental properties were replacing the cleaning company due to a change in ownership.

The articles you gave Trent sent a chill of memories over me. I had managed to paint black over those memories, and your discovery of three missing girls was like throwing turpentine over my mind. I am so very lucky that nothing happened. If our theory is correct, three women had their lives shortened by this man's personal vendetta. That night, I would have been the fourth, but Trent changed my fate. I wanted to say thank you for reminding me that I am so lucky to be alive and well."

JoAnn reached out and gave Trina an embrace. It was a woman-to-woman hug of strength and friendship. JoAnn pulled back and wiped tears off her cheeks.

"I hope I didn't scare you aware from being a friend by sharing this story, but I couldn't seem to get it off my mind. Yesterday, you offered me only genuine kindness. I truly felt that I had discovered a very special person who I could trust. Making friends has never been easy for me. But you made me feel like I could just be myself which unlocked so many hidden emotions. Trent is and always has been there for me, but it feels good to be able to share my story with you. Thank you for listening." JoAnn smiled and squeezed Trina's hand as a sign of friendship.

Trina reached out and hugged JoAnn again. They held their embrace for several minutes and then pulled back and looked at one another. Trina was at a loss for words. The horror of being attacked must have had a ripple effect on JoAnn's life. Trina tried to recenter herself to help repair her new friend's fragile state of mind.

"JoAnn there simply are no words. I will never claim to understand what you went through, but please believe me when I tell you I am always here for you if you want to talk. I am so very grateful Trent was there for you that night. He has my gratitude forever. Now I understand what might have prompted him to be a detective. I am so sorry that trudging up history by finding that skeleton had such a pronounced effect on your buried memories. Your confidence in my trust means more to me than you realize," Trina said calmly, though she knew she was speaking more clearly than she felt on the inside.

The ladies hugged one more time and made a coffee date for the following Friday. Trina locked up the store and drove home in a stupor.

Trina felt like she had time traveled and body swapped. She could feel herself lying on the ground underneath a strange man, the fight or flight instinct pumping through her limbs. She could envision staring at the black night sky, arms held above her head. She could hear Trent's southern accent calling her name. *"Trina! Trina! I'm coming to get you, Trina."* Her chest felt the weight of a man's body compressing her and straining her muscles. She could hear the man breathing by her neck. She could hear him speaking. *"I know where to find you!"* Trina was a mess. She sat in her driveway, eyes closed, breathing hard, her fingers unconsciously rubbing her scar, over and over again. She was pulled from her thoughts by a knock on the driver's window.

"Trina, are you OK? Did you fall asleep?" David stood outside her window holding Phoenix in his arms. Freckles' paws were propped up on side of her door.

Trina shook her head two or three times and wiped salty tears from her cheeks. She grabbed her purse and opened the door. "Hey, David, I must have dosed off. I had a long day and needed a moment to decompress. What time is it?" she asked as they walked into the house.

"It's almost six. I saw you pull in, but after twenty minutes realized you never actually came into the house. You never sit in your car and rest. Was it busy today?" David didn't wait for her answer and kept on talking. "By the way, the detectives dropped off your mom's old newspaper clippings. Also, Trudy dropped off a newspaper article she wanted you to read and two bags of fresh vegetables. I put all the paperwork on your desk. I also heard on the news that the dental records were inconclusive, so the Sheriff's office is planning on releasing an artist rendering to the public." David reported the update while he washed a couple of dishes that were in the sink.

"Oh, you are never going to believe this. Sean stopped by today and told me that he received a call from the police. That Jeep that he restored years ago is tied to the man's death. I don't know all the details, but the police found car parts near the body and with Sean's help they were able to tie the parts to his Jeep. When he found it abandoned in the trail years ago, it must have been right next to where the body was. Sort of creepy that he didn't even know there was a human lying nearby. So weird, right?"

Being home alone all day, David gushed out all the details of his day. He finished his dishes and opened a bottle of Moone Tsai Cabernet Sauvignon and poured two glasses. "Oh, before I forget, I'm headed to Sean's tomorrow to try to rebuild the brake calipers on my '63. Anyways, I'm starving. What's for dinner?" David finished his dump of data and now stared at the inside of the refrigerator.

Trina felt like a ghost. She was visibly but not mentally here. She took two long, slow gulps of wine. "Would you be OK if we grab a Grace Pizza tonight? I'm beat and need to lie down." Trina, truly exhausted, didn't wait for his answer and walked to the couch to lie down.

"I'm up for pizza. Do you want your Sweet Perfection on cauliflower crust? I'll get the Mediterranean. I'll call it in and pick it up. I'm going to pack up my calibers, so I'll be ready to go to Sean's tomorrow." David picked up his phone and called Grace Pizza while he walked into the garage.

Trina lay on the couch for a while. She drank two glasses of wine and fell asleep. She woke up a couple of hours later and realized that David had already come home from Grace Pizza, eaten his portion, and was watching TV. She ate two pieces of pizza and walked over to her desk to check the day's mail. She glanced through the advertisements and pleading charitable donation letters and threw everything that had come in the mail in the trash. Picking up the newspaper clippings the police had brought back, she reread them all. None of the stories mentioned that girls had been attacked, but of course the girls disappeared so they really didn't know what happened to them before they were taken. Could these disappearances be linked to the man who attacked JoAnn? How did he get away with this for so many years? Why did he disappear after JoAnn's assault? She needed to ask JoAnn the property owner's name.

Why was she feeling such empathy for JoAnn? She felt like she had lived through that paralyzing night herself. She almost felt the bruises on her arms where the man held JoAnn. She struggled to breathe because she felt like her mouth was stuffed with cloth. She was a mess. She placed the articles back on her desk and then saw the envelope from Trudy.

She used a letter opener to open the envelope and pulled out an old newspaper clipping from 1995. The article was a fluff piece about two local businessmen, the Flanigan brothers. It talked about the Salty Bar and how the previously thriving business was struggling to compete now that the Red Bar had opened. Danny said they would not have a problem retaining their business because they knew what true beachgoers wanted to eat and that their bar welcomed people of all ages and had a resident following for over fifteen years. Grayton Beach vacationers flocked to their restaurant establishment and the Red Bar would have to get creative to keep up.

Jerry, the older brother, gloated about how he had developed an empire of beach properties with long rental waiting lists for future vacancies. He was quoted as saying, "I was the first property manager to tie the benefits of restaurant ownership in with our rental properties. Our visitors enjoy the safety and comfort of beautiful beach access in one of five great beach bungalows, with the added benefit of 20% discounts at the Salty Bar. We provide amenities like beach views, paddleboards, and bikes. Our repeat customers enjoy the benefits of our top-notch properties while having access to our lunch and dinner specialties. We truly get to know our customers. We meet each family, we learn their habits, their likes, and dislikes. Their kids are like our kids. We treat them like family. They, in turn, respect my professionalism and the concierge level of service that I offer. Flanigan Brothers, LLC is a company that will thrive here on 30A forever. New businesses can try, but they can't compete with history and years of success."

The article went on and on about how the Salty Bar was one of the early establishments along 30A and that Flanigan Brothers were determined to remain a historic landmark in Grayton Beach.

Reading the missing girl articles, learning about the Flanigan brothers, finding out Sean's Jeep was found in the vicinity of the body, and trying to process her empathy for JoAnn's attack was a storm brewing inside her. Trina felt ill. Reading about Danny and Jerry, Trina tried to call on her memories, but they were gray and fuzzy, like her mind had blocked them out. She was completely frazzled and needed a good night's rest.

She let her dogs out for their last time of the night, washed her face and brushed her teeth. She felt dirty. She felt like she needed to wash her body of the dirt, the mud, the potential of being sexually assaulted. She stepped into a steaming hot shower. She used a washcloth and scrubbed her arms, her legs, her chest. She washed her face repeatedly. She felt like she was trying to help JoAnn rid herself of those awful memories.

She wished JoAnn had reported it so they could have caught that bastard. If she had gone to the police, they could have taken evidence from her. His fingerprints might have been on her body and clothes. His hair could have been trapped in the fabric of her clothing. She may have even had his skin under her nails. Trina scrubbed her nails, scrubbed them raw. She was red all over. Thirty minutes after stepping into the shower, she walked out of the foggy, sauna-like bathroom. She climbed into bed, turned on a sleep app and tried to wipe her mind clear. She crashed. The wine helped. Trina didn't dream, toss, or turn. She slept.

At four o'clock, she blinked her eyes wide open. She realized she was sweating. Her chest and face were damp, and her heart was racing. *Number four. The book of matches said number four. If JoAnn's theory was correct, she would have been the fourth girl to go missing. That's what the number four in the matchbook meant.* Trina jolted herself awake.

Wait. That can't be right. The note also mentioned a shift. Trina assumed a shift correlated to someone's work shift. Since JoAnn worked for her mom, she wouldn't have had a shift. Trina rested her fingers on her forehead. *Maybe the number four doesn't relate to the missing girls.*

Still, she should call Trent in case he hadn't put two and two together. She needed a cup of coffee to clear her head. Trina crept quietly into the bathroom and washed her body, brushed her teeth, and got dressed before sneaking out of the bedroom. David was snoring, oblivious to her departure.

It was too early to call anyone, so she decided to go through her mother's boxes of photographs. She sat down on the couch with the dogs nestled to her side and flipped through several photo albums. Viewing photos of her family spending time on the beach, bike riding and laughing at neighborhood backyard barbeques made Trina smile from the inside out. She couldn't help but chuckle at the out-of-date hairstyles, parachute pants, animal print tops and acid-washed denim skirts. By the time high school rolled around, the pictures documented how Trina and her sisters were feeling confident in cropped T-shirts, long plaid skirts, and overalls. Their hairstyles transitioned from the high and mighty nineteen-eighties style to more simple and tailored cuts mimicking Jennifer Aniston's Rachel character. Trina cherished the pictures that captured her mom packing big coolers full of sandwiches for the beach, her dad leaning over the hood of various cars and both standing near the backyard picnic table with martini glasses in their hands. The family albums woke up feelings of nostalgia for so many years of summer vacations in the bungalow. The stress she'd had when she woke up had dissipated. Relaxed now, she enjoyed the nostalgia that studying the photo albums generated.

After going through six or seven albums, she decided to open the box of random photos shoved in the plastic tub. She immediately realized these were pictures she must have taken with her camera because most of the prints were of her friends. Trina laughed out loud at the image of Monica in her tight apron and T-shirt that revealed excessive cleavage. There were pictures of Wendy and Angela smoking cigarettes sitting by a beach bonfire. Dawn, wearing cutoff shorts and a vintage tee, was sitting on the edge of the picnic table behind Grayton General Store holding a six-pack in her hand. Blurry photos of random kids sitting on beach blankets or near various firepits. Trina found a couple of prints of their friend group paddleboarding at Vortex Springs and jumping off docks. She saw many faces she remembered, but as many she either didn't recognize or had forgotten who they were.

Almost two hours had gone by when Trina heard David stirring and taking a shower. Needing another pick-me-up, Trina made herself another cup of coffee and made David a fresh cup. She let the dogs out and got settled back on the couch to go through more pictures. So far, she hasn't seen too many pictures of adults in the bin. There were a few of her neighbors and her parents' friends in the background, but Trina had hoped she might see more.

At the bottom of the box were pictures taken at the Salty Bar. Trina recognized the cheap, laminated bar that was covered in various random stickers and disposable coasters. The images showed groups of families sitting in booths with their bathing suits on and beach towels wrapped around their waists. Occasionally there were pictures of her friends during a work shift holding up large trays filled with beer glasses filled to the brim. A couple of pictures showed the kitchen staff at the end of the night sitting out back smoking their cigarettes or busboys chumming it up to the pretty waitresses. There were several pictures of men at the bar with their arms around Trina's waitressing friends or pictures of them doing shots.

Trina found one picture of the main cook, Danny, passing orders through the kitchen to the dining room. She had forgotten what he looked like, but once Trina saw his gentle smile, she remembered how kind and protective he was of 'his girls.' Trina finished looking at all the photos and was about to pack them back in the box when her brain processed something she'd seen in one of the photos. She was going to look at them again when her phone rang. It was a few minutes before seven thirty, and Trina was not expecting any phone calls. She looked at the receiver and saw that it was JoAnn who she had only exchanged numbers with yesterday.

Trina tapped the green accept button on her iPhone. "Good morning."

"Trina, it's him!" JoAnn said firmly and with clear trepidation.

"I'm sorry, it's who? What are you talking about, JoAnn?" Trina asked with honest concern.

Freckles and Phoenix both jumped up and nuzzled up to Trina hearing the pitch of her voice. David was standing with his back resting on the island countertop in the kitchen. He took a sip of coffee but tilted his head and raised his left hand questioningly.

"Trent showed me the facial composite of the man you found in the woods. It is him. Trina, you found the property owner who attacked me. I recognized him from the night that Labor Day weekend that he met me at the house. Although I never validated the sound of his voice, I recognize his face. Trent agrees with me but will continue investigating to make 100% sure. We can't publicize this yet, but his disappearance that night, the timeline of death, and the facial composite seem like a match. Trina, so many emotions came over me this morning. Your discovery closed a huge door for me. I lived my life with so much hidden trepidation not knowing what happened to him. If we confirm it's him, I owe you a debt of gratitude," JoAnn said, then let out a long, heavy sigh.

"Oh, JoAnn, I am so relieved this case has brought you closure. It must be terrifying to see his face after all these years. Thank you so much for sharing with me. I owe you a big hug the next time I see you."

The ladies shared a few more words of compassion and acceptance, then Trina said her goodbyes and told JoAnn they should meet up next week. Trina hung up and let out an exasperated sigh. David put down his coffee cup and asked her who she was talking to.

"This week at the shop I met a wonderful new friend. Ironically, she's married to the chief detective on the case, Detective Trent. Since JoAnn grew up here, we found out we had a lot in common. We ended up spending several hours discussing our teenage years. Since we bonded so quickly, she ending up sharing details of a harrowing event she experienced as a teenager. Just thinking about what she went through still rattles my nerves. I guess when she was in high school, she was assaulted one night after work. Luckily, Trent rescued her before the attacker could cause too much harm but the effect on JoAnn was the same. You're never going to believe this, but she just called because she thinks the man I found in the woods was her attacker. Is that crazy or what?" Trina said, still in shock.

"Whoa! That is insane. How old was she when this happened? Was the attack serious? Who was the guy?" David spewed out questions.

"I think she said she was about fifteen years or sixteen old. Luckily, he was stopped before he caused her any physical harm, but he left an emotional scar that will never truly heal." Trina couldn't help but feel a sense of accomplishment at maybe having a tiny part in providing JoAnn solace. David finished his coffee, rinsed out his cup and turned it upside down on a towel. He told JoAnn he had to jump on a couple of work conference calls, then headed to his home office.

Could she really have found that horrible man? And if so, why had the man end up in the state park? Would they be able to confirm his identity? How did he die? Trina was aghast. Did his accidental death stop a string of attacks that could have gone on for years? The deep pit of pain in Trina's stomach had returned. Glimpses of a man straddling a woman. Horrible images of girls being pinned to the ground filled her head. Would they ever find the three missing girls, or would that remain a mystery forever?

She picked up the pictures to put them back in the box, then remembered an image triggered a recollection. She grabbed the stack and began looking through them again. As she came across one photo, she sucked in a sudden breath.

Him. His face had been wiped from Trina's memory. Now, a tsunami of memories crashed into Trina's mind.

That night.

Fear. Suffocating. Fighting.

The sounds of a crash.

Panicking.

Running barefoot. Hiding. Panting.

Packing and leaving.

Forgetting.

Last Week Before
Her First Week

1995

Trina had survived her senior year without Christopher. Unfortunately, she had spent an enormous amount of time thinking about their last date of the summer before.

She had been so excited, so eager. She had been ready to truly be with Christopher, her last chance before he left for college. Christopher had made a dinner reservation for the two of them, and they ate a fabulous meal and walked Grayton Beach for hours. They talked about post college, how much money they needed to pay for all their wishes and dreams, and of course they talked about his departure. Trina's stomach had both butterflies and sparks of fire in anticipation of the night's end. She had come prepared. She wore her prettiest undergarments and sprayed herself with her sister's perfume.

Having recently celebrated her eighteenth birthday, she felt more mature and ready to dive into her sexuality. She was mentally ready and emotionally committed. Even though she had spent four years with Christopher and knew his body language very well, she couldn't figure out what he was thinking that night. They sat on their favorite spot in a secluded part of the beach situated at an abandoned, broken-down boardwalk that was hidden between two dunes. Lying on their backs, they could hear the water and see the gorgeous scattering of stars in the black sky.

Eventually, their hand holding led to kissing, then gentle touching and eventually exploring. Trina's heart felt like it was going to explode out of her chest. She was trying to be in the moment, but all she could think about was going all the way. They moved from the boardwalk to the beach blanket. No one was around as it was late on a Sunday night. She was not holding back, and her willingness was obvious. Christopher explored her body as she did her fair share of exploring as well. When she thought they couldn't control themselves any longer, she spoke up.

"I'm ready," Trina said in a desperate whisper. The only thing she had on was her panties, and he was down to his boxers.

Christopher groaned, but it was more of exasperation than pleasure. He leaned in and gave her one of the very best French kisses she had ever had. "Trina," he said slowly, almost painfully as he pulled away from her lips. "I have been waiting for you to say those words to me for an excruciatingly long time. I really don't know how I have controlled myself for so long. Your body would drive any guy crazy." Christopher sat up with his legs straddled to each side of her stomach.

She was trying to listen to what he was saying, but his actions didn't match his words. She didn't want to think about it anymore. She almost said, 'Just do it already!' but she held back, waiting for him to make the final move. She had dreamt of this moment. She knew Christopher was going to make her feel extremely special, and she was ready to make that final connection.

"Babe, I really want to finish what we started." He paused. "But I can't. I'm leaving for college in four days. I can't take your virginity and then just leave you." He sighed and bent over to kiss her.

"Yes, you can, Christopher. I'm telling you, yes," Trina said, thinking he was playing a game.

"I can't do it, Trina. I care for you so much, and I don't know how to tell you this." A long moment of silence passed.

"Tell me what, Christopher?" Trina said and propped herself up on her elbows, her long hair flowing over her shoulders.

"I think it's best if we... I think we should take a break. I'm headed to college in Pennsylvania, you're heading into your senior year." Christopher shifted so he was sitting beside her.

"Are you serious? Christopher, look at me. Look at me! You're serious? Just like that you've decided it's over? Christopher, you must be joking, right? After everything we have experienced together. We're perfect for one another. I know being apart will be difficult, but you can't do this. You won't. You would never break my heart, Christopher."

Trina sat up, dumbfounded, and put her bra and shirt back on. Was she dreaming? Was this a nightmare? Was he just messing with her? The only sound was the waves crashing onto the shore.

"Are you actually breaking up with me right now?"

"Yeah. Sort of," he said, still not making eye contact.

"You called me your slice of heaven. Was it all meaningless? Is this what you really want? Why? Is it because I didn't sleep with you? Is that why? I just said I was ready. I'm finally ready!" She stood up and started pacing.

"No. No, Trina. It's not that. Believe me. I would love to make love to you. You mean so much to me. I respect you so much, Trina. I do. I know how much you've valued this moment, and I couldn't live with myself if I took it from you and then left. I'm leaving soon and I don't think it's fair to make promises about the future.

Trina put her hands to her face and cried heavy, emotional tears. She bawled. He wrapped his arms around her and held her. After a few minutes, she grabbed her bag and ran barefoot down the beach in the dark night. She ran with tears of anger, frustration and disbelief raging down her face. When she made it to the back of her neighborhood, she crawled over the dunes and ran to the boardwalk. Her breathing started to settle as she sulked her way home.

She was in complete shock. She had thought about this night for so long. She had performed the act so many times in her head. He was going to be so gentle, so caring, so loving. Instead, he shattered her heart. Christopher had been her everything. How could he spend the night showing her how much he cared for her, doing pretty much everything except that one thing. *How could he lead me on? How could he do this?* She'd thought she knew him. Understood him. Loved him, even.

Unbeknownst to her, Christopher had followed her home to make sure she got there safely. He tried to talk to her on the porch, but she went inside without a word and locked the door. He continued to reach out over the next couple of days, but she was devastated and refused to talk to him.

Finally, about a month later, she relented, and they had a long conversation over the phone. He told her there was a chance they could reconnect in the future, but for now, he wanted to explore the college world. She continued to be in shock and couldn't seem to let go of what they'd shared over four years. She refused to throw away her charm necklace, wrapping it around her wrist and wearing it as a bracelet instead. She looked at the charms as a reminder that you never truly know someone.

She spent her last year of high school motivated to excel personally becoming stronger and more independent. She convinced herself that she didn't need a man to be happy. She thought about Christopher often early on, but by the end of the year, she was ready to move on. After graduation, she left in her CRX and headed to Florida alone. Christopher had secured a summer job in Pennsylvania and would not be returning to the Panhandle. She had been accepted to several colleges and was headed to Auburn University in the fall.

She made up her mind she was going to stay far away from boys this summer and concentrate on work to save up for college. Her parents were only going to spend a couple of weeks in Florida over the summer so they could continue supporting Jane and her new bakery shop back home. Trina was basically on her own this summer. She couldn't believe she had only had eight weeks left before she headed off to college. She felt like she'd grown so much the past four years. She knew much more about herself and felt way more confident.

Since Trina was living by herself, several of her friends moved in with her at the bungalow. The BBB were committed to having the best, last summer before college. Monica, Wendy, and Angela kept most of their clothes at Trina's house, and the girls enjoyed cooking dinner together on their nights off, sitting in the backyard drinking wine coolers and simply enjoying each other's company. Monica tried to get Trina to flirt with the college guys who came into the restaurant, but Trina was not interested. She was determined to be independent and concentrate on her own needs. She read one new mystery a week and spent her free time lounging on the beach engrossed in one chapter after another.

About three weeks into summer, Trina spent the day shopping at the outlet mall about thirty minutes away. She was dressed casually, and although it was hot and humid outside, she had left her hair hanging loosely down her shoulders and was wearing her glasses. Normally, Trina only wore her glasses to drive or watch TV. She learned to function without wearing them on a day-to-day basis, but her vision was getting progressively worse the older she got. She didn't like to wear her glasses unless she had to, but she figured she wouldn't see anyone she knew this far from 30A. She decided to stop in at a small Thai place in Destin to grab a Pad Thai to take home and enjoy on her night off.

It was early in the afternoon, so the place was almost deserted. Trina sat in a small booth waiting for her meal to be ready. When she heard her name, she went up to the counter to grab her bag, a waiter accidentally bumped into her as he came out of the kitchen, spilling a bowl of soup all over Trina's shirt. The owner of the shop apologized profusely. He told her that her meal would be free, and she could go clean up in the bathroom down the hall. Being a waitress herself, she didn't get mad at the accident. She'd had similar accidents herself while carrying trays of food. As Trina walked toward the bathroom, she heard a voice coming from the men's room as the door was slightly ajar. She recognized the voice as Danny's. Trina stopped and listened.

"You know I need to get back. Billy is going to wonder where I am," he whispered in a low growl.

"He can handle it. It's Wednesday night, and it's overcast today. The place will be slow for the next couple of hours. Come on, Danny, please. I need more of you," a woman said in a sultry tone.

Trina felt immobilized. That didn't sound like Janice. Trina was extremely curious. Who was he with? Should she risk walking past them to get to the ladies' room? She felt guilty for listening, but she couldn't help herself. The sounds slowly escalated. The woman was obviously enjoying herself. Trina felt so awkward. She spun around and walked back to the front register. If they came out of the bathroom, would they recognize her with her glasses on and hair down? Trina felt like running out without grabbing her food, but the manager said, "Hey, don't forget your meal."

"I decided not to clean up." Trina said.

"Are you sure? Your entire shirt is stained. If you don't wash that out, your shirt will be ruined," the manager said, nodding at her shirt.

"No, I'm going to be late for a meeting. I'll clean up when I get home. No worries," Trina said, trying to hurry him up.

"Sorry for our clumsiness. Here is your meal. Again, we apologize."

Trina was about to turn and leave when she heard Danny and the woman laughing and passing behind her. Trina waited a beat, then turned around slowly and watched their backs as they went out the front door.

"Oh my God!" Trina exclaimed.

"Is everything OK, miss?" asked the manager.

"Oh, yes. Sorry. Thank you." Trina grabbed her bag and slowly walked to the front of the restaurant, peering out the windows. She looked closely at Danny and the woman, who had climbed into Danny's Jeep.

Trina's eyes were not playing tricks on her. Danny was fooling around with Jerry's wife, Sherry Lee. Trina was in shock. She never in a million years would have guessed Danny would cheat on his wife, and never in a billion years that he would do it with his brother's wife. Damn!

Trina waited until they drove away before she walked outside. She sat in her car completely exasperated by what she had just witnessed. Danny. Good. Hardworking. Polite. Respectful. Kind. And she'd thought, trustworthy. She wasn't shocked that Sherry Lee would cheat. She was always fooling around. But Danny? Trina could not fathom why he would do such a thing.

She drove home in a daze. She pulled into her driveway and waved at her neighbor, Miss Trudy, who was outside gardening. She parked near the side door and sat in the car for a minute thinking. Should she approach Danny? Should she tell anyone about what she heard? After about two minutes of sitting there, she convinced herself it was not her place to spread rumors. She would have to keep this to herself. She got out of the car and walked to the side door, only then realizing that Bobby had been sitting on the porch steps the whole time.

"Bobby, what are you doing here?" Trina blurted out.

"Hello to you too, Trina," he said with a wide white smile that glowed off his deep, dark tan. He was wearing a button-down, white shirt with the top three buttons unclasped revealing a muscular, slightly hairy chest. He was also wearing light-brown khaki shorts that fit his physique very complimentary. He pulled his arm out from his back and held a to-go bag in his hand as he stood up.

"I stopped by the Salty Bar, and they said you had the night off. I wanted to see if we could enjoy dinner together. I brought your favorite, Danny's special fish tacos with a side of his famous broccoli salad."

"How on earth do you know what I like to eat? And hello, by the way," Trina said, walking up to greet him with a small side hug.

"I know more about you than you might think. Come on, let's eat. We may need to warm these tacos up in your microwave."

Trina walked to the side of him and unlocked the door. "That is so nice of you to bring me dinner, but I brought home Thai food," she said, raising the bag in her hand like show-n-tell.

"I don't care what we eat as long as I am with you."

Trina was about to turn him down. She really didn't want to be around guys after witnessing what she had thirty minutes ago. But when she looked up at him, he looked so happy to be there. Plus, he was looking extremely good, she had to admit.

"Monica, Angela, and Wendy will be coming home soon since they basically live here. They're all on shift tonight but ever since the Red Bar opened, business has slowed down." Trina said hoping the implication was clear; someone could walk in at any minute.

"Yes, I know. They're the ones who told me you would spend your night off sitting on the couch reading a book."

"Ah. OK, then. I guess we are eating dinner together. Come on in." Trina opened the door, allowing him to walk in front of her. As he passed, she couldn't help but breathe in his smell. He didn't wear cologne, but there was a natural, masculine scent about Bobby. Geez, why did he have to be so darn attractive? She would only eat dinner with him and then send him on his way.

They spent the first hour sitting at the back patio table sharing each other's food and sipping on wine coolers and the beer he had brought. Bobby asked her questions about the books she liked to read, inquired what kind of music she enjoyed and delved into her plans for college. He shared with her that he was working toward a bachelor's degree in criminology, which surprised her. He said it was going to take him several years because he could only take a couple of classes a semester since he still needed to run the General Store. The more they sat together and drank, the more comfortable she felt. Trina was enjoying the slight buzz as she opened her third wine cooler. She was not a big drinker, so it didn't take much. With or without alcohol, he was extremely easy to talk to, which surprised her because he rarely spoke to anyone else when they stopped in at the store.

"You look absolutely adorable with those glasses on and your hair down," Bobby said.

Trina had totally forgotten she had her glasses on and immediately felt self-conscious about her appearance. She raised her hand to remove her glasses.

"No, leave them on. I like them."

She dropped her hand but nibbled on her fingernail because the intensity with which Bobby looked at her made her so aware of herself. He grabbed her hand and pulled her up.

"Let me play music for you. Do you have a radio? I know exactly what station to play. This station plays the best songs."

Trina grabbed a radio from the patio cabinet. Several songs played and he danced with her. When "Call Me" by Deee-Lite started playing, he said, "Oh this is perfect."

Trina had never heard it before. Bobby had her cracking up as he sung the words to her. While he sang, he pretended to hold a phone in his hand, and he spun her around with his hands. She couldn't help but laugh at his foolishness.

The next song he didn't like, so he fiddled with the stations until he recognized another song. The song he picked was "Never Get Enough" by Waterliliies. Again, Trina had never heard the song. This time, he knelt on his knees while holding her right hand, singing into an invisible microphone. He was a horrible singer. Totally off key, not that she knew what the song was supposed to sound like. He had her laughing hysterically. He sang along with several more songs on the radio. Finally, he wrapped his arms around Trina and sang "I Want You (She's So Heavy)" without any background music. This song, by the Beatles, Trina recognized. He sang slowly and purposefully while standing up close and personal. He placed her hands up to the center of her chest and held them.

When he finished, he tilted his head down and kissed her. She didn't stop him. The kiss was soft and long-lasting, and he didn't press her to do more. He finished the kiss and pulled away a little, moving his hands to her waist.

"Trina, you are so special. You're smart. Hard-working. You're gentle, caring, and kind. Respected and responsible. There is something so genuine about you that attracts me to you. It's like you have a magnet inside your heart that pulls me to you. I am infatuated with— "

He didn't get to finish his sentence. Trina reached up and kissed him. She went all in. She wrapped her right hand around his blond locks, her left around his upper arm muscles. He accepted her offer. They made out for several minutes and then he slowly moved her back against the wall of the house. He took off her glasses and tossed them on the patio. With her back against the wall, Trina had an internal conversation while he started to explore.

What the hell are you doing? You didn't even invite him over. You've never even been on a date with him. Heck, you've never had more than a two-minute conversation with him before today. Why are you letting him touch you in this way? Oh gosh, you know why. He's absolutely gorgeous, and he's obviously attracted to you. Oh man! This is feeling way too damn good, and those wine coolers aren't hurting either.

He was moving down her neck. His mouth and tongue found her chest. Trina was breathing in and out slowly trying to contain herself. She pulled him back up to her mouth. After several minutes, she pushed him away slightly. She slowly unbuttoned the rest of his shirt and tossed it to the patio floor. She reached up and felt his muscles. She moved from the shoulder down to his pecks, then let her finger slowly trace the center of his stomach until it reached the top of his shorts.

He looked at her and whispered the words to the Beatles song again while her finger rested at the top of his pants. His voice was soft and tender as he slowly, purposefully spoke instead of sang the words, telling her he wanted her so bad it was driving him mad.

Trina pulled his head to hers and kissed him savagely. She felt like she couldn't get enough. He had a magical touch. She might take this farther than she knew she should. He walked her backward toward the door while their mouths were still connected. They stumbled over Trina's flip-flop but kept navigating toward the door. He stepped on Trina's glasses, and they heard a crack. They stopped for a half a second and then reunited without saying a thing. They stepped over the threshold. He pulled away only long enough to take her shirt off, dropping it on the kitchen floor. They reconnected like there truly was a magnet pulling them together. He bent down and picked her up, so she was straddling his waist. They slowly made it over to the couch in the living room.

As he gently rested her down and he began to stretch out beside her, they heard a car door shut. They separated, looked at each other and laughed. They jumped off the couch and found their shirts, pulling them back on as they ran outside and quickly sat at the table, where their dirty plates still rested next to the empty food containers.

Wendy and Angela walked in, chatting away, and went into the kitchen and opened the refrigerator. After about two minutes, Trina and Bobby were discovered sitting at the table in the backyard. Both girls joined them. Wendy and Angela of course gave Trina lots of eye contact, trying to discern what exactly had been going on. Trina and Bobby initiated small talk to hide the fact they had been fooling around. After a few minutes, the girls excused themselves to go take showers, but they made sure to give Trina serious looks as they walked back inside.

"So, let's pick up where we left off," Bobby said with a wolf's grin. He easily picked her up and had her legs wrapped around him before she could object.

"Wait," Trina said, laughing. "They'll be watching us from the bedroom window, I'm sure of it."

"Being watched will make it that much more interesting," he said as he slyly walked her to the backside of the shed in the backyard. He laid her on the grass and was not shy about picking up where they'd left off. Trina initially was hesitant, but soon tumbled like a sandcastle. What had gotten into her. It took her years to let Christopher touch her this way. Why was she giving in so easily to Bobby?

"Oh gosh! Bobby, too fast. You're going too fast," she whispered as he centered in on her chest.

"You are symmetry in motion, Trina. Every inch of you is perfect. I have wished." His tongue reached inside her mouth. "I have dreamed." He tugged on her tongue. "I have fantasized." He kissed her in ways she didn't know you could receive. "I'll stop if you want me to. If this is too much," he said as he went lower and showed her what he had been fantasizing about.

"Oh gosh. You have to stop!" Trina pushed him off. "I'm not going to lie. I didn't know I could feel this way. But Bobby, we haven't even gone on a date," she said, laughing and putting her shirt back on.

"I can take you on a date. I can take you on as many dates as you want. I know that you and I are meant to be together. I've known that since the first time I saw you when you saved a deer." He sat next to her and grabbed her hand.

"Let's see if we can reverse this motion picture back a couple of reels," she said as she stood up, extending a hand to help him stand. "I'm only working the lunch shift over the next two days, so why don't we grab dinner and see if we really are compatible or whether we both drank too much tonight."

"It's a date. I'll pick you up at six tomorrow," he said, leaning down and planting another amazing kiss on her lips. "I mean it, Trina. We are meant to be." He let go of her hand and walked out the fence's side gate to the driveway. "I'll be counting down the hours and dreaming of you tonight. I can think of so many ways to make you happy." He smiled, waved, got into his car, and drove off.

Trina couldn't help but smile. Witnessing her boss's affair and getting down and dirty unexpectedly with Bobby; she'd had quite an eventful day. And she had to admit, after a yearlong stretch with no physical contact, it had woken up her senses. But what was she doing? She was going to be leaving for college in a couple of weeks. She shouldn't be getting in a relationship. Did he even want a relationship, or did he want only to get physical? Who knew.

She grabbed the dirty plates, broken eyeglasses and walked back into the kitchen. Both the girls were standing at the kitchen counter.

"Sooooo. Did you finally get down and dirty with Bobby?" Wendy asked.

"What? What makes you say that?" Trina said, not making any eye contact with either of them.

"Well, your face is flushed. Your hair is tousled. You're holding broken glasses. Your shirt is on inside out, and more importantly, we saw you! The back of the shed is totally visible from the second-floor bedroom window," Angela said with a huge grin on her face.

"What? No way. Is it really?" Trina said, putting her hand to her face in shame.

"Gotcha! It isn't, but we figured that's what you were doing back there," Wendy said. "Was he as good as he looks?"

"Better!" Trina said, walking away from the girls and heading upstairs, leaving them begging for more! She looked at herself in the bathroom mirror. A magnet pulled us together. The pull was real. It was strong. If her girlfriends hadn't come home, Trina wasn't sure how far she would have gone. Bobby melted away her inhibitions. She felt sexy with him. She had been more connected to her body's desires. Shockingly, she admitted to herself that she had always found Bobby attractive, but she'd locked those feelings away in an attempt to stay true to Christopher. Tonight proved to her that she was free to explore, and Bobby would be a nice field trip. Very nice indeed!

Before she left for work, she left her broken glasses on the counter with a note addressed to her mom to drop them off for repair. She couldn't help but laugh out loud remembering the sound of plastic and glass breaking as they navigated backward into the house. Her mom, who was arriving back in Florida today, didn't need to know those tiny details. She only needed to know Trina needed the repair done quickly before she left for college. Leaving the house in a great mood, Trina grabbed her camera before heading to work in hopes of taking more pictures to finish out her roll of film for the end of summer.

As they waited for their first set of lunch customers, Monica and Trina talked about all the things they had successfully manipulated Jerry into doing at the restaurant over the last year. The list included washing silverware, stacking bar glasses, opening a jar of mayonnaise, and their favorite, carrying food out to customers. Trina had never been able to capture Jerry on camera completing a manual task, but today was the day.

Danny had informed the girls that a local newspaper was stopping by to interview them for an article about restaurants on 30A. Jerry and Danny had cleaned themselves up and both their wives were there looking prim and proper. Danny was the first one to be interviewed. He stood by his grill wearing blue jeans, a white T-shirt and an apron and answered the reporter's questions about their most popular dishes, their primary clientele, and their ability to attract customers. He spoke about menu concoctions and remained relatively humble while attempting to elicit excitement for several of his upcoming menu additions.

Jerry stood behind the bar wearing a white, crisp, colored shirt, lightly faded blue jeans, perfected coiffed hair, and hint of cologne. Jerry's physical attractiveness initially captivated the reporter's attention, but once he began spewing his better than thou attitude, Trina and Monica recognized the growth of disdain in the reporter's questions.

"What makes your restaurant stand out from your neighboring local hot spots?"

"Our attention to detail, the consistency of our service and our ever-changing menu pushes our restaurant to the top. I have generated a devoted following of customers. Stop in at the restaurant seven days a week and you will find every table filled with both Florida residents and annual visitors. I took this restaurant from a tiny food stand to an elevated, full-service restaurant. It was my business expertise and vision that transformed the Salty Bar. No other restaurant on 30A, or the entire Panhandle for that matter, can compete with our offerings."

"The Red Bar seems to have quickly attracted both a consistent flow of consumers as well as stellar food reviews. Is your restaurant as relevant in today's market as you think it is?" the reporter asked.

Trina could see Jerry's nostrils flare as he listened to her questions. He spewed information about how he'd created a new business model by mixing rental properties with restaurant discounts. Trina could read the contempt in the reporter's face as Jerry continued to rattle on.

"In five years, do you think the Salty Bar will still be in business, and if so, why?"

"The Salty Bar will not only be in business in five years, but it will also be ranked as one of the top five dining establishments along 30A. Customers appreciate our food and our fantastic views. They, in turn, respect me for my professionalism and the concierge level of service that I offer. The Flanigan Brothers, LLC is a company that will thrive here on 30A forever."

Monica and Trina rolled their eyes at Jerry's confidence. He was a narcissist for sure. They'd heard enough and began cleaning up from lunch shift. Monica grabbed the trash bag from the bar and Trina filled a tray full of dirty dishes.

"Do you agree?" asked the reporter, looking at Monica and Trina seeking their opinion.

The girls both agreed that customers lined up daily to enjoy the great views and tasty dishes.

The reporter turned back to Jerry. "How involved are you, Jerry, in the day-to-day running of the business?"

"I support Danny and the staff in every respect. If they need me, I am here. 100%. Right, girls?" Jerry looked at Monica and Trina with a death stare hidden beneath his sly smile.

Monica jumped at the chance. "Jerry may manage the finances, but he is never timid about lending a helping hand." Monica raised the big bag of trash in her hand toward him.

Jerry's eyes widened, and his smile slipped into a frown. The reporter turned and looked at him. Jerry put on a happy face and said, "Like I said, always happy to help. Let me take that for you girls so you can make our customers a priority." He grabbed the bag and begrudgingly walked to the back door.

Trina ran to the staff cubby, grabbed her camera, and followed him. As he threw the bag in the trash, Trina aimed the camera through the back window and snapped three pictures. The last captured Jerry's face, which was a mixture of hatred and false teamwork. Trina quickly returned the camera to the cubby before Jerry returned.

The reporter completed her interview after asking a couple more questions. Jerry kept his cool while she was there, but as soon as she walked out the door, he expressed his irritation by rattling off ridiculous tasks for the girls to complete before they finished their shift. The girls spent thirty extra minutes knocking out his commands, and Trina headed to the shed to grab a few boxes of supplies. She laughed to herself when she saw that Jerry had a big tray full of Red Bar matches, flyers and copies of their cocktail menu on his desk. She thought it was hysterical that he collected them off the tables, as if removing them would erase the Red Bar's existence.

She noticed a glint of shiny silver on the floor by his desk. She walked over and saw a girl's purse sticking out from under his desk. Covered in sequins, the small purse was something a teenager would carry. She wondered if that was a lost and found purse from the restaurant. People left things all the time, and they tossed them in a bin in the shed once a week. She was about to pick it up when she heard Jerry talking to Danny outside.

"She should be able to publish a strong, positive article. Let's hope it becomes free advertisement. You are looking worn down, Danny. How much weight have you lost?" Jerry asked.

"I don't know. Maybe a couple pounds. Not a big deal. You look like you've lost weight too. We both need belts to keep our pants up," Danny joked.

"I needed to lose weight so it's fine. Alright, I need to head to the rentals. Get some rest. Labor Day Weekend will be here before we know it. I hope you're ready. How are we going to handle everything once the college kids leave?" Jerry said.

"I'll figure something out," Danny replied confidently.

"You better, Danny. I'm relying on you. We have too much invested in this place." Jerry walked off in a huff.

Trina waited a minute and then slowly closed the shed door and locked it. She turned around, expecting no one to be there, but Danny was sitting on one of the chairs puffing on a cigarette.

"Pretty slick getting Jerry to do another task," Danny said with a tiny grin on his face.

"What? What are you talking about?" Trina asked, wondering how Danny knew.

"Trina, nothing goes on around here that I don't know about. I think it's kind of funny. It's good for him. Make him eat his own words," Danny said, pushing his cigarette butt in the empty dish and walking back into the restaurant.

Monica walked out right after Danny walked in. She told Trina she had clocked them out for the day. As they walked to the car, they couldn't help but exclaim a little joy at their successful Jerk Jerry Challenge. Trina told Monica that she'd ask her mom to develop the roll of film with Jerk Jerry pictures. It would give them something to laugh about when they returned next summer. Monica hugged Trina and left in her own car, as she had plans with her parents. Once Trina got back home, she jumped in the shower to get ready for her date with Bobby. She was nervous, but as soon as she saw him at the front door, all the jitters went away.

The date went fabulously. They really enjoyed each other's company. A new relationship was ignited. After that date, she spent every spare moment with Bobby, and the final weeks of summer flew by. Between working at the restaurant, preparing for college, and spending time with her girlfriends, she was shocked one day to realize she only had one week left before she drove to Auburn University. She was teetering back and forth between anticipation and regret, knowing that her new relationship complicated things.

Before she knew it, Labor Day weekend was upon them. She was working a crazy number of hours but scheduled Thursday night off. The rest of her friend group had left Florida to head to their own colleges for sorority rush week, leaving only Monica and Trina for the Labor Day shifts. She was so tired of working and wanted to have a couple of days off to relax before driving to college. She reminded Danny, twice, that Saturday would be her very last shift since she was leaving for college on Tuesday. Her parents would drive up the following weekend to help her put the finishing touches on her dorm room.

She decided to get a little dolled up for her potential last night together in Florida with Bobby. He took her to dinner at Café Thirty-A. Trina really enjoyed the meal and the relaxed ambiance. After dinner, Bobby took her to a small, deserted section of the beach where there was an adorable little covered gazebo that looked out on the water. Bobby pulled out a bottle of champagne to celebrate Trina's departure for college. They sat on a small blanket, drinking, talking, and planning. Bobby asked if he could come up and visit her at Auburn. She didn't say yes, but she didn't say no. He joked that she better not find a hot college kid who was going to break his heart by tearing her heart away and made sure she knew he had eyes for no one else. He'd brought a small radio and was playing romantic music. While they talked, he held her hand, not initiating anything more, simply enjoying her company.

Knowing this could truly be their last night to be together, Trina decided to be the aggressor. She climbed on top of him, caressing his chiseled chin, firm chest, and sculpted biceps. "Bobby, I can't make any promises about the future or tell you I'll wait for you. I can tell you that it has been a surprisingly fun couple of weeks. Can you help me remember my last Thursday night here before life as I know it changes?"

She grabbed a hold of his hands and held them above his head. She leaned in, her chest resting on his chest. She whispered in his ears; so soft he could barely hear her. "Bobby, can you show me how much you are going to miss me?" Trina could feel his body respond to her question. Trina leaned back and looked into his eyes.

"With your permission," Bobby said, "I will make you remember Thursday night for the rest of your life. Let me show you what your body is capable of"

And with that, Trina and Bobby explored each other's bodies and discovered new heights of pleasure. Trina might not be ready to commit to a long-distance relationship, but she was fully committed to Bobby tonight, and Bobby showed her many ways that fantasies can become reality.

Trina was going to go to college with more experience than she'd had when the night began.

The Flat Tire That Changed Her Life

1995

Bobby dropped Trina off at her house very late Thursday night. To say that she was a different person after her evening on the beach with Bobby was an understatement. Bobby was attentive, generous even. He had successfully bulldozed the mystique that hovered over Trina's idea about what sex should be opening her eyes to things she had only dreamed about. Although she thoroughly enjoyed her evening with Bobby, she had to be honest with herself that she still reminisced about Christopher. Bobby was sweet and funny, and his personality was a seamless fit with her own. Frustratingly, though, it was still difficult to give 100% of her emotional self to him, or to anyone for that matter. The anticipation of heading to college was overpowering. She didn't think she should lead Bobby on by offering a commitment, and she only had a couple days left to think about her situation.

Trina woke up with dread on Friday morning. Knowing she had two days off before she was going to drive to Auburn gave her a glimpse of her approaching freedom, but she'd promised Danny she would work doubles Friday and Saturday. She was going to have to put on a false happy face over the next forty-eight hours to trudge through. Still, she appreciated the hours that Danny had passed her way. Saving over five thousand dollars was a solid base before heading to college. Trina's work-load also made family time a precious commodity. Her parents were looking forward to spending two solid days with her before she left, as her departure would turn them into empty nesters.

She drove to work absentmindedly, in a daydream thinking about her evening with Bobby. She couldn't help but remember his caresses, his kisses, and his patience. She wished they had more time to get to know each other. Her thoughts bounced from his warm, strong hands on her hip to his—.

Trina felt a bump, followed by a hissing sound. The car swerved, hitting a parking barrier, and Trina quickly pulled over to the side of the road. She stepped out of the car and immediately noticed it appeared to be resting at a slant. As she approached the rear of the car, she was frustrated to see a flat tire. Bending down to inspect, she saw a broken piece of brown glass stuck in the rubber. The metal rim resting on the ground. She must have driven over a beer bottle. What horrible timing! Just what she needed right before she was going to head to college. Luckily, she was close enough to work to walk the rest of the way. She was going to have to call her dad and see if her parents could rescue the car. Trina grabbed her backpack and keys and walked the rest of the way to work.

Eight minutes later, hot, and sweaty, she walked into the back of the restaurant and clocked in. September heat in Florida was a killer. She called her parents as soon as she arrived and requested a car rescue. While she waited for her parents to stop by, she jumped right into the pre-lunch tasks, performing them in a zombielike mode. She was physically there but mentally elsewhere. She was thinking about Bobby and comparing him to Christopher. Thinking about all the packing she had to do to get ready for college. Anxiously contemplating how her life was going to change when she moved onto campus.

About forty minutes later, her mom came in to grab Trina's key ring. Before she took the key chain, she asked Trina if she had the backup can of mace. Trina confirmed that it was hanging off her backpack. Her mom told her to call later if she couldn't find a ride home. Monica, having overhead their conversation, offered to drop Trina off after work. Once Trina's mom left, Monica teased Trina.

"It's sweet that she's worried about you, but does she really think a can of mace is going to protect you from a potential kidnapping or sexual assault? I would be more worried about your car. What will you do if they can't fix it in time for you to leave on Tuesday?" Monica asked as she waited for meals at the kitchen window for her party of five.

"It's more of a security blanket. I've gotten in the habit of holding it in my hand when I leave. I still think about poor Jasmine whenever I walk out of here alone," Trina said as she stood beside Monica waiting for her appetizers for a family of four. "I don't have a big, strapping man to protect me anymore. And if it makes my mom and dad feel better, I don't mind hanging on to it."

"Speaking of a strapping man, how was your date with Bobby last night? Did he show you a good time?" Monica said as she filled up her tray with the final plate.

"As a matter of fact, he showed me a very good time. It was a Thursday night I will remember for a very long time." Trina smiled at Monica.

"Oh, do tell, girl. Let me drop this off and meet me by the bar to tell me all the juicy details!"

Monica rushed off with her tray, and a couple minutes later they both stood behind the bar making themselves useful by stacking clean beer mugs. Trina gave Monica the lowdown on the dinner and the drive to the private beach spot. She tiptoed around the juicy details, but Monica squeezed out enough information that she could tell Trina had a momentous evening.

"Does this mean Bobby and you are a thing? Warning you now frat boys will not be as good looking or hardworking as Bobby. He may be a keeper," Monica suggested.

"To be honest, last night was *amazing!* But Bobby lives here, and I'm going to college. I'm hesitant to commit."

"Well, first things first. You need to take off Christopher's necklace. I noticed you moved it from your neck to your wrist, but it is time to move on from your first true love. Especially after last night. Obviously, you must have gotten over Christopher. He had his moment, but you need to move on." Monica gave Trina a little hug and left Trina at the bar to go check on one of her tables.

Trina's back was to the kitchen, so she didn't notice that Sherry Lee had sauntered into the main room and was sitting at the end of the bar.

"Boy troubles, Trina?" Sherry Lee asked.

"Not really. Just time for me to see what is right in front of me, I guess."

"Take advice from someone who has seen it all. If a man knows how to keep you wondering, keep you eager with anticipation, then he is a keeper. The comfort of sticking with the steady as a rock person is the easy choice but not always the right one. Finding both is like hitting the jackpot, and you know the chances of getting all six numbers is like one in a million. I don't know your situation, but I do know you're headed off to college. Let new opportunities lead you to where your heart, and more importantly, body, tells you to go." And with that, Sherry Lee left her bar stool and walked into the kitchen.

That was the most Sherry Lee had spoken to Trina in over five years. She didn't know how much weight to give her advice considering what Trina knew about Sherry Lee and Danny, but she had a point. Following both her heart and her body should be equally important. She spent the rest of her lunch and dinner shift smiling and serving customers while she weighed the pros and cons of committing Bobby. By the end of the night, she had decided she needed to call him.

Monica dropped her off at home after a long, exhausting day. Labor Day weekend crowds kept the restaurant busy. The Salty Bar had benefited from the customer overflow from the Red Bar, which had been garnering a ton of attention down on 30A since its grand opening. The line to get a seat would be twenty to thirty people long, and the wait times could exceed an hour. Customers who were tired of waiting headed over to the Salty Bar as a backup destination. The gossip around town was that the Red Bar was quickly becoming one of the best restaurants in the area. Not only was the food receiving praise, but the patrons were clamoring to take in the unique vibe and the live music.

Jerry made it very clear that he did not understand what all the hysteria was about. He thought the Red Bar was serving very similar food to the Salty Bar. He told anyone who would listen that once vacationers got over the excitement of eating at a new place, they would all come back to the Salty Bar because he had created a committed following of customers over the last thirty years. Jerry even went so far as to walk around the restaurant at night and collect all the Red Bar matchbooks, koozies and other promotional items that people left behind. He hated seeing the red color anywhere in the restaurant.

Trina could not have cared less. If the Salty Bar was full due to overflow, it was still putting money in her pocket. Plus, with only one day left, she was not concerned about the sustainability of the restaurant. She had other things on her mind.

Her dad was still awake when she walked in. He told her he had good and bad news. The bad news was not only did she have a flat tire, but the rim and axle had gotten damaged. The good news was that although the repair shop didn't have time to fit the repair job in during Labor Day weekend, they agreed to sell him the parts. He had it towed to the house and he hoped they could get the parts to him tomorrow so he would have two days to work on it. Trina was not happy about chipping away at her savings but there wasn't much she could do. She thanked her dad and sulked upstairs.

Her room had become a small disaster over the last week. Although most of her friends had left for college already, it seemed like her floor was a hodgepodge of the BBB's leftover clothes. She was exhausted, but she was running out of time to get ready for her departure. She knew she had to start packing. She spent two hours doing laundry, separating her clothes from her friends' clothes, and packing boxes of her belongings. She had already packed most of her wardrobe, keeping the bare minimum in her closet to get by over the last couple of days. All she had left to pack was her shoes and bathroom supplies and she would be good to go. By the time she looked at the clock, it was a couple minutes before one in the morning. She knew she should call Bobby but was too tired to tackle that conversation. She would have to save it for tomorrow.

Monica picked her up the next day and they drove to work midmorning. "Can you believe today is our last shift before we head to college? It seems so strange, doesn't it? It doesn't seem real."

"Agree. College feels like this abyss of the unknown. Meeting new people and trying to reestablish yourself from scratch seems overwhelming. I'm glad today is our last shift, though, I am so over working as a waitress. It has been fun, but I'm ready to hang the apron up for good."

"By the way, can I sleep over tonight? I know your parents are back, but I would love for us to have one more night before we leave," Monica said.

"Yes, that sounds great. Fair warning, I only got a couple hours of sleep last night, so I'm not sure how great of company I will be. Are you already packed?"

"Yes, I have everything ready to go. Mentally, I have been ready for weeks. I might convince my parents to leave tomorrow morning so I can go ahead and move in and get to know my roommate. The dorms are already open since rush started last week." Monica parked and the girls walked the rest of the way to work.

Saturday was as busy as Friday. The Red Bar was playing music outside, so the streets were overflowing with vacationers. The girls struggled to keep up with the flow of patrons. Since the Red Bar stayed at full capacity all day, patrons who couldn't find a seat found their way over to the Salty Bar as their consolation prize. Jerry spent lots of time standing outside listening to the conversations and watching the streams of people. His temper came to a rapid boil, as all everyone could talk about was the Red Bar. Monica and Trina did their best to stay away from Jerry, as they didn't know what was going to set him off. He was finding any reason to criticize the staff and was breathing down Danny's neck to keep the food tickets moving. Trina felt bad for the brand-new waitresses Danny had hired. Jerry was yelling at them all day long. Trina wasn't surprised when one of the new high school girls quit in the middle of dinner service. She ran out in tears after Jerry belittled her for delivering food to the wrong table. Jerry was not handling the heat of another eating establishment chipping away at his clientele.

By the end of the night, Monica and Trina were glad to be finished. They gave Danny big hugs and wished him the best of luck. He graciously thanked them for all their hard work and wished them the best of luck as well. Monica and Trina rode home with the windows down and music cranked. When they got home, it was nearly ten. Trina read a note from her dad that the car parts came in late this afternoon, and he would begin the repairs tomorrow. The girls grabbed food and clamored upstairs. They washed their faces and threw on some of Jane's leftover T-shirts since Trina's were all packed. They sat on the bed chatting for an hour. Around eleven thirty the phone rang. It was Bobby.

Trina and Bobby talked for over an hour. Bobby was asking for a commitment, and he wanted to see her tomorrow knowing that she was leaving Tuesday. She felt terrible, but she finally worked up the courage to tell Bobby that she didn't want to go to college in a relationship. He was devastated, and she truly understood. She remembered when Christopher had broken up with her. The raw emotions and pain that she experienced all came back to her. No matter how many compliments she gave him, it couldn't make up for the fact she wasn't prepared to begin a relationship. She felt guilty. She shouldn't have gone all the way with him if she wasn't ready to commit. But for once in her life, she had done something selfishly. Saying goodbye to Bobby felt like she was making the right decision as much as she felt like she was making the wrong one. When she hung up, she realized that Monica had fallen asleep. Trina closed her eyes, hoping a day off would make her feel better.

"Honey, wake up. Trina, honey, you have a phone call." Trina's mom was standing next to her bed. Trina wiped her eyes and sat up. She grabbed the phone, mouthing a *thank you* to her mom.

"Trina, it's Danny. I am so sorry to call you. I know yesterday was supposed to be your last day, but I am desperate. All three of the new girls quit. I have no one available to work today or tomorrow. I wouldn't ask you if it wasn't Labor Day weekend. I don't know how to get through it without you. All the other waitresses have left for college."

"Danny, I really need time off. I'm leaving for college on Tuesday, I haven't spent any time with my parents, and I'm exhausted."

"I know, Trina. I know. Jerry has been flipping out all weekend. No matter what I do, it's the wrong thing. I don't know if I can emotionally deal with him if I can't open over the next two days. I'm desperate! Listen, I didn't want to tell you this, especially this way, but... Trina, I have cancer. I've been going to treatment for a while now, and Jerry is not taking the news too well. My future is unknown and that stresses Jerry out. I really could use your support. Can you please help me for two more days?"

Trina was speechless. Cancer. That was a gut punch. She didn't want to leave Danny stranded. He had done so much for her and her sisters over the years. She wouldn't be able to live with herself if she didn't help him. How could she say no? She relented and told him she would get there as soon as she could. Now she knew why he looked so tired all the time.

Trina suddenly realized Monica wasn't there. She saw a note on the dresser that said: *To my ride or die! See you on the other side! Cheers! Monica.* Trina chuckled but was sad that she'd missed saying goodbye. After washing up, she grabbed her apron from the dirty pile of clothes and sulked downstairs. She shared the news with her parents, who were disappointed, but they were also proud of her for helping Danny out. Her dad promised to work on her car in hopes of getting it fixed in time.

Trina decided to ride her bike to work since her parents were knee-deep in their own Sunday chores. She arrived about midway through the lunch shift. The place was a chaotic mess. Sherry Lee and Janice were standing in as waitresses, and Jerry was running food back and forth. Everyone sighed with relief at the sight of Trina. She knew the situation was bad because Sherry Lee and Janice both hugged her when she walked in. Jerry said, "Thank you for showing up," which was, in itself, astonishing. However, it didn't take him long to switch back to his grumpy self. The ladies quickly assigned her tables and turned over duties. Within forty-five minutes, Trina had caught up on the tables, orders were back on schedule and customers were smiling again.

Regardless of how hard Trina worked, however, Jerry could not control his habit of nitpicking over little stuff. She wasn't refilling customers' drinks fast enough. Appetizers were not being sold to every table. Trina should be upselling top-tier alcohol and tacking on desserts. She was putting too much bread and butter on the tables, which generated unnecessary costs. After listening to him for two hours, Trina was at her wit's end.

When she overheard Jerry comment to Danny that she sold too many burgers when she should be selling more fish entrees, she reached the tipping point. She laid her tray of food down and walked with poised frustration up to Jerry. She took her apron off, hung it on her index finger and held it out toward him. "Jerry yesterday was officially my last day. You should be thanking your lucky stars that I agreed to support *Danny* by coming in today. If you don't like what I am doing, please step right up, and take over. I will happily hand you my apron and walk right out the door. But I am done listening to you rant like a toddler. It's like your sole mission is to find mistakes when there are none to find. If you want to compete with the Red Bar, you're going to have to treat your staff more professionally. For that matter, you need to start treating your brother like a human being. He runs circles around you. Why can't you ever focus on the positive? I have been listening to your bullshit for five years. Shut the hell up or I am walking out of here." Trina stared him down.

Danny, Billy, Sherry Lee, and Janice all stood there with their mouths wide open. Jerry stood perfectly still. If his eyes were lasers, they would have drilled a hole in her chest. She could almost see the steam puffing out of his ears. Everyone stood speechless, staring at Jerry. The only sounds were the chattering of customers from the front of the restaurant. Finally, the sound of the bell ringing as the front door opened broke the spell. She tied her apron and stormed out of the kitchen with a tray full of food.

She couldn't believe she just did that. It felt exhilarating! She felt lighter. Like a huge stress ball had been pulled out of her stomach. Standing up for herself felt unsettling, but at the same time, it felt amazing. Jerry needed to grow up, and it wasn't her job to be his mother. The cumulation of excessively working, processing her inner relationship demons, and mentally training for the unknown of her approaching college days had overloaded her system.

Adrenaline was still pulsing through her veins after her explosion at Jerry. Trina breathed in and out a couple of times to reel herself back to a settled calm. About an hour later, Billy snuck out of the kitchen and told Trina that Jerry had stormed out of the kitchen with Danny following soon after. Billy had to hold the fort down alone until Danny returned ten minutes later. Billy said he was a little worried about Danny. When he had returned to the kitchen, his complexion was paler, and his stamina appeared weaker. Billy heard him mumble that he was running out of steam. Guilt washed over Trina. She hoped she hadn't caused more stress for Danny. But she couldn't take her words back now, she had to get through the shift.

The final lunch crowd left the restaurant, and Trina took her first break before the evening happy hour began. She ate her sandwich in a booth in the back by herself. Sherry Lee and Janice agreed to get the prep work done for dinner to allow Trina to recover. The restaurant was empty for the first time all day, and Trina appreciated the peace and quiet. She finished eating and was staring down at the necklace Christopher had given her. She had taken it off and wrapped it around her wrist. She kept thinking about her conversation with Bobby last night. Had she made the right decision? Should she have given Bobby a chance?

They did click well, and he did make her feel special. She might have to reconsider after she spent a little time at college.

While she was lost in her internal musing, Jerry came out of the kitchen and walked over to Trina. He stood rod straight and the end of the booth staring at her. "No one has ever— " He stopped, took a breath, and continued. "You don't know what I go through daily to keep this place alive. This restaurant would crumble without me. You might have saved us today, and we may need you for the next twenty-four hours, but we will survive without you, Trina. If Danny hadn't pled with me to keep you here, I would have fired you on the spot for being so—"

He stopped, and she could tell he was biting back the words that he wanted to say. He turned to walk away, then turned back. She felt surprisingly unaffected by his comments. The words he'd hoped to pierce her with fell flat. She had built up an emotional wall when it came to Jerry.

"Girls like you think you are so special. There is nothing special about you. That boyfriend of yours. What was his name... Christopher? You think he was so good to you. You think he put you on a pedestal. Let me break it to you, you were not his only girl. That boy had a side hustle going and you were his eye candy. So how special do you think you are now, Trina Scotsdale?" Jerry smirked and walked out of the front door of the restaurant.

That struck deep. She felt like she was standing on a glass elevator looking down into an abyss and the floor dropped open. She was falling, falling with nothing to hold on to. Was that true? Had Christopher cheated? Impossible! There was no way. He'd been the best boyfriend anyone could ask for.

Jerry was just jealous. And mean. He couldn't stand to see anyone happy and had never been put in his place before. He was retaliating against her by saying Christopher had cheated. She knew Jerry was lying, but still, Trina was devastated at the thought. Her mind was rehashing all her significant Christopher relationship moments. With each one, she convinced herself that Christopher was a saint and Jerry was horribly mistaken.

She finished the shift in a complete daze. Danny let her go at nine o'clock and begged her to come back tomorrow. Although he had no idea what Jerry had told her at the table, Danny profusely apologized for Jerry's actions all day. Danny handed her a two hundred dollar cash bonus for coming in on her day off and promised her a three hundred dollar cash bonus if she came back tomorrow.

Trina threw her backpack on and rode her bike home in the dark. It was difficult to see the path at night since her glasses were still broken. There were no streetlights in Grayton, so riding a bike at night was not the safest option, but it was easier than waiting for her parents. She walked into the house and noticed the reflection of the garage light. Opening the garage door, she saw both her parents were standing by the CRX propped up on a car lift. After having spent the day repairing the damage, her dad was having a slight issue with balancing the tires. He promised to have it completed by the end of the day tomorrow. Trina asked her dad if he would mind loading up her boxes tomorrow while she was at work so she could leave early Tuesday morning. They worked out a plan as her mom ushered Trina into the kitchen. She'd cooked a special dinner earlier that evening and had kept it warm in the oven. Her parents joined her at the dinner table, taking advantage of their last moments of quality time with Trina.

She didn't tell them about Jerry's rudeness or her blowup. Nor did she tell them about breaking up with Bobby or what she'd heard about Christopher. She didn't want her last night with her parents to be filled with negativity. She listened to her parents give advice, offer her guidance on adjusting to a new environment, and prop her up for her hard work and ethical standards. They were proud of Trina and knew she would excel in college. Trina called it a night. She needed to catch up on her sleep since the last couple of days had been a whirlwind. Although her emotions were raw, adrenaline from conflicting thoughts had wiped her out. She fell asleep before she could even put her pajamas on.

She woke up at nine still wearing a bathroom towel from her shower the night before. She looked around the room for any clean clothes. She found an old T-shirt in the back of her dresser but couldn't find a clean apron to save her life. All the aprons were filthy and stinky. She finally found Monica's apron under a pile of clothes. Trina sniffed it and decided it was passable. She really didn't care at this point. She tied it around her waist and looked at herself in the mirror. She looked haggard. She had bags under her eyes, and her normal energetic disposition was depleted. She was in desperate need of several days of make-up sleep. She walked into the kitchen, grabbed a blueberry muffin, kissed her parents on the cheeks, and grabbed her backpack. She climbed on the bike and pedaled her way over to the Salty Bar for the very last time.

After yesterday's interaction with Jerry, the Salty Bar didn't deserve to have her, but Danny looked awful yesterday. With his medical condition weighing on her heart, guilt was the fuel that pushed her to pedal to work. She convinced herself she could work for one more day. Christopher consumed her thoughts. She could deal with Jerry's immaturity and his ridiculous complaining. Trying to swallow that she was cheated on was a reality she couldn't come to grips with.

It was Labor Day, and the volume of customers dropped. Most renters were checking out and leaving their dreamland of 30A behind. There was a consistent flow, but it was dramatically less than the last three days. Luckily, Jerry stayed hidden away in the shed. One less thing to deal with. Trina took advantage of the dip in business to cozy up to Sherry Lee. Maybe she'd heard gossip that would confirm or refute Jerry's accusations. She began the conversation with generic topics and threw in a couple of compliments acknowledging Sherry Lee's impressive connections to the community knowing Sherry Lee would eat it up. Eventually, Trina transitioned the conversation to her relationship with Christopher. Trina planted a seed that they had broken up because he wasn't committed to the relationship and asked if Sherry Lee had ever seen him with anyone.

Sherry Lee was hesitant at first but relented after Trina pleaded. "Listen, hon, I don't like to get into other people's business. You are a sweet girl. Don't let a guy break your heart. I don't know how serious the two of you were, but yes, I occasionally bumped into him when he was with this other girl. I think her name was Jennie. No. No. That's not it." Sherry Lee paused, trying to remember.

Trina processed what she had heard and threw out a hesitant guess. "Could it have been Pennie?"

"Yeah, I think that was her name. She was always hanging on to different guys, not just Christopher. Hate to break it to you this way, but I did see them hooking up once. It was late at night after a bonfire. I glanced in a car parked on the side of the road out of natural curiosity. I recognized Christopher immediately. I wasn't quite sure who the girl was, but right when I passed the car, she turned her head and saw me. She laughed, winked at me, and went right back to it. I remember seeing that girl at the restaurant a lot. She liked to get all the attention. Sorry, babe. Be glad you are moving on and going to college. Forget your old boyfriends and have fun finding new ones," Sherry said.

Christopher and Pennie? That was like oil and water. Christopher had been so respectful of her decision to wait. He loved that about her, respected her for her decision to hold off until she was emotionally ready. He always seemed supportive; even told her it made her more appealing. *We were together for years! How did I not know he was hooking up on the side?* The images that Trina were creating in her head were making her sick. She ran out the door in the back of the restaurant and threw up in the bushes. It took her a couple of minutes to regain her composure. She stood against the building with her eyes closed, taking deep breaths.

Trina pulled it together and returned to work. She looked at the three charms dangling from Christopher's gifted necklace and ripped it off her wrist, stuffing it in the pocket of her apron. Who else knew? How long was she being deceived? Was their relationship one big lie? The more she thought about it, the angrier she became. She deserved better than that. Her gut disbelief soon morphed into pure, intense hatred. She became grumpy with customers and messed up orders. She made it through lunch but was barely functioning during dinner shift. She had one more table to get through and then she was going to go home to cry in peace.

Jerry told Danny, who looked like a walking ghost, to go home and get some rest. Trina gave Danny a tight hug and wished him well. He handed her an envelope full of cash and thanked her for helping him out. To Trina's dismay, Jerry said he would close the restaurant with her. After closing out her last tab of the evening, Trina locked the front door. She really didn't want to perform the closing duties but everyone else had gone home. Jerry was the only one left, and he wasn't going to help. She wanted to get out of there as quickly as she could, and she went through the evening checklist with the speed of an experienced staff person. While she was cleaning, Jerry sat at the bar moaning about bad luck and bad timing, complaining about one of his rental properties. A renter wanted to check in tomorrow, and he had to scramble to find a cleaner on short notice. He sat there fidgeting with a book of matches and mumbling about missing his chance. Trina didn't let his grumbling rustle her feathers. She was in her own swirling tornado of thoughts.

"Are you even listening to me?" Jerry snapped.

"What? Sorry, I didn't realize you were talking to me. What did you say?" Trina said as she wiped down the last set of condiment bottles.

Jerry took a long, slow drag on his cigarette as he sat there for a moment contemplating. He pushed his cigarette butt into the ashtray, grabbed the book of matches, stood up and walked to the back door. Trina didn't know what his problem was, but she finished her final task, grabbed her backpack, and clocked out.

She walked outside and saw that he was standing with his back against the wall in front of her bike. "Jerry, can you please move? I need to get going," she said as she slipped her backpack on her back to get ready for the ride home.

"Tell me one thing, Trina. Who do you think deserves more respect, Danny who cooks burgers for a living or me for building an empire from scratch?"

"What do you care what I think?" Trina replied without much fanfare.

"I hold people to a higher standard, and in return, people view me with elevated respect. The list of people who struggled to comply is small. I can recall a couple of females who failed to respond to my wit and charm, but with the right kind of motivation, they changed their opinions." He rested his hand on the wheel of her bike. "Not everyone can be trusted, Trina. Human beings are dishonest creatures. We all craft perceptions of ourselves because seeing the truth in the mirror is disheartening. Your boyfriend took advantage of your gullibility. You fell for it, lock stock and barrel. My brother hides behind his nice guy image, but his true self is blatantly obvious to me. My own wife does a damn good job of acting like the doting wife but all she cares about are dollar signs. But you, Trina, you don't put on a show. You have never wavered from being you. And you are the first person to ever stand up to me. I need to know. Who do you respect more, Danny or me?"

Trina let out an exasperated sigh. She was so tired. Physically drained after pulling four double shifts. Self-doubt bubbled within as she tried to come to terms with Christopher's deception. The last thing she wanted to deal with was her egomaniac boss who thought his good looks warranted respect. Summer after summer she had bowed down to his demands, watching him walk all over the staff like he was the only human and the rest of them were ants in his way. This was the last time she would ever have to see this man again, and she wasn't holding back anymore.

"Jerry, you may be the brains behind this restaurant. Danny might not have the financial aptitude to operate a restaurant, but he has the personality, humanity, ethics, and the heart that keeps this place going. We work here because we want Danny to be proud of us. Danny shows us that he deserves our respect because every day he shows up and never complains. He works harder than any of us. His passion for creating fabulous food while caring for all the people who support him makes him the winner in my eyes. So, to answer your question, it's Danny. Danny deserves more respect." Trina stood there under the shimmer of the spotlight. She had her hands wrapped around the straps of her backpack. She wanted to grab her bike, but he was blocking her.

He finally straightened up, flicked a pocketknife out of his pocket, and stabbed it straight into her bike tire. Jerry dropped the knife and slapped Trina across the face so hard she fell backward. As she was falling to the ground, the last thing she heard was, "Wrong answer."

A Broken Neck and
a Broken Heart `

1995

Trina felt like she was riding in a horse and buggy. The repeated rise and fall of riding over bumps made her feel nauseous. Where was she? Was she dreaming? Why did the side of her head hurt so much? Why did her cheeks feel raw? She was enveloped in darkness. Slowly the lids of her eyes fluttered open. She was curled up in the fetal position in the back of a moving vehicle. Her hands were tied in the back with string, and her shoes and socks had been removed. *Think, Trina, think. What happened? Where are you?* She tried to focus but it was pitch-black outside. She could see the shadow of the top of pine trees off the glare of the moon. As she tried to sit up, she realized she was in the back of a Jeep. Then the memory came back to her—Jerry had struck her.

The vehicle came to a stop. The sound of a door opening and shutting echoed through the forest. Footsteps. He had left the front lights on, but her ability to see clearly was limited. Jerry pulled down the back of the Jeep and yanked her to the ground. A box of supplies and her backpack tumbled out with her as she fell with a thud, her right shoulder landing on a big rock. Pain pulsed and reverberated down her arm. She was fully awake now. She was in the middle of the woods surrounded by trees.

He cut her hands free with a knife but held her down. He yanked off the apron that was still tied around her waist and methodically wrapped the straps around his hands. He pulled it taut, making a snapping sound as he made a tight band of fabric. She tried to scream but no sound came out. Something thick and heavy was blocking her mouth. She tried to scramble backward, but he straddled her.

"Me, Trina. I deserve your respect. Not Danny. Not your cheating boyfriend. Me." He pulled the material out of her mouth. "Say it! I want to hear you say it."

Adrenaline pulsed through her veins. She knew she should answer him, but her brain was deadlocked with fear. What was he going to do to her? What was Jerry capable of?

"I have it all. Good Looks. Charm. Brains. A history of turning shit into gold. I am the one who made the Salty Bar what it is, not Danny. Anyone can cook a damn burger! Look at me, damn it! I want to hear you, Trina. I want you to tell me that I deserve your respect. Say it!"

She was in shock. She couldn't form any words. She had always known Jerry was mean, unlikable, even creepy, but never had she thought he would hurt her. Did he take Jasmine? Had he killed her? *Is he going to kill me?*

He leaned over her and wrapped the strings of the apron around her neck and pulled. It felt like her neck was wrapped in a steel encasement, squeezing the air. Her lungs fought for oxygen. She reached up and tried to pull it off, but he was so strong. She could see his smile. That creepy smile. Her eyes were closing. Struggling. Her thoughts drifted to her family. And then suddenly she could breathe. He had released his choke hold. She took a desperate breath.

He ripped her shirt in half leaving her feeling naked. He picked up his pocketknife and carved into her skin. Blood seeped out. The pain of it seared through her, but she had no leverage to dislodge him. Even in the darkness, she could see him staring at her. Through her. Her eyes became large, white circles of pure terror. He took his index finger and rubbed it through her blood and licked his finger.

"If you weren't so damn beautiful, I wouldn't give you a second chance. I think I deserve to enjoy myself before I get rid of you like the other hussies in my life. No one. No one disrespects Jerry Flanigan!" He wiped the remnants of the blood onto the apron, then took the apron straps and tied her hands above her head. To her absolute horror, he unbuckled his belt and unzipped his pants. She was banging him with her fists, but her tied hands were making the impact futile.

She found her voice. "Jerry, please! Please, I'll say whatever you want. Please don't do this."

Her words seem to refocus him. His right hand reached up and covered her mouth with the strength of a vice. She couldn't move her head. All she could do was stare at him.

"Teeny boppers, beautiful woman, even the old hags. They all yearn for my attention. I see them undress me with their eyes. How many slutty girls have I rewarded by giving them exactly what they wanted? But you, Trina. You strut around my empire in tiny shorts and skimpy tank tops, but you never once offered those eyes. Well, now my fantasies can be a reality."

His hand pushed down on her mouth harder. She was forcing air through her nostrils, terrified at what he was going to do next. His free hand dragged down her chest, down her belly button. Her heart raced as she struggled to free herself, but his hand was pressing her head into the dirt. She felt like her skull was digging a hole in the ground.

"You belong to me, Trina. No one is going to find you. No one is going to save you. Seeing the fear in your eyes will keep me busy all night long." His finger slid lower. She squeezed her body in protest. His finger felt like red-hot fire on her skin. His enjoyment at her fear was evident. *This can't be happening.* He released his hold on her head and untied her hands. He removed his finger and slid it slowly back up her torso. It felt like a burning match leaving a scorched path on her chest. His touch repulsed her.

"I finally have your attention. I don't think I enjoyed the other three as much as I am going to enjoy you. Another disrespectful tramp was meant to be my next lesson. It didn't go as planned, but now I know this was meant to be. Tonight is your lucky night, Trina. Your gaze alone makes me excited. I can't believe I'm saying this, but you're worth the wait." His hands moved to her thighs, and with pure hatred in his eyes, he pushed her legs apart.

"I never compete with Danny over anything. The thought of you liking Danny ignites rage and fire in me. Look at me, Trina Scotsdale. I want you to look into my eyes and dare tell me Danny is better. Go ahead. I want to hear your words slowly and clearly. Try again. Tell me who deserves your respect. I want those damn lips of yours to tell me what I want to hear." His head bent down, approaching her belly button.

"You are way better than Danny! You are my hero!" She spoke with false conviction.

His head popped up; eyes locked on hers. "Go on." He was captivated.

"You're who I admire. You're the man I want to go to bed with at night." She said it with little emotion, but the effect was the same. He removed his hand from her inner thighs and reached for his pants. Trina recognized an opportunity.

"I dream of you-" She paused. She wanted him to want her to continue.

"Tell me how." He stood up and loomed over her, his legs on either side of her body. He closed his eyes.

"After work. I dream of you taking me to your office. Locking the door."

Trina saw this as her chance. She pushed herself into a sitting position. "I can't stand the way other women look at you. Admire you. Get to have you." She slowly stood up. His eyes remained closed as he focused on her words.

"I lie in bed at night. Jerry, I dream of you. Us. Alone on the beach."

"More. Tell me more."

"You are the only man for me."

Trina bent down to grab the large rock her shoulder had landed on. She stood up and edged behind him, whispering in the best soft and sexy voice she could muster. "I want you, Jerry Flanigan. My body aches for you. I have no self-control around you. You are my fantasy."

Jerry groaned. Totally lost in his own world. Seizing the opportunity, Trina raised the rock high over her head with both hands and slammed it into the back of his head. He staggered backward and fell hard. She heard a loud crack as he landed. In shock, she walked slowly backward until her back hit the Jeep. She could see the silhouette of him lying crooked at the trunk of a tree. Trina dropped the rock, which hit the Jeep before tumbling to the forest floor.

Adrenaline surged. She'd stopped the sick bastard! Emotions charged hard on the heels of adrenaline. She felt filthy. Used. Betrayed. She had to focus. She had no idea where she was, but she knew she needed to get out of there before he woke up. She needed the keys. She nervously walked over to him.

His neck was bent awkwardly over a huge tree branch on the forest floor. She felt for his pulse. Nothing. Was he dead? She needed a light. She went back to the Jeep and found her backpack on the ground. She grabbed the clip that had the mace spray and small flashlight. Returning to him, she shined the light in his face.

Dead. She had never seen a dead person before, but he was absolutely, no way around it, dead. She had killed a man. She sat there in a squat just staring at his contorted face. That face would haunt her for the rest of her life. An hour ago, she was an eighteen-year-old headed to college. Now, she was a killer. She stood up and the knots in her stomach erupted. She threw up for several long, stomach-cramping minutes.

It took Trina a while to pull herself together. She sat on the forest floor in a fog trying to process what just happened. Trying to come to terms with her actions. A mantra began in her head. She repeated it over and over again.

He was going to rape me. He was going to kill me.
I killed him in self-defense.
I had no choice. I had no choice. I had no choice.

She had no concept of how long she squatted on the ground rocking back and forth. Her ripped shirt hung off her shoulders. She was covered in brown, mulchy earth. She hugged her knees, rocking and repeating.

Suddenly, she robotically rose into a standing position. She yanked her torn shirt off and threw it in the Jeep. She had a promising future to protect. She was not going to let this man destroy her. She was going to get out of here and then never think about this night ever again.

She had read enough crime books to know evidence meant everything. She walked over to his limp body. She stuck her hand in his back pocket and pulled out his wallet and threw it into the front seat. One of the straps from the apron was sticking out from under his body. She tugged, but his weight made it impossible. She gave up on the apron. Methodically, she covered him in leaves and random tree branches. She shined the light over the forest floor looking for anything else that might tie her to the scene. She searched for the rock and found it lying on the ground next to broken fragments of the Jeep. She dropped the rock on the passenger seat and turned back around and swung her flashlight left to right over the ground.

The last thing she needed to do was grab the box of supplies that had fallen out of the back of the Jeep. The contents had splattered, leaving hotel-sized soaps and shampoos littered across the dirt. She rested the flashlight flat on the ground so she could see a wider path. Getting on her hands and knees, she swept her hand across the earth, stuffing any toiletries she found back in the broken box. As she crept on the ground, she accidentally bumped into Jerry's limp body. The instant her bare foot touched his skin, she felt instantaneously repulsed. She picked the box up and dropped it over the open window into the passenger seat, then scooted around to the driver's side, hoping she found everything and jumped in. Thankfully, his keys were still in the ignition.

She sat there and breathed deeply. She mentally recited her mantra, rested her hand on the rock, and exhaled. She started the engine. The forest was dark. He had driven the Jeep down into the bush off the hard-packed service road. She was not familiar with driving a Jeep and didn't have her glasses to help her see, but fear and revulsion wrapped a blanket of motivation over her. She put it in gear and hit the gas. Even though the headlights were on, she had to squint to see. She drove over tree limbs, roots and even bushes trying to find a way out. After a minute of treacherous driving, she made it out of the thickness to a dirt service road, but unfortunately, she didn't ease off the gas in time and bumped into a tree that was directly across the road. The impact caused her to lurch forward, but she wasn't going fast enough to get hurt. She looked out over the front dashboard and could see that she had run into a *No Trespassing, Bears Live Here* sign that had been nailed to the tree. She recognized the sign from their beer and bear parties and knew she was now on one of the service roads she was familiar with. She backed up and corrected the angle of the vehicle, then slowly navigated the path. She drove for a couple of minutes, the shadows of pine trees and the silence of the night keeping her company.

Out of nowhere, white eyes stared straight at her on the path. Trina swerved, slamming the front of the Jeep into a thick pine tree. The impact this time was louder and more forceful. Her head slammed into the steering wheel. She touched her forehead and wiped blood from her head. A family of three deer stood in the road, all six eyes staring at her. They walked up closer to the Jeep's lights. The doe walked to the driver's door and stuck her head in the open window. She sniffed, looked up into Trina's eyes, licked her head wound and then sauntered away, followed by her little ones. Trina felt a wave of motherly protection hug her like a warm blanket.

She tried to start the engine, but it was dead. She got out and looked around. She had to be close to the exit that would bring her back to the main road. She grabbed his wallet from the passenger seat and stuffed it in a zippered pocket of her backpack. She grabbed her torn shirt and used it to wipe down the steering wheel, the stick shift, and the door handles. She picked up the rock from the floormat and chucked it deeply into the forest. She went to the rear to find her socks and shoes, but they must have fallen out at the last crash. She strapped her backpack on, wrapped her left arm around the supply box and started off.

Immediately realizing it was pitch-black outside without the Jeep lights, she searched her bag for her clip with the flashlight. Her bad luck was unrelenting tonight. She had left the flashlight back in the forest. She looked up at the moon, adjusted her eyesight and took one step after another. Soon, she was running, barefoot and half naked. She felt blind in the black night, but her adrenaline forced her forward.

Her heart was broken. All her life, she had trusted that people are inherently good. Tonight's events had blown that assumption to microscopic pieces. She had never *liked* Jerry, but her youthful innocence had trusted him. How could she ever trust a man ever again? How could she trust herself?

She'd killed a man. She was a murderer.

He broke her heart. She broke his neck.

I had no choice. I had no choice. I had no choice.

Truth May Set You Free

Present Day

Trina sat staring at the image in the old photograph. A picture of a man walking back from throwing trash in a trash bin. His cruel smile. The hatred in his eyes.

The realization hit her like an ocean wave crashing her memories. She had blocked out this man, that night. That night so many moons ago. Completely, totally, irrevocably blocked it from her mind. It was like it had never happened. She held the picture and lost herself in her own horror. Jerry Flanigan was her deep, dark secret. She could feel him on top of her. She could hear his breathing. Her skin prickled at the thought of him touching her. Touching himself.

She ran to the bathroom and hugged the toilet, emptying her stomach. When she could give no more, she stood up and splashed water on her face. Slowly, painstakingly, she looked up at the image in the mirror.

I have been searching for myself. I am the murderer.

It was no longer a mystery. The body she'd found was Jerry Flanigan. His death was in fact accidental; she didn't kill him with intent. The slam

335

of the rock to the head was purely a deterrent. His neck breaking on impact was accidental.

The black curtain had been lifted. She subconsciously rubbed the scar that was embedded in her skin. Her scar!

She ran into the bathroom to stare into the mirror. She traced the bump on her shoulder with a finger. She had always told everyone she fell off her bike and cut herself on the metal fender. Now, she stared at the squiggly line from a different angle. Using her cell phone, she snapped a photo and spun the image around —the number four. *I was his fourth victim*.

She had erased the memory so purely, so perfectly. It was like she had dumped bleach over the night. Clorox wiped it away from her thoughts. Now, she was re-living glimpses. The desperate desire to flee. The deep guttural fear that had coursed through her veins. The searing pain from his knife. The disgust at his arousal. Her innocence obliterated. Her willingness and ability to trust others had been devoured by the demons of that night.

Memories of running home in the dark. Chasing the darkness for the forest's exit. The strain of carrying a box, then dumping it in a trash bin to hide the evidence trail. The excruciating desire to get back to the safety of her home. She had been a mess. She was filthy, dirty, the souls of her feet were black and sore. Luckily, her parents had already gone to bed by the time she made it home. Her father's note said the car was fixed and her bags were packed. They would see her in the morning before she left for college.

Trina had taken a shower, scrubbing herself raw. She removed any ounce, every fragment of DNA, saliva, semen, and hair. Could she scrub away his smile? His touch? Could the soap cleanse her of the indecency? The feeling of having no control. Not being able to breathe. His hand. His breath. Scrub. Wash. Scrub. She must wash all the evidence down the drain. By the time she was done, she didn't think she had any skin cells left. She would never leave a trace of herself anywhere again, she vowed. She would forever be careful, cautious, methodical, aware.

Exhausted but determined, she packed her shoes and toiletries in one final bag. She wrote a loving note to her parents telling them she was so excited about college she couldn't wait for them to wake up. She would call them when she arrived on campus. She drove through the night, arriving at Auburn at four in the morning. She sat in her car and fell asleep. When a security guard knocked on her window at seven, Trina opened her door and never looked back

***

Thirty years later, she sat in a booth at the Red Bar waiting for Detective Trent to join her for lunch. She sipped on a Bloody Mary with an umbrella and pink straw sticking out of the glass. Last month, the news had released the official sketch of the man associated with the skeleton, but she refused to watch. David had told her that they identified the man, but Trina feigned little interest. JoAnn and Trina had become fast friends, spending time together for coffee and mahjong. She'd met several other local ladies over the last month as more locals heard about the identification of the body. Trina masked her responses with controlled disinterest.

337

Trent walked in, waving at the hostess. He slid into the seat, nodding politely at Trina. "Mrs. Scotsdale, so nice to see you again."

"Same to you, Detective."

They ordered another round of drinks, and lunch, and sat silently looking at one another.

"JoAnn is my everything. A long time ago, someone tried to steal her innocence. Thanks to your discovery, the fear that has haunted my wife for three decades is now gone. Vanished. I have you to thank for that, Trina. I will forever be grateful."

Trina nodded and took a sip of her drink.

"Proving the past is a tedious and precarious job. Interpretation of evidence, well, let's just say interpretation can change the direction of an investigation. With your help, we uncovered several facts that lead us to the right conclusion. Your newspaper articles, the discovery of Freeport Clean, and the link to the current owner of the Jeep were all leads that we relied on heavily." Trent flipped open a police folder. "As investigators, we rely on tips from various sources. You proved yourself to be a valuable source. Jerry Flanigan's body has been conclusively identified. We'll continue to work on the cold cases of three missing girls, but we now have a defined path to move forward. I'm closing my official investigation into his accidental death, but I wanted to confirm one more time what you touched when you found the human remains. Please correct me if I am mistaken. A piece of denim."

Trina nodded.

"A leather belt and belt buckle."

Trina nodded.

"The Red Bar grand opening matchbook."

Trina nodded.

Detective Trent cleared his throat and looked at Trina for a moment. "A white apron."

Trina stared back without nodding.

"A necklace with three charms," he said, looking at her with such intensity she thought she would melt right there in the booth.

"I don't believe I told you that—" Trina started to say.

"You also touched a small flashlight that was connected to a can of mace. Does that about wrap it up? Is that everything you touched *the day* you found the skeleton?"

Trina sat there dumbfounded. She knew she had not touched those things when she found the body. Trent knew this too. He'd saved JoAnn, but now he understood that Trina had saved herself.

"You forgot the metal sign. I touched the metal sign."

"Thank you. Yes, you're right. I forgot to mention the metal sign. Thank you for confirming that my records are correct." He closed his folder. "Thirty years ago, three women were not lucky. One extremely brave, independent, and resilient woman survived on her own, but was haunted her entire life. She deserves to live free of buried memories. I hope the closing of this case releases her from those chains."

"Me too, Detective Trent. Me too."

The cell phone rang, and Trenton answered it. "Detective Trent. Yes. Uh huh. I understand. Where was the body found? Who found it? I'll be right there." He hung up and stood, leaving cash on the table.

"Are you coming, Trina?"

Biography

After raising three kids and juggling a full-time career, I left the corporate world in 2021 and moved to Florida. I quickly developed an immediate connection to the Scenic Highway 30A community, which unconditionally promotes entrepreneurial pursuits and artist creativity. Inspired by local southern authors and my own lifetime of fiction consumption, I was unexpectedly inspired to write my debut novel, using the charm and uniqueness of my small beach town as the backdrop for mystery.

I wrote The Panhandle Predicament to explore one woman's drive to achieve a lifelong dream of solving a mystery, while at the same time struggling with her own inner demons. In the process, I hope I have created a story that both conveys the breathtaking beauty and serenity of the Florida Panhandle while providing readers with an engaging mystery. For those who already love 30A, you will recognize many restaurants, state parks and community organizations. For those who have not yet ventured to the Panhandle, I hope I sparked your curiosity.

The Panhandle
Picasso

Did you enjoy The Panhandle Predicament?

Keep reading for a sneak peek at Kendra's second novel

H er instincts were stirring. A well-known artist from the coveted 30A Panhandle of Florida was dead at the hands of his own art. As soon as she heard how he died, that rumbling in her gut had started. Maybe she was simply letting her ego take the driver's seat after Detective Trent's compliment earlier that day. At least she thought it had been a compliment. The reality was she was blatantly guessing, but Trina didn't think the sculptor had died accidentally. Something didn't feel right, and that's why Detective Trent had asked her to come to the crime scene.

Maybe it was the incessant chatter from the standing-room only mob of gawkers. Or the lack of true sadness floating above the group like a rain cloud waiting to burst. Silently observing the crowd, Trina felt like she was witnessing a casting call of potential actors practicing emotional devastation. The tears drowning the hodgepodge of artists seemed legitimate, but were they crying over his death or the cancellation of today's art installation?

No, that wasn't it. It was something she'd heard when she first walked in. She didn't know who amongst the crowd of forty or so strangers had said it, but she'd heard it clear as day:

"Killed by his own creation. If that's not genius, I don't know what is. His art is going to be worth millions now."

She knew absolutely nothing, yet she knew something was off. Someone had killed Ian Scott.

Today was the day Ian's sculpture, along with three other handpicked artists' pieces, were scheduled to be transported on a barge from Destin to the beautiful, clear waters of Grayton Beach and purposefully placed in the Gulf of Mexico's Underwater Museum of Art (UMA). The Cultural Arts Alliance, in conjunction with the South Walton Artificial Reef Association, created the UMA in 2018. The sixth annual installation of one-of-a-kind sculptures to support and stabilize marine habitat with eco-friendly artwork was scheduled for 11:00 a.m. Unfortunately, the devasting discovery of Ian's untimely death had indefinitely postponed the event.

Trina stood on the gravel driveway in front of the Santa Rosa Beach Art Warehouse Studios on Route 393 behind the growing cluster of police cars, television vans, yellow police tape and patrol officers. Wearing a light-blue T-shirt, an athletic skirt, and a pair of walking sneakers, she stood silently and effortlessly blended in. While others wrapped their arms around one another and tissues miraculously materialized, Trina was in Sherlock Homes mode. She was assessing body language that didn't match communication. Skittish eye contact. Exaggerated levels of sorrow. Masked signs of anger. Hidden signs of satisfaction. As her own eyes darted from person to person, she eavesdropped and observed.

She knew she looked like the rest of the nosy neighbors, and once that realization hit her, she understood. Over the last few months, she had successfully uncovered evidence that helped the local police close a case. Her methods of discovery were simple. Immersion. As a resident living her best life in the serene vacation town of Grayton Beach, Florida, part of the nationally recognized 30A communities, Trina simply lived her life as a Local. Conversations happened. Tidbits of seemingly meaningless information slipped through the cracks. Being in the right place at the right time had its benefits. Detective Trent had not come out and said it to her directly, but she didn't think he'd asked her to come along just to give her a joy ride.

He knew she had the potential to be useful in this investigation. She had proven she had the ability to camouflage herself. She effortlessly bonded with other "OG" 30A locals who lived on this twenty-six-mile stretch of pristine beach. As a retired businesswoman, she had generated rapport working alongside an endless stream of volunteers at monthly cultural events and charitable organizations. As a part-time employee at a local gift shop, she interacted with visitors from all over the country, while also developing loyal relationships with local shoppers. Her secret weapon was literally the best source of information in any community—other women. Trina could find out things the police couldn't.

Trina wasn't naive, though. There were hundreds of local residents who could say the same thing. Trina was not a detective. Her only claim to sleuthing was that she possessed quirky, obsessive-compulsive behaviors like the character on the show *Monk*. This compulsion to hide her own evidence trail made her keenly aware of outliers, the Waldo in a room of red, blue, and white. She had an eye for seeing what others didn't. What did Detective Trenton Oliver hope she observed today?

A piece of art obviously could not be guilty of murder. Who in this crowd could be? Ignoring the reporters and the police, Trina quickly categorized the crowd:

Pry-ers — Serving a five-course meal to their own selfish curiosity.

Criers — Sharing sorrow but immensely thankful it happened to someone else.

Storm chasers — Creating (versus collecting) facts to capture social media worthy pictures.

Connivers — Planning ways to replace Ian Scott in the art community.

Show Must Go Oners — Analyzing obstacles and identifying opportunities.

Who had a motive? Opportunity? Was anyone jealous of his new-found fame? Maybe it was an accident? Trina's mind was spinning.

She really had no business being here, but that feeling in her gut told her she should.

30A

Now that you have read *The Panhandle Predicament*, maybe you are ready to come and explore 30A in Santa Rosa Beach, Florida. Although this is a work of fiction, some of the destinations mentioned in the story are current business establishments.

Next time you book your 30A vacation, support local!

Dining

The Red Bar

Goatfeathers Seafood Market

Red Fish Taco

Blue Mountain Bakery

Noli South Kombucha

Black Bear Bakery

Café Thirty-A

Amavida Coffee

Chiringo

Grayton Seafood Co.

Crackings Breakfast & Brunch

Bad Ass Coffee

Grace Pizza

Bud & Alleys

Retail/Service

Frank's Hardware Store

Grayton General Store

The Zoo Gallery

Grayton Beach Fitness

Sundog Books

Aura Home & Living

Happy Nails

Destinations

Point Washington State Park

Vortex Springs

Charitable Organizations

Cultural Arts Alliance

Caring & Sharing of South Walton

Follow on Instagram

@panhandlemysteryseries

Made in the USA
Columbia, SC
05 March 2025

54714581R00212